"YOU CAN TOUCH ME ALL YOU WANT, BUT I WON'T ABANDON THE JOB."

"I know that." Her gaze tracked her hands as she slid them down his chest and over his flat belly.

He sucked in air, his jeans becoming way too tight. "Then what are you doing?"

"Exploring." Her thumbs brushed slightly beneath his waistband, and she smoothed around to the small of his back. "I'm tired of being two steps behind you on this job. I want to be equal partners. If you're going to be my handler, I'm going to handle you, too."

He nearly burst out of his zipper. Oh, she was good. Brave, even. "You're playing with fire, little girl." His Southern drawl came out low and natural, surprising him. Being home seemed to have centered his wild redhead, and now she was trying to take control. "I'm not one to give up control. Don't even try."

Her smile was that of a siren used to getting her own way. "Is that a challenge?"

Also by Rebecca Zanetti

The Dark Protector series

Fated
Claimed
Tempted
Hunted
Consumed
Provoked
Twisted
Shadowed
Tamed
Marked
Talen
Vampire's Faith
Demon's Mercy
Alpha's Promise
Hero's Haven

The Realm Enforcers series

Wicked Ride
Wicked Edge
Wicked Burn
Wicked Kiss
Wicked Bite

The Scorpius Syndrome series

Scorpius Rising
Mercury Striking
Shadow Falling
Justice Ascending

The Deep Ops series

Hidden
Taken

FALLEN

REBECCA
ZANETTI

ZEBRA BOOKS
KENSINGTON PUBLISHING CORP.
www.kensingtonbooks.com

ZEBRA BOOKS are published by

Kensington Publishing Corp.
119 West 40th Street
New York, NY 10018

All Kensington titles, imprints, and distributed lines are available at special quantity discounts for bulk purchases for sales promotion, premiums, fund-raising, educational, or institutional use.

Special book excerpts or customized printings can also be created to fit specific needs. For details, write or phone the office of the Kensington Sales Manager: Attn.: Sales Department. Kensington Publishing Corp., 119 West 40th Street, New York, NY 10018. Phone: 1-800-221-2647.

First Printing: October 2019
ISBN-13: 978-1-4201-4583-0
ISBN-10: 1-4201-4583-5

ISBN-13: 978-1-4201-4584-7 (eBook)
ISBN-10: 1-4201-4584-3 (eBook)

10 9 8 7 6 5 4 3 2 1

Printed in the United States of America

This one is dedicated
to all of my family members and friends
who wonder if I'm writing about them
with some of my odd characters.
Spoiler alert.
I am.

ACKNOWLEDGMENTS

I'm so excited about this new Deep Ops series! I have many people to thank for getting this book to readers, and I sincerely apologize to anyone I've forgotten:

A HUGE thank you to Tony Zanetti for being the best husband in the world, and who deserves his own page of acknowledgments for each book! Thank you to Gabe and Karlina for being such awesome kids. Being your mom is my biggest blessing. I can't believe how much you've both grown, and I'm excited to see what you do next;

Thank you to Jim Dorohovich, who came up with the perfect name for this series as well as how to improve on a Moscow Mule (change out vodka for Maker's Mark);

Thank you to my hardworking editor, Alicia Condon;

Thank you to the rest of the Kensington gang: Alexandra Nicolajsen, Steven Zacharius, Adam Zacharius, Ross Plotkin, Lynn Cully, Vida Engstrand, Jane Nutter, Lauren Vasallo, Lauren Jernigan, Kimberly Richardson, Tory Groshong, and Rebecca Cremonese;

Thank you to my wonderful agent, Caitlin Blasdell, and to Liza Dawson and the entire Dawson group, who work so very hard for me;

Thank you to Jillian Stein for the absolutely fantastic work and for being such an amazing friend;

Thanks to my fantastic street team, Rebecca's Rebels, and their creative and hardworking leader, Minga Portillo;

Thanks to the fans who've been so supportive about *Hidden* and *Taken* so far in this series!

Thanks also to my constant support system: Gail and Jim English, Debbie and Travis Smith, Stephanie and Don West, Jessica and Jonah Namson, Kathy and Herb Zanetti, and Liz and Steve Berry.

Chapter One

The smell of wood polish and lemons mixed with the smooth male scent of the way too respectable man sitting across the round table from Brigid. Everything about Raider Tanaka was clean-cut, upstanding, and unyielding. Even his perfectly tailored navy-blue suit with striped green power tie made him appear like a guy who daily helped old ladies cross the street. "You look like a Fed," she whispered.

His black eyes glimmered. "I am a Fed," he whispered back, his voice low and cultured.

Yeah, and that was a problem. She looked around the darkened Boston tavern, where the attire of the patrons ranged from guys wearing worn dock clothes at the long counter to handmade silk suits over in the corner. Bodyguards with bulges beneath their jackets stood point near the guys with nice suits.

She shivered and smoothed down her black T-shirt featuring Dr. Who. The new one. "I don't think we blend in."

"I believe that's the point, Irish," Raider said, using the nickname he'd given her the first day they'd met. He finished off his club sandwich. His angular features showed his part-Japanese heritage, giving him an edgy look that contrasted intriguingly with his stockbroker suit. Just who was this man?

She shook her head. "I don't get it. Angus sent us here just to have lunch?" The plane ride alone from DC would've cost a mint, even though they'd sat in coach. Of course.

"The boss always has a plan," Raider said, tipping back his iced tea while eyeing the suits in the corner.

Aye, but it would be nice to know the plan. Brigid enjoyed temporarily working for the ragtag Homeland Defense unit run by Angus Force, but her job was hacking computer systems or writing code. Certainly not having a weird lunch with her handler in Boston. "Shouldn't we be doing something?"

Raider shrugged and gestured toward her Cobb salad. "You going to finish that?"

"No." Her stomach was all wobbly.

"Okay." He slid his empty plate to the side and tugged hers toward him, digging in.

Her mouth gaped open. Straitlaced Raider Tanaka did not seem like the kind of guy to share somebody else's food. Not a chance. She'd figured him for some dorky germophobe, albeit a good-looking one.

"What?" His dark eyebrows lifted. When she didn't answer, he glanced down at the lettuce. "When you grow up on the streets or in foster care, you take food where you can get it." Then he munched contentedly on a crouton.

She blinked, her mind spinning. "You grew up in foster care?" She'd have bet her last dollar, if she had one, that he'd grown up in Beverly Hills somewhere with a maid or two cleaning up his room and making his bed. His suits had to cost a fortune, and he had that prep-school look.

"Yes." Raider leaned back in his chair. "You're not the only one who's tough to figure out."

Well, that explained why he was such a control freak.

Growing up in the system probably did that to a guy. She tried to keep eye contact but found it difficult. Her abdomen warmed, and an interesting tingling licked along her skin. She had to do something about this disastrous attraction she had for him.

His gaze narrowed, while his back somehow straightened even more. That quickly, he went from lazily amused to alert and tense.

Her breathing quickened in response.

A man appeared by their table. One of the guys with the bulging jackets. "Can I help you?"

Raider looked up, a polite smile curving his lips. "Not unless you're serving dessert."

Brigid breathed in through her nose and exhaled slowly. Adrenaline flooded her system. This was bad. Was she even supposed to be involved in a side job to her already side job? "We're fine," she said.

The guy didn't look at her. His hair was slicked back, revealing beady brown eyes and a nose that had been flattened permanently to the left. A scar cut through the side of his bottom lip. "You look like a Fed."

Raider smiled, flashing even white teeth. "So I've heard."

"It's time for you to leave," the guy said, resting his hand on his belt.

"No," Raider said, his voice almost cheerful.

Brigid began to rise, feeling exposed and way too far out in the open. "Raider, I think—"

"Sit down." Raider kept his gaze on the man with the gun, but the barked command in his voice had her butt hitting the seat in instant response.

She blinked. What the heck had just happened? "Um."

The armed man leaned in toward Raider. "I tear apart Feds for fun. Now get the pretty redhead out of here before

I decide to rip off your face and show her what a real man can do with an hour or two."

Brigid's hands curled over the table, and she looked around frantically. The door was so close. She focused back on Raider.

If anything, he looked a little bored. "My money would be on the redhead," he said, losing his smile. "Now, friend. You can either go get us a dessert menu, or you can fuck off and slink back to your bodyguard duties."

Brigid swallowed a gasp. Had Raider just said the F-word? She glanced toward the corner, where one of the other bodyguards had started strutting their way. This was about to get bad. She wasn't armed. Was Raider? He couldn't be. They'd flown commercially, and he hadn't declared a gun.

They had to get out of there. Right now.

The guy grabbed Raider by the tie, and then everything happened so quickly that Brigid froze in place.

Raider stood in one easy motion, manacled the back of the guy's neck, and smashed his head down so hard into the table that the wood cracked in two. Dishes and utensils flew in every direction while the guy and the table crashed to the floor.

Brigid's chair rocked back, and she yelped, scrambling to her feet to keep from falling. The guy on the floor didn't move.

Raider's easy and brutal violence shocked her more than the fight itself.

"Hey!" The other bodyguard, a redheaded man with a barrel of a chest, ran forward while yanking out his gun.

Raider pivoted and kicked the guy beneath the chin, following his downward spiral in a blur of motion. Three punches and a quick twist, and Raider stood with the gun pointed at the back table. When he lifted his chin, the two men there raised their hands.

The remaining patrons looked on, not moving.

Raider straightened his tie and tossed a business card on the table. "Have your boss call me if he wants to get serious."

Brigid could only gape, her mind fuzzing. What had just happened?

Raider backed toward her. "Door. Now."

She stumbled for it just as sirens echoed down the street. Running outside into a light rain, she rushed to the passenger side of the compact they'd rented at the airport. Raider calmly entered the driver's seat, started the engine, and drove away from the restaurant.

Brigid gulped down panic, struggling to secure her seat belt. "I don't understand. Why in the hell were we sent to that restaurant?"

Raider set the confiscated gun between them and maneuvered around traffic. "I have a feeling our mission went according to plan." His hands were light on the steering wheel, but his voice held a tone she couldn't identify. She scrutinized him. He looked as if he'd been out for a relaxing lunch with a friend and hadn't probably just put two guys—two tough guys—in the hospital for a week.

Just who was Raider Tanaka?

After a silent plane ride back to DC, where Raider read a series of HDD reports and refused to answer any of Brigid's questions, especially about the darn business card, they finally ended up at their headquarters just as night began to fall. As usual, the dilapidated elevator hitched at the bottom floor and then remained quiet.

"I hate this thing." Raider smacked his palm against the door. "Open, darn it."

The door shuddered open.

Amusement bubbled through the unease in Brigid. "You're magic."

He looked over his shoulder. "You have no idea, Irish." Then he crossed into the small, dimly lit vestibule of the basement offices.

Had he just flirted with her? For Pete's sake. She moved out of the claustrophobic space on wobbly legs. This day was overwhelming on way too many levels. Enough of that silliness. Reaching the wide-open room, she sighed. A coat of fresh paint had brightened the office a bit, but the myriad of desks were still old and scarred, and the overhead lights old, yellow, and buzzing. They'd arranged four desks in a pod belonging to Raider and his colleagues, Malcolm West and Clarence Wolfe. The fourth was empty so far.

Raider looked down at the cracked concrete floor and shook his head.

"We're supposed to paint that next," Brigid said, coming up on his side. Wasn't that the plan? Though she probably wouldn't be left in place that long. She shivered and tried to stay in the moment. "I think there's art coming, or screens that show outside scenes." The basement headquarters were a step down from depressing, even with the fresh paint. This evening, the big room was eerily silent.

Three doors in the far wall led to an office and two conference rooms, while one more door, a closet for the shrink, was situated to the west.

A German shepherd padded out of the far office, munching contentedly on something bright red. It coated his mouth and stained the light fur around his chin.

"Roscoe," Brigid breathed, her entire body finally relaxing. Animals and computer code, she knew. It was people who threw her.

The dog seemed to grin and bounded toward her, his tail wagging wildly. She ducked to pet him. "What in the world do you have?" Close up, she could see that the stuff was thick and matted in his fur. She frowned and tried to force open his mouth. "Roscoe?"

As if on cue, Angus Force stepped out of the second conference room, also known as case room two. "Hey, you two. How was Boston?"

Brigid looked up. "Roscoe has something."

"Damn it." Angus made it through the desks in record time. "Is it Jack Daniel's?"

Brigid craned her neck to see. "No. It's red." The dog had a well-known drinking problem.

Angus glared at his dog. "Drop it. Now." The command in his voice held absolutely no patience.

The dog sighed and spit out a gold-plated lipstick.

Brigid winced. "That looks expensive."

The dog licked his lips.

Angus sighed. "I told everyone not to leave makeup around. He likes the taste."

"No, you didn't," Brigid countered.

Angus pierced her with a look. "Well, I meant to. Roscoe, get back to the office. Now."

The dog gave her a "what a butthead" type of look and turned to slink back to Angus's office.

"You two, come with me." Angus turned and headed back to the case room, no doubt expecting them to follow.

Raider motioned her ahead of him. Yeah. Like she'd return to that death trap of an elevator. Though it was preferable to dealing with Angus Force. The former FBI profiler now headed up this ragtag division of the HDD, and he seemed almost able to read people's minds. Was he reading hers? Did he have one clue that she wasn't who she was supposed to be? How much had he guessed? More importantly, why had he sent her to Boston?

She crossed into the case room to face a whiteboard

across from a conference table. Several pictures of men, aged twenty to seventy, were taped evenly across the expanse. "New case?" she asked.

"Yes." Angus gestured for them to sit. "Did anybody recognize you in Boston?"

It took her a second to realize he was talking to her and not to Raider. "Me?"

"Yes," Angus said.

What the heck? "Why would anybody have recognized me?" she asked, her senses thrumming. Was she being set up? Again?

Raider eyed her and then Angus. "Nobody recognized her. My best suit, which you asked me to wear, did get some attention, however. And I left that business card as ordered. I take it somebody will be calling soon?"

Angus nodded. "I've already read the Boston police report, and yes, somebody will be calling your new ID, which we're still creating."

Curiosity took Brigid as she sat down with Raider beside her.

Angus moved to the board. "New case I requested from the HDD. They think it's crap, and I think it has merit. Either that, or somebody is messing with us."

Raider stiffened just enough that Brigid could feel his tension. "How so?"

"While the Irish mob no longer exists in Boston, there are criminals, past associates of the mob, that have risen in the ranks and become threats recently," Angus said, standing big and broad on the other side of the table.

Brigid perched in her seat, still not seeing the connection. She had no problem hacking into criminal affairs, so perhaps that's why she was included on this op?

"How so?" Raider asked, all business.

"Instead of working within the usual, or rather former,

hierarchy of the mob, these guys are outsourcing work to incredibly skilled computer criminals for everything from laundering money to shipping schedules," Angus said.

"Like me," Brigid said quietly. Oh, the fine line between hacking for the government and for criminals. In fact, was there even a line? She couldn't see it anymore. Bad guys were everywhere.

Angus nodded. "Exactly. We have a lead on a group using a site on the dark web. They're running drugs, and I'm telling you, I think there's more." He scrubbed a hand across his eyes. "In fact, I think I've found what."

The dark web was nearly impossible to hack. "I can't just find a site without knowing where it is," Brigid said. "The key to bringing down somebody on the dark web is—"

"Getting them to meet you in person," Raider said. "Guess that's my part of this op."

"Partially," Angus said, eyeing them both. "There's something else."

Warning ticked through Brigid. Why, she didn't know. But her instincts rose instantly, and she stiffened. "What?"

"We think this might be one of the key players." Angus turned and taped one more picture to the board.

Brigid stopped breathing. She stared at the picture. He had aged. His skin was leathery, his nose broken more than once, and his hair now all gray.

Raider glanced at her. "Who is that?"

"My father," she whispered. The man she only spoke to out of duty these days. She coughed. "You're crazy. He's a farmer. Always has been."

Angus winced. "No. He was involved with the Irish mob, more specifically the Coonan family, for years. Formative ones. Then he supposedly got out, but now we think he's back in, and he's part of what's happening now."

That couldn't be true. No way. "That's why you sent us

to Boston? Those guys in the corner were mobsters?" Brigid gasped.

"Yep. Just wanted to see if you'd be recognized, and I also needed Raider to leave his new calling card," Angus said.

"Damn it," Raider muttered. "You could've given me a heads-up."

Brigid tried to rein in her temper. "Of course nobody recognized me. You're wrong about my father."

"Prove it," Angus said mildly. "You and Raider go talk to him and prove I'm wrong. But be prepared to be incorrect about this."

Brigid shook her head. "You want me to take an obvious government agent to my father's farm and what? Just ask him if he's involved in cybercrime?" No way. "Believe me. My dad wouldn't talk to a Fed if he was dying."

Angus's smile didn't provide reassurance. "No. You're going home to reconcile with your father because you've finally found your way in life with the man next to you—one with possible criminal ties that we're still working out. The man you want to introduce to your father before you marry."

"Marry?" Brigid blurted, her mind spinning wildly. "Are you nuts?" She turned to the straitlaced hottie next to her. "Tell him this won't work."

Raider hadn't moved. "This is important, Force?"

"Crucial," Angus affirmed. "There's more going on here than drugs. I just know it."

Raider turned and studied her with those deep, dark eyes. "Well, Irish. Looks like we're engaged." His smile sent butterflies winging through her abdomen. "This is going to be interesting. Now that you're mine, I will finally figure you out."

Chapter Two

Anticipation rushed through Raider's veins, yet he sat still in his seat, schooling his expression into mild interest.

Force smiled at Brigid. "I need you to reach out to Wolfe's new friend Dana. The journalist? Supposedly she's been working on a story about the Irish mob and credit card fraud."

Supposedly? There was no such thing with Angus Force. "How did you tip her off?" Raider lifted his head.

Force shrugged. "It wasn't hard. She's a good investigator, and I planted a few crumbs. She picked them up easily, which is good, because we need her sources."

"We've only been back a week. Now Dana is Wolfe's friend?" They'd met the woman the week before in Kentucky on another assignment, and he hadn't thought the two had hit it off. Clarence Wolfe was the muscle for the unit, and dollars to donuts, he was insane. Or else he had a really weird sense of humor. Raider hadn't pinned him down yet. "He's not going to like you messing with her life."

Force tugged his T-shirt free of his neck. "He's a good soldier and he'll understand the mission. Well, probably. Brigid? After you call Dana, I need one more thing from you today. There was a new possible sighting of Henry

Wayne Lassiter in Malibu the other day. Would you mind dodging into your computer room and running it down?"

"Sure." Brigid stood, her gaze flicking to Raider and back. The woman's green eyes had captivated him from the first second, followed closely by that slight Irish brogue with a hint of Boston in it. The brogue was strong, but the eyes vulnerable. She tried to hide it, but he was a master at figuring people out. What scared her? She was all wrong for him, but the flashes of fear she let slip drew him. If she needed protection, he could provide that. It was his job, after all.

She bit her lip before continuing. "You know we haven't found any proof that Lassiter is alive, right?" Her voice was tentative and her glance sympathetic as she focused back on Force.

"I'm aware," Force said dryly. "And if one more of you gives me a copy of *Moby-Dick*, I'm going to fire you all."

Well, the guy was searching for a whale that didn't exist. Lassiter was a serial killer Force had shot and supposedly killed five years ago who maybe, just maybe, was actually alive. Raider thought Force was tilting at windmills, but so long as the guy didn't get in the way of Raider's op, he didn't much care.

Brigid moved silently from the room, and the air somehow grew heavy. Roscoe lifted his head from his bed in the corner, sniffed, and jumped to his feet, following the woman, his tail wagging.

Force stood by the board, his muscled arms crossed, his green eyes shrewd.

Raider studied him. "Why now, Force?" The guy had impeccable timing. "There's a ticking clock on all that you do."

Force nodded. "Yeah. The HDD tracked some of Coonan's money to Thailand, where there are several missing girls."

Ah, crap. "You think they're trafficking kids?" Raider grunted.

"Maybe. Gut feeling? Yes. And those kids are somehow being moved right now." Fury darkened Angus's gaze.

Raider swallowed. "Then put Brigid on it. Why didn't you tell her?"

Angus shook his head. "Tell her that her father might be part of a human trafficking ring? Right. For now, you don't tell her this part of the operation."

Fair enough. She didn't need to know that. "Fine."

Angus's chin lowered. "What about you? Are you okay with this assignment?"

Raider lifted a shoulder. "Of course."

A muscle ticked right beneath Force's jaw. His gaze narrowed, and his hands were steady. Too steady. Had he been dipping into the bottle again?

Raider waited. He'd learned patience at a young age, too young of an age, and he could sit still all day.

Force's upper lip curved. "Did you think I wouldn't find out?"

Well, that was ambiguous. Raider kept silent and didn't avert his gaze.

Force smiled then, and it wasn't a pretty sight. Oh, he was probably good-looking to most women, and most men, but Raider knew a predator on the edge when he saw one. And the former FBI profiler definitely rode a razor these days. "Raider?" Force asked softly. Way too softly. "I can send Wolfe in with her and fire your ass."

As a threat, it was spot on. Force hadn't been the best for nothing.

Raider shifted gears and strategies in a nanosecond. "How long have you known?"

Force snorted. "I'm a profiler. Jesus. I knew from day one you shouldn't be in the HDD's secret and embarrassing unit." He gestured around the room, encompassing the old yellowed tiles on the floor and dented panel walls. "Is the story even true?"

Raider thought about forcing a blanch but figured Force would see through it. So he went with the truth instead. "That I slept with a superior's wife and got my balls busted? Yeah. That's true." Of course, he hadn't known the woman he'd picked up in a bar that night was married to his boss's boss. But still. He'd never been a guy to pick up a one-night stand, and he deserved a slap-down for doing that, because a government agent, one at his level, had too much to lose. But he'd just lost his partner, and he'd been out drinking, and things had gone from bad to worse. The sex hadn't even been that good. "But it was just an excuse to get transferred."

"So you have friends high enough to get you exactly what you want," Force said, no judgment in his tone.

"Not friends," Raider returned. He could count his friends on one hand, and most of those had grown up with him in foster care. This team, well now. He was starting to count them, too, and he didn't need that distraction. Keeping his distance should be second nature to him, especially since he was a much colder bastard now than he'd ever been—and he hadn't exactly started out warm and fuzzy. "People who want the Coonan family taken down as badly as I do. We saw the opportunity with Brigid and your Deep Ops unit, and we took it. *I* took it." This was on him. Nobody else.

Force yanked out a chair and dropped into it. "I read the report. You were a good handler, and it wasn't your fault Treeson died."

Mel Treeson had been a thirty-year-old smartass with a heart of gold, and nobody deserved to die the way he had at the hands of the Coonans. "I was *his* handler," Raider repeated. Mel's death was on him. Life was simple and true. Shitty but simple.

Force sighed. "How long had you worked together?"

"Off and on for about three years and then two years solid on this op, which centered on the Coonans' drug trade before the patriarch died." Mel had gone undercover in Boston as an enforcer in the Coonan family organization, and to this day, Raider didn't know how he'd been found out. "I've waited a year to figure out another way in." He knew all the players, and even though Brigid's father had supposedly been out for decades, he'd kept feelers out. It had been fortuitous that he'd found out about Brigid—Wait a minute. Raider straightened his already ramrod posture. "You fucker."

Force's face split in a smile. "That's the first time I've heard your real voice."

Ah, shit. His Southern drawl, the one he'd worked so hard to banish, had rolled out with his anger. Raider cleared his throat, sharpening his diction and regaining his necessary and always present control. "You engineered this." He'd forgotten. In his ego, in this rush to get back to the case and take down the people who'd killed his friend, he'd forgotten what a master manipulator Angus Force really was.

Force shrugged. "Meh."

Fury spiraled up Raider's spine, and he breathed deep, holding on to his temper with sheer will. "Meh?"

Force's green eyes glittered. "You've been playing at being an easygoing Fed for over two months in my unit, and you think you have a right to be pissed?"

"Yes," Raider said evenly.

Force snorted. "Fair enough. When I discovered the case, my research led me to Brigid, who was serving time for hacking. I may have requested her release, and I might've ensured you were made aware of her possible transfer to this unit." He flattened large hands on the dented conference table. "The bait was there—but you jumped at it faster than a trout spotting a worm."

Raider aligned the new information with his plans, which didn't change one iota, really. It was good the gloves were off with Force, because now he could drop the pretense. "You already knew about the Coonan family. This case didn't just arrive on your desk." Sometimes he wanted to shoot Force between the eyes.

"Yep." Force slid a manila file toward him. "I have several cases I'm looking into, and this is one of them, and you were a necessary piece on the chessboard. So tomorrow, you be here with your files, since I'm sure you kept copies. We'll add those to the records I've compiled, and we'll come up with a plan."

Yeah, Raider had records. "Do our handlers know about this?" The unit, unfortunately, had a couple of HDD handlers who wanted nothing more than for them to fail.

Angus scratched his chin. "Agents Rutherford and Fields may or may not know. I'm not sending them reports, but that doesn't mean they aren't keeping track."

Oh, those two were definitely keeping track. One problem at a time, though. Raider cleared his throat. "I don't need Brigid to go undercover with me. She's untrained, Force." Plus, he liked the redhead. She was sweet, and even though she'd followed the wrong path and gotten in trouble, he fully planned to help her find a good second chance. The woman deserved it.

Force shook his head. "Don't tell me you're falling for her."

Raider snorted before he could stop himself. "For a wild hacker who keeps getting in trouble with the law? Um, no."

Force's gaze narrowed, and his upper lip tipped. "Not your type?"

"Not even close." Sure, she was pretty and had that fragile underside, but his type was a nice girl with a calm life and no criminal record. One who'd fit in with his life and ambitions at the agency. Someday. Not now. "Regardless, I don't require Brigid on this case."

Force shook his head. "Yes, you do. There's a time crunch, and you need to get through to her father. She's an asset. But to work with her, you need to understand her. Here's when Brigid first found herself on the wrong side of the law." He pushed the manila file folder even closer.

Raider ignored the folder and fought against the curiosity grabbing him. "I already know she was caught hacking into a secure governmental server, sentenced, and yanked from prison by you to work for the unit. Free pass."

Force rolled his eyes. "She's too smart to get caught. Look beyond the pretty face that irritates you so much."

That pretty face kept him up nights, but he'd never admit it. Raider flipped open the folder to quickly read an arrest warrant from years ago. Her first of many arrests. "She was seventeen." He frowned, reading more. "She hacked into a hospital system to research a new drug trial."

"Yep. Her mother had esophagus cancer, and Brigid was looking for hope. Thus began her life of crime," Force said, sliding a second folder his way. "This one is on the arrest three months ago that sent her to federal prison until I pulled her out. Can have her returned any time I want."

Raider glanced at the contents, but he'd already read these. She'd been working for a nonprofit and had hacked into a computer to bust a guy downloading child pornography, but he worked for the Pentagon, and the computer was on a federal server.

"Of course." Force slid the third and last folder, this one a light blue, across the table. "Here's the profile our shrink and I created for Brigid." Once again, he apparently refused to use the name of Nari, the HDD shrink who had been assigned to the unit. What was his problem with her? "To sum up, Brigid's mother died shortly after she was first caught hacking, and her father, a farmer, basically turned away. She left home and has had problems ever since."

Yeah, Raider knew all of that. "What else?"

"Her choice in men. She definitely has a type, and your cover as a criminal who might want to do business with the Coonan organization is perfect." Force cracked his neck.

Raider wanted to look inside the folder, so he purposely kept the top closed. "Has my cover been created?"

"Not yet. I have the team working on it, and we should have it in place within the next couple of days. Brigid will create an online presence for you." Force smiled. "You'll have to lose the suit. Definitely not the type of guy she has gone for in the past, and her daddy will know that."

Figured. "Don't tell me. I have to become a computer geek who gets a hard-on for Comic-Con every year." Raider tapped one finger on the blue folder.

Force snorted. "First of all, Comic-Con is awesome. Secondly, um, no."

Curiosity overcame him, and Raider opened the file to read profiles of three men. One Brigid dated in high school, the other in her early twenties, and the final one just before getting caught this last time. "They're all assholes."

"Apparently, so are you," Force returned. "Read the entire file."

Raider read through the entire file, finally looking up. "All right. She likes rule breakers. The first kid was a petty thief, the second guy a computer hacker who stole credit cards, and the third a vigilante going after bad guys. Forget rule breakers. She likes criminals."

Force rubbed his chin. "They all make their own rules, and they are in control of the situation. It probably suits her mathematical mind."

Amusement ticked through Raider. "Control?" He'd been told by people who actually cared about him that he was a control freak, so that characteristic might be perfect for this assignment. Yet he thought through what he'd just read. "Maybe these guys were in control of certain aspects of their criminal acts, but not one of them controlled her. She hates having a handler."

"She craves stability, Raider," Force said evenly. "Her world was turned on its head when her mother died, and she was left with an absentee father who she's estranged from. She wouldn't be the first person to fall for the illusion of strength in a jackass." He leaned forward. "If I let you continue with this op, her safety is on you."

The pretty redhead's safety had been on him since the second he'd agreed to become her handler. "She won't be harmed."

"I'm not talking physical harm," Force retorted.

Raider looked at a man he truly respected. Oh, Force had problems, but he was a good agent. An obsessed one. "I'll use anybody and anything to take the Coonans down, and you know it. But I'll do my best to protect her." He opened the first folder again to take out a picture of a seventeen-year-old Brigid. Her big green eyes filled her entire face, and at that age, she looked even more fragile than she had after he'd picked her up from prison in her orange jumpsuit. Heat flashed through his chest with the need to protect and shield. A sense he'd only felt for his foster family before now.

A barely there smile crossed Force's face. As if he knew a secret. "Fair enough."

Raider shoved down irritation. "Her falling for the wrong guy—repeatedly—isn't an excuse for breaking the law," he murmured.

"Didn't say it was," Force said, his voice cheerful again. "But you need to turn into a badass criminal with an attitude. The reason I'm telling you this is that when we turn you into her type, she may fall for you, and I don't want personnel problems here."

"What a line of malarkey," came from the door.

Raider winced and looked over his shoulder to find

Brigid standing there, her pale skin flushed a very pretty pink. "I do not have a type, and no way on God's green earth would I fall for Raider Tanaka." Her Irish brogue came out stronger than usual.

If that wasn't a challenge, Raider didn't know what was. "Don't push it, sweetheart."

Her chin snapped up. "Bite me, Tanaka."

Force coughed in the lamest attempt to cover a chuckle ever. "Apparently we'd better get started tomorrow with you two falling in love."

Chapter Three

How freaking unbelievable. The nerve and the ego. Brigid stomped ahead of Raider. "You're such a jerk."

He paused at his desk and drew out his gun, then jammed it at the back of his waist. The weapon was a SIG DAK, and she knew that because Raider and Wolfe had gotten into a mild disagreement the other day about DAK and DA/SA triggers, and she'd had to drown them out to work on her computer. Guns made her itchy.

She swallowed and shrugged off the unease, reminding herself that she now worked for the Homeland Defense Department. Then she turned and maneuvered around the dingy desks to the small foyer, saying a quick prayer before striding into the crappy elevator, which was probably a death trap.

The Fed followed her calmly, his body warm behind her. His weight rocked the car before he pressed the button for the main floor. Then he took up all the space in the delapidated elevator as it ascended and faltered alarmingly every once in a while. He stole all the oxygen as well. Brigid studied the six-foot-two government agent from beneath her lashes. "I am not drawn to controlling individuals," she said with as much force as she could muster.

He moved then, faster than a whip training a new colt.

His big body bracketed her into a corner. "Let's test that theory." When he leaned down, the scent of woodsy musk washed over her like a warning. "And the word 'individuals' wasn't what you meant." His voice went low and hard. "What word did you really mean?"

She blinked twice, up into his incredibly dark eyes. A shiver ticked from her shoulders down her spine, licking each vertebra on the way. This was not the same man she'd been dealing with for the last couple of months. "Step back."

His face lowered, his eyes blazing. "No."

Holy crap. She tried to meet his gaze, but her stomach had gone all mushy and her head fuzzy. What in the world was happening? He was like a code that didn't add up. Unfortunately, she was drawn to a mystery like that as much as to a seriously sexy man. This one she should *so* not find sexy. He wasn't even close to her type. "Raider," she breathed.

He watched her more closely than anybody ever had, his gaze running from her widened eyes down her heated face to her throat as she convulsively swallowed. His chin lifted. "Interesting. Score one for the profilers."

Panic melded with anger, and she let both loose. She shoved him with hands set on either side of his perfect tie.

He didn't move. Hard muscle, cut and warm, lurked beneath the pristinely pressed shirt. His head cocked to the side. "I asked you a question, Brigid." The commanding tone alone would've caught her attention, but a thread beneath, a hint of something new, stilled her. Was that a Southern accent?

She needed more words from him. "Men. Man. Males," she muttered. "I don't like controlling men."

"Of course, you don't," he agreed, stepping back just enough to let her breathe. "But you do like men who are in control." The accent was gone.

"There's no difference," she snapped.

"Oh, sugar. There's definitely a difference." There it was again.

Very faint, but so intriguing she leaned toward him. "Do you have an accent?" she asked.

His smile provided both warning and invitation. "You'll know me well enough to be able to answer that question soon."

She tried to swallow again. The man was throwing her completely off balance. Seeing him in action earlier had set her hormones into overdrive, and that was a huge problem. A betrayal by her own body, for Pete's sake. He was all about control and loyalty to the team, and he'd never understand that she wasn't. She couldn't be. Even so, she couldn't help but study him as the stupid elevator took its time deciding whether to take them up two floors or just drop them according to gravitational laws. Man, he was something to look at.

Jet-black hair, thick and a bit wavy, showcased a hard-ridged and symmetrical face. His eyes were as dark as his hair, and they often seemed to look right through her. His lean physique was muscular, and she'd thought he moved with the grace of a swimmer. Apparently, based on the fight at the diner, a swimmer who could kick your ass if necessary. The guy probably had an exercise regimen he kept to religiously. He seemed like the type.

He returned the survey, *not* beneath his lashes. The man had no problem keeping an eye on her.

That was part of his job, of course.

"Stop looking at me," she murmured.

"You're looking at me," he returned easily as the elevator stopped abruptly and jumped twice. The door did not open. He frowned, finally releasing her gaze from his spell. "This thing can't be safe."

No doubt. Finally, as he focused elsewhere, she could breathe. Brigid pushed her unruly hair away from her face and forced thoughts of small spaces out of her head. Kind of. "You know we can't pretend to be engaged, right?"

Raider shrugged. "That's the assignment, Irish." His tone remained unconcerned, and he appeared relaxed. Yet a tension, a promise that he could leap into action in a nanosecond, always emanated from him. It both fascinated and irritated the heck out of her.

Brigid bit her lip and stared at the closed elevator door. "Shouldn't this be opening about now?"

"Yes," he said, leaning back against the scarred wooden wall. "The door will open soon. Probably. Who knows. It's ancient."

Wonderful. Being stuck in a rickety elevator with Raider, especially this new unmasked version of him, was the last place on earth she wanted to be. Well, the second to the last place. Prison had sucked—royally. "You don't have to come with me to see my father. I can handle the mission on my own."

Raider didn't answer.

Irritation clawed Brigid's throat. She couldn't handle him pretending to be all bad-boy on her. It was too much. "I said you're not needed."

He lowered his chin, his gaze more than a little direct. Oddly so. "I'm your handler. Where you go, I go."

Handler. The way he said it, or maybe the way she heard it, sent sparking tingles through her that she did not need. Not at all. It was crazy, insane actually, to look at Raider as anything other than another governmental drone put on earth to make her life painful and frightening.

Yet there was something about him, a respect or just politeness when he dealt with her that she couldn't figure out. Especially since she'd seen him so casually use violence against those guys in Boston. She was a former con, and he was an HDD agent. Yet he treated her with respect, watchful though it might be, and never once had been unkind. Not once. "Why are you here?" she whispered.

He looked at the closed door, as if contemplating what to do about it. The elevator was so old that there wasn't even a phone inside. Or an emergency button. "I told you."

"No." The walls were starting to close in on her, and she took a deep breath. "Come on, Raider. I've now seen you leap into action." Far faster and more efficiently than what she would've imagined. Even when relaxed, he was way too alert. Sure, she'd heard he got into trouble by sleeping with his boss's wife without knowing who she was, but something told Brigid that he could've fought being demoted. "Why are you stuck babysitting me?" Or now agreeing to pretend to be her fiancé?

"You're a threat." He said the words simply, his gaze meeting hers again. "Your ability with computers, with hacking and coding, make you dangerous to this country and everything I believe in. Watching you, making sure you don't create a disaster, is an important job." He scrubbed a hand through his thick hair, giving her more space, as if somehow knowing she needed it.

There was something else. She could sense it beneath his surface just like a hidden line of code. "What else?"

"Keeping you safe is just as important."

Her eyebrows lifted on their own accord. That wasn't it, but his claim was interesting. "Keeping me safe? I'm not in danger."

He gave her that look then. The one she'd seen more than a dozen times in the last two months, since they'd met. The look that said he thought she was slightly nuts. "You're one of the best. You've been able to hack into systems that are unhackable."

"Nothing, no system, is ever unhackable," she returned without thinking.

"Exactly. You're known now. After being arrested and

incarcerated, your name is known worldwide. Do you have any idea what a foreign enemy would do to get their hands on you?" he asked, his voice soft.

What about *his* hands? Her mind had to knock it off. "You're overestimating me."

"Not even close, Irish."

She blinked. "My accent isn't strong enough to warrant the nickname," she muttered. Her father had been Irish, her mother Bostonian, and her speech pattern held slight, very slight, hints of both. That's all. She grew up on a farm in the USA, for Pete's sake.

"I think it does." Raider moved toward the doors and placed his hands in the middle, digging his fingers between them. Or rather, he tried to do so.

Nothing happened.

Brigid's breath quickened. That fast, she was back in a cell. Her lungs hurt. Her vision narrowed from the outside, making her eyes sting. Were they even on the top level? How far would they have to fall? God, she had to get out of there. She sucked in air.

He turned then, narrowing his focus onto her again. "Whoa." Stepping in, he grasped her chin and lifted her face enough to meet his eyes. "Take a deep breath."

She couldn't breathe.

"Now, Brigid." The command in his voice shot through her panicked mind.

She instinctively heeded it and pulled in air, filling her lungs. Automatically obeying him just as she had in the pub. What was *wrong* with her?

"Now let it out. Slowly." He waited until she did so. "Again."

She obeyed his order, and her heart rate slowed down. Then she started to focus on something other than her imminent death in a small space. His size. His scent of male and musk. His nearness and warmth.

Her heart kicked back in along with her libido. Heat flushed through her, igniting nerves, softening something deep inside her. His grip remained gentle yet firm on her chin. If he lowered his head, his mouth could be on hers.

Where the heck had that thought come from? Heat burst into her face, no doubt turning her a very unappealing crimson.

"It's okay," he murmured, the tone deep and reassuring. "The door will open."

The door? What door? She coughed. "You don't like me." The words tumbled out. Was she reminding him or herself?

Both of his dark eyebrows rose. "That's not true." He released her and stepped back.

"Yes, it is." She wanted to cross her arms but forced herself to remain still and in control.

"No. I just haven't figured you out." He turned for the door again.

She frowned at his broad back. "So?"

"I figure everyone out." He smacked his palm against the door. "Open, darn it." The doors shook and then inched open awkwardly. He'd done it again.

"You sure have a way with elevators," she breathed, jumping out into the dingy hallway.

"Just wait until you see how good I am with a fiancée," he murmured, moving out behind her and bringing heat and power with him.

She shivered. Was that a threat or a promise?

Chapter Four

Raider held the outside door open for the charming computer expert, his gaze automatically scanning the area for danger. Dim streetlights cut through the dark night, illuminating the barren area. The wind blew pine needles across the dew-covered grass, landing against an ancient picnic table placed beneath trees in an odd and deserted park next to the nearly vacant parking lot. The lone building, erected sometime in the late seventies, was set among trees about an hour outside of DC.

The Homeland Defense Department didn't want Angus Force's small unit to be comfortable, that was for sure. That was fine with Raider. He might wear thousand-dollar suits once in a while, but most of his life, he'd felt lucky if he had food in his belly and some sort of roof over his head—especially if nobody wanted to hurt him right at that moment.

Of course, pain came from unexpected places. He placed his hand at the small of Brigid's back and then grinned when she jumped. "We're engaged, Irish." His hand remained in place. "You'll need to get used to me touching you."

She hurried her walk. "Whatever."

Skittish, wasn't she? He easily followed the redhead toward his truck, which was parked in the center of the lot. Her skin was warm beneath her blouse. Keeping her off balance was necessary. It'd be easier if she wasn't so damn likable. They'd forged a natural friendship, and he actually trusted her, which was odd for him. It made his job more difficult.

She was smart, and now that she had her feet under her with the Deep Ops unit, she was starting to ask questions. Ones that showed she saw beneath the surface. He needed to be careful with her. With what he showed her. His single goal was to bring down the Coonan family, and if that included her father, so be it.

An energy-efficient light green car whipped into the lot, and Raider instinctively pivoted to put Brigid against his truck, blocking her with his body. The car lurched to a stop, rocking slightly. The door opened, and Clarence Wolfe unfolded his six-foot-six frame with the grace of a panther on the hunt.

Raider fought amusement. The guy looked like he'd gotten out of one of those crazy clown cars. "What the hell are you driving?"

Wolfe's blunt features widened in a smile as he drew out a tray holding three lattes, complete with mounds of whipped cream covered in sprinkles. "I was undercover, watching Dana's six. She was meeting with a source."

There was no way the massive ex-soldier could blend in, especially in the minuscule car. In fact, with his buzz cut hair, scar down his jaw, and cut muscles, he stood out wherever he went. "Okay," Raider said. He tried to keep from blanching as Wolfe handed over a latte, one that no doubt would cause a sugar high from hell. "Thanks."

Brigid leaned around Raider to accept hers. "Yum."

Raider sipped on the straw, and the sugar hit his stomach instantly.

Wolfe nodded. "Just one shot of coffee since it's nighttime. The flavor is candy cane."

Brigid gave a barely there sigh behind Raider. For some reason, Wolfe was obsessed with giving everyone lattes laden with sugar, and the massive soldier seemed so happy about it that nobody could ruin his delight. Especially since he was usually planning how to take out their enemies. Real or imagined. "Are you here to see Angus?" she asked.

"Nope. Force texted me to take you guys to Dana's place and promised he'd spring for pizza. Said you should talk to her about a mob story she's working on." Wolfe dropped his head and sucked coffee through his straw, draining half the drink. "Though she doesn't share stories, even ones that Force obviously tipped her off about. I'll talk to him later regarding that situation."

Oh, she'd share this one. Raider cocked his head. Would he have to go through Wolfe to get to the journalist? "How close are you and Dana?"

Wolfe lifted a shoulder. "Just friends. I can't take on more than that right now. Until I finish my mission."

"What is that mission?" Brigid asked, stirring the whipped cream.

Wolfe's eyes lost all expression. "I'll let you know when it's time."

Awareness danced up Raider's spine and spread across his shoulders. Sometimes he saw a glimpse of the cunning predator beneath Wolfe's easygoing, goofy, and sometimes crazy façade. "You know we're a team, right?"

"Yep." Wolfe's good nature returned immediately, and he finished his latte. "I wouldn't spring for the good sprinkles if we weren't a team." A plaintive meow sounded from the left pocket of his battered leather jacket, and he glanced down as a furry white head popped out. The kitten blinked bright green and blue eyes, and his damaged left ear twitched. "Kat. What the heck, dude? You just went to the can."

"Oh, you sweetie." Brigid handed off her latte to Raider and gingerly lifted the kitten out of Wolfe's pocket. "Come on, baby. I'll take you over to the grass." She cuddled the animal to her chest and strode across the ripped-up asphalt serving as their parking lot.

Lucky cat. Raider watched her go, along with Wolfe. There were no threats near the barren park, even though parts of it were dark. "Stay in the light, Brigid," he called out.

Wolfe sipped his drink. "That cat is such a chick magnet."

Raider blinked. The ex-soldier had rescued the kitten by the side of the road and quickly adopted it. "You know, at some point, he's going to be too big for your pocket."

Wolfe scratched his whiskered jaw. "I'll just get bigger pockets." He finished his drink with one long pull on the straw. "Or maybe he won't want to stay in pockets any longer. It's his life." The wind picked up and scattered wet leaves across their boots. Wolfe shifted, and the SIG Sauer at his waist caught the dim light for a moment. "But I do feed him tuna fish, goldfish crackers, and steak. So he'll probably stay with me. Unless he finds the right kitty to settle down with."

"Do you try to sound nutty?" Raider asked, keeping Brigid within sight.

Wolfe grinned. "Rumor has it we have to turn you into the ideal man for Brigid. You're gonna have to lose the suit." He lifted his head toward the park. "You should smile at her more. Shotgun." He strode around the truck and jumped into the passenger seat, rocking the entire vehicle as he did so.

Brigid snagged the kitten as he began to climb a tree and turned back for Raider, her expression unguarded as she snuggled the cat. In that moment, she looked young and vulnerable. Even fragile.

And he planned to ruin her father. Sometimes, he wished he'd become a dentist instead of an operative, like his favorite foster mom had suggested. But even then, he'd known something lived inside him that needed to seek and destroy those who caused pain, and out of deference to Miss A and her rules, he'd gone the legal route. It was unfortunate that Brigid's father had not.

Brigid played with the kitten on the silent drive to the reporter's apartment outside of DC, her mind spinning. No way was her father involved in the mob. Not the grumbly old farmer who'd gone through the motions of raising her. He'd been all about rules and guidelines with a strong dislike for modern technology. Her dad had thought television was for the news only, and that social media would lead to the destruction of civilization. He might've been right.

But he had not broken the law. Just because he was from Ireland, decades and decades ago, didn't make him an Irish mobster.

Although she rarely spoke to him since going off on her own, she'd clear his name. It was the least she could do—especially for her mother.

"Damn it." Wolfe leaned slightly forward to read the face of his phone, the light washing over his blunt face. "Go here." He gave an address in a suburb outside of DC.

Brigid leaned to the side to study his profile better.

Raider drove off the Interstate. "What's happening?" he asked, his tone calm.

"Dana followed a lead and needs a pickup," Wolfe said. "She's been working on a story about a dentist selling prescription drugs out of the back of his practice, mainly to bored housewives, and one of her sources must've given her a call after I left her apartment."

Raider glanced back at Brigid. "Why is Dana calling you?"

"Can't get to her car," Wolfe said, urgency lowering his voice. "What the hell is she doing? I told her not to go without backup. That moronic camera guy she uses has never even shot a gun, and chances are she didn't even take him."

Brigid petted the purring kitten, her heart rate accelerating. "Isn't Dana a crime reporter with the *Post*? And she's telling you all about her stories?"

"She's freelance now," Wolfe said, drawing his gun from the back of his waist. "And she didn't exactly tell me about her cases." Darkness and then light alternated inside the cab as they drove quickly past the streetlights. "I might have broken into her apartment and then her computer so I could find out what she's working on. Her password was almost too easy to guess," Wolfe admitted, his hand on the gun.

Brigid swallowed. There seemed to be no boundaries to Wolfe's friendship. Just how dangerous was the ex-soldier? She only knew him in passing at this point, and the lattes and the kitten had disarmed her. Had that all been intentional? "Wolfe, she probably won't like that invasion of her privacy." Brigid squinted out the window at a commercial area with a few boarded-up buildings with bars on the windows and doors.

Wolfe pointed down a side street. "Drive to the mom-and-pop convenience store and park there." A few dented and older vehicles occupied the parking area, while a car or two pulsing with loud, pounding music drove by.

Raider did so, easily pulling into the lot and scanning the area. "Montegue Dentistry?" He pointed to a darkened strip mall directly across the street. "Where is she?"

Wolfe texted something. "She stopped answering." He

glanced back at Brigid. "You and Kat stay down. Raider, I'll take the back. You go in the front."

Brigid's breath quickened. "Wait a minute. If she's working, did she ask you to come in with guns blazing?"

Just then, a woman dressed in all black burst around the side of the building, running full bore toward them. Her blond hair was secured through a dark baseball cap, and she clutched a camera to her chest. Two men ran behind her, and one fired a shot that missed the woman and pinged off the curb.

"Get down," Raider ordered, already jumping out of the truck.

Brigid gasped and ducked down, curling over the kitten. How was any of this even happening?

Wolfe leaped out and immediately fired back, slamming the door.

"Our unit can't go public right now. Try not to hit anybody," Raider snapped, ducking low and shutting his door.

Brigid barely leaned up to peer out the window. Raider and Wolfe kept pace with each other, both firing across the street at the two men but hitting the building. Dana kept running toward them, and vehicles swerved out of the way. She reached them, and Wolfe grabbed her arm and tossed her behind him. She landed on her feet, wobbled, and then ran between a couple of cars into the parking lot.

Wolfe and Raider continued to advance, and the two other guys retreated and ran around the building again.

Dana reached the truck and opened the back door, jumping inside. "Hi."

Brigid blinked. "Hi."

Dana leaned over and sucked in several deep breaths. "Got pictures and everything." She held up a camera, her green eyes sparkling. "Pretended to be a buyer and have all the evidence for a story." Her face was flushed and her voice high.

Raider and Wolfe ran back to the truck and shoved their way inside.

Wolfe turned around. "What the holy hell were you doing?" he snapped. He shoved his gun in the jockey box.

Kat jerked on Brigid's lap and gave a little meow. Brigid swallowed and turned to look at Dana.

Raider turned around. "Do we need to call the police? If so, we have to do it on the run."

Dana shook her head. "No. I can file the story online in about an hour, and then I'll call the police. Those morons won't get far." She held the digital camera to her chest. "You said you wanted to provide backup, Wolfe."

"Then I needed to be here to be backup," Wolfe countered, his face harder than ever. "We are going to have a long and uncomfortable discussion about this later."

Dana rolled her eyes. "Not your place, *friend*."

Okey doke. Wow. There were some emotions here that even Brigid could sense.

Raider fired up the truck and pulled out of the lot. "As I see it, Dana, now you owe us a favor." After engaging in an illegal shootout and damaging a building, he was as calm as if he'd been at the beach all day. How did he do that? What kind of a childhood did it take to learn that type of control?

Dana stiffened. "All right. That's fair. What do you want?"

Raider looked at her through the rearview mirror. "All of your research into the current status of the Irish mob, the Coonan organization, and anything else that ties in so far. I want it tonight so I can read it all before our debriefing tomorrow."

Dana pursed her lips. "How in the heck did you know about my story?"

"My boss is the one who tipped you off initially." Wolfe turned fully in his seat to look at her. "Then, just to make sure, I read your computer files. *Friend*." He smiled, and the sight was nowhere near reassuring.

Raider sighed. "We don't have time for this."

Chapter Five

Brigid awoke early in her miniscule apartment, her heart thundering. Rain pattered outside, and she stilled, listening for any sound of an intruder. Nothing. No shuffles, or moved air, or the too quiet sense of somebody holding their breath. Muscle by muscle, she forced her body to relax in the uncomfortably soft bed that had come with the apartment. Then she pushed off the bedspread, staying as silent as possible, and padded outside of the tiny bedroom to the living area.

The round dining table was still in front of the door, where she shoved it every night, her muscles straining. Biting her lip, she moved over to the sole window to see the old screwdriver placed in the sill and shoved slightly beneath the sliding glass. Nobody could get in.

Oh, they might try, but she would hear them.

She was just as imprisoned now as if she were still in that cell. Or in one of the dark holes they'd threatened to throw her in if she didn't cooperate.

Sweat broke out down her back. Her breathing quickened, and she tried to halt the oncoming panic attack, but it hit anyway. She could call her friend Pippa, who also had attacks and would understand. But she had to be careful with Pippa, who was now living with Malcolm, one of the Deep Ops agents.

She couldn't tell the truth to anybody. She sank to the floor and pressed her forehead to her knees, letting the fear take her for a moment. Until it didn't want her any longer.

Her phone buzzed, and she let out a muffled scream. Damn it. Scrambling for the counter, she tugged the phone down where she could continue to sit on the floor. "What?" she answered.

"Agent Banaghan. Where's your report on your unscheduled trip to Boston?" Agent Tom Rutherford asked, his tone authoritative and somehow threatening.

She gulped down air and tried to calm her voice. "I don't have a report. We went, there was a fight, and we returned home. I don't even know what the case is about, yet." She could probably get away with that lie for a day or so. No longer.

Rutherford sighed. The jerk was probably at the office dressed in a hugely expensive suit with his perfect blond hair swept back. What a jackass. "Do I have to remind you—"

"No. Stop reminding me," she whispered. He held the cards and she did not. She got it. "I'll get a report to you today, although I don't have much to say."

"Good." He clicked off.

She set the phone down and knocked her head against the cupboard. Life sucked.

Once she could breathe again, she moved like an old woman to the bathroom to get ready for the day. Raider would soon be there to pick her up, and he'd see the sleepless night on her face. She'd worried about her father all night.

After quickly getting ready, she waited for Raider, who seemed to be in his own head for the morning. The drive to work was blissfully silent, though she'd admired his strong hands on the steering wheel for much too long. When she walked into the dingy HDD offices, she was pathetically grateful for the sugar-laden lattes already waiting.

She took a latte off the battered first desk, the one that Wolfe had claimed. The room was vacant, though. "I don't see why you always have to drive," she said, taking a big drink, now ready to engage in dialogue.

Raider eyed the remaining drink. "It's my truck."

Yeah, but something told her he'd want to drive even if it was her vehicle. "I think you're a control freak."

"Okay." He'd dressed down today in a plain black T-shirt and jeans, and his body looked harder than ever. "I can live with that."

Her gray T-shirt illustrated a joke about string theory with a puppy all wrapped up in string.

Wolfe strode out of the second case room, with Kat perched on his shoulder. "They're almost ready. Nari was up all night adding your records to Force's and Dana's, and they have a good slide show ready to go." He tilted his head toward the remaining latte, his dark eyes even darker than usual. "That's yours, Raider."

"Thanks." Raider took the drink and swirled it around, watching the whipped cream. "Appreciate it." He barely hid his wince.

A side door opened, and Malcolm West and the very petite Nari Zhang strode out of Nari's office. Malcolm was their field specialist, and Nari their shrink.

"Morning," Nari said, her black hair in a ponytail and her pretty brown eyes studying them. For casual Saturday, she'd dressed in cream-colored slacks and a pretty floral blouse with silver jewelry.

Brigid tugged on her T-shirt. She always felt frumpy next to the fashionable psychiatrist. Even the woman's ankle boots were an off-cream with cool green accents, which gave her a couple extra inches in height. She still looked dainty next to Malcolm.

"Morning," Brigid said, looking at the agent. Malcolm was a former cop, an undercover specialist, and a decent guy. He had dark hair, sharp eyes, and was as tall as Raider. He'd recently solved a case and fallen in love with the woman he was supposed to investigate. "How's Pippa doing?" Brigid had enjoyed getting to know the quiet woman while they'd painted the offices the previous week, and had barely kept herself from calling Pippa for support after the panic attack earlier.

"Good," Malcolm said, his eyes softening. "She's been out a lot lately and needs some downtime at home. Away from people."

"It's a good idea," Nari said, moving closer, her boots alive on the worn concrete. "With her anxiety disorder, she's doing the right thing in giving herself time alone. She's managing very well."

"Plus"—Wolfe smiled as the kitten rubbed against his chin—"if Pippa is home, she's probably doing some baking while working on the Internet. I'm expecting cookies or pie tomorrow, Mal." The kitten nipped at his ear and batted at his cheekbone, perfectly content on the big soldier's shoulder.

Brigid nodded. "Those sugar doodles she made last week were amazing." The woman could really bake.

Malcolm grinned before he turned and headed for the elevators. "I'll see what I can do."

Wolfe followed him. "Maybe I'll come with you. I'm free this morning since the police picked up the dentist Dana busted. Did you read her article? It'll be in the print edition today." He kept talking as they walked onto the terrible elevator and the doors finally closed.

Angus Force poked his head out of the case room. "Are we getting to work, or what?" His short dark hair was ruffled, and his eyes were bloodshot. Had he been up all night?

Raider gave her a look and strode toward the room, gingerly sipping his latte.

Brigid liked the sugar. She followed him into the room and took a seat at the dented conference table, careful not to snag her shirt on the top's wooden slivers. Angus had pulled down a yellowed screen in front of the whiteboard, and he moved to the head of the table, where a laptop had been set up.

Raider sat on her left, and Nari took the seat at the other end of the table from Angus. As usual.

Brigid looked around. "Hey. Where's Roscoe?"

Nari's nostrils flared. "Grounded in my office. He ate my best lipstick yesterday."

Brigid bit back a smile. Being grounded in the shrink's office meant Roscoe was sleeping on a cushy bed in the corner with doggie treats and a bowl of water nearby. Poor dog. It was nice to be around animals again. Sometimes she missed the farm so badly, the pain felt physical.

"I told you not to leave makeup or booze around," Angus muttered, setting his hands on the keyboard.

He typed slowly with two fingers, and finally a face came up on the screen. The man had short black hair, blue eyes, square features, and a flattened nose. His eyes lacked emotion, and he appeared to be in his midforties. "Meet Eddie Coonan, son of the recently deceased Patrick Coonan, head of the Coonan crime family. His daddy died three months ago."

The guy looked like a mobster. A brawler. "He's the leader?" Brigid asked.

"Yes," Nari said, shuffling a series of manila files in front of her. "He's been running drugs and extorting money since he was a teenager, and don't let his looks fool you.

He's brilliant. Probably a sociopath, from what I've been able to glean."

No way did Brigid's father know this guy. "If you give me an hour, I'll get you everything else on him."

Angus nodded. "That's the plan. Among other crimes, the Coonans have a first-class laundering system in place using hair-styling salons, laundromats, and motels, among a few other businesses that are hard to audit and easy to exploit."

Brigid studied the man on the screen. "The motels are the cheap kind? Where cash is still okay?"

"Exactly," Angus said.

Made sense. There was no way to really know if one person or a hundred checked into an inexpensive hotel in a night.

Angus continued. "Before I have you do a deeper dive, let me show you what else we have." He clicked another button, and two men came up on the screen. The first guy had blondish-gray hair, was wiry and slender with direct blue eyes. The second guy had brown hair, brown eyes, and a broad chest. "Say hello to Jonny P and Josh the Bear."

Raider let out a whistle. "I know these two. They're Coonan's enforcers, and his best friends. Coonan and Jonny P have been besties since birth, I think. Jonny's dad was in the organization but disappeared in a mob war a decade ago."

"You know them?" Brigid asked, swiveling to stare at Raider. What was going on?

He sighed. "Yes. I was in on a mob case dealing with drug running a while ago, and I'm familiar with most of the players."

There was more to his story. Her mind started to click facts into place. Betrayal rankled her like poison ivy.

"Later," Angus said. "You two will have plenty of time

to talk when you start dating. For now, work." He looked at Raider's latte. "You going to drink that?"

"Hell no," Raider said, nudging it toward Angus. "Wolfe isn't here, so please take this. You actually want it?"

"Rough night. It's either sugar or Jack Daniel's," Force muttered, taking the drink.

Oh, Raider had some explaining to do. For now, Brigid would listen to her boss. "What about Josh the Bear?" she asked. The guy looked like a muscled teddy bear.

"Fascinating guy," Nari said, studying the screen. "He just showed up out of nowhere about fifteen years ago and immediately befriended Jonny P."

Raider nodded. "We couldn't find anything on him before that time. He didn't exist."

Brigid sipped her drink, and the warmth pooled in her stomach. "Any chance he's undercover?"

"No," Force said shortly. "Though he is interesting. Volunteers at the food bank, plays Santa every holiday season, and then calmly goes out and buries bodies for the Coonans with the same smile on his face. While Jonny P likes to take his time and enjoys his work with a knife, Josh is quick and efficient with a gun. Just gets the job done. That much I was able to learn on my other case."

Brigid shivered. "So, they're killers."

"Absolutely," Nari said thoughtfully. "Though I can't tell if Josh's loyalty is to the mob, to Coonan, to Jonny P, or if it's just a job. I would love to get into his head."

Angus studied her. "Probably not going to happen. Also, everyone be aware that Jonny P is an expert in explosives. Guy loves to blow things up, and he likes to make a statement. He's the perfect enforcer for the Coonans." The screen went dark. "Raider? We have an identity almost in place for you as a cybercriminal with an extensive history of phishing, identity theft, and credit card fraud. You are too successful and need somebody to launder your illegal gains, and the Coonans are the best around. Your skills and resources will be appealing to the Coonans and their new venture into cybercrime, and it also explains your hooking up with Brigid."

Raider sat back, his gaze on the blank screen. "If her father is still a player, and that's my background, he'll think I'm using Brigid to get to him."

"Exactly," Force said quietly. "He won't play games with you. Either he'll confront you, or he'll just try to take you out."

Brigid shoved back her chair. "My father is not a killer." Though he sure wouldn't like a guy cozying up to Brigid just to get to her dad. That was a crazy play.

"He was," Force said, almost gently, typing again. A picture of her father in his early twenties flashed onto the screen, standing next to a younger and harder version of Eddie Coonan, right down to the smashed nose. Eddie had inherited his looks from his daddy, without question. The picture was yellowed with age, and her dad had his arm around Patrick Coonan. "Your dad and Patrick were close. And your dad has a record." He pushed another manila file across the table. "Extortion, blackmail, assault and battery."

Brigid couldn't breathe.

Raider stopped the file before it could reach her. "This isn't necessary. If her dad thinks I'm using her, the less she knows about his past, the better. She needs to look innocent."

She grasped the file with two fingers and tried to tug it free. "I want to know."

Nari tapped manicured nails on the crappy wooden table. "His life of crime ended when he fell in love with a Bostonian waitress named Janet Larington. They got married, bought a farm far away from Boston, and moved there to have a daughter about ten years later." She leaned forward, her chocolate-colored eyes earnest. "It's possible he gave up crime for Janet. That he's not involved."

"He's involved," Force countered, pointing to the file. "Jonny P and Josh the Bear made two trips to your family farm in upstate New York last quarter. They've also reached out via email, but we haven't been able to track down a response. That's your next job."

Brigid's stomach cramped. "No. My dad wouldn't be anywhere near a computer. Or email." He still read the *Farmers' Almanac*, for goodness' sake. "And just because two men went to upstate New York doesn't mean they saw my father. You're reaching, Angus." Heat filtered through her chest.

"You haven't talked to him in quite a while," Angus countered, his green eyes darkening. "You don't know what he's doing."

The words cut deep, even though the tone had been sympathetic. Her temper rose. "That may be true, but a person doesn't just change everything about themselves. He hates technology and wants nothing to do with pretty much anybody but his cows and the farm. You don't know him."

Raider flattened his hand on top of the file folder. "Maybe you don't know him as well as you think," he said, almost gently.

"Maybe not." She tried to think rationally, but her stomach kept flip-flopping. "Is there any record of members of the Coonan organization traveling to the farming community before these two trips?"

"No," Angus said, his gaze narrowing. "We haven't done a deep dive, and I'll have you look for that. But if you find nothing, it does bring up an interesting question."

"Why now?" Brigid asked softly, and the air grew heavy.

Angus nodded. "Exactly. I need you to figure out what has changed, if anything. Coonan senior has died, but my gut says it's more than that."

Her throat went dry. "My dad is a good guy." Period.

Raider turned toward her. "Look at me, Brigid."

She looked up, surprised once again by the intensity in his black eyes. How had she not realized how much he hid beneath his agent façade and meticulous motions? "What?"

"You don't have to read these documents, and you don't have to know anything about your dad besides what you believe in order for us to get this job done. It might be better if you don't know anything." Raider leaned toward her, bringing his warmth with him. "I want to protect you from this. Let me." His voice was low and coaxing with that intriguing hint of the South.

Tempting. Man, it was tempting, and that tone of voice zinged around her erogenous zones. Would he still want to protect her if he knew the full truth? Probably not. But curiosity had always ridden her, and that wasn't stopping now. Plus, she had a job to do. "I can't hack into this enterprise without finding everything," she whispered. It was true. "So I might as well begin with a head start."

Regret flashed for the briefest of seconds across the hard planes of his face. He lifted his hand so she could take the file folder. "Fair enough."

Chapter Six

After a truly rotten day of reading police records and hacking into personal email accounts, Brigid's temples pounded and her chest hurt. She'd confirmed that the two mobsters had traveled to her small hometown, but what they'd done there, she had no clue. There was absolutely no evidence that they'd met with her father. But why would they go to such a rural area if not to meet him?

The manila file folders in her hands felt heavy. Aye, her father had been a criminal before meeting her mother. She wasn't sure what to think about that. He'd given her such a hard time the first time she'd been arrested.

Maybe that was why.

She stood outside Raider's apartment as he unlocked his door. The HDD had put them both up in an older complex just about ten miles from the office in a sprawling neighborhood full of commuters. He'd been inside her apartment many times, usually doing a sweep after he brought her home, but she'd never set foot inside his.

He opened the door. "I don't think I need assistance."

Her stomach clenched and her curiosity took over. "Angus asked me to help you with a wardrobe that makes sense." No way would she take a guy in a suit home to meet her father. The idea of seeing her dad again strengthened her headache.

Raider flipped on the small hallway light and walked inside a living room furnished with low-end leather furniture and end tables that had come with the apartment. They were the exact same ones she had. "We need to start looking for new places," he muttered, moving into the utilitarian kitchen with blue Formica countertops. Hers were yellow. They both had contractor-grade gray carpet and plain white tiles in the kitchen. "The HDD only gave us three months of rent."

She hadn't had time to search for a new apartment, since she wasn't sure how long she'd be with the Deep Ops unit.

The place smelled like Raider. Clean and musky with a hint of something spicy. A guitar leaned against the far wall, near a window that looked out at more apartment buildings. "You play the guitar?" she asked, turning to view the agent. He was full of surprises, wasn't he? Just how good was he with that incredible voice?

"Yes." He pulled his gun out of his waistband and set it on the counter, then took his cell phone and speed dialed. "What kind of pizza do you like?"

She shrugged. "Anything without anchovies that isn't too spicy."

"Ham and pineapple?" he asked, his gaze raking her.

She turned away. She had to. "Sure." There wasn't another personal touch in the living room other than the guitar, and she itched to check out his bedroom. Would there be more clues about him there? Somehow, she doubted it. Straightening her shoulders, she set the folders on the counter next to his gun. "One of these is the cover that Force and Nari came up with. We both need to memorize it as well as our history together." She rubbed her eyes.

He finished ordering the food. "I'm sorry you have to lie to your father."

Yeah, that was bugging her. She hadn't seen him forever, and lying to her father now didn't feel right. But she had to clear his name. She was confident of his innocence. How could she not know the man who'd raised her? "Force is wrong about him."

"Maybe, but Force is rarely wrong." Raider brushed her long hair off her shoulder.

She jerked.

He grinned. "We're gonna have to work on that if we're going to convince anybody we're lovers."

"Lovers?" she snorted, ignoring the instant tingling through her skin. "You are such a dork."

"Maybe." He brushed her hair from her other shoulder, and this time she didn't react. "Better," he murmured, his gaze heating. "Are you ready to turn me from a dork into a bad boy?"

She lifted her chin to meet his gaze more directly. "It's hard to turn you into anything when I don't really know the true you." Apparently, he was a master at remaining anonymous. Yet, so was she.

"Meaning?" he asked.

She glanced at the guitar. "Well, in the last couple of days, I've learned that you grew up in foster care, play a guitar, and were already investigating the Irish mob before taking this job with Angus Force." Yeah, she wasn't stupid. "Were you after my father all along?"

"After him, no. Aware of him, yes." Raider slid his hand into his dark jeans. "I can't help it if people look at me and make assumptions."

"You like that," she said, studying him. "You like people not knowing the real you."

His chin lifted. "Maybe. I was seven when I entered the foster system, and some places were good and some not so much. Holding life close to the vest was necessary. At least until I landed at Miss A's when I was twelve."

Miss A. Brigid knew Raider had just gone back to a small Kentucky town to see Miss A and help out a foster brother. Everything in Brigid wanted to meet this mysterious woman who made Raider's voice and eyes go all soft and gentle. She must be quite a lady. "You grew up in the South," she said.

He grinned. "Yes, ma'am. I did." The pure Southern accent rolled right over her skin, tunneled down, and spread warmth throughout her entire body. It was probably safer for females everywhere that he kept that under wraps. "Learned diction and different accents while in training with the HDD."

Wow. Just wow. "Do you speak Japanese?" she asked.

He nodded. "My mother grew up in Seattle and was Japanese, and she taught me both Japanese and English before she died when I was seven. I kept up my studies, no matter where I went. It's a way to keep a part of her with me."

Brigid's heart stuttered. Finally. The real Raider. The more she knew him, the more she liked him, and the worse she felt about the entire situation. Yet she couldn't stop delving into him. "And your father?"

"A marine who died in action before they had a chance to get married, hence my last name," Raider said. "I don't remember him at all, but she sure loved him, so he must've been a good man. They were engaged. I hold that close, too." He leaned back, effectively withdrawing. "All right. Shall we go through my closet for anything that might work?"

She wanted to keep talking and learning about him, but the temptation to see his bedroom was too much to ignore. "Sure, and you don't have to hide the accent from me." Okay. Maybe she wanted to hear it again.

"It's habit by now," he said, sounding like he came from the Midwest. "This way." Brushing by her, he moved into the bedroom, and she followed, her heartbeat quickening just enough for her palms to grow a little sweaty. Raider Tanaka's bedroom.

A big bed with a blue comforter, standard dresser, tables and lamps. And one personal touch. Two pictures on the dresser. She moved to the larger picture, lifting it to see a teenaged Raider with two other boys, a pretty blond girl, and an African American woman with salt-and-pepper hair and smiling brown eyes.

He looked over her shoulder. "Miss A, Hunter, Faye, Mark, and me." His voice cracked just enough on Mark's name that she paused and looked at him. "We lost Mark in the line of duty. Faye and Hunter are getting married sometime next year, and Miss A is going strong." He paused, obviously searching for the right words.

She set it down and picked up the other photo—this one of two boys and two girls, all younger than the kids in Raider's picture. "These?"

"The next crop of kids to go through." His smile was soft. "We crossed time there." Then he sobered and pointed to the cute brunette in the middle. "That's Wendy. She was with Mark, and when he died, she just took off. I mean, I know she's safe right now, but I wish she'd reach out." His smiled widened as he pointed to the tiny blond girl with deep brown eyes. "That's Michelle, who was always the wild one. Poor kid spent time in foster homes across the entire country, based on whether her mom was clean or not. She's in Portland now and doing well."

The fondness in his voice was alluring. Brigid set the picture down. "Looks like a nice group."

His voice softened. "My family."

Family. Something told her Raider would do anything for family. Anything for those he loved. "I like that about you," she whispered.

He blinked. "Like what?"

Instead of answering, she turned and gently placed the

picture on the dresser. "Let's see those uptight clothes of yours, Agent Tanaka." Trying to force her feelings back into a box, she turned to his closet, because she also knew he'd do his duty, and if he was determined to bring down her father, nothing would make him stop. That put them on opposite sides of their mission, and that didn't take into consideration her other duties. The ones he had no clue about and didn't control, which would definitely irritate him. "Please tell me you have jeans that aren't dark and perfectly pressed."

He sighed and tugged open the bottom drawer of the dresser, pulling out several faded and ripped pairs of jeans. Everything was neatly folded and color coded. Totally organized. Control freak. "Of course. I mean, come on."

Those were perfect. The idea of his tight butt in them made her mouth water. She had to get a grip on herself. "Okay." She opened the closet door and shoved several nice suits out of the way. "Ah, Raider," she breathed, pulling out a well-worn black leather jacket that was made for long rides on a motorcycle. "This is beautiful." And so freaking sexy she wasn't sure she wanted to see him in it.

He took the jacket, his lips curving into a light smile. "We bought them the first chance we could after getting jobs. Hunter's is dark brown, Faye's is a light camel color, and Mark's was a lighter brown." He took the jacket and shrugged into it, looking like a guy who'd just found home.

Her ovaries flipped over. Just right over and then danced around. "It's nice," she croaked, heat flooding her face. "What else is in here?" She buried her head in the closet, seeing more dress shirts and fancy clothes. All hanging perfectly and organized both by color and fabric. Man. The guy really did have control issues. "Where are your T-shirts?" After she'd gotten herself under control, she turned back toward him.

He moved to the dresser again. "Before you ask, I like

boxer-briefs. I am not getting tighty-whities, or full-on boxers, or going commando. That's nonnegotiable."

His underwear. They were discussing his underwear. Her breasts tightened in total betrayal of her mind. This assignment might actually kill her. Could a woman die from a sexual attraction that was so wrong for her? How was she going to pretend to be his fiancée? Though, that would give her an excuse to touch him. Maybe a little. Just a little. Okay, she'd have to keep it to a little—like just his arm and maybe his tough-guy neck. Or his chest. Just how hard was it?

"Brigid?" Raider turned from pulling out a stack of perfectly folded T-shirts.

What had he asked her? Her mind went blank. "Shoes," she gasped. "What about shoes?" Loafers wouldn't do it.

Raider tossed the shirts on the bed and headed for the closet, leaning over her somehow. "Box in the bottom."

Her breath heated, and she turned, ducking down and pulling out a box. Her butt brushed his knees on the way down, and was that a groan? She glanced over her shoulder and up, and his face was a polite mask. She must've imagined it. When she drew the box out, he backed away.

Then she flipped open the top to reveal black cowboy boots—the real kind. No heel, square toe, broken in. "Wow," she breathed.

He nodded. "They're good for riding motorcycles as well as moving pipe."

She shook her head like a dog with a face full of water. "You've moved pipe?" The term meant moving sprinklers to water all of a field, and she'd spent half her life doing it for low pay at their farm.

"Yep. In Kentucky, summer job as kids. We didn't move those fancy ones with the wheels. No." He smiled at the boots. "We unhooked, lifted, moved, set down, and rehooked them up."

Good God. Raider Tanaka had moved pipe. She was so

far down the rabbit hole, she'd never find her way back up. Had he been shirtless in the sun moving those sprinklers? The idea was almost too much. She stood and handed him the box. "You look so smooth and put together. Fancy," she murmured.

His smile this time was all for her. "You can become anybody you want to in this world, baby girl. Just who do you want to be?"

A slow shiver wound down her spine, spreading out across her lower back. That tone. It was a killer.

Chapter Seven

Raider couldn't help but glance again at the closed door to the Deep Ops computer room, where Brigid had disappeared with the kitten. The cheap lights buzzed above his head, and water audibly dripped somewhere in the distance.

"Drink." Wolfe shoved a shot glass of rotgut across the desks.

"Not thirsty." Raider kept his hand near the glass, since Roscoe had stood up from his perch outside Nari's door. He'd seen how fast the dog could move when there was alcohol there for the plucking.

Force tipped his own glass down from the adjacent desk and then repoured. "Is it just me, or are the women irritated with us?"

Raider twirled his glass around. "We shouldn't have given Brigid her father's records." The feeling in the pit of his stomach wouldn't go away, although there was a warmth about sitting around with his team and having a drink. He'd missed having a team. He considered his foster siblings family, and he'd found a team in the HDD before his last op had gone wrong. Now he had this ragtag group of truly excellent fighters to call his own.

"She deserves the truth." Wolfe looked toward Nari's closed door. "What pissed the shrink off?"

Raider finally found a hint of amusement. "She suggested, again, that Force start counseling sessions with her. He kindly refused." Not true. The refusal had been delivered in a voice harder than concrete.

Wolfe snorted. "The rest of us are supposed to talk to her. Why not you, Force?"

Force rolled his eyes. "The deal with HDD is that you all talk to her, since you're a bunch of troublemakers. I'm the one they want to keep quiet, so I can get away without expressing every damn feeling I might have about anything."

Raider rubbed his cleanly shaven chin. "The fact that they let you get away with blackmail really does lend credence to the fact that Lassiter is alive." Lassiter was a prolific serial killer that Force had caught and supposedly killed, but an informant had sent Force information that indicated otherwise before disappearing, which was why Force had created the Deep Ops unit. The HDD would want to keep the secret because Lassiter had been an HDD employee. Hence, case room one. "Any new leads?"

"No." Force downed another shot, and the dog whined from the corner. "Roscoe, knock it off. No more booze for you." The dog barked once and then snorted, obviously not happy at being left out of the drinking.

The elevator door dinged, and Wolfe instantly drew out his weapon.

"Jesus." Force wiped his eyes. "Put your gun away. Nobody even knows we have this crappy office."

Wolfe didn't move.

Raider's blood pressure rose slightly. Not enough to move his body, but the tension was there, nonetheless. Why was Wolfe always so on edge? Force and Wolfe definitely suffered from PTSD, and Raider guessed West did as well. Hell. Sometimes his nightmares made him wonder if he shouldn't be seeing Nari for real. She was a specialist in many disorders, including PTSD.

The door opened, and Malcolm West loped inside with a platter of cookies in his hands. "Lose the gun, Wolfe."

Wolfe calmly placed the gun to the side of the bottle. "Figured it was you."

West set the platter down on the desk. "I don't want to know your plan in case it wasn't me."

True enough. Raider took an oatmeal cookie and bit in, nearly humming at the pure taste. Delicious. He chewed, his mood lifting, but they had to get back to work soon. The idea of missing girls from Thailand was keeping him up at night. He wanted to tell Brigid about that part of the case, but Angus had been dead set against it, at least until they had some proof that Coonan was trafficking in humans. Raider chewed again, forcing himself to enjoy the calm moments. "How is Pippa?"

"Good." West pulled out the chair at his desk, which abutted and faced Raider's. "She's baking and has a lot of work to do for several of her Internet clients. Something about tax time. I think she and Nari have lunch plans later in the week, if she's ready to venture out into the world again. If not, they can talk on the phone. Whatever she needs works for me." He looked at Force. "What's my job on this op?"

"Backup for now," Force said, munching contentedly on a sugar cookie. "Raider and Brigid will go undercover, and the rest of us will be ready if we have to go in." He watched as Wolfe downed a third cookie. "You should weigh a thousand pounds."

Wolfe patted his flat stomach. "Good genes, baby." He took another cookie.

Force shook his head. “I need you to keep an eye on your reporter. Her records, which she was nice enough to share with you since you saved her ass last night, are good. Her research and contacts are impressive, but we need her out of the way for this. Is she angry I had somebody tip her off about the story?”

“She doesn’t have enough sense to be angry,” Wolfe said, sipping his drink. “Besides, she has a big story she’s been working on for a while, one she won’t dish about, and she thinks she would’ve found this one, anyway. But I doubt it.”

Force’s eyebrows rose. “Her last few articles have all centered on pretty dangerous criminals.”

“Yes,” Wolfe said, looking toward Nari’s door. “I’ve been providing some backup, but she takes too many risks. I’m not sure why.”

Raider cut Wolfe a look. “What is happening between you two, anyway?” They couldn’t have one of their members feeding materials to a reporter, especially one as good as Dana seemed to be.

Wolfe shrugged. “Just friends. I like her, but emotions aren’t my thing.”

That was the understatement of the century. Or rather, Raider guessed there were a whole mess of emotions in the hulking man. Kind of like a volcano with magma just bubbling beneath the surface. He wasn’t sure he wanted to be in the vicinity when Wolfe blew.

Wolfe grinned and looked at the three men. “I like our team meetings with cookies and booze, even if Brigid and Nari are irritated with us. It’s nice just to be with soldiers for a few minutes. Or agents. You’re kind of like soldiers. I mean, everyone here has been shot. Right?”

They all nodded.

Wolfe poured a fourth glass and leaned over to hand it to West. Then he held up his glass. “To the brotherhood of still breathing after being shot.”

Raider lifted his glass as the other men did the same. Brotherhood. Responsibility and something else, something warm and comfortable, settled onto his shoulders. They'd cover each other's backs, and they'd get the job done. He'd figure out a way to protect Brigid in the process. "Amen to that."

Brigid finished her deep background check on her father, finding no additional arrests or records. Her hands shook a little, and her palms were slightly sweaty. How could she not have known her dad had been arrested several times as a younger man? Did she know him at all? There had been nothing on her mother, thank goodness. Brigid picked up Kat and walked out of the computer room. The four male members of the team were kicked back in the middle of the room at the old desks, drinking whiskey. Giving them a nod and purposely not meeting Raider's gaze, she walked past them to Nari's office, where she knocked and waited for the shrink to give her a call to come in.

Why was her heart rate picking up? She could almost feel Raider's gaze on her back. *Don't look back. Don't look back.*

"Come in," Nari called.

Brigid twisted the knob and stepped inside, shutting the door instantly and sighing. "I received your email to come see you when I got the chance."

Nari looked up from the other side of her desk, surprise in her dark eyes. "You're flushed. What's going on?"

"Men are morons." Brigid moved two feet and drew out a chair in what was more of a big closet than an actual office. Nari's small desk touched one side wall and barely gave her room to move past it on the other side. Behind her was a plain and dingy wall holding a painting of a beach scene with plenty of sun and sand. "They're all out there having a drink."

Nari pushed her laptop to the left. A stack of papers rested to her right along with a myriad of manila folders. "It's how they bond. At least, it's how those four bond when bullets aren't flying and bombs aren't being defused."

Brigid shared a smile with the brilliant doctor. "True that." She smoothed her hands down her jeans. Today Nari had dressed in dark slacks with a pink shirt and one of those delicate scarves tied in the front in a way that some women seemed to naturally know how to do. The woman looked more out of place in the dilapidated office than did the German shepherd camped right outside the door. "It, ah, seems like most of us are screwups here," Brigid said quietly.

Nari's dark eyebrows arched. "I wouldn't put it that way."

How else could it be put? Brigid was a hacker out from prison, Angus an obsessed agent, Wolfe a nutjob, Malcolm a wounded agent, and Raider out for blood from an assignment gone wrong. What about the shrink? "Why are you here, anyway?"

Nari sighed. "HDD wants me here keeping an eye on all of you. I haven't hidden that."

Which meant she was probably informing on them to the powers that be. "All right."

Nari tapped a gold-plated pen on a notepad. "But everything you tell me is confidential. I would not break patient confidentiality for any job. Ever." Her voice, low and cultured, remained measured and sure. "You have my word."

There was more to the woman's story, and Brigid knew it. But she hadn't had a chance to delve into Nari's records, and she really didn't want to get caught doing it. "If you say so," she murmured.

"I do." Nari smiled. "Shall we talk about your next mission? When was the last time you saw your father?"

A male voice boomed through the door. "Nari? Come look at this, would you?" Angus bellowed.

Nari rolled her eyes. "He's been waiting for a profile from an expert at some college, and he wants me to look at it immediately. Geez." Grumbling under her breath, she stood and strode gracefully through the narrow opening between desk and wall. "I'll be right back." She shut the door behind herself.

Brigid pushed unruly hair away from her face. Her father. The thought of him hurt somewhere deep in her chest. Closing her eyes, she remembered their last encounter.

They'd stood on the well-kept wooden front porch near the swing where she'd spent hours swinging while typing on her laptop through the years. The smell of grass, alfalfa, and hay wafted on the sweet breeze from the farm, and in the distance, a tractor droned methodically.

"You should not have hacked into that medical program's computers. A federal grant is part of the package, so you broke federal laws," her dad said, his green eyes dark and his hard jaw set. His Irish had come out in full force in a way it rarely did.

Her anger matched his. "Mom should've been part of that study. She might've lived."

"No," her dad said. "She wasn't a good candidate, and she wanted to live her last days here, not being poisoned. It was her decision." He looked toward the boy on the motorcycle waiting for Brigid. "Don't leave with that idiot."

The idiot was a fun guy, and she had to get away from the farm. Her father should've made her mom take part in the study. She'd still be alive—maybe. "I'm eighteen," she said, needing to get out of there. Away from the quaint farmhouse surrounded by barns and fields. "I can go."

She'd gotten arrested for hacking just six months before, but her probation was up now, and she could leave town.

"This is a mistake. Stay on the farm and go to the community college," her dad said, dirt on his overalls and his gloves hanging out of one pocket. Emotion was stamped hard on his square face. "It's a good living. A safe one."

Her chest ached, and her eyes pricked. She'd miss him. But he'd been on her since her arrest, and she needed freedom. People and places instead of land and cows and more land. She couldn't go on with just the two of them and a bunch of old farmhands. They needed distance from each other, at least for a while. "There's a world out there, Daddy. I want to see it," she whispered. Why couldn't he understand?

"Then find a way without a computer," he growled. "You'll just get into more trouble, and I can't help you with that. Please."

Life without a computer? She'd rather lose her arms. "I can't." Her skin chilled, and her eyes ached now. "Please understand."

"No," he snapped, looking big and strong on the porch. "If you leave, don't come back."

The office door opened, and Brigid jerked back to the present.

Nari retook her seat on the opposite side of the desk. "So. Before you go see your father, you and Raider have to become lovers. Well, at least seem like it. Are you ready to start practicing?"

Chapter Eight

"I thought this would be better without an audience," Raider said, pressing his hand to the small of Brigid's back as they entered the local sports bar. She jumped and quickly calmed. He sighed and steered her toward a booth in the back, waiting until she'd settled herself across from him. Her face was flushed a pretty pink, making her green eyes stand out even more than usual. "Are you averse to being touched?" Did she have trauma in her past? His chest filled. Had somebody hurt her?

"No." Her voice was breathy. "It's just you."

Ego hit him first, followed by a strong dose of masculine pride. Yeah, he was an ass sometimes. "Let's start there. What is it about me?" He wasn't fishing for compliments. The problem couldn't be tackled until he understood it.

"You don't make sense to me." She pushed curly red hair away from her oval-shaped face. "Like a code missing a line or two."

What was wrong with him that his body flared wide awake and ready to play when she talked computer nerd? "Okay. That's easy to fix. Ask me anything, and I'll answer it." As a promise, it was risky, but not nearly as risky as their failing in the field. If she had to really know him to lose her skittishness, he'd give her everything he could. Except the promise that he'd leave her father alone. He'd do his job there. Plus, she'd been honest with him since he'd become her handler, and he could easily do the same. She deserved it.

"All right." She plucked at her paper napkin. "Favorite color?"

The green of her eyes at the moment. "Blue," he murmured.

"Favorite movie?"

"*Rambo*." He smiled. "And *Christmas Vacation*."

She returned the smile, visibly relaxing her shoulders. "First love?"

He sat back, memories returning. "Latesha Jones, tenth grade, volleyball player. Broke my heart when she dumped me for a guy named Bert."

"Bert?" Brigid's eyes lit up with humor.

"Bartholomew Jordan the Fourth," Raider confirmed. "Hunter wanted to go beat him up, but I didn't see the reason. I couldn't blame her. He had a hell of a lot more to offer." Like car rides and fancy dinners. All he'd had was an attitude, and potential that was iffy at best right then.

"She chose wrong," Brigid said softly. "Where is she today?"

He shrugged. "No clue." In fact, he hadn't thought about her in years. "Your first love?"

"Bad boy who liked to shoplift," she admitted. "Never had good taste in men, but that's the point here, right? You're going to pretend to be a criminal." Her light eyebrows slanted down as she looked him over. "Even with the leather jacket, I don't see it. My dad will know you're a Fed. Or at least not a bad guy."

"I can become almost anybody," he admitted, adding a Scottish accent. "It's training plus a decent gift. Probably from a crappy childhood." This time he threw in a Japanese accent that felt as right as his Southern one. "Any other questions?"

"Favorite sexual position," she threw out, challenge lifting her chin.

Damn, she was cute. If she thought to embarrass him, she'd read him wrong. "Helm of the Bobsled," he drawled. "Behind you, over a table, my fist in your hair. Right where I'd want you." He met her gaze, more than a little amused when that pink flush turned a lovely rose.

"Aren't you unflappable?" she forced out.

Yeah. That was him. He'd learned the skill at way too young an age. Yet his jeans had just become uncomfortably tight. "What about you? Slow and soft or fast and hard?"

She tilted her head, and her tongue flicked out to wet her lips in a nervous action.

He bit back a groan and tried to shift his weight in his jeans.

"I guess both?" She jumped as the waitress plunked down two ice waters. They ordered dinner, and Brigid took a couple of sips from the sweating glass. "I've never been a good liar. My dad will see through me."

Raider twirled his glass. "Then I guess we start to date for real. We're attracted to each other, and if we didn't work together, I can see us hooking up."

She blinked. "You're a government drone, and I'm a convicted hacker. We wouldn't have hooked up in a million years. Not even for a one-night stand, which I've never had, by the way."

"Opposites attract," he returned, leaning toward her. "Listen. Here's the deal. The best undercover identities are built on as much truth as possible. The only real lie we have to tell is about my profession, and truth be told, half the time I've worked with undercover teams, which means we lie all the time. Which is okay in the professional world." Not in the personal one, though. Loyalty was all he had.

She lifted her gaze. "I hear a line drawn there."

"Yes. Lying is unacceptable in friendship or anything more," he affirmed. "It's unforgivable." Did she turn pale? Shoot. He hadn't meant to scare her. "I'm sorry. I know I'm asking you to lie to your father, which contradicts my personal beliefs and no doubt yours. But it's the only way to prove him innocent." Which Raider knew wouldn't happen. There was no way Sean Banaghan was innocent, based on the fact that Jonny P and Josh the Bear had visited him twice in farm country during the last month. "So your motives are pure. Right?" Man, he hated manipulating her like this.

"You're so full of crap," she returned, setting down her glass. "You're lying to me right now."

Yeah, but it was professional. "Good point. Okay. New promise. We only tell each other the truth, even if it isn't pretty." He reached across the table and took her hand. Her skin was smooth and soft, and he gentled his touch. "What do you say?"

She swallowed but left her hand in place.

Sometimes he forgot that not everybody could see bright lines between right and wrong. Also that some people didn't see that the ends often justified the means, which meant she was a heck of a better person than was he. But they had to get this right. So, keeping his hand on hers, he stood and slid in next to her on her side of the booth. Then he put his arm around her and pulled her close. "Are you ready to start dating?"

A slow shiver tumbled through Brigid as Raider's hand settled on her shoulder. The entire left side of her body warmed against him. How could she pretend to date him when she was lying to everyone? Not that she had a choice. "What are you doing?" she croaked.

He turned his head and brushed his lips across her forehead. "Getting you used to my touch."

Heat flashed down through her body with an intensity that stole her breath. "I'm not a skittish colt," she returned, wanting to lean into him more as if she had a right to do so.

"Oh, you're definitely skittish," he murmured, running his hand down her arm. "I just want to gentle, not break." He grinned at his own wordplay.

She rolled her eyes, her body humming. "You are such a complete dork."

"Look there." He tugged her closer in a half hug. "We're getting nicknames for each other. I'm sticking with Irish for you. Dork is fine for me."

He seemed more like a lethal weapon than a dork, but she couldn't exactly give him that much. The guy had an ego already. A sizable one. "I think I'll find another nickname for you. Maybe something to do with the fact that you play the guitar." Which intrigued the heck out of her.

"Sounds good." He paused as the waitress set down their food and then released Brigid to dig in.

The man certainly took food seriously. She dumped the dressing onto her Cobb salad. "Do you cook?"

"Yep. Every chance I get. I'll make you something while we date," he said, nudging her plate toward her. "Eat up. We have to go for a walk and learn to hold hands after this."

Her stomach flip-flopped. It was so silly. Holding hands didn't mean anything, and yet, she felt like she was fifteen years old again with her first crush. Why? What was it about him? "When was the last time you dated somebody?" she asked, taking a bite.

He chewed thoughtfully. "Seriously dated? Probably

about three years ago before we started working on the mob case. Her name was Louise, and she was a veterinarian. Nice woman, but we kind of frittered away."

Frittered? Brigid hadn't heard that term in way too long. Her phone buzzed, and she read the face. "Finished a deeper background check on Jonny P and Josh the Bear. Jonny has a pretty good rap sheet, but even I couldn't find a hint of Josh before he met up with Jonny." She pursed her lips. It was rare, very, for somebody to be that anonymous. "I'll keep looking."

Raider finished his burger. "Good luck. Even HDD can't find a history for him."

Brigid ate her salad and started to relax at having the hard-bodied Fed next to her. She was almost sorry when he paid the check and escorted her outside to the vacant sidewalk. A slight rain had begun to fall, and dark clouds rolled across the sky.

Raider ushered her to his truck. "Guess our walk will have to wait."

She jumped inside and waited for him to start the engine and drive toward their apartment building. Even though she knew better, this felt like a date. How far would he take it? As if in answer, he reached across the seat and took her hand when he drove away from the curb.

His palm was warm and calloused. Raider Tanaka hadn't spent his life behind a desk, now had he? She cleared her throat. "With all the intrigue and going undercover, how do you keep your life straight? I mean, how do you ever trust anybody?" She tried to keep her tone emotionless, but it wasn't easy. Sometimes it was difficult to know what the truth was when dealing with people. Computer code never lied.

His hold tightened. "You have to know who you trust. There has to be somebody you give all the truth to, or you'll go nuts. For this case, it's you and me. No lies." The rain splattered the windshield harder, and he flicked on the wipers.

She couldn't do this. Not really. But she couldn't tell him that. "I don't really trust well."

"You trust me, right?" he asked.

She wasn't sure. "Yes."

"And I can trust you, correct?" He drove onto the Interstate.

She mulled over the question for several miles. It was true. He could trust her, even though she couldn't tell him everything. "I won't let you down." It was the truth. That had to count, right?

"I know," he murmured. He exited the Interstate and drove down the street, his free hand more than capable on the steering wheel. Finally, they pulled into the parking area, and he shut off the engine. "I enjoyed our dinner. You're a lovely date." He opened his door and pulled her across the seat to lift her against his chest before shutting his door. Ducking his head over her and shielding her from the rain, he leaped over a mud puddle.

She bounced up, and he caught her, running faster.

Exhilaration swept through her, and she manacled her arm around his neck, laughing as he ran into the building and up the two flights of stairs as if she weighed nothing. Finally, he set her on her feet at her door.

Her hair fell down around her shoulders, barely wet. Her breath came in gasps, and nothing could've prevented the smile that curved her mouth. "You are seriously strong and in good shape." She laughed. She wasn't exactly a lightweight, and he wasn't even close to being out of breath. This side of Raider, the fun side, was way too appealing, and she was getting caught up in the fantasy of being with him.

"I do all right." He brushed a wild curl away from her temple before gently grasping her chin.

The amusement inside her popped and dissipated, leaving electricity arcing through her. "Raider." She had to tell him everything. Keeping secrets was too hard for her.

His eyes darkened. "Yeah." Lifting her chin, he lowered his head, and his lips touched hers. Firm and warm, his mouth curved against hers, and then he kissed her. Slow and sweet, seeking, his muscled body backing her against the door at the same time.

Heat pooled in her abdomen, sliding desire through her veins to brush every nerve into languid awareness. She let a soft sigh escape her, and she levered herself up on her toes, kissing him back. She curled her hands over his strong shoulders, pressing against him, opening her mouth.

He took advantage, kissing her deeper, brushing his tongue against hers.

She jerked at the contact, wanting more. Needing more.

He gentled the kiss and released her mouth, leaning back. "Ah, Irish. You're a sweet thing, aren't you?" The Southern drawl came out low and hungry.

She shivered. Wow. Just holy wow. "Um."

He smiled and took her key to open her door. "Stay here." Then he searched the apartment, returning to drop the key in her hand. Finally, he placed a soft kiss on her nose. "Have a good night. We'll practice touching more tomorrow."

She wandered into her apartment, her mind spinning and her body fluid. This was such a huge mistake. They had to trust each other? She couldn't even come close. Letting a sigh loose, she bunched her legs for balance and pushed the dining table across the room to bar the door. Once again.

Chapter Nine

After a sleepless night, a rushed morning, and a turbulent flight on a commuter jet to upstate New York, during which Raider kept his promise to touch her lightly on the hand, on the face, just casually, Brigid was ready to crawl out of her own skin from need. They landed after dinnertime, but it was still nice and bright outside. She stood off to the side of the car rental counter in the tiny regional airport while Raider efficiently filled out paperwork and accepted keys to one of three cars sitting outside the door.

He moved toward her, all grace in motion. The torn jeans, worn T-shirt, and battered leather jacket made him look like a badass out for a good time. The shadow along his jawline added temptation to an already appealing male. The perfect guy for some nice girl to try and tame. "Our car is the one in the middle," he said absently, folding the rental agreement into perfect lines before grasping the handle of his carry-on luggage.

"So you're talking to me now?" she muttered, rolling her bag toward the door.

"I wasn't not talking to you," he said, sliding a pair of sunglasses out of his pocket to shield his eyes. "Did you memorize our cover story?"

"Of course." She'd spent most of the flight studying their backgrounds, which were similar to their real backgrounds. Except that Raider headed a criminal enterprise that used computers for all sorts of crimes. "My father isn't going to like you."

"I think that's the point," Raider murmured, holding the door open for her to step into the evening sunshine.

She blinked and tugged her glasses out of her purse, slipping them into place. Once they'd secured their bags in the trunk, she fastened her seat belt and waited as Raider adjusted his seat and finally ignited the engine. "You seem upset about the kiss last night," she said, unable to keep quiet any longer.

"Not at all." His gaze focused. "Sorry. I always take a little time to myself before an op. I didn't mean to shut you out. At all."

Oh. Well, then. "Okay." So he hadn't been stewing over the fantastic kiss like she had. Maybe he'd even slept like a baby. That didn't seem fair. "I don't have much of a cover. It's just me going for the wrong guy." Something she'd done plenty of times in her life.

"I'm sorry you have to do this," Raider allowed, driving the vehicle onto the main road, which was empty of traffic. "It isn't fun lying to people you care about, but you have to trust your partner in the mission. I trust you, so just trust me to make sure everything is okay."

"Okay," she murmured, watching rolling hills speed by outside. This sucked. She couldn't tell him the full truth, and he definitely wasn't going to like that. Maybe he'd never find out. Right.

"Run me through your most recent arrest," Raider said, settling in his seat. "I want your take on it and not the recording officer's."

Okay. What was her cover? "Well, I had a record for helping a boyfriend steal money from rival criminals, and that was definitely wrong. But then I was trying to do some good. I was working with a nonprofit that combatted child pornography, and I hacked into one of the pervert's computers." She shook her head. "Turned out the guy was a low-level employee at the Pentagon, and I hacked into a federally owned system. Should've known better."

Raider's hands remained steady on the wheel. "Tell me they arrested the guy."

She nodded. "That was part of the plea deal." Of course, that had been part of it. No way would she let that guy go free. In fact, his arrest had led to several more arrests, which was why she hadn't had to spend much jail time. "I'm really trying to make up for my past mistakes." Which was the absolute truth. But the why of the crimes didn't matter, just that she'd committed them.

"I understand," Raider said, speeding up on the quiet roadway. "We're all trying to make up for things in the past. Honesty is what matters."

Irritation swept over her skin like a rash. "Oh yeah? Like you've been so honest." She partially turned on her leather seat to face him. "You were working this Irish mob case from the beginning, and you knew you'd have to maybe take down my father, if you're right about him and his mob connections. Which you're not, by the way."

His lips compressed. She could almost see the squirrel running in his head. Finally, he sighed. "You're right. I'm sorry."

Whoa. An apology? From a man? Her mouth gaped open.

He sent her a sideways glance and then grinned. "Seriously?"

Yeah. Wow. "Are you manipulating me right now?" She had to ask. "Since we're going undercover soon?"

He focused back on the road. "No. I was wrong to use

you and expect you to tell me everything and trust me. I am sorry."

Wow. As an apology, it was darn good. "How about we don't lie to each other from now on?" she asked.

His chin lowered. "That's not the same as being honest with each other."

Yeah, she knew that. But if there was a chance her father was in trouble, she'd do what she had to do to protect him. She thought back to those pictures of his foster family Raider kept in his bedroom. "If Miss A was in trouble, what would you do to save her?"

Raider was quiet for a moment. "Absolutely anything and everything I had to do."

"Then you understand," she said.

He shook his head. "Miss A would never do anything illegal. Her past is pure."

"As far as you know," Brigid countered. "And I think my dad's past is pure. You have to be wrong about him."

Raider slid his glasses up on his head as clouds began to cover the sun. "So long as you understand, I'm very good at my job, Brigid."

"Is that a threat?" she muttered.

"No." He sighed, and his large chest filled. "But it is a fact."

Raider kept the car steady as they sped down the narrow road. Night shrouded the landscape, but the headlights picked out alfalfa on one side of the road and hay on the other. The silhouettes of mountains rose in the far distance, but they were definitely in farm country. He'd never been this north in New York before. "How big is your dad's farm?" he asked, breathing in the smell of hay.

"About two hundred acres, with one hundred acres of farmland under a lower-pressure pivot system," she said, her gaze on the dark fields outside the window. "Fifty acres for cattle."

It was hard to reconcile the computer hacker with a farm girl. "Bet you were cute in overalls."

She didn't turn his way, her hands plucking at her jeans. Her anxiety was strong enough to ratchet up the tension in the car. "Thanks."

He tightened his hold on the steering wheel to keep from reaching for her hand. They were colleagues, and his one mission, his only mission, was to take down the people who'd killed his friend. And now, if Force's connecting the dots was accurate, he had to save a bunch of girls being trafficked in a way he couldn't find. The ticking clock of that increased his blood pressure.

He felt a little guilty keeping that part of the op from Brigid, even though he was under orders.

By the end of this assignment, she'd probably hate him, and he'd more than likely be looking for another job. Unless the success of the mission kept him at the HDD, which was certainly possible. While he needed the win to get back in the good graces of the higher-ups, right now, he didn't give a crap about that. The people who'd murdered Treeson would pay. That was a vow he'd taken over his friend's grave, and he never failed to keep a vow.

No matter the cost.

But if there was a way to protect Brigid, he'd find that, too. It was the least he could do, even if she wanted him dead.

"When was the last time you talked to your dad?" Raider asked.

She hunched her shoulders forward. "I call him on his birthday and Christmas every year, and I send a card for Father's Day. He calls on my birthday." Her voice was low and soft. "It's awkward." She settled her head back on the seat rest and shut her eyes. "My mom was a candidate for a drug trial, and I felt like my dad didn't encourage her enough to try it."

"Wasn't it her decision?" Raider asked quietly.

"Yeah, and at the time, I didn't understand that." She sighed and opened her eyes. "I should've come home years ago and made amends, but first I was breaking the law, and then I was working for the HDD, and time flew by." She shook her head, and her red curls bounced around. "That's no excuse."

"Maybe this will be a good chance to do that," Raider said, feeling like an ass, considering his motivations.

"Sure. Showing up with a fake boyfriend who wants to put my dad in jail is a great way to make amends." She turned startling green eyes his way. "Don't try to act like my friend. We both know what you are."

Yeah, they did. "Fair enough." He handed over a small case from his backpack. "It's a camera that will be recording everything around you. Put it on."

The necklace was a dainty-looking silver cross. The camera was in a moonstone right in the middle. Though he expected her to object, she didn't. Sighing, she secured the necklace at the back of her neck. "I'm not wearing this the whole time."

"Yes, you are—and it's Agents Rutherford and Fields watching, not Angus Force, so keep that in mind." Those two were the unit's official liaisons with the HDD, and they were uptight and a pain in the butt. He didn't like it any more than she did, no doubt. "I'm sorry about that."

"Whatever."

He took her hand this time, holding tight when she tried to pull away. "Remember your role, too. And Brigid? If your dad has knowledge, his best bet is to work with us once everything goes down. I'll make sure he has a chance to make a deal, somehow. So long as he wasn't in on Agent

Treeson's killing." If he had been, which was doubtful, Raider would put him in the ground himself. It was only fair to warn her.

"There's no record of my dad working with any criminal organization after he left Boston and bought the farm here with my mother," Brigid snapped.

Was she going to be able to pull this off? Raider had no experience working with civilians, and emotional ones at that. How she channeled that emotion into cracking computer code fascinated the hell out of him, and that was before taking in her stunning eyes and wild curves. He had to think of her as a job and nothing more.

As darkness deepened, he worked it through in his mind.

"How about you trust me to do the right thing?" He surprised himself by asking the question. By how much her answer meant to him.

"Not a chance," she muttered, turning back to the window.

Humor attacked him, and he barked out a laugh. Man, Miss A would love Brigid. The thought sobered him. There was next to no possibility the two women would ever meet. After this op was over, they'd probably go their separate ways.

A faded red barn came into the circle of the headlights next to what looked like a bunkhouse. Then another barn and a lot of equipment. He kept driving, and soon a white clapboard farmhouse with a wide porch appeared between several trees with a creek running between it and another huge barn. "Wow." It was his perfect image of a family home. One he hadn't had until he'd met Miss A.

Brigid nodded. "There used to be a picket fence, but the cows get loose every once in a while and run through it. My mom finally gave up on it and tulips, because the deer eat tulips no matter what they have to jump over to reach the buds."

The remaining flowers were purple and apparently deer resistant. Wildflowers sprang up on either side of the winding creek.

A tall older man with a barrel of a chest stepped through the screen door to the wooden porch, a shotgun in his hand.

Brigid sighed. “My father.”

Chapter Ten

Brigid couldn't breathe. She pulled her hand loose from Raider's, and he let her. She shivered, and nausea tumbled around in her belly. It had been too long. Was her dad still mad at her? Their conversations through the last several years had been short but friendly. Well, not friendly, but not adversarial. Her father had never been much for talking on the phone. Or talking in general. Why did Raider have to be here for this?

He pulled the car to a stop, and she jumped out, striding up the stone path and wooden stairs, her gaze on her father. He'd aged. His hair was gray and still thick, his beard almost all gray, and his eyes the green of an Irish hill. He wore overalls with work boots, and at seeing her, he set the shotgun near the door. "Brigid."

She moved to him, settling in for a hug. He awkwardly patted her back, smelling like hay, alfalfa, and cigar. The scent of home. Tears pricked her eyes, and she wanted to tell him everything. To blurt it out. But the necklace lay heavy on her chest, and she leaned back. "I'm sorry it took so long."

"You're here now." He'd always been a man of few

words, and his gaze had already gone over her shoulder to Raider.

She almost reluctantly turned to see Raider striding toward them and barely kept her mouth from gaping open. His easy gait had turned into a strut, his intelligent eyes were somehow belligerent, and he had a sense of toughness about him that was usually veiled. In the worn leather jacket, boots, and torn jeans, he looked like her teenaged fantasies of a bad boy who could be tamed by the right girl. Now she knew better. Bad boys were never tamed, and this one, not a chance. It wasn't all an act, either.

"Daddy?" She swallowed several times. "This is Raider Times, my, ah, fiancé."

Her dad stiffened.

She winced. Yep. This was going to go just great. "Raider? This is my father, Sean Banaghan."

Raider jumped up the steps and held out a hand. "It's nice to meet you." His accent was all streets of New York.

Brigid blinked. How in the world did he do that? Was the guy a chameleon, or what?

Her father shook hands. "So. You're engaged." He didn't sound happy and instead opened the door. "Why don't we go inside and have a beer?" That was her father. If he had an emotion, it was carefully shoved down and hidden.

If she had a heart attack, all of this would be over. Instead, she turned and entered the house first, forgetting for a moment that the men were behind her. The living room still held her mother's furniture. Comfortable floral sofa and chairs in front of a fireplace. Tons of pictures of them as a family and some of friends on the mantel and even on the walls. A pang hit Brigid. Things would be so different if her mother had lived.

The place smelled faintly of polish. She walked inside and turned to look over her shoulder. "Everything is so nice and clean."

A fascinating red colored her father's weathered face for a moment. "Some ladies from town help out. They clean during harvest season and sometimes bring food." He shuffled his big boots. "I don't ask them to."

Brigid bit back a grin, forgetting briefly about the mission. Of course the biddies in town were interested in her father. Was he interested back? Why hadn't she come home before now? "It's nice that they do that, Dad."

He moved past her into the country-style kitchen, a slight limp in his gait.

She knew better than to ask if he was okay. If he was moving, he was all right, and that'd be the end of it. It wouldn't be the first time he'd been kicked by a bull. The life of a farmer was rarely relaxing, even in the good years.

Her dad took three jelly jars out of a cupboard along with a bottle of Glendalough single malt. "Since we're celebrating." He poured three generous doses and handed them out. "*Sláinte*."

"*Sláinte*," Brigid said, downing hers in one gulp. The whiskey landed in her stomach and splashed out instant warmth and tingles to counteract the nausea in a nicely numbing way. The room smelled faintly of a casserole, and she was taken back to her early years. Her mother had been an incredible cook, and her father much happier when she'd been alive. Why did life have to take such devastating turns?

Raider downed his drink. "Nice farm you have here."

She jumped at the odd accent. "Things are good, Dad?"

"Yep." He poured three more shots and leaned against the tall fridge that had stood in the same place for twenty years. "When's the wedding?"

"We're thinking a Christmas wedding," Raider said smoothly. "Pretty pictures with snow and red poinsettias."

That did sound lovely. Brigid sipped more of her drink, trying to look innocent. Her face heated.

Her dad looked over her warm face. "You pregnant?"

She coughed up the whiskey, sputtering. "God, no. Dad. Geez." She patted her chest, and the cold metal of the necklace pressed into her palm. "We might wait until next June for a spring wedding. It's not set in stone."

"Humph." Her dad eyed Raider. "What do you do for a livin'?"

Leave it to her father to get right to the point.

Raider smiled, his eyes somehow gleaming. "A little of this and a little of that. I'm in exports, actually."

"Well, shit," her dad muttered, turning on her. "He's another criminal? You still haven't learned your lesson?"

She blinked, wanting to hide under the table. Her dad had never hit her—never even yelled at her. But his disappointment weighed as heavily on her shoulders as a hay baler. "He's not a criminal, and neither am I. I've been working for a nonprofit for years." Well, she had before getting arrested.

Her dad shook his head. "Fine. Why don't you go get settled in your room, and Raider and I will have a talk before I show him the guest room." He looked at Raider. "Unless you want to come out and see the barn. I just made improvements."

Brigid faltered.

"How about tomorrow?" Raider downed his drink and set the glass on the counter. In one smooth motion, he grasped Brigid's arm, tugged her close, and planted a kiss on her forehead. "We've been traveling all day and should get some sleep. I'm happy to use the guest room."

"You don't have a choice." Her dad led the way out of the kitchen.

Raider didn't like leaving Brigid with that vulnerable look on her face, but he didn't have a choice. He'd underestimated the emotional impact on her of returning home, probably since he hadn't had a home before he was a teenager. So he'd arranged for her to get some space and rest before they continued with the charade. The old man was pretty much what Raider had expected.

After being shown the comfortable guest room, Raider waited about two hours and then got to work. Every floorboard in the old house creaked at the slightest step, and it took all of his substantial training to move quietly. He searched the entire house, the outside barn, and even some of the surrounding property. There were no signs that the place was anything other than a working farm. Even the cellar, which he'd accessed by an outside door, just held more cobwebs and forgotten canning jars than anything else. He checked the barn again, finding only tools and farming equipment.

"What in the heck are you doing?" Brigid whispered, her body nicely outlined by the moon behind her. She'd changed into leggings and a mint-green T-shirt with a barcode across her breasts. With her wildly curly hair and smooth curves, she looked like every wet dream he'd ever had. Not that he'd dreamed of having sex in a barn before.

"Searching." He moved to her and drew her inside, shutting the door. Her skin was soft and chilled beneath his touch. "What are you doing out?"

"I couldn't sleep." Moonlight poured in through the upper rafters, highlighting her pretty face. "Lying to my dad is a bad idea. He always finds out the truth."

"We don't have time to ease him into the truth," Raider countered, unable to stop himself from running his hands down her arms to warm her. "Force's intel says that Coonan has something big cooking up, but we don't know what. We have to get in there, and now. Maybe your dad will make the introduction if I agree to dump you." He would love to see her smile.

She rolled her eyes. "You'd never dump me. I'd do the dumping. My dad knows that."

Cute. Adorable, even. And she was getting used to his touch. It was unfortunate for him that he liked touching her way too much. She was smart and sweet, and stubborn as all get-out. It showed what a deviant he was that that fact turned him on. He brushed the hair off her shoulder and slid his knuckles over the smooth skin of her neck.

Her eyes darkened. "What are you doing?"

Something he definitely shouldn't. "We have to be more natural with each other to fool anybody." Could he be any more full of crap? Leaning in, he brushed his lips against her temple, inhaling the sweet scent of her thick hair. Honeysuckle and vanilla. The dual scent was always around her, and it had drawn him since the first day they'd met. "You're getting used to me."

She slid her hands up and over his chest. "I've wanted to touch you for a while. Not because I like you." Her hands continued their exploration, and then her knuckles brushed up both sides of his neck. "You're just so hard and angled that I've been curious. When I saw you fight the other day, you moved so gracefully."

His body went from alert to full-on burn. Her touch was going to kill him. This was an assignment, and he had to keep that thought in his mind. Another thought, one from the back of his brain, spiraled forward. Was she manipulating him? Not once had she hidden her intention to protect her father. If she was working him, she was doing a damn good job of it. Maybe it was time to see how far she'd go. "I've wanted to touch you, too." He tangled his hand in her hair like he'd wanted to for so long.

Her gasp was involuntary and honest.

He liked that. "You can touch me all you want, but I won't abandon the job."

"I know that." Her gaze tracked her hands as she slid them down his chest and over his flat abdomen.

He sucked in air, his jeans becoming way too tight. "What are you doing?"

"Exploring." Her thumbs brushed slightly beneath his waistband, and she caressed around to the small of his back. "I'm tired of being two steps behind you on this job. I want to be equal partners. If you're going to be my handler, I'm going to handle you, too."

He nearly burst out of his zipper. Oh, she was good. Brave, even. "You're playing with fire, little girl." His Southern drawl came out low and natural, surprising him. Being home seemed to have centered his wild redhead, and now she was trying to take over. "I'm not one to give up control. Don't even try."

Her smile was that of a siren accustomed to getting her own way. "Is that a challenge?"

Yes. God, yes. "No. Just a fact." He twisted his fingers and tightened his hold in her hair, tugging back slightly. "Tell me you get me."

Her eyes flared hot and bright. A pretty pink flushed beneath her pale skin. Her nails dug into the skin at the small of his back, even through the cotton. "I don't think I get you, Raider." Her voice was a challenging blend of a sarcastic Southern accent and her true Irish tone. "It feels like you don't have control."

Well. If that wasn't a gauntlet, he didn't know what was. "All right. Let's change that feeling." Nothing in the world could've stopped him from taking her mouth.

Hard.

Chapter Eleven

Brigid caught her breath in her throat as Raider kissed her, delving deep and possessing with a heat he hadn't shown before. All of the emotions roused by coming home had prompted her to challenge the biggest predator in the area just to be taken away for a moment. She'd always ventured too close to the flame, and she often got burned.

But the dance was one that pulled her in every time.

His tongue dueled with hers, the taste of whiskey on his breath warming her. His hold was unrelenting and his mouth seeking, taking. Warm and firm and seductive.

What had she done?

His free hand grasped her hip and partially lifted her against him, his fingers branding her through the thin cotton. Her core met his erection, and she moaned at the sweet friction.

Raider Tanaka knew how to kiss. Really knew how to kiss.

She returned the kiss, rising up on her toes and caressing the hard planes of his chest again. Smooth muscle and natural strength filled her palms. Desire spread through her with the heat of a wildfire this time, pooling in her lower belly with a yearning she couldn't fight.

He lifted her against the wall, forcing her legs open while deepening the kiss somehow.

She grabbed onto his shoulders for balance and clasped her thighs against his hips as his heated hand slid down to cup her butt and keep her against him. The smooth wood of the barn door bracketed her back, and she tilted her pelvis against him, rubbing against all that hardness.

He growled low and deep, sending the vibrations down her throat with an intimacy that should've given her pause. Instead, she let the feeling spiral through her, flashing need beneath her skin, delving deep. Yeah, she'd wanted to wrestle control away from him, and she'd wanted to touch him. Both had led to her being held against the wall by a man far sexier than she'd realized.

Sure, he was handsome and smooth and always in control. But this heat, this scalding wildness in him, was unexpected. Exhilarating and frightening. And she wanted more of it. Wanted to see how wild he could get. What could she bring out in him?

He released her mouth, and she gulped in several deep breaths, trying to fill her lungs. "Raider."

His eyes glittered a hungry onyx, while his hold remained strong and sure. "Don't start anything you don't want to finish." His Southern tone had gone low and gritty.

The sound alone bit along her nerves, firing them into need. She did want to finish this. At least, her body wanted to. Her mind finally tried to force reason into the moment. The blood roared through her veins, pulsing in her head with the sound of a tumultuous river. "Who says I want to stop?" Her mouth. Damn, her mouth. It couldn't resist a challenge, even though her brain knew better.

Like any predator, his nostrils flared at the hunt. Both of his hands tightened their hold, reminding her of her precarious position. If he didn't want her to move, she couldn't.

How and why that fact shot desire through her body like heated whiskey, she'd figure out later.

"Brigid." He pulled her head back more with one easy twist, revealing her neck to him. "You're gonna have to learn that every time you throw down a challenge, I'll take it, twist it, and make it mine." He lowered his head, and his lips scraped down the delicate skin of her neck, sucking hard for a second on her clavicle.

The sharp pull shot to her nipples, pebbling them both into hard points. She gasped, her eyelashes fluttering. "Did you just mark me?" she breathed.

"You're lucky it's just your neck." He licked across her collarbone and nipped the other side this time, not hard enough to leave another mark. Then he licked up the other side of her neck, touching every inch and leaving tingles in his wake. He kissed across her cheekbone, the edge of her nose, and then her temple. Finally, his lips touched hers, firm and sweet.

The strength wrapped in such gentleness nearly undid her. She had to keep her wits about her, but it was way too late for that. She let him kiss her, sinking into the moment. So warm and firm and sensual. The man could write a book about kissing alone.

What else was he good at?

She blinked her eyelids open, and he lifted his head, his mouth curving into a smile.

"What?" he asked. "No more challenges?"

She couldn't find any words. Her body thrummed with need, and her mind had gone fuzzy. A good part of her wanted to take him down to the hay-filled floor and have her way with him. The other part knew she should run for the house and her safe and solitary bed.

"Yeah," he murmured, letting her slide against his angled body until her feet found purchase on the floor. "I'm not going to say no for your own good, Brigid. You come to me, offering what you almost offered, and I'm going to take it." His hand in her hair slowly untangled. "If you're lookin' for a voice of reason, you're lookin' in the wrong place."

She swallowed, her body pulsating with need. At least she knew he wouldn't reject her. Humor tried to filter through her desire, but all of it mingled into an ache that was almost too much. Could she even walk back to the house? Her face warmed.

He released her and took a step back. "Go back inside."

Cool air washed over her, and she had to fight her instincts to step right back into his heat. "What are you going to do?"

A rueful smile curved his talented lips. "Probably go jump in the creek over there. For a while."

She returned the smile and backed out of the barn, all but running for the house when every impulse she owned wanted her to turn back around and take what he'd just offered.

After a sleepless night, and a day spent with a skittish Brigid showing him the ranch, Raider was about ready to lose his mind. Sean had been absent most of the day, working the farm, and Raider didn't have time for this crap.

So after dinner, when Sean offered to show him the barn that Raider had already spent too much time in the night before, he jumped up and followed. It was time to lay his cards on the table and see if Sean wanted to play the hand. He had to make this good. Sean led the way outside, not speaking.

The moon rose high and bright and round, looking closer than it did in the city. Almost as if the glowing orb hovered specifically over the rows and rows of hay.

Sean hauled open the heavy door and stepped inside, flicking on a light as he did so.

Raider followed, his boots snapping straw and hay as he stepped inside to see the tractor, empty stalls, and a myriad of tools lined neatly on one wall just as they'd been the night before.

In a surprisingly graceful move, Sean grabbed a shovel leaning against a post, turned, and swung it at Raider's head.

Raider ducked, out of pure instinct, and the metal brushed his hair. He jumped back. "What the hell, man?" It was a sad testament to his training that his accent came out just like he'd grown up on the streets of New York.

Sean held the shovel with both hands, his stance set. "Who the hell are you?"

Raider forced himself into character. "I'm your daughter's fiancé."

"Right. Maybe so, but that's not why you're here." Sean tapped one part of the handle against his left hand. "Start talking, or I'll take off your head. Brigid will be pissed, but she ain't marrying you."

Raider took another step back. If Sean swung again, he'd have to take the shovel, and he didn't want to hurt Brigid's father. "Fine. I have an organization that needs your connections." He held up a hand as Sean's chin lowered. "All I need is an introduction to the Coonans. Nothing more."

Sean's eyes glittered an angry emerald. "Who the hell are the Coonans?"

Nice try. Raider forced a scoff. "I have your police records and rap sheet. It helps to have friends in high places." His smile even felt dirty. "I know you were an enforcer with the Coonans, and I know you're still in contact with them. Introduce me, vouch for my organization, and I'll never bug you again."

Sean's nostrils flared. "And Brigid?"

"I like her. Am happy to marry her." The next words

burned through Raider's throat. "If you want me gone after the introduction, I'll be gone. But she likes me. If this new enterprise goes well, I can make her a very wealthy woman. Give her anything she wants."

Sean snarled. "I haven't talked to the Coonans in two decades. There is no reason under God's green earth that I'd reach out to them, and they'd know that. You'd be dead the second you showed for a meeting. You stupid sonofabitch."

The man was lying. There was no question Jonny and Josh had visited the farm at least twice. Why? "I don't think you understand the connections I have," Raider drawled.

Sean's face turned a motley red. "Did you have this enterprise in mind before or after you met my daughter?"

Raider swallowed, looking for the right answer. "I met her, started dating her, fell in love with her, and then had her investigated." He shrugged. "Had to know everything. When I found out about you and your connections to the Coonans, I started to think of a way to expand my business. It's—"

Sean held up a hand. "I don't want to know a thing about it. Does Brigid know what you do?"

Again, Raider tried to read the man's expression, but it was blank. He must've been an excellent enforcer at some point. "No. The less she knows, the better. It's safer for her." He tried to look earnest. "I'm only into cybercrimes, Sean. Don't move drugs, don't move guns, and don't move people. Well, guns once in a while. Just odd jobs." Maybe that would make him more palatable to the old guy. "If I partnered with the Coonans, and they used their current system to launder my money, I could do very well. So could they."

Sean lowered the tip of the shovel and leaned it against the post again. "Well, here's your problem. I'm not in touch with the Coonans, and even if I was, I wouldn't help you. I left that life a long time ago." He wiped his hands down his overalls. "I plan on telling Brigid the truth, but I doubt that will change a thing. She's always had terrible taste in men." He rubbed his weathered hands together and moved closer to the door. "Probably karma for my past sins. So you're going to end it with her."

Against all logic, Raider kind of liked the guy. Yeah, he was lying, but he definitely cared about his daughter. "What incentive would I have to do that?" he asked.

Sean smiled for the first time. "Well, end it, and I won't kill you." He pivoted on his left foot.

The punch came out of nowhere, full on, and with a farmer's strength. Pain exploded in Raider's temple, his brain instantly swelled, and he dropped like a boulder to the barn floor. Hay filled his nostrils, and then the entire world went black as unconsciousness took him under.

Chapter Twelve

Brigid sat on her handmade wedding-band quilt and looked around her childhood room. Lightning zigged outside, and fat raindrops started to fall against the window. She loved a good rainstorm on the farm.

Pictures and pom-poms and sports trophies covered her dresser and end tables, and a collage of more pictures and souvenirs took up the entire wall space above her desk. She'd forgotten. Her dad had coached her in softball and in soccer for her early years, until she'd played at school.

Then she'd discovered her first computer and had turned away from sports. Had her father felt she'd turned away from him, too? Her mother had died, and they'd both retreated, and then she'd walked a little on the wild side.

Would he be proud of her now? Of the good she did? She fingered the necklace and started to release the clasp.

A knock sounded on her door, and she jumped, dropping her hands instantly. "Come in."

The door opened, and her father walked in, wiping his hands off on a faded yellow bandana. He'd removed his boots, but his hair and overalls were wet. "How are you settling in?" he asked. The smell of the outdoors came with him. Thunder crackled outside.

"Good." She cleared her throat. He and Raider had been outside for a couple of hours. "How did it go with Raider?"

Her dad shook his head. "I'd hoped your decision making would've improved as you got older."

His disappointment hit her like a wet hay bale. So Raider had done a good job with his cover. "He's a good man, Daddy." That was the truth, but at the moment, she kind of wanted to punch Raider in the balls. This was a disaster.

"No, he's not. He's looking to break the law, and even though I think he does care for you, he'll end up in prison." Her dad shoved his hands in his pockets, his gaze barely meeting hers. "I'm afraid you'll end up there, too. You have to stop using your skills for the wrong man."

She'd give anything to toss the camera necklace out of the window and tell her dad the truth. She'd take it off to sleep and then forget it in the morning. He'd be out early with the cattle, so she could catch him then. For the night, the stupid HDD agents could believe what they wanted. Nothing was worth making her dad think she was still a moron. She couldn't take that look on his stubborn face any longer. "Dad, I don't want to fight."

"Me either." He sighed, and the lines in his face seemed to deepen. "We can talk more tomorrow. Raider ain't sleeping in here."

Warmth flooded cheeks. "I know." She couldn't even imagine sleeping with a man under her father's roof. The guy was so old-fashioned. "He's a good man, Daddy. I hope you gave him a chance." Except Raider wasn't acting like a good man.

"It might not be an issue," her dad muttered. "Guys like that don't seem to stick around for long." He looked around the room and then backed out. "'Night."

"'Night," she repeated as he shut the door. The second she was alone, she dropped her head into her hands. "You guys are dicks," she whispered toward the necklace. Before undressing for bed, she removed the heavy silver and placed it in the wooden jewelry box her dad had made her years ago. No way was Rutherford getting a show. Settling into bed felt like coming home, especially with the rain pattering against the window.

Her mind spun through the last day or so. She enjoyed working for the government. Enjoyed being one of the good guys putting away bad guys.

Until now.

She drifted off to sleep in worn flannel sheets that smelled faintly of fresh air and sunshine. Did her dad have her sheets changed regularly in case she came home? He could be so sweet when he wasn't in the room. The idea made her snuggle deeper into the sense of home and family. Her sleep was calm and her dreams languid.

A sound jerked her straight up in bed before dawn.

Her heartbeat sped and she looked around, trying to get her bearings. Had she been dreaming? Rain still fell outside, and she took several deep breaths.

The boom of a shotgun firing had her jumping out of bed and running for the door. "Dad?" she yelled, running through the hallway and down the stairs. Her dad wouldn't shoot Raider, would he? An explosion bellowed through the early morning, and she rushed for the front door, bursting onto the porch.

Fire billowed from the closest barn. Slats of burning wood rained down from the demolished structure along with heavy tools. Another explosion rocked the buildings, and she ducked her head as fire heated the rainy air around her. "Dad?" she called.

Her father came around the side of the house, firing toward the barn. "Get off my property, you sons of bitches," he bellowed, dressed only in a pair of old jeans and boots.

Oh, God. She started down the steps in her bare feet, which instantly chilled from the hard wood. "What is going on? Raider?" She looked frantically around as the fire crackled. Where was he?

"Get back inside," her dad yelled, rain matting his gray hair to his head as he advanced toward the fire.

Her vision blurred, and her body shook. Then she caught sight of a black SUV on the other side of the burning barn. She squinted to see better, and just then a man from the other side of the vehicle fired toward her father. Letting out a yelp, she ducked and hit the wet grass, rolling toward the side of the house for cover. She was a sitting duck on the porch. Where the heck was Raider?

Then a bullet hit her dad, and he went down. Two men with guns rushed her way. She screamed.

Rain splattered against the side of Raider's face, and he groaned, spitting out grass. Or was that hay? Pain pounded in his face, and he gingerly rolled over, letting the water cool what felt like fire. He blinked and opened his eyes. More pain, agony really, slashed into his skull. "Son of a bitch," he muttered, forcing himself to sit.

The alfalfa stalks swayed around him from wind and rain. Even with the rain, the moon was strong enough to barely lighten the clouds above him, enough that he could see a bit, but it wasn't dawn yet. Not even close.

He rubbed his burning temple and jaw, feeling for a fracture. Dizziness swamped him, followed by surprise. The old farmer had dropped him with one punch. He smiled and then winced at the instant agony. Okay. If he didn't want to puke so badly, he'd be impressed. Nobody got the drop on him, and he'd learned to take a hit years ago. In fact, he hadn't lost a fight in a decade.

Until now.

He pushed himself off the wet ground and tried to get his bearings. He stood off to the side of a barely there dirt road. Stalks and more stalks of alfalfa surrounded him. The old bastard had knocked him out and then driven him to the middle of nowhere. Raider snorted a laugh. The unit would be in hysterics right now. Apparently, Sean Banaghan didn't want Raider dating his daughter.

It'd be funny if his face wasn't broken. Raider ducked his head against the rain and studied the road. It narrowed farther to the left, so he should probably go right. It was as good a plan as any. He reached for his phone in his back pocket. Nope. Gone. Also his wallet with his fake identification.

Good thing he'd left his authentic license and badge beneath the seat in the rental vehicle. What he wouldn't give for a cell phone right now.

The wind picked up, slamming against him as if it was on the farmer's side. The smell of wet hay filled his nose as he began walking down the muddy road. What was the difference between hay and alfalfa, anyway? Just the color? It all smelled the same.

Was he concussed? A hit to the temple would do that to a guy.

He put one foot in front of the other as his mind finally started to clear. The chilly wind and unrelenting rain actually helped. What was he going to tell Brigid? More importantly, how was he going to handle Sean? This was obviously a warning—and not a subtle one. The ex-enforcer would probably go with a bullet next.

Raider had to respect that.

He walked for about an hour, his boots and lower legs soon coated with mud. The smell of smoke on the breeze caught his attention, and he lifted his head. Maybe somebody had a fire going. But the smell was different. Like an outdoor campfire instead of an indoor fireplace.

His instincts humming, his face aching, he increased his pace.

The dirt road forked in three directions, and he paused, looking toward the horizon. A faint glow showed from what he guessed was north. What the hell was that? Was something on fire?

He pivoted and launched into a jog, running full out after about a mile as the glow turned the clouds a tumultuous orange. Was that the house? It couldn't be.

His heart rate accelerated and he ran faster, soon seeing fire extending toward the sky. It was the barn. He ducked his head and ran faster. Was Brigid in danger? Trying to put out the fire? He turned and ran through a row of tall alfalfa, taking a shortcut and forgetting the road. Stalks whipped at his cheeks and arms, but he ran faster, bursting out of the crop behind a black SUV.

A man with a gun in hand partially turned, and Raider reacted on instinct.

He dodged to the side, ducked his head, and charged, hitting the guy square in the chest before he could get off a shot. They landed on burning wood and rolled toward the creek, both already punching and trying for leverage. Raider knocked the gun out of the guy's hand, charged up, and landed on the gunman's chest. It took him a second to recognize Jonny P. What the hell was the mobster doing there?

Jonny punched beneath Raider's chin, and Raider's head snapped back, more pain exploding in his already damaged temple. He swayed, and Jonny shoved him off, trying to stand.

Raider fell to his side and kicked out, knocking Jonny back down. He scrambled for purchase, punching the mobster in the side before Jonny turned and manacled him, rolling them both into the damn water.

"Stop or I'll shoot her," a male voice called out, the tone low and calm.

Raider blinked water from his eyes and shoved himself away from Jonny to stand. Then the world narrowed in sound and focus. Josh the Bear held Brigid in front of him with a Glock pressed against her temple. Rain had soaked the pink shirt and yoga pants she'd worn to bed, and her dark red hair curled wildly around her face. Her eyes were a wide and shocked green.

Raider slipped over wet rocks to reach the grass. "Put the gun down."

"No." Josh kept his grip firm as the fire raged through the destroyed barn behind him.

Jonny sloshed out of the creek and shook off water. He ducked to grab his gun and stomped toward the SUV. "Let's get out of here."

Brigid tried to angle away from Josh, her eyes darkening. Her shoulders tensed.

Raider gave a subtle shake of his head. If she tried to fight, the gun would go off. His hands curled into fists. He couldn't get to Josh before he could shoot her. "Let her go. Whatever you want, I'll make sure you get."

Jonny smiled, revealing a chipped tooth. "Oh, we'll get what we want. Tell the farmer he has twenty-four hours, and we'd better have that damn journal. All evidence, in fact." With that, he dragged Brigid to the SUV and shoved her in the back seat, following as Josh started the engine and whipped a U-turn to speed down the private driveway.

Raider ran to his rental to find the tires had been slashed. Damn it. He looked wildly around. Where the hell was Sean?

Chapter Thirteen

Brigid craned her neck to peer out the back of the SUV, but smoke from the burning barn hampered visibility. She shoved against Jonny P, who scooted over but kept the gun pointed at her. "Did you kill my father?" she choked out.

"You'd better hope not," Jonny said, wiping rain off his forehead. "It's not like the old coot hasn't been shot before."

Brigid shoved her hair away from her face. Did she have time to open the door and jump out before he could fire off a shot?

"I will shoot you," Jonny said, easily reading her thoughts. "Just behave yourself, and you'll be fine when your dad gives us the journal." He reached up with his free hand and knocked Josh in the shoulder. "Good plan, buddy."

There was too much to decipher. Why the hell had she taken off the damn camera necklace? "Plan?"

Jonny nodded. "It's all about leverage. We knew Sean had a daughter, so we've had the regional airport staked out for a year in case you showed up." His blue eyes raked her. "You're not a good daughter. This took way too long."

"Screw you," she retorted, trying not to feel vulnerable in her wet T-shirt. "You've been here before, right?"

"Yeah," Jonny snorted. "Sean finally blipped on our

radar a few months ago by showing up at a county planning hearing to stop some development. Dumbass."

She swallowed. "What's your plan now? I'm not getting on a plane with you." Her voice remained steady, but anxiety spiraled through her, making her throat scratchy. These guys were killers, and she was unarmed. She didn't even have on shoes.

"You'll get where we want you to get," Jonny said.

Okay. This was crazy. "My dad isn't in the mob," she said, eyeing the stalks flying by outside the car.

"He was," Jonny said. "That loyalty shouldn't ever go away, right, Josh?"

Josh didn't twitch. Did the guy even talk?

Brigid ran through scenarios in her mind. She was an HDD consultant, and she had a job to do. "What journal do you want from my father?"

Jonny sighed. "If you don't know, then you don't need to know. How about you shut up for a while?"

What an ass. Brigid inched closer to the door.

Jonny manacled his hand around her arm and yanked her toward the middle of the seat. "I don't want to shoot you, but I will."

"Banaghan will want proof of life," Josh said, his voice a low rumble.

So the guy did speak. "Yeah. Proof of life," she repeated.

Jonny tightened his hold until her skin bruised. "You can be shot and still be alive. In fact, the sight of you bleeding out would probably be decent motivation for the old guy."

Brigid's stomach rolled over. Her mind spun. She could deal with this. "It's not my father you need to worry about."

"Oh?" Jonny snorted. "I'll admit that your boyfriend can fight, but the guy didn't even have a gun with him. Not a good sign."

"Fiancé," Brigid retorted. Where had Raider come from,

anyway? She hadn't heard him leave the house. "Raider Times isn't a man you want to cross. Believe me." She almost stumbled on the false last name.

Jonny stiffened. "Raider Times?" He frowned toward Josh. "Isn't that the guy—"

"Who left a business card after taking out Milo and Aiden at that bar downtown," Josh affirmed, his cold gaze meeting hers through the rearview mirror. "This is interesting."

Brigid swallowed and dove all the way in. "We were in town to see if my father would get us an introduction to Eddie Coonan. Raider has a business proposition." Could she sound any more like a stupid female? Her voice shook, and that wasn't part of the cover. If she stopped scrambling long enough, she'd probably start throwing up. "Surely you researched him."

"We did," Jonny affirmed.

Good. The cover they'd created for Raider showed him as a ruthless businessman who had no problem getting his hands bloody in truly creative ways. Maybe that would keep them from killing her. For now, anyway. "Yet you didn't call," she muttered.

"We had something else to do first," Jonny said, his hand steady on the gun. His gaze ran over her again, turning calculating this time. "Our dive into his background didn't show a fiancée. It sure as hell didn't show you as the fiancée."

"Raider likes to keep me under wraps, for obvious reasons. I think once he got to know me and found out about my father, his idea for a new venture with you took place." She tried to simper but had to sniff instead. "You're welcome." If she moved to the left, she could punch his wrist, and he'd drop the gun. But could she grab it before he could? And if so, did she have time to shoot him before Josh did anything? He probably had a gun up there.

Jonny's gaze narrowed. "Do you know where the journal is?"

She blinked. "I don't know what you're talking about. What's in the journal?"

Jonny pursed his lips. "If you're lying to me, you're going to bleed. However, if you're telling the truth, you might be of more use than I originally thought."

She rolled her eyes. "Raider won't negotiate for me. He'll come in with knives flying and just cut out your throat. You have to know that from checking him out." Just how good were the Coonan hackers? Raider's cover was solid, but no fake ID would hold up forever.

They drove for about an hour toward the mountains, finally reaching a small dirt runway used for crop dusters. Rain sluiced over a small private jet at the end. She shook her head. "That's crazy. There's not enough runway."

Josh chortled from the front seat. "You should've seen us land. Nearly hit that mountain."

She eyed the gun pointed at her. Should she make a run for it?

Raider kicked his slashed tire, frustration roaring through him so quickly he swayed. Turning, he leaped over the creek and ran for the house while the fire crackled wildly behind him. Where the hell was Sean? Old-fashioned storm cellar doors were wide open on the side of the house, and he ran to them, jogging down crumbling stairs where blood drops and rain mingled.

He paused at the dank bottom. A bulb hung suspended from the ceiling, swinging and revealing rickety shelves holding cracked and discarded canning jars. He ran past them and turned left, into another room with a heavy metal door.

"Holy crap," Raider muttered at seeing Sean in the middle of a weapons room. Handguns, automatic shotguns, even some grenades in the corner. And dynamite. A bloody bandana was wrapped around Sean's upper arm as he shoved guns and knives in his waistband. "What the hell?"

Sean looked over his shoulder, his serious eyes the same shade as Brigid's. "Can you shoot?"

"Yes." Raider's nostrils flared.

Sean tossed him a SIG Sauer and a shotgun, which Raider easily caught. He shoved the SIG in his waistband. "Where would they take her?" Raider asked.

Sean shook his head. "Either a cabin they've secured, which I doubt, or out of here to Boston. There's only one landing strip long enough for a private plane, and it's about thirty miles east of here on federal land between farms."

"My tires are slashed," Raider said.

"Mine, too," Sean muttered. "We'll have to run to the barn a mile away. I have a summer car there." He looked Raider over. "You going to be of help or be in the way?"

If he was in the way, there was no doubt Sean would just shoot him. "Where the hell's my phone?" Raider snarled.

"Don't need it." Sean shoved past him and ran up the old stairs.

Raider followed and grabbed the older man, swinging him around. "I need my phone. Now."

Sean started jogging toward the road. "I threw it in your rental car."

Raider gave him a look and ran across the small bridge this time, reaching the car. The phone was on the dash. He grabbed it, pulled his badge and ID from under the seat, and launched into a run down the road after the older man, already dialing Force for backup.

"What?" Force growled for answer over the phone line.

"Brigid's been taken by the Coonans, and I think she'll keep her cover in place. They're probably going to try and fly her to Boston," Raider said, his head pounding every time his boots hit the ground. "I'll need a lift out of here sooner rather than later. There's a federally owned small landing strip about thirty miles east of the farm. I'm counting on you." He clicked off before Force could protest and then sped up to run beside Sean.

"These are the guys you wanted to meet, you jackass," Sean coughed out, his bleeding arm not seeming to slow him any.

"What do they want from you?" Raider tucked the phone in his pocket in a smooth move and ignored the raging pain in his head.

"None of your damn business," Sean returned, speeding up and splashing mud over Raider's legs.

Raider sped up as well. "That's where you're wrong. They took my fiancée. Tell me the truth."

"She ain't yours, and she won't be." The Irishman's jaw firmed into what looked like solid rock. He moved fast for an old guy and was definitely in good shape. "I could've cut your throat and left you for the buzzards."

"Yeah. Thanks for that." Raider's aching face heated. "I'm not usually easy to knock out."

"One punch," Sean snorted, his shoulders going back.

Raider's shoulders went back. "A sucker punch right to the temple. You could level a moose like that." He tensed his neck, fighting embarrassment. "I really can fight, you know," he muttered under his breath.

Sean cut him a look as the next barn came into view. "Aye. I saw you take down Jonny P before I ran to get guns. He's actually quite the scrapper."

Well. At least that was something. They reached the

barn and Sean tugged open the large door, wincing as he did so. Raider jumped in to help. "How bad you hit?"

"Just went through my upper arm," Sean grunted, looking pale for the first time before jogging into the dark interior of the barn. He reached a car and quickly pulled off the blue car cover to reveal a 1977 Pontiac Firebird polished to perfection and ready to go.

Raider whistled. A real *Smokey and the Bandit* car. "You're injured. I'll drive."

Sean faltered.

Raider moved toward the driver's door. "We're talking about Brigid here."

Sean grimaced but strode for the passenger's side and slid inside.

Raider yanked open the door and sat on the smooth leather, instinctively pulling down the sun visor. The keys dropped into his hand, and he inserted one, twisting. The engine roared to life with a rumble he felt to his bones. Putting the car in gear, he peeled out of the barn and swung around to the main road, punching the gas. "We have a chance to catch them."

"Yep." Sean rested one gun on his lap and put the shotgun on the floor. "I don't know nothin' about you, but if I need to shoot them, I will. Stay out of my way."

Raider swallowed. "Stay out of mine, Sean. I'll get Brigid back." He'd brought her on this assignment, and he was her handler. No way in hell was he going to lose another agent. Especially this one. He had no problem dropping the entire op to save her.

The car fought him over the bumpy road as he increased his speed and followed Sean's directions, but they burst out onto the runway just as a small plane lifted into the lightening sky.

"No!" Sean jumped out of the car, already firing his gun.

"Stop it." Raider flung himself over the console, out of

the car, and tackled the older man to the muddy ground, spinning the gun out of his hand. "You could hit Brigid or the fuel tank."

Sean punched him, and that was the end for Raider. He flipped the ex-mobster onto his stomach and secured his hands at the back of his waist in a classic police take-down move.

"Let me go," Sean said, struggling. "They're getting away."

Raider hung his head and let his neck relax. "I have friends coming. We'll get her back." He didn't loosen his hold. "Trust me, Sean." The man continued to struggle but finally subsided, blood flowing more freely from the wound in his arm.

"Why should I trust you?" Sean snapped, his face pressed against the dirt.

Raider sighed. "Because I'm HDD. I have the entire federal government on my side in this." Well, sort of.

Sean stilled. "Ah, shit."

Chapter Fourteen

The private plane that picked them up was owned by some buddy of Force's, and the pilots weren't happy about having to work on what should've been their week off, apparently. They'd frisked them both and tossed all weapons out in the brush, probably on orders from Force, actually. Once Raider and Sean had boarded and taken their seats, the pilots shut the cockpit door and didn't emerge once for the rather short flight.

Sean didn't utter a word, either. Instead, he closed his eyes and slept the entire time.

Raider sat across from him, a table between them. When they were close to DC, he tried again. "Sean. I'm telling you the truth. I'm with Homeland Defense, and you need to tell me what your job is with the Coonans."

Sean's green eyes slowly opened, already clear and focused. "I don't work for the Coonans."

Since Jonny P had just blown up Sean's barn, that was probably the truth. "You did," Raider said softly.

Sean didn't even blink.

Fine. Raider ignored the constant worry that Brigid had been taken. She'd be safe for the twenty-four hours Jonny P had promised. "What do you have that they want?" It was a simple question, and Raider would get an answer. Period.

Sean just stared at him.

Raider slapped his badge and ID down on the table between them. “I already told you who I work for.”

“Those can be faked. Easily,” Sean said, crossing his arms across his still bare chest. Dried blood crusted the bandana now. “My girl wouldn’t be caught dead with a Fed.” Regret flashed for the briefest moment across his blunt features. “Unfortunately.”

“You think the government wouldn’t use her skills?” Raider countered. “She’s invaluable.”

Sean finally blinked.

“Yeah.” Raider pressed his point. “She got in a little trouble—doing a good thing, by the way—and the Feds made her a deal. She hacks and does a lot of good now. She’s helped more people than I can count, and I’ve only been her handler for a month.”

Sean’s chin lifted. “Her handler?”

Okay. That did sound wrong. “We’re not really engaged. It was a cover to get to you, because we thought you were working with the Coonans.” Raider watched Sean carefully for any tells. He still wasn’t sure the guy was out of the business, notwithstanding the burning barn. Was it possible that Jonny P and Josh were making a move against the Coonans? Unlikely, but he’d seen odder situations in the mob. “Whose side are you on, anyway?”

“Brigid’s,” Sean said, his arms flexing. “My girl is in the arms of mobsters because you tried to use her for a mission. I’m going to kill you when this is done.”

Raider forced a smile. “Your girl is in the arms of mobsters because you used to be one, maybe still are, and they want something from you that you won’t hand over. Jonny called it a journal.” Of course, that was code for something. A ledger, perhaps? After all this time, what info would still matter? “And better men than you have tried to kill me. Good luck.”

Sean's cheekbone twitched in what appeared to be a muscle spasm. "Brigid wouldn't have been at the farm to get caught if you hadn't brought her, asshole. This is on you."

"This is on both of us," Raider shot back, meaning every word. But he had to stay on track. What the heck was in that journal? What did Sean know? He followed the logic. "The elder Coonan died, what? Maybe three months ago?" Wasn't that the first time Jonny and Josh had visited the small farming community? "What information do you have that his son lacks? And is it Eddie Coonan sending these guys to blow up your barn, or are they working their own angle?" If they were on their own, Brigid's life just became more precarious.

Sean's lids half lowered as the plane began to descend. "When we land, we're going our separate ways. I'll get my girl back."

Oh, hell no. "Good luck with that," Raider said.

The plane landed with a soft bump and rolled to a stop at a private airstrip outside the city. Sean was up and out of his seat to open the door, quickly bounding down the stairs.

Raider followed more sedately, not surprised to see Angus Force, Clarence Wolfe, and Malcolm West waiting patiently against a black Chevy Suburban, all three with weapons strapped to their thighs. Roscoe sat on his haunches next to Force, the German shepherd's gaze alert and sharp. It was the first time Raider had seen the dog actually at attention.

Sean paused at the bottom of the steps, his gaze on the animal.

Raider drew abreast of him and made quick introductions before taking in the vehicle. The SUV was riddled with bullet holes and had several long scratches across the hood. The back window was covered with a black tarp, and the tires lacked hubcaps. Yep. It was exactly what he'd expect for their unit.

"That's a piece of crap," Sean muttered.

True. Very true. "Nice plane, though," Raider said to Force. "Good connection."

"Wasn't mine," Force returned easily. "Nari had a friend of a friend. Turns out the shrink is good for something."

Those two should just get a room and get it over with. Raider refrained from making the comment and instead gestured Sean forward. "If you like our ride, just wait until you see our offices." Just how hard was he going to have to go at the guy to get the journal?

As a mob house, the mansion in Marblehead had a surprising country-family feel, with a stunning view of the Atlantic Ocean. Brigid sat in a cozy home office with fireplace, view of a wide stone terrace that led down to the water, and comfortable furnishings. Everything was nice but not over-the-top.

"Are you sure I can't get you anything?" Eddie Coonan asked again from the leather chair that was across a sofa table from her own.

"I don't think so. This is my first kidnapping," she said, tugging down her now dry T-shirt picturing the cast of *The Big Bang Theory*. Her leggings were dry, but her bare feet still hadn't warmed up.

Eddie grinned. He had to be in his early forties, with black hair, blunt features, and a flattened nose. He looked like one of those boxers from the early twentieth century, but intelligence shone in his deep blue eyes, and his diction sounded educated. There was something slightly off about the guy, but she couldn't place what. "We'll have to make it a good kidnapping, then."

A chill slithered down her spine, and she hid it. "Did our fathers really work together?" Maybe if she could find common ground with him, he wouldn't want to torture or kill her. Her mind kept making logical plans while her body heated and chilled, sending anxiety through her limbs. The disconnect was probably due to shock, but even knowing that fact didn't help her grab onto reality. So she went with what she had. "Were they friends?"

Eddie nodded. "Yeah. Your dad was a hell of an enforcer, believe me. I was just getting into the business then, after college, when he met your mom and decided he wanted out." Eddie leaned forward. "Truth be told, I think it hurt my dad's feelings. They were tight."

She didn't want to know what her father had done as an enforcer. As a dad, he'd been distant but loving. He'd done his best. "Something tells me people don't just walk away from your, ah, organization."

"Good insight," Eddie said, reaching for a crystal glass of what smelled like whiskey, even across the table. He took a taste, swirled it around, and then set it down to pour a second glass. He nudged it across the table and gestured with his head for her to take it. Her hand shook, but she did so. He lifted his glass. "To our fathers."

She clinked her glass with his and took a small sip. Warmth slid down her throat. She took another drink, just to warm up. "This is so strange."

Eddie finished his glass. "It's the new age of the mob. Our businesses are virtual, and we rarely get our hands dirty. Even a simple kidnapping can be civil, and death can be rendered quickly." His eyes gleamed. "I'm a good friend to have, Brigid."

She had enough friends. But she forced a smile, anyway. She knew more about the guy than he realized, and his hands were incredibly dirty. The ticking clock over her head nearly drove her crazy, but she fought to stay in character. "Your men just blew up my dad's barn. Then one guy shot my dad." Although he was still moving, so it obviously hadn't been fatal. "But, my fiancé wants to work with you, so maybe this all will turn out okay." If Eddie thought she wanted something from him, or that she was okay dating a criminal, then maybe he wouldn't be worried she'd go to the police.

"I've looked into your fiancé." Eddie sat back and crossed his legs in perfectly pressed black slacks. A crisp white button-down shirt covered his wide chest. "The guy has a past but seems to make money. A lot of blood on his hands."

Had they overdone the cover identity? "He's civilized now," Brigid said. "Uses computers somehow."

"And how do you fit in?" Eddie asked, looking her over.

She barely shoved away a shiver. "I don't understand a lot of it, but I can make a good website. With pretty colors and a nice design." Lying about her abilities burned her throat almost as much as her fear of the mob. "But he doesn't usually need that, so I just freelance when I get the chance."

A phone buzzed, saving her from trying to sound like an airhead any longer.

Eddie drew it out from his pocket and set it on the table between them before swiping across the face. "Eddie Coonan."

"This is Raider Times. Where's my woman?" Raider's voice came through low and hoarse with that New York accent he'd used before.

Her heart leapt, and all the sound roared in, taking her away from the haze of shock. "Raider." She leaned forward and only inched back when Eddie's gaze narrowed. "I'm okay. Not hurt."

"Good. Because if you're hurt, I'll burn the entire Coonan organization to the ground," he growled. Then his voice smoothed out. "However, if you're all right, then maybe Eddie and I can talk some business. I believe there's a journal you'd really like to get your hands on, Coonan."

Eddie's legs uncrossed, and his eyes gleamed with something not quite right. "You have the journal?"

"Not yet, but I will soon. You don't get it until Brigid is returned safely. One bruise, and I'll destroy you." The threat sounded real and freaking weird when made so calmly.

Eddie flicked open a knife that he'd drawn out of nowhere. "Here's the deal. You have one hour to bring the journal to my home." He gave the address. "At the sixty-minute mark, at every sixty-minute mark, I'm cutting off a piece of your fiancée." His smile was chilling. "Don't worry. I'll start with the pinkie fingers; it will take time to get to anything interesting."

"I'm outside of DC and need to fetch the journal," Raider countered.

Eddie eyed her, and she tried not to shake. "Fine. You have two hours. But I want to use my knife at least once."

"I'll be in touch." Raider clicked off.

Brigid tried to hide her surprise. He'd just hung up? That was it?

"Cool son of a bitch, isn't he?" Eddie slipped the phone back into his pocket.

"You should see him with a knife in his hand," Brigid said softly. Raider would need to get on a plane right now to make it to Boston within two hours, and it would still be close. "Not an ounce of emotion, and yet . . ." She forced a shiver.

Eddie's upper lip curled. "Nice try, sweetheart. Your boy might be dangerous, but no way does he let a sweet thing like you get near the action. Don't try to play me." He stood and grasped a blanket off the back of his seat to toss at her. "Your lips are turning blue. Warm up, and I'll have dinner brought in soon." He pointed to a remote control. "Feel free to watch television while you wait."

She tucked the blanket around herself as if settling in and reached for the remote control. A large flat-screen television had been mounted on the wall between two sets of double doors that led outside to the wide lawn.

Eddie strode for the door to the rest of the house. "I have guards outside, and you won't make it two feet. Be a good girl and stay inside." He paused. "I don't want to kill you, but I will. You should know that." He opened the door. "I don't enjoy the killing, but there's something about releasing a soul that has always done it for me. I feel I capture a part of it somehow." The door shut quietly behind him.

She shuddered. What kind of insanity lived in the well-dressed mobster? There was time to figure out that later. For now, she flipped on the television to a rerun of *Parks and Rec* and then set the remote to the side. There was no reason to try to go outside. Quietly sliding the blanket out of her way, she padded across the office to his desk and computer. Everything she needed was right there. Biting her lip, she got to work.

Chapter Fifteen

Raider was about to break the old man's face as they sat in the main room of the HDD unit's headquarters. He had to leave in less than ten minutes to get to Boston within the time frame, and he'd have to risk his life in the shitty helicopter waiting in the parking lot. Angus had bought it during the last mission, and the thing was a death trap, but it was all he had right now. The private plane they'd used earlier had headed back to upstate New York.

Roscoe lay on top of the desk, his nose on his paws. Wolfe kept leaning over to check out Raider's bruised temple, poking it every once in a while. "Stop it," Raider snapped.

Wolfe probed again. "Man, you got hit hard." He smiled at Sean. "You must have fists like anvils."

Sean eyed the ex-soldier. "I boxed in my youth."

Malcolm and Angus had gone to the main HDD headquarters to use resources there, and Raider had spent precious moments trying to talk Sean into giving up whatever the journal might be. Wolfe had provided backup, sort of, by pretty much admiring the bruise swelling over Raider's face. "Listen, Sean."

"No." Sean crossed his arms, seemingly content even though his daughter was in danger. "Let me go, so I can save Brigid. You're just in the way, Fed."

At least the guy finally realized Raider was a Fed.

The elevator door opened, and Raider partially turned as Wolfe drew a gun from his desk drawer. The gun quickly disappeared as Nari Zhang clip-clopped into the room in sparkly pink heels.

The dog perked up, his gaze on the shoes.

The petite woman rolled her eyes. "You are neither wearing or eating these, Roscoe."

With a soft whimper, the dog put his head back down.

Sean looked at the animal. "He wears heels?"

"Yes." Nari pulled out Malcolm's empty chair and sat, sliding a manila file toward Sean. "He has a short-dog complex, even though he isn't short, and often tries to make himself taller." She swept her hand toward the dog sitting on top of the desk instead of below it. "The problem is, he then tries to eat the heels. It has become expensive."

Raider cleared his throat and tried to force thoughts of Brigid to the back of his mind. "Dr. Nari Zhang, this is Sean Banaghan, Brigid's dad."

"Hello." The shrink held out a hand with light pink nails, and Sean took it gingerly. When he released her, she pointed to the folder. "Eddie Coonan has criminal enterprises all over the world, and he's expanding quickly in ways his father never would've approved. He's going to get caught, and when he does, he's going to talk about everything and everybody."

Sean took the folder with one gnarled hand and opened it, reading the information. "Let him." Anger glittered in his eyes.

"Okay," Nari murmured. "But right now he has your daughter, and we want to help her. Please, trust us. What's in the journal?"

Sean shut the file folder and set it down on the desk, flattening his hand over it. He was quiet for a moment, obviously working things out in his head. Finally, he spoke.

"When I got out, I had to take leverage with me. Otherwise they would've hunted me down, friends or not."

Raider breathed out, not wanting to spook the guy. Was he finally going to spill?

Sean sighed. "In the journal, I have records of transactions with certain officials, some high up by now, as well as carefully detailed records of crimes that don't have statutes of limitations."

In other words, homicides. Raider kept his gaze stoic. "Just records? Why is Eddie so consumed by this?"

Sean smiled. "Well, the journal isn't all. I have recordings, pictures, and even a couple of documents."

Raider mulled over the facts. "Why come after you now? I mean, Brigid or your wife could've been used for leverage at any point through the years. I understand that Patrick Coonan is dead, and Eddie has taken over, but that information has been safely in your hands for decades."

"Pat was my friend," Sean said simply. "The leverage gave me freedom and him a way to save face and let me out of the organization. We were brothers, although we'd gone down different paths. He knew I wouldn't betray him, and I knew he didn't want me dead." He focused on the pretty shrink. "It probably doesn't make sense to you, especially since we bonded in crime, but there was still loyalty between us."

It did make sense to Raider. Loyalty mattered. Period. "Eddie shares no such loyalty."

"Nah. Eddie has always been over-the-top paranoid, and having information like that out there probably keeps him up at night," Sean admitted. "Plus, I'm getting up there in years, and he's probably afraid of what will happen to the information if I pass on. Jackass doesn't realize I have a good forty years in me yet."

Reaching a hundred years old wasn't impossible. "Where's the journal and box of evidence?" Raider asked, trying to profile the man. Where in the world would he hide something like that for decades?

"Buried in a cemetery right outside of Boston," Sean admitted. "I didn't have a backup plan in case Pat Coonan took me out, because I knew he wouldn't. So I secured the box and forgot about it to live my new life."

Was the evidence even safe? Sitting in the ground for decades didn't sound like an ideal situation. "You know that whatever we find will implicate you as well," Raider warned. Not that he cared. Brigid's safety took precedence over everything else.

Sean shrugged. "Good luck."

Smart, wasn't he? Well, the guy had walked away in one piece from the mob. "I need that journal," Raider said.

Sean scoffed. "You going to just walk in the front door with it?"

Raider glanced at Nari and then back. Sean was holding something back. He could feel it. But he'd have to figure out what later. "No. I'm going in without it first." He jerked his head at Wolfe. "We can't leave Brigid in there by herself any longer. We'll have Force get the information, but we have to go right now."

Sean shook his head. "You go in there without something to trade, and you'll be dead in less than a minute."

Raider breathed out. It was a chance he'd have to take.

Brigid had unraveled Eddie's passwords in about ten minutes and delved deep into his home accounts, making mental notes of anybody he emailed often. There was no evidence of crime on the computer or in the emails, but she found a trail to a series of computers she pinged to a bar on the outskirts of Boston. There was a computer system there, but she couldn't get into it. The server must be local and it was protected well. She memorized the address.

She caught sight of another protected file and went to work, using an encryption code she'd created. She found numbers and dates and other numbers. What were those? Latitude and longitude? She memorized the page, trying to make sense of it. Some of the material was a code, and she ran through several she knew, finally unraveling a series of places: Thailand, India, and Haiti. She memorized the entire sheet.

Then she scrolled through his email. Nothing. What about another account? Humming, she ran another algorithm and found a secret account where Eddie was named Bulldog. It kind of fit. The recipient was called Lion. Interesting. Dogs and cats didn't usually get along. Her blood quickened as she caught a scent. She traced it, following it, and found Lion on another site. Then another, and finally, a name. "Scot Tyson," she murmured. How did she know that name?

Then a sound echoed down the hall and she quickly exited the computer and rushed to sit, settling the blanket over her legs.

The door opened, and Eddie Coonan walked in, knife in hand.

She jumped over the side of the chair and edged around it, her mind spinning. She'd taken some defense classes at the HDD, but securing a knife from an experienced killer was out of her skill set. "Get away from me."

He walked inside, his clothes somehow still perfectly pressed. "I'll only take a pinkie or an earlobe. It's your choice."

Her stomach lurched. She eyed the door, but the outline of a man with a gun proved Eddie's claim that guards patrolled the property. She needed her pinkies to work hack, and she liked her earlobes.

Eddie moved forward. "Don't fight me, and it'll go a lot easier."

The saliva in her mouth dried up. She clutched the back of the chair and angled to the side in case he gave her an opening to run for the door.

The doorbell rang.

Her head snapped up.

Eddie's shoulders went down, and he sighed. Then he glanced at his watch. "One minute to go."

Was he disappointed or just messing with her? She gulped in air, her legs trembling and barely holding her up.

A ruckus sounded and then the doors opened. Two men brought in Raider, who was bleeding from the mouth and had an ugly purple bruise on his temple. He'd changed into a dark green T-shirt and another pair of faded jeans, along with what looked like motorcycle boots.

Relief filled her so quickly she became dizzy.

He ignored Eddie and focused on her, his black eyes intense. "You okay?"

Gulping in air, she forced herself to speak. "Still all in one piece. Barely." She released her death grip on the chair and tried to focus in case he made a move.

He shrugged off the two men she now recognized as Jonny P and Josh.

Eddie slipped his knife back into his pocket. "You search him?"

Jonny P nodded. "He's clean. No weapons or wires."

"Good." Eddie motioned toward the chair next to the one Brigid had leaped out of. "Sit."

Raider moved gracefully across the room, took her hand, and sat her down before taking the other seat. His touch seemed to calm her while somehow also ratcheting up her anxiety.

Eddie followed suit, removing a gun from the back of

his waist and setting it on his thigh, while his enforcers shut the door and remained in place behind Eddie. "Where's the journal?"

Raider sat back as if they were having a nice discussion about fall football and cheered for the same team. "You knew I couldn't get to it in two hours. My men are fetching it now, and I'll have what you need by tomorrow morning."

Eddie's dark eyebrows rose over his damaged nose. "I told you to bring it or I'll cut her."

Raider's chin lowered. "Again, the box of evidence, much more than a journal, has been secured for decades. Do you really think I could just go open a safe-deposit box in downtown Boston?"

"Where is it?" Eddie asked softly.

Raider laughed out loud this time, the tone from the streets. "Give me a break, Coonan."

Eddie cocked his head to the side to study Raider and then slowly, very slowly, lifted the gun to point it at Brigid. "Let's try this again. Tell me where the information is being kept, and I won't shoot your girlfriend in the head."

"Fiancée," Brigid said, her lungs compressing.

Eddie blinked.

Good. Maybe if he thought she was crazy, or that Raider was nuts, he'd give them a break.

Raider didn't move. "You shoot her, and my men will send the information, all of it, to the HDD, the FBI, the CIA, and the news."

"The news?" Eddie snapped.

Raider nodded. "Yeah. I like that Darla Perintino. She's analytical and looks beneath the surface. And she likes dogs."

What the heck was he talking about? Brigid's back started to ache from the tenseness of her muscles. "I think that's a good plan. How about we go find a nice place to stay in Marblehead and call Eddie in the morning once you have the journal?"

"I like that." Raider kept her chilled hand in his as if knowing she needed some serious reassuring.

Eddie shook his head. "Not the way I do things. The fiancée has to get shot."

Raider sighed heavily, released her hand, and slid his phone from his pocket. Scrolling through, he found a picture and set the device down on the table, twirling it to face Eddie. "That's your wife through the scope of a sniper rifle." He leaned over and swiped left. "That's your mistress—different rifle actually." His voice calm, almost bored, he swiped again. "Your other mistress." Raider looked up at Eddie. "She's a little young for you."

"She's twenty," Eddie returned, his eyes hardening.

Raider swiped again. "Jonny P in a scope, Joshua in a scope here."

Eddie winced, while Josh straightened behind him, looking deadly. "The last guy who used Josh's full name is blind from a broken eye socket that was truly gross," Eddie said.

"My apologies," Raider said smoothly, swiping one more time. "You in a scope, Eddie. You ever see the damage a Knight's Armament SR-25 can do to the human skull? It's fucking impressive, man."

How had they had time to get these photographs? Brigid kept her expression clear. Angus Force must've been working background on this mission longer than any of them had realized. "I've never seen that, but sniper rifles scare the heck out of me." She shivered, playing along. "To think you were in a scope and didn't feel it, Eddie. That's terrifying."

"So." Raider stood and tugged Brigid to her feet. He wiped the blood off his mouth. "We'll be going now but will call tomorrow."

Eddie also stood, his face a hard mask. “Actually, you’ll be staying the night. You have until nine tomorrow morning for your men to deliver the journal and any accompanying evidence.” His smile revealed unusually long canines. “Or I shoot you both, and I’m taking my time with the pretty redhead.”

Chapter Sixteen

After a truly late and uncomfortable dinner with Eddie in his palatial dining room, Brigid paced the lovely guest room with a view of the ocean. While Raider had kept his cover perfectly in place during the meal, his eyes blazed with a light she'd never seen before. It had to be terrible to sit across from the man who'd killed Raider's friend and partner. "We have to get out of here," she said, rubbing her hands down her chilled arms.

Raider shook his head, looked around the room, and headed for a corner, scouting clockwise.

What was he doing? Brigid studied the area. The bed was covered in purple silk and faced a quaint fireplace flanked by a wide reading bench beneath a window with a view of the ocean. The furniture was high-end wicker, and the lights inset in the ceiling. Paintings of sailboats adorned the walls.

He removed a knickknack from the mantel and tugged out a camera, which he dropped to the wooden floor and ground beneath his boot. "I missed you." Finally, he turned his full attention on her. "Are you sure you're all right?"

She gestured around. Were there more cameras or bugs?

He shrugged and moved to her, taking her hand. "You look cold still. Let's get you warmed up." The New York accent remained in place, and the gritty tone helped warm her, anyway.

Numbly, she followed him into the luxurious guest bath and waited until he'd turned on the shower. He smoothly toed off his boots, revealing a small burner phone hidden beneath his left foot. Smart. She grinned.

He leaned in. "Honey, you need to get into the shower and warm up." He reached for the hem of her dirty top.

She slapped his hands. "What are you doing?"

He leaned in. "Can't be sure they didn't plant anything on you. Take off your clothes."

She shivered, and it wasn't all from shock. He had a point. This whole espionage thing was new to her. "Turn around," she mouthed.

"Can't." His mouth was so close to her ear that heat slid down her neck. Beneath her skin. "We had a scuffle, and I was out for a bit. I could be tagged, too." In one smooth motion, he whipped off his shirt.

She took a step back. Holy cow, Batman. Smooth, hard muscle with his darker skin tone was beyond sexy. The bruises along his rib cage only made him look more dangerous. She gingerly ran her fingers over the welts. "Are you okay?"

He nodded, his gaze intense. "Bruised and not broken. Take off your clothes, Brigid."

She so wasn't made for undercover work. Not this kind. She twirled her finger for him to turn around. With an exasperated eye roll, he did so, dropping his jeans as he moved. Steam started to fill the room.

She knew not to look. Honest. But when faced with one of the tightest butts in history, how could she not? She shook her head. This was a job. A game, even. And it wasn't like she was overly shy. But this was also Raider. Biting her lip again, she quickly tossed her clothes to the floor and walked into the stone-tiled shower, letting the steam cover her as much as possible.

Raider followed her and shut the door, keeping his gaze on her face.

But just how good was his peripheral vision? It took every ounce of stubbornness she had to keep from covering herself with her hands like some old-fashioned virgin in a classic movie.

He leaned toward her, not touching. "They can't hear us now. Seriously. How are you?"

Shockingly aroused all of a sudden. No. None of that. He was talking about the case. She could do that, too. "Freaking out," she hissed, her mouth close to his ear. If they were close, he couldn't see her bare boobs. "The guy wanted to cut off my earlobe. He's nuts."

Raider smoothed both hands down her arms. "He might've just been trying to scare you, but either way, he's definitely off. As soon as Force gets his hands on the journal, we'll get you out of here. I'll continue the op on my own and work with Eddie after this."

She shook her head, her chin brushing his while she stood on her tiptoes. The steam and warmth created a sense of privacy that was somehow sexy when combined with the danger they were in. "I hacked into his computer, and he has a business outside of Boston with more records. It's a secure server, and I'll have to actually be in that room to get into them. I think the shipping manifests and plans are on there." And who knew what else.

He leaned back slightly. "Your lips really are blue. Get under the spray, Brigid. I'll turn my back." He turned around.

Her gaze slid to his butt again, and she mentally smacked herself, stepping to the side and into the warm spray. A soft moan escaped her, and darn if his body didn't jerk. She angled her view to see a tattoo of a four-point Celtic knot that swirled over his left shoulder and bicep. "I like your ink," she whispered.

He turned then, his broad chest now covered in water from the other nozzle. "My foster brothers and sister have the same one. There were four of us during that time, hence the four points."

"Why the Celtic knot?" she asked, her heritage kicking into gear. She absolutely would not look lower.

He smiled. "Faye thought it had protective properties and we all needed that." His eyes darkened.

The mood changed, and her body flared alive. The steam and intimacy and naked hard body hit her all at once, and her knees wobbled. Yeah, the urgency of their situation and the inherent danger of being kept prisoner in a mob house also contributed to her heightened emotions.

Or maybe it was just the sensual man facing her in a steamy shower, his gaze still remaining on her face in a disciplined show of self-control that was just plain and simply sexy. "How close are we to death?" she whispered.

Amusement filtered across the hard planes of his face. "So long as Force gets the journal, we'll be okay. Leverage is how you survive this type of situation."

Oh. So there wasn't a last-ditch chance to touch his body. She had to appreciate that he didn't lie to her.

He lifted one smoothly muscled shoulder. The guy was built like a runner who could fight. "But we're undercover with a mob boss who seems to enjoy the killing part of his job. He may take us out just for fun. Who knows." Raider reached over and tapped her nose. "Wash your hair, warm up, and then we'll try and make weapons from items in the room." He ducked out of the shower, leaving her wet and alone and slightly turned on.

Okay. More than slightly.

* * *

Raider dried and dressed quickly, checking his clothes for bugs, when every impulse he had wanted to leap back into the shower and touch all of that smooth, pale skin. He'd been the gentleman Miss A had taught him to be, but he wanted to forget the gentle part and be all man. So he strode out of the bathroom and shut the door, surprised to see women's clothing on the bed.

A flashy dress had been laid next to yoga pants and a T-shirt that had the word "Shopping" across it in red sequins. More importantly, unopened packs containing a G-string and thick socks were there, too. Brigid needed the socks. He would not give another thought to the G-string. He took the casual clothes, socks, and underwear and left them on a bench in the huge bathroom after conducting a cursory check for any bugs.

Then, he turned and surveyed the bedroom, heading for the first painting of sailboats. By the time Brigid emerged, dressed, her hair in wild and wet curls over her shoulders, he'd already torn apart two frames and twisted them into sharper objects. The wicker furniture was useless, and no tools surrounded the fireplace, so no poker or lighter; the glass from a lightbulb would cut his hands to bits before he could do anything good with it. He eyed the mattress.

"What can I do?" Brigid asked.

He turned. The color was back in her face, and with her skin so freshly scrubbed, she looked young and innocent. Her eyes had lightened to the color of a meadow in a Kentucky spring, beautiful and clear. "Get in the bed," he said, his voice rougher then he'd intended. Then he pressed a finger to his lips. There was no way to tell if the room was still bugged or not.

"Backup?" she mouthed.

He nodded. "Wolfe," he mouthed back. Unfortunately, Wolfe was at least a mile or two away and couldn't reach them quickly. "I told you to get into bed."

Her eyebrows rose, but she did as he said, crossing the room and sliding beneath the covers. He turned off the bedroom light and moved silently to the reading nook, taking a seat where he could watch the backyard area. The moon was high and dim, but he could make out figures below. He looked back toward the bed for a brief moment. The light slid inside the room enough to make her visible. "'Night, Brigid."

"'Night," she said softly, watching him.

He watched the outside for about an hour, memorizing the movements of the guards. Their pattern was well thought out and even better organized, but he still calculated the best route to the dock on the ocean below. As far as he could see, there was only one boat. The open garage revealed several vehicles. If they had to make a run for it, a car would be faster than a boat and get them where they needed to go.

Why the heck hadn't Force called yet?

Raider's body ached and his head felt sluggish. The concussion from Sean's punch would've been enough pain without the impact of a fight with Eddie's guards earlier. But at least he'd knocked two of them out.

Shaking off the pain, he moved for the bed, leaving his T-shirt and jeans on the floor, taking out his phone. If he didn't get some decent sleep, he'd be useless the next day. He slid under the covers and quickly texted Force. Where the heck are you? Have the journal?

A text came back immediately from Force: Here with West and Sean. Journal not in our possession yet. Will contact you immediately when it is. No worries.

No worries? That wasn't good. They should definitely have the journal by now if it had been where Sean claimed. Had the old farmer lied? Bastard. Force had only added the "no worries" in case anybody else read the text. There was something wrong.

"Everything okay?" Brigid asked sleepily, rolling toward him.

His chest heated. "Yes." His body vibrated with need. When was the last time he'd had sex, anyway? Way too long ago, and anyway, it was the woman next to him he wanted. None other right now. What was it about her?

She moved closer to him, snuggling her nose into his ear. "What's going on?" she whispered, sending heat zinging through his body right to his groin.

He shook his head and rolled onto his side to face her. There was no way to know how strong a bug might be. So he kissed her, making noise.

She started and then kissed him back, moving into him. Not what he'd expected. He lightened the kiss before he completely lost his mind and rolled her onto her back and took what he needed. Instead, he moved his mouth against hers, forming the word "bug."

Against all rational thought, she burst out laughing, her mouth warm against his.

Amusement took him, and he smiled. Okay. Not his most seductive moment, he could admit.

She caressed the side of his bruised face. "My dad?"

Raider barely kept from prodding the bruise. How had they not had a chance to talk about this? Way too much had happened. "Yes. Sucker punch to the head and then I woke up in a field in the rain." He didn't care if Eddie tried to decipher that statement.

"I'm sorry." Brigid explored his cheekbone down to his now-whiskered jaw.

"He wants to protect you," Raider whispered, wanting to do the same thing. Even if it was from himself.

She leaned in and kissed him. "I don't need protecting."

Ah, but she did. Even though she'd been in trouble for hacking, she still hadn't seen the darker side of life. Not really. Now she was making a move in a situation where they needed to keep their minds alert and ready to fight. That was sweet and naïve in a way that touched him much deeper than he liked.

But the first time he had sex with her, he wasn't going to have an audience.

His phone buzzed, and he reached for it, his eyebrows rising at seeing it was a call and not a text. He put it to his ear. "Tanaka," he whispered as quietly as he could.

"Hey. It's Force. We have a problem. The stuff isn't in the grave where Sean said it'd be." A tractor droned in the distance.

Raider breathed deep, keeping his body and voice as calm as possible. "Copy that."

Force muttered something beneath his breath. "This is a shitshow. We're not going to have anything by the deadline in the morning. I don't want to storm the house, even if HDD will give us resources, because that'd tip off Eddie. But if you want me to, I'll do it. We can sabotage the case and then try to break him."

Eddie didn't seem easy to break. Raider closed his eyes for a moment. "No. We'll just talk to you in the morning. Good work tonight." He'd have to get Brigid out of there somehow.

"You sure?" Force asked.

"Yes. 'Night." He clicked off and then rolled over, pressing Brigid onto her back, allowing his voice to return to normal volume. "Now. Where were we?"

Chapter Seventeen

Brigid's body went from interested to full-on aroused as Raider planted himself on top of her, even though he was so tense he felt like a ton of bricks. "All right," she murmured, turning her head and giving him better access to her ear. Something was going on.

He kissed her loudly on the cheek and then wandered over to her ear. "We need to get in a slight argument, get quiet as we go to sleep, and then silently go out that window." His voice was barely there.

She jerked, blinking rapidly. Out the window? They were two stories up. She swallowed, digging deep for courage. And trust. So she nodded.

"Good girl," he whispered. "You can do this."

Man, this was crazy. "Wait," she said in her normal voice. What should they argue about? An idea struck her. "Isn't there a guard at the door?"

"Yeah," Raider said lazily. "So what? Let's give him a show."

She pushed at him. "I don't give shows." Was there still a bug somewhere? Could she be as silent as Raider when crossing the room?

"Come on, baby. Let's show the man what I own," Raider said.

She couldn't help it. Even in character, she rolled her eyes. "You don't own me. I bet that stupid blonde from the DC bar would give a show. She was a hooker, right?"

"Not a hooker. An accountant." Raider's chest shook against hers. Was he laughing? "That was just one night, and you and I weren't engaged yet. I've been patient enough with you about it, and if you don't knock it off, I will give you something to really regret." His tone was actually a good imitation of a complete asshole with a hint of scary to it.

"Whatever." She pushed him off her completely, and this time, he let her. "I'm going to sleep."

"Fine," Raider grumbled, moving loudly to the other side of the bed. "My head hurts, anyway. But baby, you're giving it up in the morning, or you're not going to like the result."

She kicked him in the shin for good measure, even though he was acting. He deserved it. The bed shook for a moment as if he couldn't help but laugh silently.

Waiting in quiet for about an hour was one of the hardest things she'd ever done. Raider gave a good impression of snoring for about twenty minutes, and even though her stomach hurt and her body had chilled from fear, an odd need to laugh rose in her. A hysterical one. So she bit it down and tried to remember that men with guns were right outside the door.

Finally, Raider slipped from the bed, not making a sound. He ducked and pulled up his jeans before tossing on his shirt. Enough moonlight illuminated the room that she could track his movements.

Holding her breath, she eased from the bed and stood in the thick socks, regaining her balance. Then she followed him to the window. He painstakingly slid the lock free and then lifted the glass in a smooth but slow motion.

Brigid's legs wobbled, but she stood still and off to the side.

Raider watched outside for a while and then took her hand, drawing her close. He pointed at a white trellis over to the side and then gently nudged her toward the sill, keeping her hand. She faltered at the sill and his face hardened as he gestured her out.

It was too far to the trellis.

She looked down, and her stomach dropped. A stone path lay right below the window two stories down. There wasn't even a bush or two to break her fall. She faltered.

He instantly pivoted, picked her up, and set her on her knees on the sill, facing him. His face was implacable. Geez. Would he actually push her?

Panicking, she grabbed the sill and eased her body outside. Cool air brushed her, and she shivered, holding on with all her strength and trying to be as quiet as possible. Raider grasped her wrists and then shoved. She gasped and kicked her legs, stilling as she realized he held her aloft. She looked up into his deep eyes. Oh. Man. Just how strong was he?

He swung her gently back and forth, giving a short nod as he swung her hard and released her left hand. She reached out and grabbed the trellis, hovering in midair for a second. He let go, letting her swing and latch on with her other hand.

She pressed her forehead against the smooth wood, panting. Okay. Down. She was totally exposed right now in the air, and she needed to get to the ground. Climbing down in the socks was easier than if she'd had on shoes, because her feet fit inside the squares better. Going as quickly as she could, praying the damn thing would hold her, she climbed down fast and let out another sigh of relief when her feet touched stone. Then she sidled toward the house, angling herself into the corner and waiting. Her heart beat so quickly, her chest ached.

In another couple of seconds, Raider dropped to the ground. He grabbed her hand and ducked low. "This way."

She gasped for air, trembling with what had to be too much adrenaline. She copied his pose and hunched her body, trying to appear smaller than usual.

He led her along the house and down the path until they reached trees.

Footsteps sounded behind him.

Raider shoved her behind a tree and covered her with his body, blocking her view of the courtyard. The footsteps continued in even time, casual and purposeful. They slowly faded away.

Her lungs felt like they were about to explode. How did he seem so calm? He checked one way and then the other, taking her hand and moving to the path again. They inched carefully down the stone steps toward a dock. The water lapped in, splashing against the dock.

A glint of gold caught her eye, and she angled her head to see part of that picture frame in his other hand. She'd forgotten about weapons.

She stumbled, and he quickly righted her. They reached the bottom of the steps and hurried to the dock.

"Hey!" a male voice yelled right before a man ran out of the trees. "Breach. Calling 'All Breach!'" he bellowed, pulling a long black rifle over his shoulder.

"Shit." Raider turned toward the man coming at them. An alarm blared from the house, and lights came on in every room, followed by floodlights all over the property. "Get in the boat, Brigid!" Raider yelled, ducking his head and charging the guy with the gun.

* * *

Raider hit the guy mid-center, throwing them both onto the sandy beach. Pain detonated in his head, followed by explosions of light behind his eyes. He ignored the on-going concussion and struck fast and hard for the guy's neck, cutting deep with the edge of the frame. The guy flopped unconscious, spraying sand. In one smooth motion, Raider grabbed the rifle and backflipped to turn and run for the boat.

Men shouted from around the house. Good. They wouldn't know where he was yet. The trees partially blocked the beach area from the floodlights, but not enough.

He ran down the beach and leaped onto the dock, where Brigid was finishing untying the only boat. A sleek black speedboat that looked like it could really move. Excellent. He grabbed her and tossed her in.

A body tackled him from nowhere, throwing him onto the dock. His forehead bounced, and his ears rang. He rolled and manacled the attacker with his feet, yanking the guy's head down and immobilizing him.

He barely had time to duck before Brigid swung a canoe paddle at the guy's head, hitting it with a hollow thump. The attacker went limp on top of Raider. The bastard weighed at least two-fifty. Groaning, Raider shoved the man off him and picked the gun back up.

He staggered to his feet, following Brigid back onto the boat. "Here." He pulled her down to the wide bench seat and rested the rifle on the back deck of the boat, putting the butt against her shoulder. He took her finger and placed it on the trigger. "Fire toward the beach." She didn't have to hit anything, but they'd slow down if there was return fire. "Make sure you stay down." He tumbled over the front seat, searching for the key. No key. Damn it.

Running boots echoed across the stone walk. He kept low and scrambled for the jockey box, ripping it open and feeling around. Something cut his hand. A bobber had caught his finger, and he pulled out the key. Bullets pinged along the beach.

Brigid returned fire, yelling as she did so. That was fine. It wasn't like the enemy had lost track of them. He glanced over his shoulder to see her spraying the beach and the stone walkway intermittently. She hit several trees as well.

He ducked and shoved the key in, hoping somebody had driven the boat lately and there weren't tons of gas fumes trapped near the engine. He didn't have time to use the blower. "Keep firing, Irish," he bellowed, hoping they weren't about to explode.

"I'm out of bullets. He didn't have many." Brigid crawled up next to him and started to rise. The boat drifted sideways toward the beach.

Bullets clacked into the wooden dock, close to the boat. He pushed her down, trying to protect her head. "Stay down there." Then he twisted the key, and the twin engines roared to life.

More men, all armed, ran down the steps toward the dock. A man up above kept firing wildly, sending water spraying up. The moron would hit the engine at some point.

Keeping calm, shoving all emotion into another world, Raider pulled out the gear shift, shoved it back in, and bent the throttle forward. The boat jumped to life, and he pressed the throttle all the way down, roaring away from the dock with a spray of water. More bullets impacted all around them, and pain lashed into his hip. He dropped to the seat, turning the wheel and driving into the darkness.

Soon only the roar of the engines filled the night.

Brigid clamped both hands on the other leather seat and hauled herself upright. The wind whipped her hair around, but she turned and looked at the other homes along the point. "I can't believe that worked," she called, her voice sounding lost.

"Me either," Raider said grimly, tugging his phone from his pocket and pressing speed dial. "Force? We're on a boat heading for shore, and I've been shot. Have Wolfe pick us up at Devereux Beach. ASAP."

A light flashed from the shoreline, and he paused for the briefest of seconds as his mind registered what he'd seen. "Shit!" He dropped the phone and dove for Brigid, taking her over the back of the speeding boat. They hit the churned-up water hard and went under.

He kept a strong hold on her and kicked to the surface just as the boat exploded, splintering fire, fiberglass, and wood in every direction. Brigid yelped, and he took her under again, letting the fire blow across the water where they'd just been. He held her under as long as he could and then looked up, finding a dark place to rise.

She sucked in air in large gasps, and he did the same. Fiery debris continued to fall all around them. "What in the world just happened?" she croaked, holding on to his shoulders as the water bobbed them around.

"Rocket launcher," he said, looking toward the dark shoreline. He'd recognized the sound in a split second. Who would've thought Eddie Coonan had a rocket launcher he could fire from the beach? The damn thing must've been on a four-wheeler. "I underestimated that jackass." His head ached, his hip hurt, and his chest felt like he'd landed on concrete. "You okay?"

"Yes." She wiped salt water out of her eyes. "We have to get out of here."

"Yes." He let the water hold them up, but it was starting to push them toward the shore. "Tell me you can swim."

Her thick hair darkened in the water. "I can swim. How about you? You were shot."

"I'm fine." They'd see if his legs continued to work or not. He pointed to a distant shore. "I'd rather swim there, if we can." It was where he'd told Angus to have Wolfe meet them. "It'll be safer than trying to run along the beach." A boat engine ignited in the distance. He grasped her arm and started to swim around burning fiberglass. "Let's get away from the wreckage and into the darkness before they reach this area."

It was their only chance.

Chapter Eighteen

Brigid could barely kick as they finally reached the dark beach, and she couldn't even imagine how Raider was still swimming. She crawled up the sand and flopped there for a moment, letting gravity take her. Sand covered the side of her face, but she didn't care.

Raider landed next to her and turned onto his back, breathing heavily. The ocean rolled in, spraying them as if sorry to let them go.

Wolfe came out of the darkness, silent and deadly. "Thought I might have to swim out and get you two. Saw the explosion and then spotted the two of you pretty quick, swimming. Trained with the SEALs for a bit, but I was meant for something else."

Tears pricked Brigid's eyes. Safe. Wolfe would have a car, and they could get out of there. First one boat, and then several, had started searching the bay and areas along the beach. She and Raider had ducked under too many times to count, and she had started losing hope they'd ever reach shore. "It's good to see you, Wolfe." She turned on her side and coughed out sea water.

"You too." Wolfe grasped Raider's arm and hauled him

up. The soldier's dark hair, clothing, and even boots blended right into the night. "Where you shot?"

"Hip," Raider said. "I can walk."

Wolfe leaned down and plucked Brigid right off the sand. "Okay. Follow me." He was warm and hard, and she wanted to snuggle into his chest, but it didn't seem right. Her body was pretty much a limp noodle at this point, and she didn't have any fight left in her. Not right now.

They reached a nondescript silver car, and Wolfe gently placed her in the back seat. No light came on when he opened the door. "I don't have a blanket." Without missing a beat, he ripped off his huge T-shirt and handed it over. "Do you need help?"

"No." She shivered violently and tried to reach for the shirt, but her fingers refused to work.

The front passenger-side door opened, and Raider fell into the car with a loud groan.

Wolfe studied her for a moment. "Okay. We're on the same team." Without giving her a chance to protest, he pulled her sopping wet shirt over her head and pulled his down to cover her. Warmth and dryness surrounded her, and she wanted to whimper. Until he pushed her back and tore off the yoga pants, underwear, and thick socks.

"Wolfe," she protested.

"It's dark, and I'm not looking." He tossed the wet clothing on the floor and shut the door.

She curled into the dry shirt, huddling to warm up.

Wolfe slid into the driver's seat and took off, somehow seeing the road in the darkness. He flicked a button, and blessed heat began to fill the car. "We'll keep the lights off until we're in town," he said. "I have two motel rooms on the other side of town ready for you in case we need to sew one or both of you up." He lifted his head, probably to look in the rearview mirror. "You cut anywhere, Bridge?"

She couldn't see in the dark like he could. "No. I mean, I don't think so." Now that she was warming up, pretty much everything hurt. "We'll take inventory when we get to the motel." She put her head back and closed her eyes, letting the heat seep into her aching bones. "Before I forget, I found a connection between Eddie Coonan and Scot Tyson. Does that name mean anything?" The information she wanted was in the back of her brain, but she couldn't find it. Where was a laptop when she needed one?

"Yeah," Wolfe said. "He's a US Senator from Massachusetts who just announced he's running for president."

Brigid stiffened. "I need a computer." Exhaustion swamped her, making her limbs impossibly heavy. The feeling of safety pushed away any remaining adrenaline, draining her and taking her under.

She awoke with a jerk, finding herself beneath the covers of a queen-size bed in a clean but utilitarian motel room. Raider sat on a table across from the bed, dressed in a pair of ripped sweats and nothing else. He was leaning to the side, focusing on the closed curtains, as Wolfe drew a needle through his skin.

Brigid sat up. "Holy crap. How bad is it?"

Raider grimaced but held perfectly still. "The bullet just grazed me."

Wolfe snorted and bent down to perform his task. "Would've been easier if it had gone through, but it ripped open your side instead. Sorry you need stitches."

Brigid blew unruly hair out of her eyes. "How long was I out?"

"About an hour," Wolfe said, tying the thread in a knot and reaching for a bandage. He'd changed into another dark T-shirt, probably from the ripped army-green go-bag sitting in the corner. "Okay. Raider? You need sleep." He efficiently cleaned up the supplies, moved to the bag, and drew out a big black gun to hand over. "I'll be in the next room, and I'm armed. You keep this one."

Raider took the gun and edged off the round table, heading for the other side of the bed.

Should she protest? She didn't want to, but there was no reason for them to share the room. It connected to Wolfe's room, so she'd be safe alone. "Raider."

"Don't want to hear it," he said, exhaustion lining his strong face. He set the gun on the night table, pulled back the covers, and all but fell in. "I'm between you and the door until we get the hell out of this town."

Brigid eyed him and then snuggled back down. Two nights in a row, in the same bed, and they kept getting shot at.

"'Night," Wolfe said cheerfully, turning off the lights. "There are more, ah, supplies in the bag if you need them." Then he crossed through the connecting doors and shut his.

Darkness swallowed the room. Brigid tried to keep her eyelids open but completely failed. "Why do you think he shut the door?"

Raider breathed deeply next to her, already asleep.

She turned on her side and cuddled a little closer to the natural heat he emanated. She yawned and then scooted close enough to rest her chin on his shoulder. He didn't so much as twitch. With a small smile, she let herself drop off to sleep.

Raider came fully awake around dawn, acutely aware of the woman molded to his side. Her nose was pressed against his neck, her hand was flattened over his belly, her leg was bent at the knee and thrown over his, and her long, curly hair cascaded across his chest. Even after being dunked in the ocean, the faint smell of honeysuckle and vanilla wafted from her.

Her scent.

He went rock hard in an instant. The ache in his cock overtook every other pain in his body, and that was saying something.

She murmured his name against his skin, and he shuddered.

Her eyelids slowly opened, revealing those staggering emerald eyes. She blinked, but her expression remained languorous, and her touch light. The hand on his stomach slid across his abs and up his chest, and she made a purring sound that nearly broke his control.

He swallowed. "Brigid." Was she even completely awake?

"Yes." Her eyes cleared, but she didn't halt her exploration. "We almost died last night."

The blood rushed so fast through his veins, he wasn't sure his heart muscle could survive it. "We lived."

She kissed his shoulder, having to turn her head to do it. "Are you in pain?"

He was about to fucking explode. "No." Was that his voice? Gritty and Southern?

"Hmmm." She walked her fingers up his neck and beneath his jaw. "You saved me. Jumped with me right out of that boat before the missile hit."

Oh. He shuddered out a breath. "I just did my job. No need for gratitude." So that's what was going on.

She chuckled and used the knee on him to give herself leverage, sliding over him, landing on top of him. "I'm not feeling all that thankful, Raider. Yet." She nipped beneath his jaw.

What the hell? He was trying to be a decent guy, but he was only a man. And sometimes not that good a one. He allowed himself the luxury of sliding his hand through her thick curls to knead her nape. Soft skin, silky hair, delicate bone structure. "Irish? I'm about at the end of my tether here," he murmured.

She partially lifted up. "Good. It's about time." Then she kissed him, her knees dropping on either side of his hips, her sex pressed against his.

His body went rigid as he let her explore him. Her kiss was sweet and gentle with just enough pressure. He enjoyed her touch, his control slipping away one chain link at a time. The kiss was easy with a hint of comfort. Of shared survival. Then she bit his lip.

The chain snapped.

And he kissed her. Hard and deep and right there with her against his body. The taste of salt from the ocean on her lips drove him on as a reminder that he could've lost her the night before. In an instant, he didn't care about being gentle. Didn't give a shit that this was a huge mistake. His mind not only changed, it stopped working against him. Against what he wanted. What he fucking needed.

Hunger burst through him with a raw edge of insanity. He twisted his hand, holding all of that thick hair, wrestling control from her as easily as if they'd been sparring. Wild and savage, he focused solely on the woman lying on him. His tongue slid over her salty lips and into her mouth, where he delved deeper than he had any right to go.

A gasp whispered from her, inflaming him beyond reason.

Her nipples tightened into sharp points against his bare chest, and her mouth opened to his, taking him from reason to lunacy faster than that boat had exploded the night before. He kissed her like he'd been roaming the desert all night and she was water.

The cold of the night before, the fear, the determination . . . all faded away.

He bit her lower lip, just enough to give her pause.

Except it didn't. She moaned and moved closer, her thighs soft on the sides of his hips. It took him a second to realize she wasn't wearing underwear. Only Wolfe's shirt. Her core pressed against his boxers, wet and ready.

He broke the kiss, staring up into her eyes. They had gone river-bottom green, dark, hot with desire. With need. Her lips were already swollen from his kiss, and her pale cheeks had turned a stunning pink. In his entire life, he'd never seen anything or anyone more beautiful.

And a madman had kidnapped her just the day before.

The idea snapped free any control he might've been able to find. "You're sure?" he asked, his biceps undulating.

"Yes."

She'd barely gotten the word out when he grasped her hip and rolled them over, his bigger body pressing her into the mattress.

He pressed against her, his cock hard and swollen. She moaned and arched against him, her pink nipples brushing his skin again. Flattening his hands on either side of her head, he leaned down and kissed her again, taking his time and enjoying the moment while trying to wrench some control back. They'd been nearly blown up the night before, and he wanted to be gentle with her.

A woman like Brigid needed finesse. He had that in him somewhere. "This changes things," he warned her, his lips moving against hers. He couldn't be who he needed to be and take this lightly. Take her lightly. There was nothing casual about Brigid Banaghan, and he wasn't going to pretend otherwise. "Tell me you understand, Brigid." He was already responsible for her on one level, and if they took this deeper, he wouldn't be able to distance himself any longer. That might be bad for both of them.

But he was beyond caring. This was her decision. He'd already made his.

"I understand," she breathed, tunneling her soft hands through his hair and tugging just hard enough to make him growl.

He wasn't sure she did. "I'm not a casual guy."

She leaned up and nipped his chin again, adding a scrape of teeth this time. "Prove it, Tanaka."

Chapter Nineteen

Brigid let the challenge loose, knowing full well how Raider responded to challenges. So be it. "I'm tired of trying to keep my distance from you. Wherever this goes, I want to jump." It was the truth, and she was done hiding it from him. Raider was a risk and a dangerous one.

She'd always flown too close to the flame. Why stop now? To emphasize her words, she bit into his shoulder, right next to the Celtic knot. If she had to keep using her teeth to show him she was serious, she would. The sense of his power, of his absolute self-control, was all around them. It was reflected in his eyes, in the way his muscles jumped. In the bruises along his face. She'd do anything to get that control to snap.

It was close, but he was still holding on. She wanted him to let go, so she scraped her nails down his back to his tight butt, digging in.

He growled low, settling against her. A warning, way too late, sounded in the back of her head. Was she making another mistake? Finding a challenge and jumping in without thinking? Her heart pounded, and she opened her mouth to speak, when he dropped his head and swept his rough tongue against her nipple.

The words sputtered in her throat. A roaring between her

ears drowned out that slight thought of caution. She dug harder into his butt. He lifted his head and kissed her again, this time commanding a response. She gave him what he wanted, kissing him back, her entire body on fire.

He scraped his whiskered jaw down her neck and paused, reaching for the bag still on the floor. "Wolfe said he had supplies."

It took her a second to follow his statement. She blinked. "Oh. He probably didn't mean—" Yep. Raider took out a box of condoms. So Wolfe had meant that? Or did the soldier always carry a big box?

Raider lifted up, his nostrils flaring. "We have supplies, but again, you sure?"

Definitely, especially since they had protection. "I'm sure," she said, her voice hoarse. This was intimate on a level she hadn't anticipated.

"All right." He nipped her neck, swirled his tongue around both nipples, and kept moving south, kissing her belly on the way. He took his time with both of her hip-bones, nipping and leaving slight marks, driving her crazy. Then he continued down her body.

She swallowed, tiny shocks zipping through her straight to her core. Then he kissed her. Right there, right where she wanted him. He stroked his thumb over her clit, lighting her entire body on fire. She mewled, her thighs shaking. Hot streaks of desire, raw and deep, seared through her.

He clamped a hand on her hip, pressing her into the mattress. Then he lowered his dark head and flicked his tongue against her needy bundle of nerves. One finger entered her, and he licked her, looking up with that black gaze.

That alone nearly sent her into orgasm.

Then he smiled against her flesh, the sight as devastating as the sensations he created. He kept her in place, kissing and licking, winding her higher and higher, and she writhed and moaned, needing to fall over. He made her ride his fingers and mouth, drawing out her need, until she detonated with a small gasp.

She cried out, latching onto his hair, her eyelids shuttering as ecstasy took her away. He played her body like he'd spent a lifetime memorizing each curve. The orgasm rolled through her and then hit harder, somehow prolonging the devastating pleasure. When she couldn't take any more, she softened to the mattress and tugged on his hair.

He nipped her one more time, and electricity shot to every nerve in her body. She jerked and a moan escaped her.

Then he took his time on his journey back up her body, licking, nipping, and touching every inch on the way. She'd had no idea the indent of her waist was such a sensitive place. Or the underside of her breasts. Even the center of her palms gained a kiss as he drew up her hands and pressed her knuckles onto the bed, holding her in place.

With him over her, so strong and attentive, she was taken away. Taken, period. Never in her life had she felt like this. A combination of need and vulnerability and desire mingled inside her until she couldn't focus on any one thing.

Except Raider. For the moment, there was nothing else in the entire world but Raider Tanaka. And she wanted him inside her. Now. He quickly rolled on a condom, his gaze piercing hers.

Holding her in place with the long line of his muscled body pressing her into the bed, he returned to her mouth, kissing her with an intensity that ratcheted up her tension at a breathless speed. His body was warm against hers, heated even, and his erection rubbed enticingly against her needy sex.

She lifted her knees on either side of his hips. "Stop holding back. I'm ready." God, she needed him to lose control. To join her in being taken over by this. "Now, Raider. Give me all of you."

He went utterly still and lifted his head, his eyes the darkest of midnights with no stars. Dark and deep and powerful. His hands flexed against hers, and then he shifted his hips, poised at her entrance. Slowly, intently, he penetrated her, all of him taking her over.

Even though she'd been ready, and wanted him, she gasped at the invasion. He took her, big and full, inching inside and giving no quarter. He went steady, and tingles exploded one after the other inside her, even as she rode the perfect edge between pleasure and pain.

Her body relaxed to take him, and the feeling was so overwhelming that she shut her eyes.

He paused, halfway inside her, and gently kissed each of her eyelids. Soft and gentle. Understanding. Tears pricked the back of her eyes, and she blinked rapidly to keep something of herself separate. But he saw everything—he felt everything. There was no hiding from Raider.

He continued pressing inside her until he'd taken her completely, going deeper than she'd realized anybody could.

She opened her eyes again to meet his gaze. The intimacy of the moment, of him all the way inside her, of his sweetness in the unexpected kiss, overtook her.

"Now," he whispered, his smile all masculine intent. He pulled out and shoved back inside her, not holding back. Then he started to pound.

Her body responded way before her mind, lifting her hips to meet his thrusts, wanting everything he could give her. The tension inside her spiraled up until she gave up breathing. She curled her fingers over his, unable to move her hands and touch him. The inability to move, the total control he kept over her body, drove her up higher than ever before.

He angled his body more over her, and slammed into her, rubbing across her clit.

She gasped, biting her lip to keep from screaming. Lights flashed behind her eyes and she climbed higher, trying to get to that peak that was so close. So damn close.

The orgasm, one that would devastate her, was preceded by sparks unleashing inside her. She breathed out, and then in once, seizing the air in her lungs, her entire body tightening almost painfully. She fought falling over, tried to keep control, and then the entire room sheeted white and finally red hot.

She cried out and arched against him, the explosion ripping through her with the force of a tornado. Every nerve fired, and lights flashed hot and bright against the back of her eyes. She forgot where she was for the briefest of moments and let the supernova of orgasms destroy her reality.

He buried his face in her neck, coming hard, shaking with it. Even so, his lips latched on to her skin, leaving his mark as he lost himself.

His scent, the feeling of him, the sensation of being under him would stay with her forever. This was way more than sex. What it was, she had no idea. As she panted out air with her body still tingling, she tried to find some path back to sanity. To control.

He lazily licked her neck to place a sweet kiss on her lips before rolling off her. Somehow, in the movement, he ended up spooning around her in a cocoon of muscled warmth.

She snuggled her butt into his groin.

He groaned, and amusement took her. Oh, it was edged with tension and need and overwhelming panic, but she smiled anyway. It was good to know he was as overtaken as she had been.

He caressed a calloused palm down the sensitized skin of her arm to hold her hand at her waist. The simple movement, the sweet touch, dug right into her heart and bloomed.

She shook her head. This couldn't happen right now. There was too much going on.

"Stop thinking so hard." His lazy voice rippled over her skin with that Southern accent. "Just enjoy the moment. Everything can go to hell when dawn arrives."

She swallowed and looked at the closed connecting door. How loud had she been? "Um, do you think Wolfe heard us?" Her own voice was hoarse and kind of sexy sounding, actually.

Raider's hold tightened. "Want me to lie to you?"

She winced. "No."

"Wolfe is ex–special forces, hardly ever sleeps, and can hear a twig crack a mile away. Chances are, he heard."

Heat flamed into her face. "Great."

Raider chuckled, his chest moving against her back. "The good news is that Wolfe's a decent guy. The second he heard something, he probably put the pillow over his head."

That was more than likely true. She cheered up. "Good point."

"Or," Raider murmured, "he went outside and scouted the entire area because he knew I wouldn't be paying attention to the door. That's more likely."

That was an even better scenario. Then he wouldn't have heard anything. "I like that," she whispered.

"I like you," Raider said easily.

She stiffened instantly. "But?"

He sighed, moving her hair. "But things are complicated. For now, I want you off this case."

She wouldn't have been more surprised if he'd asked her to shave her head. "Are you kidding? It's a computer case, and you need me."

"Yeah, but your dad lied to us, and I think he knows more about what's going on than he's telling us," Raider said with his "trying to be reasonable" voice. "I'm going at him hard, and you want to protect him. I get that, I really do. But I'm going to protect you no matter what. I told you things would change."

She wasn't going to argue with him while naked and vulnerable. Instead, she turned in his arms and ran both hands down the hard and impressive planes of his chest. "Well, then. I say we make the most of this night. Let's fight tomorrow."

His smile was pure sin. "Now that's a plan." He leaned in and kissed her, drawing her even closer. "We have several hours until dawn. Let's see what we can do with them."

She kissed him back. Tomorrow would come, but for now, she had this moment. She let him take her away again.

Chapter Twenty

Angus Force leaned back in control room one, looking at the murder board that haunted his nights. Henry Wayne Lassiter was still alive, and there was no way he wasn't killing regularly. The guy couldn't help it. So where were the missing women? Where were the bodies?

His once good source in the HDD, the guy who'd given him the heads-up about Lassiter, had disappeared months ago. No trace. Probably on assignment in Siberia somewhere.

The cheap and probably dangerous lights emitted an annoying buzzing, and his dog snored lightly in the corner on a new and way too plush bed Nari had brought in the day before.

His phone rang, and he looked down. "Hi, Wolfe. What's up?" His team had better be safe outside of Boston.

"Just doing a perimeter search around the motel," Wolfe said over the traffic sounds in the distance. "I think Coonan is still searching the water for bodies, but I wouldn't be surprised if he starts looking in Boston soon. We'll be out of here around dawn, so he won't know anything until we contact him. Any news on the journal?"

"No," Angus said, wiping his eyes. "It wasn't in the

grave Banaghan claimed, and he gave a good imitation of a shocked man." But the guy was a former mob enforcer and surely knew how to lie. "If I didn't know his background, I'd believe him."

"What now?" A siren sounded in the far distance across the phone line.

"I have him under guard for the night. The cemetery was flooded about ten years ago, and things shifted both above and beneath ground." Which wouldn't be a terrible problem if Angus had any juice with the HDD, but he didn't. "I have Mal working on getting a court order to let us sweep the cemetery or at least use equipment that can search underground for what Sean promises is a box."

Wolfe was silent for a moment. "You think he's jerking us around?"

"It's possible," Angus admitted, his attention caught by the German shepherd as he whimpered and started running in his sleep, his legs twitching. "Banaghan doesn't trust us, that's for sure." The guy had been stonily silent after Brigid and Raider had gone on mission. "He's not going to do anything until his daughter is in front of his face." It was Angus's last chance with Sean. "Maybe she can talk him into working with us." It pissed Angus off that he wasn't sure whether Sean was lying or not. He was a fucking profiler, or used to be, anyway.

"I don't think we could beat it out of him," Wolfe said, as if discussing pizza toppings.

"Agreed," Angus said. Oh, every man had a breaking point, but Sean Banaghan's wasn't physical. His daughter was his weakness, and Angus had to be careful there. Not only was she part of his team, he liked the young hacker. But if he had to, he'd use her to motivate her father. "How are Brigid and Raider?"

"Wet and exhausted, and I sewed up Raider's hip. The guy is solid, man. Gets the job done."

Angus nodded. Raider was definitely solid, if obsessed with taking down the Irish organization. He should probably feel bad about using that obsession, but Angus felt an impending deadline in his gut. There was a reason Coonan was making a move now, and he had to figure out what it was before all hell broke loose. "Are Brigid and Raider working together or in opposition?" That was a serious concern, especially since he'd need Brigid's hacking skills soon.

Wolfe sighed. "Well, being nearly blown up bonded them, but you're talking family relationships versus revenge obsession. They're getting along right now, but who knows if that'll last. If things go south, it's gonna be ugly."

Angus had already determined that. "The only way to keep things from going south is to get Sean Banaghan to work with us, and I may have to use Brigid."

"Do what you have to do," Wolfe returned, seeing only black and white, as usual. "They're in this business and not weaving serapes somewhere. They chose their paths."

Weaving serapes? Man, sometimes Wolfe's brain worked at odd angles. "Any news from your reporter?" Angus asked.

"No. She gave us intel but doesn't have anything new. If we find enough evidence to take down the Coonan organization, I'll give her an exclusive."

"You trust her?" Angus asked.

"Yep." Wolfe's footsteps increased in pace.

The elevator door dinged in the other room, and heels clipped across the rough cement. "Call in with anything else," Angus said, clicking off. He turned as Nari Zhang strode into the room. "What the hell are you doing here at three in the morning?"

Her fine eyebrows arched. "Hello to you, too."

The dog awoke and yawned, his ears picking up.

"Hi, sweetie." Nari strode for the dog and handed him a

bone from her leather purse. She turned around. "I've been reading the profile and all records on Sean Banaghan and figured you'd be here."

Where else would he be at three in the morning? Angus studied the shrink. She wore dark pressed jeans, a white sweater, and black boots that had made that clipping sound. Her dark hair was secured at the top of her head with some sort of clip, and tendrils rained down in a casual manner that looked cool. Her dusky skin was free of makeup, her lips a light rose, and her deep brown eyes tired. "Why are you here, Nari?"

She blinked and drew out a chair. "I told you."

"No. At the HDD. I know you were sent in to report back on us, but what did you do to get here?" He'd wondered for a while but didn't have access to her files.

She gave a sardonic cough. "I volunteered for this one. Needed a change, saw you were all on the edge, and figured a shrink would keep this place from imploding." Her gaze moved to the dog munching happily on his bone. "Then I decided I like it here." She looked around the dingy room. "Well, not here, but I like the people. A nicer office would be better for all of us."

Right. That wasn't going to happen. "What did you determine from Banaghan's file?" They needed to stick to business, and his eyes had to stop dropping to her petite body.

She sighed. "He's lying. The first chance he gets, he's making a break for it to handle things on his own. And my guess? Taking out Eddie Coonan is the first item on his to-do list."

Raider awoke after the best few hours of sleep he'd had in a couple of years. His face ached, his hip burned, and his body just plain and simple hurt. But damn, he felt good.

He eyed the sleeping redhead next to him. Her curly hair was splayed across the pillow, and she'd curled onto her side. Her breathing was easy and light.

What the hell had he done? Not once in his career had he risked a mission by letting it get personal. Not like this. Moving silently, he slid from the bed and yanked up his jeans, heading for the door and walking outside into a rainy morning, remaining dry under the overhang from the floor above.

Wolfe emerged from the other bedroom, already dressed in jeans and a jacket. He handed over a latte topped with a mile of whipped cream and what appeared to be drizzles of both caramel and chocolate. "How's the hip?"

"Good." Raider took the drink and guzzled half of it down, not caring that the sugar would probably kill him. He needed the caffeine. "What's the plan?"

"Transport gets here in thirty to take us back to DC for at least the night. No news on the journal or evidence." Wolfe tucked his thumbs in his pockets. "We're gonna have to go at Sean Banaghan pretty hard." The soldier gazed out at the many cars and trucks in the wet parking lot. "Thought you should know."

Raider took another drink. "No lecture about last night?"

"I don't lecture." Wolfe straightened as a portly guy in a business suit exited a door farther down the way, pulling a small suitcase. He watched the man get into a green Chrysler and then drive away without looking their way once. "I like you and I like Brigid. But I don't see this going down a good path. Not with the facts we have."

Raider nodded. "Agreed. Unless we get Banaghan to work with us and put Brigid somewhere safe for the time being. She's been in enough danger, and Coonan knows of her. He'll try to get to her again." Raider had a job to do, and he couldn't think unless Brigid was safe. Whether he liked that fact or not, he wouldn't lie to himself, and he refused to lie to the guy who had his back.

Wolfe snorted. "One night with her and you want to lock her down. Forget Coonan. I'm worried where your brain is right now. We need Brigid on this."

"Sure. We need her in the computer room." Heat clawed its way up Raider's neck to his face. The last person he needed personal advice from was Clarence Wolfe. "She's not an operative, Wolfe. She's a computer hacker more comfortable in a quiet room than in the field. And she spent time with a lunatic who wanted to cut off her finger, before nearly being blown up by a fucking missile." Raider's drawl rolled out against his will.

"Well. So long as you're not personally involved," Wolfe drawled right back, sarcasm heavy in his gritty tone.

"Shut up," Raider muttered.

Wolfe relaxed against his door again. "You shut up."

Raider snorted as the caffeine and sugar hit his system and woke him completely up. "We should check in with Force again."

"Talked to him about three in the morning," Wolfe returned. "He's obsessing about Lassiter again. Not sleeping."

"He never stopped obsessing," Raider said. "At some point, that's the case we need to work full out." Of course, first they had to take down the Coonan organization. It seemed like horrific deadlines kept cropping up to prevent them from dealing with Force's ghost.

"One thing at a time," Wolfe said, as if reading Raider's mind. "Malcolm is getting a court order to search the entire cemetery where Banaghan said he buried the shit. If you ask me, he's lying."

"Would you trust us?" Raider asked.

Wolfe shrugged. "In his situation? Probably not. But his daughter is with us, and that has to mean something."

"His daughter who has made questionable choices since

she was a young teenager," Raider said thoughtfully. "Can't blame Sean for being cautious." Though time was running out for caution.

A rustle sounded from the motel room.

"Your lady is up," Wolfe said, straightening.

His lady? Raider drew in a deep breath before the day ran away from him.

Wolfe's phone dinged, and he pulled it from his back pocket to read the face. His expression darkened. "Huh."

"What is it?" Raider asked, his instincts thrumming.

Wolfe looked his way. "Apparently Sean Banaghan knocked out both of the HDD guards on him and is now in the wind."

Raider took a moment to let the words penetrate his brain. "Well, shit."

"Yep." Wolfe slid the phone back into place. "Get Brigid to move faster. We have to return to DC. Now."

Chapter Twenty-One

Brigid settled back into her computer room at the Deep Ops unit after a short but way too bumpy flight, a quick shower, and a change of clothing. Her body ached from the tumble into the water and the long swim, and her muscles felt like somebody had stretched them out of place. But her windowless room with three consoles, wondrous hard drives, and two laptops eased her stress. An L-shaped desk spanned all three walls except the one with the door, and she had three rolling chairs set around.

She had different young farm animals up as her screen-savers. The calf was probably her favorite.

She quickly diagrammed on a piece of paper the one page she remembered from Eddie's computer, with the odd countries and dates. Obviously he was conducting some sort of international business, but the page didn't give any clue as to what kind. She'd run those by Angus later.

The computer blinked at her, and she typed a program into place. Where the heck was her dad? Before the last week, she would've bet anything he would return to the farm. Now, who knew?

Nari clipped inside and drew out a chair. Her hair was neatly held back in a cool sparkly clip, and her lipstick was a pretty pink today. She held a cup of peppermint-scented tea in her smooth hands. "Any luck finding your father?"

Brigid looked toward a computer displaying all traffic cams in the area. "Not yet. He hot-wired a blue truck from a Walmart, and I'm trying to find where he went from there." Who knew her dad could hot-wire a car? She was oddly impressed.

Nari had donned a pair of glasses, making her look even more brilliant than usual. But she probably didn't know that. Her voice remained soft and her gaze focused. "Is this difficult for you? Helping us find your dad?"

Brigid barely kept from rolling her eyes. "Don't shrink me."

"It's my job." Nari reached over and placed a cool hand on Brigid's arm. "Plus, we're friends. I want to help."

Brigid looked at the psychiatrist. "This situation is difficult for me, because I think my dad is probably planning to kill Eddie Coonan, if this enforcer stuff is all true. Eddie is well armed, and he could hurt my dad."

Nari eyed the other computers. "Sounds logical, Brigid." She cocked her head. "What else do you have going on in here?"

Brigid turned toward the second screen. "Deep dive on Senator Scot Tyson to connect him with Eddie Coonan. So far, nothing. But I just got started." The man was powerful, that was for sure.

Nari turned to the final screen. "That one?"

"Another search. I took info off Eddie's computer and am trying to find out what he's into now and why he's trying to get ahold of my father. Say there is a journal, and my dad has it, why track Dad down now? But I need access to the computers in that bar outside of Boston. I can't search them remotely."

Nari pointed to an open laptop in the corner. "And that one?"

"The Lassiter case. Anything that could possibly prove the guy is alive," Brigid said, wanting to return to her keyboards. "Nothing yet."

Nari looked around. “We need to get something for your walls. Anything. A cork board and maybe a picture.”

Brigid didn’t much care about the walls. It was the hardware that mattered. “Fine by me.” Then she turned toward the shrink. “If we’re friends, why don’t you tell me something about youself? I mean, like, where are you from?”

Nari turned from the screen to Brigid. “I was born in Los Angles, and both of my parents are from Macau.” When Brigid kept staring at her, she crossed her legs. “All right. My mom owns a jewelry store in LA, and my dad is a lawyer. Corporate tax.”

That sounded like a nice background. “Are you close to them?”

Nari’s eyes softened. “Very. I miss them, being across the country now. But I love my job.”

“Why psychiatry with an emphasis in PTSD?” Brigid asked. The shrink was good at helping people and she seemed nice enough, but that was quite the field to study.

Nari just smiled. “There are reasons for everything we do, right?”

“Yes. And your reason?”

Nari exhaled. “I was kidnapped as a child and survived.” She held up a hand when Brigid gasped. “I was frightened but not physically harmed, but PTSD often doesn’t care about how trauma comes about.”

A chill clacked down Brigid’s spine. “I’m sorry. I didn’t know.” Curiosity almost made Brigid ask questions, but it wasn’t right. If Nari wanted to share more, she would. The shrink didn’t say anything else.

“No worries. I hadn’t told you,” Nari said.

What was a lighter subject? They needed to get back to a comfortable situation. “How many languages do you speak?” Brigid only spoke English and computer nerd.

“Three. English, Chinese, and French.” Nari leaned

closer to the first computer, her eyes widening. "Oh my. Is that your father?"

Brigid turned toward the monitor to see two uniformed police officers handcuffing her dad right beyond an intersection. He wasn't fighting them and instead hung his head, letting them place him in a police car. How in the heck? Wait a minute. "I take it Force put out a BOLO?"

Nari chewed on her pink lipstick. "Apparently. Well, the good news is that you'll see your dad soon."

Geez. Force could've told her he'd plastered her dad's face all over town. Maybe she could've helped with the search, if she'd known the police were involved. But at least her father looked safe right now.

Force poked his head in the door. "We just had the state police pick up your dad."

"We saw it in live time," Brigid said, her chest pounding. "What now?"

"The cops will turn him over to us, even though they want to charge him with grand theft. He's only about thirty miles away." Force leaned against the doorway, his dark hair ruffled, and his green eyes blazing. He'd dressed in his usual jeans, boots, and button-down shirt with the sleeves rolled up. His last name certainly fit. "I need you to be the one to get through to him. If he doesn't tell us where the evidence is, we have no leverage against Eddie, and we can't get into that computer room you want so badly."

Brigid swallowed. Her next words hurt to say, but they were the truth. "My dad doesn't trust me, Angus."

Force lifted a shoulder. "Don't care. Make him trust you." He turned his grumpy gaze toward Nari. "You're the famous shrink here. How can she get through to her dad?"

"Hey. Be nice," Brigid ordered. The guy didn't have to be so cranky with Nari all the time. He obviously didn't know about her past, and while Brigid wanted to tell him, it wasn't her business.

Nari placed her hand on Brigid's shoulder. "That is nice for Angus." She rolled her eyes. "Your dad is thrilled you're back in his life, and he's going to want to help you. You have to show him that telling you the truth is the best thing for you, not him. It's you he cares about."

Brigid pushed the keyboard away. That was true. "Okay. I can work with that."

Angus clamped a hand on the doorframe. "Tell him whatever you need to in order to get the truth. Time is running out."

"Fine." She'd do her best.

He looked around. "What else is going on?"

Brigid gestured toward the second computer. "I'm trying to find the link between Eddie and Senator Tyson. The fact that Tyson is running for president is interesting."

Angus nodded. "That is interesting, timing wise. What all did you find in those emails?"

She shook her head. "Nothing that made sense. Just talk about tennis and boating. I'm sure it's all in code, but I didn't have time to print anything out or even email it." Darn it. "And I'm trying to get back into the account, but I'm having trouble." Which meant that she might've left a trace, and the senator was on to her. That wouldn't be good. "I'm doing my best."

"I know. Just keep it up." He started to turn and the piece of paper on the table caught his attention. "What is that?" His tone dropped low.

Brigid instinctively stilled. "I copied that from information I found on Eddie's computer at his house."

Angus took the paper and lifted it, reading it over. "Exactly?"

"Yes," she whispered. "Why? Do you recognize it?"

She partially stood to look over his arm. "I think it's some sort of shipping plan with dates but not destinations."

Angus's gaze hardened somehow. "I knew it. I just fucking knew it."

"What?" Nari asked, also standing.

"I wanted to be wrong." He dropped his chin and took a deep breath before lifting his head. "Those are shipping manifests, and based on the origination points, Eddie has expanded into human trafficking. My source suspected he was moving girls, but the Coonan organization has stayed away from that crime up until now."

"Until Eddie's father died," Nari said quietly.

Brigid's breath caught. "Why didn't you tell me this was part of the op?" She could've been doing research into those girls. Somehow.

Angus sighed. "Because we thought your dad was involved. We wanted you solely focused on him."

"We?" she asked.

"Me," Angus returned.

Oh, Raider had known. How could he not tell her? They were so going to talk about that soon. No wonder he seemed to be on full speed ahead. There was a time limit to this. She leaned closer to the paper. "The delivery date for all three shipments is Thursday, but the how and where of the destination isn't here." She grabbed Angus's arm. "The information wasn't on Eddie's computer, or I would've found it. We have to access his main computer hub."

"Agreed," Angus said. "Get back on the computer and research the situation from this angle, now that we have it. Do what you can." He pivoted and disappeared from the room.

"Isn't he just a ray of sunshine?" Nari muttered. A plaintive meow sounded outside, and she stood to let Kat in. "Do you mind if the kitty keeps you company?" She retook her seat, watching the laptop handling the Lassiter case.

"No." Brigid turned back to the computer to watch the

police car drive her father away from the blue truck. Okay. Her dad was safe. So she typed a new search command for information regarding Coonan's human trafficking enterprise. The sense of urgency made her type faster, but there was nothing else on the web.

Kat jumped up on the table and then moved in front of Brigid, rubbing his little furry head against her chest. She snuggled him close, trying to keep her feelings shoved down. Too much was happening. Between her father and Raider, she couldn't seem to find the calm she'd always wanted.

Nari cleared her throat. "I'm here to listen, if you want. I'd never disclose personal information to anybody."

Brigid turned toward the woman, petting the kitten. Could she trust the shrink? Even if she could, what the heck would she say? "Everything has gotten so complicated."

Nari's eyes softened. "I'm sure. It's been a long time since you saw your dad. There has to be a lot of feelings there to deal with."

And she'd slept with Raider. Brigid bit her lip, deciding against sharing that fact. Right now, anyway. She wasn't sure how she felt about it, so how could she even explain it? "Thanks, Nari. I'll talk when I'm ready." Keeping the kitten close, she focused back to the screen. *When all else fails, it's time to turn to the computers.*

Kat meowed happily as if in perfect agreement.

Chapter Twenty-Two

Raider met the cops and Sean Banaghan outside to take custody of the Irish bastard. Sean's thick hair was slicked back, and he'd stolen jeans and a blue flannel shirt from somewhere. "This way." Raider nudged him toward the old elevator, and it hitched the second the doors closed. "What the hell did you think you were doing?" Raider burst out as they started to descend.

Sean turned stoic eyes on him. "What needed to be done. If you'd get out of my way, I'd take care of Eddie Coonan for you."

Raider barely kept hold of his temper, wanting to beat the stubborn farmer over the head until logic was drummed into it. "While you were dicking around, he kidnapped your daughter, threatened to cut off her fingers, and then launched a missile at a boat she was in."

Sean pivoted, grabbed Raider's shirt, and threw him up against the fake wood paneling. It cracked, raining down pieces. "You put my girl in harm's way."

That was it. Just completely it. Raider brought up both arms, breaking Sean's hold. He went low, punched Sean in the gut, and then swept the guy's feet out from under him. Just as he moved to grab Sean's arms and press a knee to his back, Sean turned and swung out, hitting Raider in the temple. Again.

Raider saw red. He punched back, and they fought, hitting and kicking, both trying to gain leverage.

The elevator door opened, and Roscoe barked. Raider manacled Sean in a choke hold, subduing the big farmer, and looked up to see Wolfe and Malcolm watching him with the dog panting between them.

Malcolm lifted an eyebrow. "Need some help there, Agent?"

Wolfe just grinned and patted the dog's head.

Raider jerked Sean to his feet and pushed him out of the elevator. It had been ages since he'd lost his temper. Then he straightened his clothing.

Sean stomped toward the dog. "Where's my daughter?"

Force came out of his office, took in the scene, and jerked his head toward the alcove right off the elevator landing area. "Take him to the first interrogation room." His chin lowered. "You can see your daughter after you're done talking."

Sean bunched his legs. "I ain't going anywhere."

The computer room door opened, and Brigid strode out, a purple file folder in her hands. She stopped cold, looked at Sean, and then shifted her gaze to Raider. "What in the holy hell is going on?"

Sean fidgeted and straightened his shirt, while Raider wiped blood off his lip. "Nothin'," they said in unison.

Wolfe snorted, Raider chuckled, and the dog whined, putting his furry head on his paws. No expression crossed Force's hard face.

"That's it." Brigid stomped toward case room two. "Dad? Get the heck in here." She disappeared into the room, and a light flipped on.

Banaghan coughed, straightened his shirt better, and ducked his head before striding around the pod of desks to the room at the end. Raider followed, his irritation melding with amusement. Finally. Somebody had made the farmer do something upon command. And where had that tone come from?

"She's not messin' around," Wolfe whispered to Malcolm.

Wasn't that the truth? Raider entered the room behind Sean and Force, and they all took a seat and looked up at Brigid.

Man, she was pretty. In anger, her eyes had turned a light emerald that glowed. Her hair was pulled back in a ponytail, revealing the smooth skin of her delicate neck. A slight bruise, more of a hickey, showed beneath her right ear. Raider shifted in his seat, his hands itching to touch her again.

She eyed each of them in turn. "Listen to me, and listen good."

If anything, they all sat taller. The atmosphere grew heavy.

She tapped the file folder against her other hand. "This isn't about any of you." Glowering, she focused on Force. "You need to get your head out of the Lassiter case and into this one hundred percent. Right now."

Force blinked and his shoulders went back, but he didn't say a word.

She looked at Raider. "And you. I understand the need to avenge your friend, and I know how badly you want to get evil off the streets. But forget all of that, for now, and work this one angle. It's what you have, and I'm tired of your attention getting diverted."

Ouch. He met her gaze evenly and didn't fidget. A part of him wanted to take her down to the floor in a hard kiss, but he refrained.

Sean snorted next to him and gave him a triumphant look.

"And you." Brigid's voice rose and she slapped the folder down on the table. Sean jerked and focused solely on his daughter. "This is not about you, either. I understand why you left the mob, but things have changed. There is no honor among thieves here, and taking out Eddie Coonan only helps you."

Sean cleared his throat.

She held up a hand. "Not yet. Not one word." She flipped open the top of the file to reveal a pretty young girl with black braids, brown eyes, and cute dimples. "I've spent the last thirty minutes since Angus told me what was happening, focusing my research. This is Hathai, and this is about her." Brigid pounded the table. "She and at least ten other girls, young and innocent, are on their way here to be sold after having been labeled as missing from a village in Thailand. Everything we do is about these girls." She pushed the picture aside to reveal several more young girls, all innocently smiling at the camera. Her voice cracked. "Stop acting like jackasses and focus on this case. On saving these girls."

God, she was magnificent. Her lips, full and rosy, pursed as she made her point. Tendrils of her hair escaped to frame her face, and the intelligence in those eyes nearly dropped him. Raider could only look at her.

Her eyebrows lifted. "Does everybody understand me?" Her voice rose to an uncomfortable pitch.

"Yes," Force said, tapping his fingers on the table.

"I do," Raider said quickly. He wasn't quite sure she wouldn't start throwing things at people.

"Yes, ma'am," Banaghan said, his tone subdued. "I'm sorry about all of this."

She reached for her father's gnarled hand and patted it.

"I know, Daddy. But we need that journal and evidence so we can get back in to Eddie's organization and find those girls. All we know is that the delivery date is supposed to be Thursday, and there is more than one shipment. I have only had time to find these girls so far. There are more kids out there who need saving, and we only have a small window to save them, if that shipping manifest is accurate. Please, help us."

Banaghan looked at his daughter, and his shoulders went up. "You don't understand. I've kept that information safe most of my life, and it's more important than ever right now."

"Why?" Force asked, his gaze hard.

Sean just shook his head.

Brigid leaned toward him and patted his hand. "It's time to let go, Dad. I'm safe, you're safe, and the Coonans won't stop coming. But I have to ask. Why are they coming right now? The timing is odd to me."

Sean looked at the blank screen and then shuddered. "All right. It's happening now because of Patrick Coonan dying, Eddie taking over, and Senator Scot Tyson running for president."

"We figured," Raider said quietly, his senses wide-awake. "What exactly do you have on the senator?"

"Not a lot, but he doesn't know that," Sean admitted. "Tyson's mom lived in the old neighborhood, and I don't know who his father was. She became one of Pat's mistresses when Tyson was about eight. The kid grew up hard, and he and Eddie were tight. Got in some trouble and went to juvie, came out and got smarter."

Raider looked at Brigid.

She rubbed her neck. "I just started digging into his past and haven't had time to deep dive yet."

Sean sighed. "Tyson took the money he earned as a runner

for Patrick Coonan, got a college degree in economics, and then went west to attend law school in Seattle. He kept his ties to the family, and in the summer, he worked off the books for the Coonans. I have a couple of pictures and some notations in the journal, but nothing that really hurts him. I've made sure he doesn't know that."

"Anybody running for president will be up for increased scrutiny," Raider murmured. "The elder Coonan might've kept a leash on Tyson all these years, but that leash is gone. Has the senator kept ties with Eddie?"

Sean shrugged. "I don't know, but it wouldn't surprise me. When I left the business, I left completely." He frowned. "There was also talk about Tyson and missing girls—one in high school and another out west, but it was just talk. I don't know any other details than that, although I might have indicated otherwise when I left."

Wolfe crunched a piece of candy and swallowed. "Dana worked for a newspaper in Seattle for years and probably has great resources. Want me to reach out to her?"

Raider grimaced. Giving a reporter information on a case didn't sit well with him. But Brigid was overwhelmed with the computer work they were already asking her to do, as well as the emotions that had to be rushing through her; maybe additional help would be good. It wasn't like the main HDD really wanted to assist them. "Do you really trust her?" he asked.

Wolfe nodded. "I do. She'll run with a story, but I trust her not to print anything until I agree. I can just give her a hint about Senator Tyson and something in Seattle, if that helps."

Force steepled his hands together, his gaze both hard and thoughtful. "Yeah. Give her the tidbit and see what she comes up with. How screwed up is it that I'd rather go with a reporter than the HDD folks?"

Wolfe snorted. "HDD doesn't like us." He looked around the room. "Raider and Nari are the only ones who were actually with the HDD before all of this started. The rest of us are here for other reasons."

Brigid glanced down and then looked up at her dad. "It's time you told us where the evidence is, Dad. Please."

The words hung in the air. Raider waited patiently, knowing there was no way anybody could refuse her, especially somebody who cared for her. He'd pretty much do anything for her, and he'd only slept with her once. His body stiffened. Yeah, he had to get control of himself. There was a good chance Eddie Coonan would end up putting a bullet in him soon. He had no business thinking about Brigid in any way other than casual. "Come on, Sean," he muttered. "It's time to trust."

Sean kept his gaze on his daughter. Finally, he nodded. "All right. I buried the box in the cemetery."

Force sighed. "Where we looked?"

"No," Banaghan said. "The last and final time I moved it was to Wilton Cemetery right outside of Boston—about twenty miles from the first one I sent you to. Everything is buried beneath a headstone that says George Willowby Smith the Third."

Brigid jerked. "After my first pig? The pig that won at the county fair?"

Banaghan shrugged. "Well, yeah."

Chapter Twenty-Three

Several hours after her father had finally told the truth, Brigid waited in the conference room for the agents to deliver the metal box they'd dug up from the grave outside of Boston. Her dad sat across from her and tossed the crust from his pizza to the happy dog in the corner. Roscoe caught the piece easily, munching with a contented doggy snort.

"Nice dog," her dad said.

She breathed out. "Thank you for telling us the truth."

He eyed her with his deep green gaze. "So you work for the government now."

She finished chewing a piece of veggie pizza, her anxiety upping a notch. She could tell him the truth. Maybe he'd finally be proud of her. "Yes. We stopped a bombing plot that would've killed tons of parade-goers last month." She took a sip of the too sweet soda Wolfe had provided before he'd disappeared into the other room. "I think I can help people this way and still use the computer." Her grin felt more natural. "It beats getting in trouble."

Her dad took another piece of pepperoni from the box. "Ain't that the truth."

She swallowed, enjoying the warmth of being near

him. "Did you leave the Coonan organization because of Mom?"

His eyes softened. "Aye. Was an enforcer, felt like a badass, had lots of money. She was workin' as a waitress in a small diner, puttin' herself through school to study accounting." His gaze seemed far away. "Took one look at her and knew I'd have to be a different man to even have a chance."

Brigid smiled. "Was it hard? Leaving the exciting life of crime?"

"Nope." He chewed some more. "Farming was exciting enough—never knew what the weather might bring. And I had her . . . and you." He ducked his head, a massive man with big muscles and thick gray hair. "I'm sorry."

Brigid held up a hand, tears pricking the back of her eyes. "I'm sorry. I should've come home sooner."

"I shoulda come and got ya," he said, his hands twisting a napkin. "So stubborn. Both of us."

"So was she," Brigid said softly. "I understand why she didn't want to go through with the medical trials. She wouldn't have been able to enjoy the time we had left. But man, was she stubborn."

Her dad barked out a laugh, his expression lightening. "Wasn't she, though? One time, when she was mad at me, I thought she'd bean me with a skillet. But no. She cooked vegan meals for two weeks. Remember?"

Laughter and love swelled through Brigid. "I do. Remember the tofu? It was flavored with lemon and . . ."

"Some sort of grass." Her dad shuddered. "Boy, did I give in on that one. Even bought her flowers."

Brigid laughed and wiped off her hands. "I remember."

Her dad cleared his throat. "So. About this Raider."

She winced. "I don't know what to say about him. Yet."

"Well, he throws a good punch." Her dad nodded as if

in approval. “And he seems smart. Definitely knows where you are at all times, which ain’t a bad thing.”

She blinked rapidly. “Are you saying you like him?” Her voice was hushed.

“Aye. There’s a lot to like.” Her dad leaned toward her. “But if he hurts you, I’ll sink him to the bottom of the Atlantic. Just say the word.”

Man, she hoped he was kidding. “Um, thanks? But I’ve got this, Dad. You can trust me.”

“I do.” He sobered. “I trust you, baby girl. You’re a smart one, you are. Just like your mama.”

Her heart swelled, and her eyes ached. Had he just said that? She pressed her lips together to keep from bawling like a moron. “I’ve missed you.”

“Me too.” Were his eyes misty? “How about you promise to come home for Christmas this year? We can do it up right. Big tree, presents, music and your mom’s Tom and Jerry recipe.” He shook himself out of it. “And you can bring that Raider, if you want. I won’t drop him in the east pasture for the night this time.”

She coughed out a laugh. That shouldn’t be funny—it really shouldn’t. But Raider was always in control, always knew exactly what he was doing. The thought that anybody could get the drop on him and leave him nearly hogtied in a field was inappropriately funny. “I don’t know. He might want payback sometime.” She couldn’t think beyond the next week with Raider right now. It all was too much.

“Aye. Can’t blame him.” Sean studied the peeling paper on the wall. “I like this place.”

She blinked, looking at the dented conference table and rough concrete floor. “Seriously? This office is a dump.”

“Yep.” Sean ran his hands over the rough wood of the table. “It’s the shiny government offices that give me the creeps. This one is well worn and remote. Obviously you all aren’t in the good graces of the HDD, and I think that's a good thing." His eyes twinkled. "You can get away with more sh—stuff that way."

Maybe. Having better resources would be nice, though.

The elevator dinged in the other room, and heat rushed through her body like she'd been plugged into an outlet. Heavy footsteps sounded, and Raider carried in a dirty metal container the size of a large postal box. "Agents just delivered this," he said.

Brigid moved the two pizza cartons, and Raider deposited the box in the middle of the table.

Angus Force followed. "Wolfe is meeting with his reporter to see if she has any new leads, Malcolm is working a lead with the coast guard, and Nari is meeting with HDD techs and should've been back an hour ago." His face didn't change expression on the last, but there was an odd note in his voice.

Brigid stood. "So. The box."

"Yep. That's it," her dad said, standing and yanking the rusty clasp away from it. "It's all yours."

Raider gauged the atmosphere in the room. Light and relaxed, at least until he'd set down the box. Good. Brigid and her dad needed to make peace. She'd be much happier that way. He tried to act natural, but their night together kept running through his head. He couldn't get enough of her. Even now, her scent was driving him nuts. "Show us what you have in there, Sean," he said.

Sean wrenched the top back. "Ah, look at that." He pulled out a worn leather journal wrapped several times in see-through plastic. "This is a record of every crime committed by the Coonan organization during my tenure there."

Tenure? Raider barely kept from shaking his head as he accepted the journal and started to unwrap it.

"And?" Force said, moving between them and leaning over the box.

Sean drew out five cassette tapes also wrapped in plastic. "I don't suppose you have a tape recorder around here."

"No," Force said, taking the tapes. "We'll have to track one down. What's on these?"

"Different recordings of crimes being planned or executed. Not many." Sean looked back in the box. "There's an interesting conversation between Tyson and Eddie Coonan in there. I'm sure they want badly to know we have that—and what exactly they said."

"Give me the short version," Raider said, still unwrapping the journal.

"Tyson, long before he was a senator, had a girlfriend in high school who disappeared. On the tape, Eddie mentions her in a way that sounds like he took care of the problem." Sean rubbed his chin. "Bodies were often buried—"

"Wait." Brigid turned, holding up her hand. "My dad wants immunity before he says anything else."

Sean chortled. "Baby doll, don't you worry. I have the recording and I'm not on it. Wasn't there. Didn't even know about the conversation until weeks later when I fetched the tape recorder I'd hidden." He shuffled his feet. "There's plenty I ain't proud of in my past, but I never killed anybody. Not once."

So any statute of limitations had run out on the crimes he had committed, unless Sean could be charged with conspiracy to commit murder. Something told Raider that even if Sean had done so, there was no evidence of it. So there was no reason to ask the question.

"Did you ever help plan a murder?" Angus Force apparently had no problem asking the question.

"Nope." Sean took out a stack of black-and-white photographs also kept safe in plastic wrap. "These were taken by a friend of mine, and I am in some of them, but I'm just sitting around and talking. Or waiting. There are a couple of Eddie and Tyson that are interesting."

"Incriminating?" Force asked.

"Not enough," Sean acknowledged. "But the senator doesn't know that. Yet."

"Who took the pictures?" Raider asked.

"Bobby Janetz, who was just a photographer. Did families, some sports events, school dances. We met up at a gambling hall, and he thought it'd be fun to help me gather a little evidence to keep safe. I paid him well." Sean handed over the pictures to Raider. "He died about a year after taking these pictures from some weird cancer. Right before I met your mother." He looked at Brigid. "She would've liked him. Nice guy. Smoked cigars all the time, and they were the stinky kind."

Raider set the pictures down and dropped the plastic from the journal to a chair. Then he started flipping through it. Dates, names, and specific crimes were all recorded in heavy, precise handwriting. "You started recording these crimes way before you met Brigid's mom."

"Yep," Sean said.

Brigid leaned around Raider to look at her dad. "So you were planning to get out even before meeting Mom."

Sean's expression sobered. "Guys in my line of work didn't last long, and I figured I'd need some security. I wasn't loving the life, but I wasn't sure what to do next. So yeah, I guess I was planning a way out, even if I didn't know which direction to take."

The relief that crossed Brigid's classic face warmed Raider's chest.

Brigid frowned. "We can just make copies of all of this before handing it over. I don't see why they want it so badly."

"They might believe Raider will keep their secrets,"

Force murmured. "Worst case scenario for them? They'll need to know what we have, in order to figure out a countermove, if necessary. Politicians deal with information, and right now, the senator doesn't have it. It's that simple."

Raider cleared his throat. "I can convince them I'm on their side, and they'll figure they can blackmail me after we do a little business together, so they won't care if I have copies. It makes sense to work with me on this. So, let's not waste any time." He set his cell phone on the table and dialed a number.

"What?" a low voice snapped.

"Raider Times calling for Eddie Coonan. I'm not at the bottom of the ocean." Raider slipped his New York accent into place.

There was a shuffling, and Eddie came on the line. "Well, shit. We've been looking for you for hours. How are you, buddy? Somebody stole my boat, and I'm thinking it was you? Should I call the cops?"

Raider sighed audibly enough that Eddie could hear him. "You're not being recorded, and at some point in this life, you and I are going to discuss you kidnapping my woman and then launching a missile at a boat. Do you have any idea how long it takes to swim across that bay?"

"Don't know what you're talking about, except I think you just admitted you stole my boat," Eddie drawled. "How is the pretty Irish lass? Does she miss me already?"

Irritation clawed through Raider's gut. "She's well out of town and your reach, Eddie. I protect what's mine." There was enough truth in the statement that Raider didn't have to force a growl into his tone.

Brigid shook her head and grabbed his arm. Oh, if she thought she was going anywhere near Eddie again, she'd lost her mind.

Raider ignored her and continued with Eddie. "But for right now, you should know that I have the journal, tapes, and photographs that Sean Banaghan has kept safe all these years."

Silence ticked for a couple of moments. "I don't know what you're talking about."

"Humph." Raider flipped through the journal, looking for an interesting entry. "Here's one. April third. Eddie and somebody named Geo Beneto met and discussed the distribution of cocaine on the east side. They want to take out a rival dealer, and they came up with a plan. Said plan is recorded on tape C, about halfway through." Raider took the tapes and shook the bag loud enough even Eddie could hear them. "I haven't listened yet. It's harder to track down a tape recorder these days than you'd think."

Eddie was quiet for a couple of heartbeats. "Who else knows about the tapes?"

"Just Sean, Brigid, and me," Raider lied easily. "They've gone underground and don't want anything to do with you."

"But you do," Eddie said.

"Yes. I could use your laundering facilities to clean my, ah, clothes." He had to at least sound like he didn't want to be recorded.

No movement sounded over the line. "I have your word you won't make copies?"

"Sure," Raider lied.

"Right," Eddie muttered. "Regardless, I need to know what you have. Keep in mind I reward loyalty, and considering you want into the business, you don't want to double-cross me. So, you'll bring the journal and tapes?"

Raider laughed. "I'll bring half of the journal and one tape. Trust takes time, Eddie. In addition, I want to see your organization and make sure it's up to the task I need."

Adrenaline ticked through his veins. They were close. He was so damn close.

"Fine," Eddie snapped. "I work from the Deoch bar outside of Boston. I can be there by four tomorrow afternoon after I take care of some business here. Be there." He clicked off.

Raider exhaled. "Well. There we go."

Chapter Twenty-Four

Brigid was ready to explode by the time she and Raider reached her apartment. She'd kept her cool while saying goodbye to her father before Angus took him to a safe house. Sean hadn't been happy with the idea until Angus had promised to keep him up-to-date on their progress, and had also given him a free pass for all the food and drink he could order.

It was better that Brigid didn't know the location of the safe house, but still, she didn't like it.

At the moment, however, she had a larger argument to mount. "I'm the one who needs to go into Eddie's organization and hack a computer." How could Raider be so stubborn that he didn't realize that one simple fact? She unlocked her door and pushed it open.

"Wait here." Keeping his hand on the butt of his gun, which was stuck in his waistband, Raider slid inside the apartment and checked every room. He returned to the door, his hand relaxing. "We're clear."

She only worried about surprise visitors at night. Sometimes the guys at the HDD were just too over-the-top. Of course, they'd all been shot and attacked more than once in their jobs. She was happy not to have any bullet holes in her, but still. Come on. She stepped inside and shut the door behind herself. "I need to go in on this one."

"No," Raider said, leaning against the wall and crossing his arms, as if settling in for a good fight.

Her skin pricked. Her throat heated, and her scalp tingled. Yep. Her temper was about to appear. "Listen, Raider. I'm part of this team, and I'm the computer expert. We have to gain access to Eddie's computers, not remotely, and find where those poor girls are being brought in. There's no other option."

Neither his expression nor his stance changed. "The deal is with me, and Eddie knows I'd never send you in alone."

"I don't have to go alone. He knows we're a team, and if you're there to distract him, maybe I can get to a computer. In fact, he thinks I design little websites, so maybe he'll let me do some work." That wasn't a bad plan.

Raider snorted. "That's a terrible plan." Pushing off the wall, he prowled into the kitchen and eyed the row of wine bottles set atop her cupboards. "Any of those full?"

"No." She placed them up there after they were empty, admiring the colorful labels. Two more empty wine bottles sat over by the toaster because she hadn't had time to climb onto the counter to place them up high.

She opened the refrigerator. "I brought some of the ones with cool labels with me when I moved here." For goodness' sake. She hadn't drunk all of those bottles during the last two months. "All I have chilled is a chardonnay and a pinot grigio. Both pretty good." Looking over her shoulder, she kept her voice level. "Or I have a cabernet in the cabinet."

"Cab." He turned and opened the cabinet, taking out the red wine. "Thought we should have a sip as we fight."

She shut the door and reached for two wineglasses hanging from the nearest cupboard. "We're not fighting. You're going to get logical, forget we slept together, and create a plan for us to do our jobs."

He opened the wine bottle and poured two generous glasses. "This has nothing to do with the fact that we slept together." Handing her a glass, he brushed by her and returned to the living room, sitting on the plain leather sofa.

Okay. Hitting him would not get her anywhere. Kicking . . . maybe? Instead, she sat in the chair set kitty-corner to the sofa, extended her feet to the utilitarian coffee table, and sipped her wine. The cab was full-bodied but could've used an hour to breathe. "It has everything to do with us sleeping together," she finally countered.

"It doesn't have to," he said, swirling the rich liquid in his glass. "Yeah, things have changed. But in this situation, even if you were Wolfe or Malcolm or even Force, I couldn't take you in. Whoever is with me just becomes leverage."

Was it whoever or whomever? She was feeling irritated enough to correct him, but she wasn't sure if she was right or not. "None of them can do what I can do with a computer." The comparison wasn't fair.

"True. But if you and I go in there with half the evidence against Eddie, he's going to start cutting off pieces of you until I get the other half of the evidence." Raider took another healthy drink of the wine. "If I go in myself, there's a better chance he'll deal with me because we really could make some money with my so-called criminal enterprises."

She sipped thoughtfully. All right. He was making a good point. "Then I should go in alone." She had to get to those computers.

Raider blinked. "He'll just torture you until I bring him everything."

"No." She shook her head. "I tell him I took the entire box and that I'm the person to work with. That I'm actually the one with the criminal ties. With my family history, he might buy it."

"Not a chance," Raider countered. "Our backstories are

already created and have been investigated by him, for sure." He looked her over. "Eddie would be suspicious. Why cut me out?"

She ran every scenario through her mind. "Well, what if I come across as a gold digger? Say I want to trade up?"

Raider's chest moved in what seemed to be an odd cough. Was that a scoff? "Right. He'd probably want proof in the form of you naked and in bed and trying to convince him. You sure you're up to going that much undercover?" His dark eyes glittered with challenge.

No. Not in a million years. "I'm sure I could get around that."

"The answer is no." He tipped his head back and finished the glass. "Give me a plan for how I secure the information you need. There has to be a way."

There was a slim chance, but he'd need to be able to plant a USB and type a command to download the information from the secured computer. And he'd have to know which computer to use. She finished her glass, trying to figure out a way she could get to those computers without his agreement. Would Dana help her? "There's no way."

"Too bad, and stop thinking of ways around me. This is my op, and you aren't coming with me. You have about seven hours to think up a good plan." He stood and drew her to her feet. "Now. How do you want to spend those seven hours?" His head dropped, and his mouth took hers.

Shock kept her immobile for two seconds. Then heat flowed through her, head to toe, and her body ignited. How did he do that? With a soft gasp, she kissed him back.

Raider delved deep, needing to touch her one more time. If she gave him another night, he'd take it and hold it tight. There was a pretty good chance he wasn't making it back from Eddie Coonan's bat cave, and he'd like something to keep him warm during the probable torture to come. He caressed his hands down her arms, grasping her wrists, even as his tongue swept against hers.

Wine and woman and something sweet filled his senses.

Her small gasp tickled his lips. She flattened her palms over his pecs, and then her nails dug in.

The slight pain shot electricity right to his balls. He grasped her jawline and lifted her face higher, giving him better access.

She twisted her head to the side, breathing heavily. Then her enticing green gaze met his. "We need to fight more before we do . . . this." Her body belied her words as she pressed closer to him, and her sexy scent nearly dropped him to his knees.

"We can do both." His Southern accent came out full force.

Her slightly swollen lips curved. "You want to fight in bed?" Was that curiosity in her eyes?

"Sure. We can roll around, wrestle, argue, and then you'll give in." He grinned, enjoying the challenge heating her expression. "We can include a healthy spanking, for good measure, if you'd like."

Her chin lowered. "You want me to spank you?"

He laughed instantly and without thought. Even irritated and aroused, she was quick on her feet. He liked that. A lot. Smart girls had always done it for him, and she was freaking brilliant. And a complete smartass, which only made her more appealing. For answer, he took her hand and placed her palm against his obviously bigger one. Much bigger. "You sure you want to play that game?"

One of her eyebrows lifted, and she studied the impressive size difference in their hands. "It's not the size of the weapon . . ."

He chuckled. God, she was cute. If she wanted to play, he was more than willing. With one smooth motion, he flipped her around, smacked her sweet ass, and then turned her back to face him. "That was a love tap."

She gasped, and her face flushed a light pink. Surprise and need glimmered in her eyes. "Oh yeah?" She grabbed his arm and shoved him. He remained in the same place. Frowning, she tugged harder, trying to turn him around to get a good aim at his butt, and yet still keep away from his bandaged hip.

His chest warmed, and realization was like a sledgehammer to the gut. He liked her. Didn't just respect or want her. He actually enjoyed the woman. So he ducked his head and tossed her over his shoulder, clamping an arm over her legs and turning for the bedroom. "I'm the one who does the spanking, Irish." For emphasis, he caressed her firm butt.

She shivered and then gave him a glancing blow to the butt, away from his injured hip. "Oh yeah?"

"Yeah." His smack resonated through her entire body.

She yelped. "You are so going to pay for that."

"Promises, promises," he murmured, entering her bedroom and flipping her onto her back on the bed.

"Oh, you'll see." Her smile was all imp as she reached down and pulled her shirt over her head. A pretty pale yellow bra curved over her full breasts.

His cock perked right up. "Race you."

With a sweet chuckle, she reached for her jeans and tried to tear them off just as he ditched his clothes in record time. "I won," he said, reaching down to help her with her socks.

"Let's hope that's the only time tonight," she snorted, now fully naked and beyond beautiful.

He pounced, landing on her and then rolling so she was on top. Had he ever laughed in bed before? Ever had so much fun while being so aroused his entire body ached with the need to be inside her? Warning ticked through him, but he ignored it. If this was his last night with her, he was taking it.

She straddled him, balancing on her knees and poised above him.

"Wait." He grasped her hips, holding her tight. "How about a little foreplay?" He wasn't exactly small, and she was incredibly tight, as he remembered. There was no reason to hurt her.

"After. We have all night." She grinned a little, arching her back. "And I'm kinda ready." Leaning down, she nipped his lip. "Maybe I liked to be spanked."

He almost came right then and there. Well, all righty. "Condom," he murmured, releasing her hips.

She blinked and in a truly graceful move, she leaned to the side and swiped the foil package from his jeans on the floor, smoothly regaining her seat. Her gaze kept his while she tore the wrapper open with her teeth.

Jesus, he might just die right now.

Levering up, she leaned back and unrolled the condom over him.

He nearly bit through his lip in an effort to keep control. Finally, he set his hands behind his head on the pillow. "Okay. Let's see what you've got, Irish." By the sweet curve of her mouth, she remembered saying those same words to him.

She began to lower herself onto him, going slow, giving herself plenty of time and pretty much killing him inch by inch. The pain from his stitched hip disappeared. His balls drew up tight, and his hands ached with the need to grab her and plant himself in her completely. But he held on to control.

Finally, her butt rested against his groin, and her wet heat surrounded him completely. For the first time in way too long, he felt like he'd come home.

"I like you inside me," she whispered, her eyes so light the green looked luminous.

The words and her sweet expression slayed him. His control shredded, he grabbed her hips and lifted her, pulling her back down.

She gasped and grabbed his shoulders, partially leaning over and helping him. They set up a hard rhythm, and he tried to keep her gaze, which was full of wonder and need and something else. An expression he couldn't recognize but felt deep inside.

Her body began to quiver, and he tilted her toward him, making sure her clit impacted every time he pulled her down and thrust up.

Her head went back as an orgasm took her, and she cried out, her internal walls vibrating along his shaft. He let her ride out the waves, waiting until her body had stopped shaking before yanking her down and holding her in place. Fire raced down his spine to explode in his groin, and he came, sparks shooting behind his eyes.

She fell forward, her nose in his neck, her body heaving against his. A soft kiss to his neck nearly took him apart. She lifted up. "So. That was a tie. Ready for round two?"

Chapter Twenty-Five

Brigid smoothed down her leggings while sitting at a vacant desk in the hub of the HDD offices. Supposedly some expert on the Lassiter case was going to use the desk at some point.

Her body was pleasantly sore from the night before, and heat filled her cheeks as she sifted through the memories. When morning had finally arrived, they'd declared the evening a tie.

Raider, of course, had asked for a rematch at the first possible opportunity. Yet there had been a seriousness, a heaviness, to his movements that morning as he left to go shower for the day. When he'd kissed her, soft and sweet, there had been a hint of goodbye in his touch.

She shifted uncomfortably on the chair. Yeah, she liked him. A lot. But he wasn't going to forgive her for lying to him. Or at least, for having kept secrets even though they'd become intimate. She felt like a jerk. But what else could she do?

Now he and Angus strategized in case room one after she'd given them very clear directions on how to find the correct computer, how to slip the USB in place while looking somewhere else, and finally what commands to type to get the download they needed. There were so many things that could go wrong.

At the moment, Malcolm and Nari were talking in Nari's office. Wolfe sat across from Brigid, his humungous feet on his desk, his head back, and his eyes closed. Kat the kitten lay on one of his shoulders, snoring softly.

Brigid cleared her throat. Kat opened sleepy green and blue eyes. Wolfe didn't move.

She did it again.

Wolfe sighed but kept his eyelids shut. "What?"

"Why are you so tired?" Brigid pushed away from the rough wood of the desk to keep her T-shirt from snagging.

Wolfe finally opened oddly focused brown eyes. "I tailed Dana all night while she met with sources for a story." He held up a hand. "It's our case, and I already told Force about what she's found out. She's concentrating on the senator angle, so backup from our unit was legitimate."

Ha. Like Wolfe cared about legitimate backup. "She seems to have pretty good sources," Brigid mused.

He nodded. "Yeah. A decade as an investigative journalist will do that. Well, if you're a good one." He tilted his chin and rubbed against Kat's furry head.

Brigid studied him. He wore a dark T-shirt with a faded flag emblem across the chest, jeans, and black boots. His jacket was tossed over his chair. His buzz cut dark hair was growing out, and he had several days' stubble across his square jaw. Even though he sprawled in the chair, a sense of danger emanated from him. He looked like a panther snuggling with a kitten.

"What?" Wolfe asked.

"You and Dana," Brigid replied quickly. "There's more than friendship." In fact, Wolfe seemed very interested in the pretty reporter's safety.

"Nope." Wolfe yawned, nearly dislodging the animal. "Just friends. Can't be anything more."

"Why not?" Could she finally get Wolfe to talk?

He exhaled, his massive chest moving. "Lots of reasons. One, I have a job to do and am working to make it happen. Two, if I get it done, I might go back to the teams. Three, after the explosion that took me off the teams, my head ain't all the way right." His smile revealed a shocking dimple in his left cheek. "And I wasn't all that right to begin with."

The elevator dinged, and they both turned, Wolfe reaching for his desk drawer. Then he paused.

A five-foot-tall woman with bright purple hair, several earrings, and hazel eyes strode out lugging a matte-black briefcase that looked heavier than she did. She looked up, drew out a badge, and flipped it open to reveal she was an HDD operative.

Wolfe set the kitten on the desk and dropped his feet to the floor with a loud clump. He stood and strode toward her, reaching for the bag. "Let me help."

She shook her head and stepped back. "Nope." The woman had to be in her midtwenties and was dressed in a flowing skirt and lime-green tank top beneath a mauve suede sweater. She looked more like a gypsy than an HDD agent.

Angus and Raider strode out of the case room and around the hub of desks.

Angus reached for the briefcase. "Agent Frost, I assume?"

Agent Frost? The name couldn't fit the woman less. "Yep." She kept hold of her briefcase and shimmied around the men toward the hub in the center. "Hi," she said to Kat before gently laying down the case.

Kat looked her over and then gingerly scampered over the desk to reach her, instantly rubbing against her belly. Agent Frost glanced down. "Whose kitten?"

Wolfe shrugged. "He stays with me, but he's his own little man."

"Can I pick him up?" she asked, her gaze softening.

"It's up to him," Wolfe predictably replied.

The woman slowly reached for the kitten, who jumped into her hands. Her laugh was high and melodious. She could probably seriously sing. "You're a sweetie." She snuggled the kitten, kissed his nose, and then set him back down before turning to face the group. "So. Who am I wiring up?"

"Wire?" Panic flushed through Brigid, and she moved toward Raider instinctively. "You can't wear a wire. They'll search you for sure." She touched his arm and then looked at Angus for backup.

Angus's gaze narrowed on her hand. His chin lifted. He stared at Raider.

Oh, crap. Brigid let her hand drop. Force probably didn't like romance among his operatives. "Well, Angus?" She put a bit of snap in her tone.

His head tilted very slightly to the left. "All right. Things to discuss later. I agree that Raider will probably be searched, and a wire is a risk."

Agent Frost snorted. "Not if I'm wiring the handsome dude." She flipped open her case and turned to look him over, head to toe. And then the other way. "You sticking with the dark shirt, ripped jeans, and boots?" At his nod, she tapped her finger on her lips. "We have a few options, but the range on these is just a few miles."

That was good since it meant backup would remain close to Raider.

Agent Frost looked him over again. "I can place the listening device on your belt buckle. For the camera, hmmm now. How do you feel about my piercing your ears?"

Raider grinned. "Had them pierced as a kid but haven't worn earrings in years."

The woman drew out a large needle. "Well, then this is gonna hurt a little."

Raider lost his smile.

* * *

All during the turbulent ride on the crappy helicopter, Raider's newly pierced ears burned, reminding him of his wild youth. Wolfe drove him near the outskirts of South Boston after departing the motel where they'd left Force to organize the surveillance equipment and weapons. Even in the rain, a few kids hung out on street corners, vaping. The buildings close to town were nicer and better preserved, but on the outskirts, there were boarded-up buildings punctuated by bars and a brick Catholic church.

"You ready?" Wolfe asked, peering into the darkened night where rain had started to fall.

"Yep." Raider would've loved to have a knife on his body, but he'd definitely be searched. His phone rang, and he answered. "Hey, West. You ready to give me undercover tips?"

"Sure," West said over the line. "Being a handler is different from being the operative."

Raider pressed the phone to his ear, being careful of the earring. Was West's head in the game? Only one way to find out. "How's Pippa doing, anyway?" Pippa and West had moved in together the month before, after West had investigated her and a cult that was hunting her down. She'd been terrorized for years and had almost become a hermit.

West chuckled. "She's doing well. Took on a new client—a high school—that's driving her a little nuts, but she actually enjoys it. Says their books are a disaster, but nothing gets her logical mind going faster."

It was nice to know one of them could find happiness. "How's it having Wolfe for a neighbor?" He cut Wolfe a look, and his partner just rolled his eyes, concentrating on driving. When West had moved out of his bungalow and into Pippa's next door, Wolfe had moved right in.

"Let's just say he shows up at dinnertime a lot," West said wryly. "It's Pippa's fault for being such a great cook and for enjoying cooking so much. She loves feeding the overgrown bastard."

Raider couldn't imagine actually enjoying cooking. Thank goodness Pippa often sent cookies and pies to the office.

"Now that you're assured I'm on the job, let's get to work." West cleared his throat. "You need to get into character and remember that Wolfe can reach you within minutes if necessary."

"Got it." Raider said.

West coughed. "You ever been undercover longer than a week?"

"No. No longer than a couple of days, really." Raider was usually the handler. He looked at his partner. Wolfe wore a yellow polo with "Hurley Water Supplies" above his left pocket, along with worn slacks and scuffed shoes. His buzz cut was growing out slightly, and when he'd checked them into the motel, he'd shuffled as if he truly was a down-on-his luck salesman and not an ex-soldier with issues. Wolfe was pretty good at this. "I don't know how you did it for two years," he said to West.

West sighed. "You have to embody the person you're supposed to be. It's not acting, it's becoming."

Raider nodded. "I acted like an ass last time."

"Then you're an ass," West said easily. "Take the worst parts of your real personality and capitalize on those aspects. Forget about the cameras in your ears. They don't exist. If you acknowledge they're in place, you'll act different and speak different from your cover. "Got it?"

"Yep. Thanks. We'll call with details." He clicked off.

"They like me eating at their house," Wolfe said, taking another turn around the block.

"I'm sure they do."

Wolfe glanced at him. "Okay. Let's get you into the right mindset. Those diamond earrings are something else. What are they?"

Raider scratched his head. "My babe Brigid bought them for me the first time I gave her cash."

"Good, though probably not enough true. Try again, and get your accent in place," Wolfe said, taking a left by a bar called Deoch that had a newly painted bright green door.

All right. "An ex-girlfriend, one with crazy purple hair who was slightly nuts, gave me the earrings after getting me drunk and shoving a needle through my ears." He barely kept from rubbing the aching lobes as he lapsed into the New York accent. "It bugs Brigid that I wear them still, but I like big diamonds."

Wolfe slowed down behind a red truck. "Better. Truth will inflect in your voice when you talk about Agent Millicent Frost and her needle."

"Millicent?" That name so did not fit the woman. Neither did Frost.

"Yep. How are the lobes? The shit she put on them after opening your piercings looked painful." Wolfe took another left.

"Burns like hell," Raider admitted. "But the gel is supposed to keep my earlobes from getting red or swelling from the recent insult to them, so I'm taking it as a good sign." He couldn't look like he'd just gotten them pierced. He ran through his cover again. "I think that Eddie's headquarters is a working tavern, so any weapons will probably be under the bar and near the cash register."

"Check," Wolfe said, watching the few cars around them. "There will be a back room."

"With computers and who knows what else." Raider put himself firmly in character. "I've locked down my girlfriend and her father to keep them safe from Eddie, and neither are happy about it, but people in my organization do as I say."

"How'd you get the bruise on your face?" Wolfe started throwing questions.

"Fight with Sean over Brigid. He doesn't think I'm good enough for his daughter. I won," Raider said.

"And Brigid? How serious?" Wolfe asked.

"Not very, at least not yet. I'm a free agent. But it'd be an insult to me if Eddie hurt her." That sounded more plausible than he had no clue how he felt, and based on Eddie's past, he'd respect Raider's claim.

"Where's the rest of the evidence?" Wolfe asked.

Raider thought through several scenarios. "I gave it to my best man, Roscoe, to hide somewhere." He had given Roscoe a good bone that had quickly disappeared. "My instructions were to put it all somewhere I'd never imagine, so if Eddie does torture me, I don't have the information." Man, hopefully Eddie would believe him. And it was true. Force had taken half of the journal, tapes, and pictures somewhere he didn't share with Raider, just in case.

"If you're bleeding out, why can't you call Roscoe?" Wolfe asked calmly.

Probably because he would be bleeding out and losing consciousness. "Roscoe doesn't have a phone. He's to contact me in a week from a burner to see if I'm still alive. Under no circumstances is he to give me the evidence." There was a slim chance that one fact would keep Raider alive.

Wolfe pulled into the vacant lot of what used to be a gas station. A rusty *Red and Sons Petrol* sign hung drunkenly from the boarded-up square building. "This is where I get out. I'll walk back to the motel and check for escape routes if we end up on foot." He leaned over and held out a hand.

Raider shook it. "Thanks, Wolfe."

"Yep. You've got this." Wolfe smiled, the sight grim. "Embrace the new identity but keep as quiet as you can. Never volunteer anything. Give the code word, and we'll come in, guns out."

Adrenaline flowed freely through Raider's veins as

he released his friend. The unit had bonded quickly, and he trusted Wolfe and Force with his life. With Brigid's life, too. "Thanks, Wolfe."

"Yep." Wolfe opened the door and jumped out, leaving the vehicle for Raider. "Just don't die, Tanaka."

Always good advice. Raider climbed over the console to the driver's seat and shut the door. It was time to become somebody else. Hopefully he wouldn't die as that person.

He put the SUV in drive and dove completely into his cover.

Chapter Twenty-Six

After a long day conducting an even deeper search into Eddie Coonan's organization, Brigid had filled a notebook with the names of every person he'd ever done business with. She'd left it at the office. She'd also spent serious time scrubbing any pictures of Raider from the web. There were only a couple, mainly from an op he'd conducted with their unit the previous month. But no scrub was complete. She'd done the best job possible, and her neck muscles felt like somebody had pounded concrete into them.

She waited at the entrance to her apartment as Malcolm and the dog conducted a cursory search. Rolling her eyes, she walked into the small living room. "I don't see the necessity of you guys checking out the place every time I come home. Nobody knows I'm here."

Malcolm prowled out of her bedroom. "You have a guy jump out of your closet one night at you, and you'll wish I had checked it out first."

Well, that was true. Geez. Though Malcolm, in his ripped shirt and facial scruff, looked tons more dangerous than any crazy guy in a closet would. Except for the furry white kitten head visible from his right pocket. Roscoe returned to her, his tail wagging, his tongue out.

Malcolm stopped right in front of her, so large she

almost backed up to look him in the face. "You sure you don't want to come and stay with Pippa and me tonight?"

She nodded. "I want to stay here, but I should be at work."

Mal shrugged. "The communication devices on Raider only work a short distance away. We can't communicate with him. Wolfe and Force are excellent backup, and they're in place. So there's nothing more for you to do than get some sleep. We need you on your game tomorrow."

Whatever. "Okay." She patted Roscoe's head and the dog nudged her, nearly knocking her over.

"Are you sure you don't want to come with me? Pippa is making some sort of fancy steak-and-noodles dish."

Okay. That sounded amazing. But being with a happy couple right now was more than Brigid could take. She wasn't sure where she was with Raider, and she needed some alone time. "I'm sure, and you can leave the kitten if you want." She was safe enough with the handgun in her bed-table drawer and the ex-soldier German shepherd at her feet. She wasn't supposed to let him sleep on the foot of the bed, but what Angus Force didn't know wouldn't hurt him.

"I promised Pippa I'd bring home Kat," Malcolm said. "But you get the dog."

She smiled. "'Night, Mal."

"'Night." Malcolm brushed past her. "Lock the doors." He gently shut the door.

She engaged the locks, and soon his heavy footsteps retreated down the hallway. She looked down at the dog. "You hungry? I bought some good treats for you."

The dog's tongue rolled out again, and he panted.

Man, he was smart. Maybe Raider should've taken Roscoe. He would've been a decent backup if things had gone bad, but taking Roscoe to a tavern was too much of a risk. "Come on. Let's have a treat, and I'll make you some lean hamburger for dinner." The pooch didn't like dog food.

He sneezed and followed her into the kitchen, where he froze. His ears went back, the fur on his neck stood up, and he growled.

She paused, looking around the small space. "What—"

Roscoe bunched his hind legs and leaped high into the air.

"Roscoe!" She tried to grab him, but he was too fast.

He landed on the counter, skidded sideways, and shoved his tongue into one of the two empty wine bottles. His yip was one of joy.

"No." She hurried to him and tried to take the bottle.

He growled, shaking his head. He whined, sounding pained.

Oh God. His tongue was stuck in the bottle. How the heck had he done that? "It's okay, baby." She patted his head as he flopped down across the stovetop, his eyes wide and his tongue in the bottle.

Was the glass rough inside? She didn't think so. Gently, she stroked his large head. "I need you to stay calm." If he freaked out, he'd break the bottle and might cut his tongue.

He whined louder.

"Honey, it's an empty bottle," she soothed, leaning forward to better see. She tilted it up. Yep. His tongue was in there but good. The neck was smaller than most wine bottles. "This was a homemade bottle from a neighbor down the way, and it wasn't even that full-bodied." She kept her voice calm as she reached for a jug of olive oil from the nearest cupboard. "We have to work on this drinking problem you have."

His nose wrinkled, his eyes widened, and he sneezed. The bottle shot across the kitchen and hit the wall, dropping to the counter and rolling to the floor, where it shattered.

He looked over the side of the counter, and she could swear he sighed.

She surveyed the mess. "Oh, Roscoe," she murmured.

He whimpered and turned his head away, facing the dials for the burners. Her heart softened. "It's okay, sweetie. We all like wine sometimes."

He hunched his powerful shoulders, and his ears twitched, but he didn't turn toward her.

She bit her lip. Broken glass tinged with red covered her kitchen floor, and a hundred-pound soldier dog lay across her stovetop, too embarrassed to look at her. Man, her world had gotten weird really fast. "All right. Just stay there and let me clean up the glass." She couldn't let his paws get cut.

He didn't move.

Just another stubborn male in her life. They all had such issues. She fetched the broom and quickly cleaned up the mess, using a wet cloth to pull up the remaining wine. Finally she moved to the dog. "It's okay, Roscoe. How about you come down and have some dinner?"

He stiffened but didn't turn toward her.

She gingerly ran a hand down his back. Just how upset was he? It seemed the canine was half human. Definitely fit in with the guys. "It's all right. Let's forget about this and just have a nice dinner."

He didn't move.

Her heart went out to him even as she tried not to laugh. "I'll tell you all my secrets." She leaned in and snuggled her face against his warm fur. "I like Raider but I haven't told him the truth. He's a guy all about truth."

Roscoe shuddered but didn't move.

She leaned back. There was only one solution. "Do you want to try on some of my shoes?"

He jerked and then slowly turned his head, his honey-brown eyes focusing on her.

She nodded. "Yeah. Come on. I have a new three inch pair I foolishly bought. I'll never wear them, but—"

The dog leaped off the counter and headed for the bedroom, pausing at the doorway to look over his shoulder with an "Are you coming?" expression.

Shaking her head at how bizarre life had become, she stepped over the wet area on the floor to help a dog try on her shoes.

At first appearance, Deoch looked like any old-time neighborhood bar with worn wood, weathered sign, and faded paint. On closer scrutiny, the door was made of heavy, impenetrable steel, and the cameras covering the area were high-end and well protected. Raider let rain slide off his leather jacket as he shoved open the heavy door and strode inside.

A long oak bar with gold railing covered the entire right side of the establishment, with bottles of liquor neatly placed on glass shelves in front of mirrors. Black bar stools spanned the entire length, and four men sat at various points along the way. Tables had been arranged in a grid pattern, with a couple of pool tables and dartboards placed at the far end. Atmospheric music played from invisible speakers, the floor was heavy wood, and the walls a mint green color. The place smelled of cleanser and booze in a comfortable combination.

The bartender, a giant of a man with a bald head and gold hoop earring, took one look at Raider and reached beneath the counter. Hopefully to push a button and not grab a shotgun. Then he strode around the bar and gestured for Raider to lift his arms.

It was the most thorough search Raider had ever endured. Finally, the guy straightened up and moved back behind the bar. "I think you owe me dinner now," Raider called after him. "And maybe a yacht."

A door at the far end of the bar opened, and Eddie Coonan motioned Raider forward.

Raider avoided the deep breath he needed to take, striding toward the mob boss. The four guys at the counter didn't turn, but the bartender watched him with no expression on his boulder-sized face. As a deterrent in the bar, that guy was better than any baseball bat or shotgun.

"Welcome," Eddie said, looking Raider up and down. "Getting blown up doesn't seem to have hurt you."

Raider forced a grin. "We jumped out. The swim was more of a pain than the missile." He frowned. "Where'd you get missiles, anyway?"

"I'm a man of many secrets," Eddie said, moving aside. "Why don't you come on back?"

Well. This was either going to be a smooth plan or a very painful disaster. Raider walked beyond the fortified door, surprised to see an ordinary-looking back room with a round poker table in the middle, just like old times when there would be secret poker parties for big money. He paused and looked back at Eddie as he closed the door. "You still play poker?"

"Yep." Eddie secured three locks and then punched in numbers on a keypad. "You play?"

"Yeah." Maybe that would be another way in if he survived the next hour. Raider memorized the layout. There were three closed doors, one each in the remaining walls—the farthest one probably was an exit to outside. "You run your entire operation out of here?" He had to get into those other rooms somehow.

The first door opened, and Jonny P walked out. His chin lifted. "I still say we just shoot him."

Eddie scowled. "That's probably gonna happen. What does Josh think?"

Jonny shrugged. "He hasn't said."

Eddie chuckled. "I know. I was just kidding." He escorted Raider to the nearest closed door, used another keypad, and pushed it open. "Josh doesn't offer up much unless we ask. I like that about him. Come this way."

Raider followed Eddie and kept his hands loose in case he needed to fight, but how the heck was he going to get out of there? The doors all had keypads. He'd known Eddie had stepped it up in the tech department, but he hadn't realized how much. Could Brigid hack those doors? Probably. But she'd still be too much leverage for Eddie to use, and they'd made the right call in leaving her at headquarters, even though she hadn't been happy about it.

Eddie's office held a cherrywood desk with green marble center, thick leather chairs, and a fish tank that took up the entire wall behind him. Odd paperweights, including a bronzed brick, cluttered the desk along with a laptop that had been pushed to the side. He took a seat behind his desk and gestured for Raider to sit.

Jonny P entered behind Raider and shut the door, his armed presence adding weight to the atmosphere.

Raider sat and angled his head to better see the many black piranhas in the tank. "Is that a shark?" he asked.

"There are two sharks; they're usually at the bottom swimming around. I just fed them all goldfish, so they're fat and happy at the moment. Where's my journal?" Eddie asked.

The air behind Raider heated as Jonny shuffled closer with the scrape of a boot. Raider reached into his jacket and pulled out half of the journal to hand over, along with two cassette tapes and one picture of Eddie with the future senator.

Eddie reached for the journal and flipped it over. "You actually cut it in two."

"Right down the middle." Raider kept his accent in

place and leaned over to point. "I used steam to loosen the glue and then just pried it apart. Unfortunately, much of your business with the future senator is in the second half. The first half mainly deals with your father, God rest his soul."

"Did you make a copy?" Eddie drawled.

"Nope. Told you I wouldn't," Raider lied, smiling.

"Right." Eddie looked at the first half of the journal. "Information is power, my friend."

Jonny P clamped a hand on Raider's shoulder. "Let me have five minutes with him and a blowtorch. I'll get the other half."

Eddie studied him, his eyes bloodshot. Had he been playing poker late? "It's an idea."

Raider shoved off Jonny's bony hand. "It is an idea, and one I already thought of." He gave Eddie an "aw shucks" expression. "A loyal friend named Roscoe has the other evidence, and I ordered him to take it somewhere I'd never consider." He folded his hands on his jeans, making sure to move his head enough that the diamond camera caught the entire room. "Roscoe is good at hiding things."

Jonny P coughed. "Within an hour, I could have you calling Roscoe with new orders."

"Well, now, that's the problem." Raider kept his attention focused on Eddie. "Roscoe doesn't like phones and has no intention of checking in for a month. I truly have no clue where he is." He smiled and forced himself to appear calm and not ready to rip out Jonny's trachea. "So, best idea? How about we get to work? There's a lot of money to be made."

Eddie's nostrils widened in his already wide face. "Can't decide. Either we should just kill you now and take our chances, or maybe we'd make good business partners." He spun a letter opener on his desk.

"I vote business," Raider said, as cheerfully as he could with the accent.

"I vote bullet, and then we can go bowling," Jonny P countered from behind him, pressing the cold metal of a gun to Raider's temple.

Chapter Twenty-Seven

Brigid helped the dog balance in white three-inch Payless heels on his front legs and two-inch floral Manolo Blahniks on his back legs. She'd bought the designer shoes after her first two paychecks from the HDD. The rest of her closet held tennis shoes and boots, which were much more in her comfort zone. "You look so much taller, Roscoe."

His head lifted even higher, and his furry body twitched with delight.

She petted him between the ears, sitting against her bed. "Though you're plenty tall already. I just don't see why you worry about your height." As she understood the story, there was a slightly taller dog on the mission in Afghanistan, and then a bombing had injured many soldiers, including both canines. Before that occurrence, Roscoe hadn't tried to be taller than he was. "When did the drinking problem start?" she asked.

He panted, his tongue out, the closest thing possible to a doggie smile on his face. He licked her chin, and she chuckled.

A knock sounded on the outside door, and she jumped up. Was Raider back? Had they decided to go another route? Her heart thundering, she ran through the apartment and yanked open the door.

"Oh, crap," she muttered, her shoulders falling. She'd forgotten. In having fun with the dog, in being part of the op, she'd actually forgotten her tormentors for a moment.

"It's nice to see you, too," Agent Tom Rutherford said smoothly, walking past her and into the apartment. As usual, the HDD handler wore a designer navy-blue suit, power tie, and polished loafers. His blond hair was cut short in a wave, and his blue eyes were shrewd and ambitious.

Agent Fields waited in the hallway. "May we come in, Brigid?" His tone was much more polite, albeit weary.

She stepped aside and gestured him in. Her stomach cramped. "Like I have a choice."

The older agent gave her a sympathetic glance, his faded brown eyes kind. In contrast to his partner, his brown suit was from the eighties, as were his striped tie and scuffed shoes. He moved like he'd been shot a few times and was just waiting for retirement to kick in so he could be done with all of this nonsense.

She shut the door, her mind reeling.

Roscoe clopped out of the bedroom, eyed the men, and then jumped out of the heels to run to Brigid. The powerful dog planted himself in front of her and barked. Twice.

Well, wasn't that nice. "I think he'd eat you both for dinner if I asked him," she said, her spirits lifting.

Fields stared at the four shoes on the floor. "Was he wearing heels?"

Brigid patted the vibrating dog. "I wanted to see what they looked like from a distance." Roscoe's height issues were nobody's business but the team's. "Decided the floral ones were the best for the dress I'm planning on wearing to your retirement, Rutherford."

The younger agent snorted. He was probably decades from retirement, but no way was that guy staying an agent. Probably had political aspirations. He even looked like the new, young, hip politician that had just been elected from New York.

He moved for the sofa to take a seat. "You haven't reported in during the last week. That's a violation of your plea agreement, *Agent* Banaghan. Surely you don't want to see Guantanamo from the inside."

The threat was getting old. Brigid had done enough good for the HDD that she was getting some juice, but she couldn't yet challenge Rutherford. She'd get there soon, and if she told Angus Force the truth, he might help her with the higher-ups. Or, he'd be so pissed she'd been sent to spy on him that he'd kick her butt out of the unit. The idea sank a heavy stone into her gut.

What would Raider say? She bit back a shudder. He was all about truth and loyalty to the unit, so he probably had even stronger feelings when it came to lovers. She shook off her unease. That was a concern for another day. "Maybe I don't have anything to report," she said, remaining by the door.

Agent Fields leaned against the counter, his suit hanging on him as if he'd lost weight recently. But his hangdog expression remained the same as the first time he'd interviewed her. "We know that Tanaka, Force, and Wolfe have flown to Boston, for some reason. What we don't know is why."

Rutherford picked dog hair off his slacks. "Angus Force is working the Irish mob case, which is fine, but we need to make sure he doesn't screw up three other cases we're working against the Coonan associates."

Brigid crossed her arms, trying to look tough. These guys and their power made her knees wobbly. The pictures they'd shown her of the detainee station before she'd signed her plea agreement still gave her nightmares sometimes. "You didn't think Angus would get this far with the case?" It was incredible. The HDD truly thought Angus was a washed-out alcoholic. How wrong they were. Well, about the washed-out part, anyway. "The case hasn't changed any. Angus has a source that says Coonan is trafficking in women and children, and we're trying to stop that. To stop him."

Rutherford's nostrils flared. "Angus's sources are crap. He listens to fortune tellers and hot chicks with Ouija boards." He stood, and dog hair clung to his pants. "The guy had a complete breakdown after the Lassiter case and ended up in a psych ward. Bet you didn't know that."

No, she hadn't. Which meant that information had been buried by some pretty good techs, because she'd done a background check. Not a deep one, obviously. "Lassiter killed Angus's sister. Of course he had problems." But a psych ward? Did the other team members know that for a fact?

Fields sighed. "Yeah, and he escaped the place and disappeared into the woods with that crazy dog guarding you."

Brigid mulled over the information. "Yet the HDD gave him a unit when he asked." There could only be one reason for that fact. "Is Lassiter alive?"

"Of course not," Rutherford snapped. "But Lassiter had worked for the HDD and was a huge embarrassment to us, so we need the case closed. We can't have the FBI agent who caught him going around spouting nonsense or looking like a lunatic. Either Force will have another breakdown and end the unit, or he'll finally accept that Lassiter is dead. Either way, don't get too comfortable."

As if their offices were anything near comfortable.

Rutherford eyed the bristling dog. "Now. What exactly is Tanaka doing in Boston? It's time you did your job, Brigid, or you'll wind up in a cell that's more like a hole in the ground. And you know what? I'm going to find a similar one for your daddy, now that we know you two are back in contact. No pretty shoes or animals for either of you. Ever again."

Raider kept his expression slightly bored as he and Eddie stared at each other, when actually his hands itched to reach across the desk and slam the mob leader's head against the wood until both broke. The idea that this bastard had killed Treeson made him want to puke. His temple buzzed from the cold gun barrel. Raider couldn't move fast enough to keep Jonny from shooting him, so he went for sarcasm. "If this is how you treat your business associates, I may be in the wrong organization."

Silence descended for a moment.

Finally, Eddie smiled. "You're a cool one, aren't you?"

Sooner or later, Raider was going to prove him wrong on that statement. "Not my first time with a gun at my head," he said calmly.

Eddie jerked his head, and the barrel disappeared.

Man, Raider was going to punch Jonny P in the kidneys at some point in this investigation.

Eddie sat back. "All right. You brought me half of the evidence I need, and you seem to be pretty damn calm. My guys have your background, and my sources have secured your federal rap sheet, Interpol rap sheet, and records from California, Massachusetts, Florida, and Idaho."

Idaho? They'd found the fake misdemeanor charge of pot possession in Idaho? Brigid had buried that one deep. Eddie's computer folks were damn good at their job. Hopefully not as good as the HDD and Brigid, or Raider would be dead soon. "I've learned not to get caught," he said, as if defending himself. "If you look closely, there are no arrests or even inquiries for the last six years."

"I noticed," Eddie said, scratching his neck.

"I've been working and making more money than ever before," Raider continued as if trying to sell himself.

Eddie studied him for a couple of long moments. "What's your offer, Times?"

Raider leaned forward to convey eagerness. "A partnership. I'm making too much money from my current enterprises, and I need help laundering it so I can set up my own legitimate businesses in the States and then launder it myself. But right now, I don't have legitimate funds to use as start-up. Not with my records, anyway."

Eddie flipped through the partial journal. "How have you made so much money?"

It was comical that the guy was so careful not to admit anything, even though the journal chronicling his criminal past was right in front of him. But Eddie hadn't avoided prison all of these years by being stupid. Raider leaned back in his chair, noting the faint scent of cigar smoke wafting from the leather. "If you've read my sheet, you know how. I just got better at it all."

Eddie reached over and tugged a silver ball on the Newton's cradle set near his laptop. It hit the next ball, sending the farthest one out and then back in. "The last guy who went into business with me gave me this. He lied to me and is no longer with us."

Raider swallowed. "It's very nice." He let just the right amount of sarcasm into his voice.

"Isn't it?" Eddie let the spheres stay in motion, their clacking sound rhythmic. "So you work in credit card and identity fraud mostly. Anything else?"

"Maybe. I wouldn't mind expanding globally to the drug or trafficking trades, but I don't have the connections yet." He sank into character to keep from grimacing.

"You think I do?" One of Eddie's dark eyebrows rose.

Raider shrugged. "Maybe you do, maybe you don't. I'm

not willing to think beyond our first contract with each other until we see if it works out. You're the first guy I've offered a deal to. There are several other organizations in the country I could approach. You were just the easiest."

Eddie's chin lifted. "It's nice when business and pleasure combine, isn't it?"

Was the asshole talking about Brigid? Yeah, probably. "Sometimes life works out," he agreed, sounding unconcerned, angling his wrist to check the USB device masquerading as a watch on his wrist. "Let's get down to business. I have five hundred million—"

"Oh, not yet." Eddie stood and walked around the desk. "We have some business to do first." Continuing past Raider, he opened his office door and strode out.

Raider stood and followed, acutely aware that Jonny P had yet to holster his gun. "Where are we going?"

Eddie strode beyond the round poker table to the door directly across from his office and used another keyboard before it clicked open to reveal a back alley. A town car was parked next to a grungy green dumpster.

Raider balked. "What exactly is happening?"

Jonny P prodded him in the center of his back with the gun. "Move."

Ah, man. This might be bad. Raider spotted Josh the Bear stepping out of the driver's side, barely visible in the rainy night. He wore black slacks and shirt with his gun holstered at his side and in plain view.

Raider shouldn't leave with them. They'd probably want to avoid blood splatter inside the building. Outside, not so much. "I'm not going anywhere until you tell me what's happening." Hopefully Wolfe was listening in.

Eddie slid into the back of the car and moved over. "Come on, New York. Let's just see if we can trust each other."

Jonny P pressed the gun against Raider's spine again.

That was it. Raider took a step forward, pivoted, and yanked the gun away from the enforcer. "Stop doing that," he snapped.

Jonny bunched his thin legs to attack.

"Stop," Eddie said, partially leaning over. "Enough with this. Either you're coming or not, Times. It's up to you."

Damn it. Raider tucked Jonny's gun in his waistband and turned to enter the car. Hopefully Josh wouldn't shoot him in the head and ruin the very nice leather upholstery.

Eddie smiled. "There you go. This is gonna be fun. The good stuff always happens after midnight, but you might want to get some shut-eye. We have about a five-hour drive ahead of us."

Raider looked at the mob boss. "Where the hell are we going?"

"You'll see." Eddie put his head back on the seat rest and closed his eyes. "By the way, if you're not who you say, I'm definitely going after the redhead. Can't seem to get her out of my mind."

The door slammed hard next to Raider, and he barely kept from jumping. This was nuts.

Chapter Twenty-Eight

Brigid managed another sleepless night with Roscoe heavy on her feet. The feeling of the dog lent a sense of safety she had been lacking. Finally, around four in the morning, she gave up. "Get up, puppy. We might as well go to work."

Roscoe opened one eye, looked at her, and then shut it again.

She pulled her feet free and headed for the shower. "I get ready quickly. You have about fifteen more minutes to sleep, and then we're going to work." The meeting with the HDD agents hadn't sat well with her, even though she'd only told them facts they could find out on their own. Where was Raider? Was he safe?

She prepared for a long day, donning comfortable jeans, boots, and a light green sweater that supposedly brought out the color of her eyes. Maybe Raider would return that day. Man, she hoped so. It was time she told him the truth about her agreement with the HDD. "Come on, Roscoe. You can use the grassy area right outside before we go."

The drive to her office was punctuated by the dog snoring loudly in the back seat of Raider's truck. He'd loaned it to her when he'd left town. Maybe she should buy herself a car at some point. Something fast and sporty. The roads were mainly empty at that early hour, so she arrived in record time and parked the vehicle. A very light rain was falling, and she huddled into her sweater.

Roscoe lifted up, looked outside at the darkness, and dropped back down.

She chuckled and jumped out, opening his door and giving his ear a tug. He sighed a long-suffering moan and then leaped to the ground, running full out for the entrance and sitting beneath the slight eave.

"It's just a little rain," she muttered, shaking her head and jogging across the lot to unlock the door. The dog shook his coat, spraying droplets over her light jeans. If she didn't know better, she'd think he'd done it on purpose. She patted his head anyway, and then led the way to the elevator and down to their dark offices. She flipped the lights, and they started to buzz, making the room look yellow. "We need new lights."

Once in her computer room, she finally relaxed and got to work. This was where she belonged—in front of a computer. What if Raider couldn't get the USB port into the correct tower?

The main phone rang in case room one, and she jumped up, running to answer it. What if it was Raider? Her heart kicked into action. "Hello."

"Um, hi. Is Wolfe around?"

Brigid bit her lip. "No. He's not here yet." She glanced at the clock. It wasn't even five yet.

"This is Dana. I've been trying to get hold of him all night, and he's not answering his cell. Is everything all right?" The woman cleared her throat. "I'm a friend of Wolfe's. He probably hasn't mentioned me."

"Sure he has." Curiosity filtered through Brigid. Man, she'd love to meet the mysterious reporter. "Wolfe is on a mission but will probably be back soon. This is Brigid. I'm the computer gal. He probably hasn't mentioned me." She chuckled at repeating the phrase. Wolfe didn't talk much.

"Oh, hi. He has mentioned you. Pretty redhead—cross between an Irish rose and a farmer's daughter."

Well. That was kinda nice. Brigid smiled, her heart warming. Wolfe was a good friend. "Can I help you with anything?"

Dana was quiet for a moment. "He asked me to reach out to contacts in Seattle, and I did so. I have an update."

Brigid perked up. "The senator?"

"Yes."

Anticipation filtered through Brigid's veins. "Well, how about you tell me? Or you can come to the office. I'm the only one here working early." Yeah, she'd get a look at Wolfe's reporter. Was there a romance brewing? Hopefully Angus wouldn't be ticked she'd invited a reporter into their offices. Yeah, he wouldn't be happy. If Dana had valuable information the team could use, he'd have to get over it.

Dana cleared her throat. "Okay, but Wolfe and I have quid pro quo."

Oh, Brigid just bet they did. She coughed away a chuckle. "Fair enough. I'll give you what I can if your information is helpful to our case." She sounded just like an HDD operative. Maybe she could get good at this job.

"Okay. Do you want a latte or anything? I'm going to grab one on the way."

Brigid's stomach growled. She hadn't even thought of eating earlier. "Sure. But, well, ah—"

"No whipped cream or sprinkles?" Dana laughed.

"Exactly." Brigid gave the address. "See you soon."

Dana clicked off, and Brigid returned to her computer room to conduct a quick dive on Dana the reporter. It wouldn't hurt to have some information in her pocket when the woman showed up. She read different reports across the screen. Dana had cracked some amazing stories ranging from falsified test scores to corruption to fraud. She'd won several awards, and her dating history was spotty.

Brigid had just turned to Dana's formative years, what she could find out about them, when the elevator dinged. She quickly closed her browser and strode into the main room, brushing her hair out of her face as she did so.

"Hi." Dana stood about five-foot-eight in flat black boots, black leggings, and an oversized cream-colored sweater. Her hair was a natural dirty blond and her eyes an intriguing mossy green. A laptop bag was slung carelessly over her shoulder, and she carried a latte in each hand. "You must be Brigid."

Brigid smiled and moved to take a latte. "It's nice to meet you. What do I owe you?"

"Information." Dana's eyes sparkled with obvious intelligence. "First, reassurance that Wolfe is okay. He's been on mission before but has still answered my calls."

"As far as I know, they're all fine," Brigid said, her stomach aching. Were they all fine? There was no way to call Raider since he hadn't taken his phone undercover. But Wolfe should have his. She glanced at the wall. Should she call Malcolm or wait until a decent hour? Better to find out. She reached for her cell phone and quickly dialed Malcolm.

"West." He answered as if he was already up.

"Hi." She winced. "I'm sorry to bother you so early, but we've lost contact with Wolfe."

"We?"

She swallowed. "Yeah. I'm with his friend Dana. The reporter?"

Malcolm rustled around. "I was just on my way in. They had to leave the motel quickly, and Wolfe left his regular phone but has the burner for this op. They're in pursuit of Raider right now, and they've been driving all night."

"Pursuit?" She couldn't breathe.

"Yeah. I'll explain when I get in." He clicked off.

She took the phone and just looked at the blank face. Something had gone wrong.

The drive to the small town of Collinsville, New York, was four hours of Raider's life he'd never get back. Josh calmly pulled off Interstate 90, driving to the outskirts of town.

None of this made a lick of sense. At any point, Eddie could've shot him. Or explained what they were doing. But no, the mob leader had slept the entire way, Josh had driven silently, and Jonny P had stared out the window into the darkness. As a mind fuck, it wasn't bad. He had to give them props for that.

So, to keep his cool, he watched the world fly by via streetlights outside, tracking his movements. His eyes grew gritty, but no way in hell would he put his head back and rest. Eddie would probably shoot him the second he did so.

The idea of Brigid's pretty face kept his attention. Her skin was smooth, and her gaze intelligent. He hadn't had enough time with her, not nearly enough, so he had to survive this. Whatever this was. Most men would be complaining or asking questions, so he purposely kept silent.

If they wanted to play games, he was all in. Being undercover meant that the less he talked, the better. Were Wolfe and Force following?

This was the first time he'd had anybody back him up while undercover. It was his job usually to determine what was needed in every situation, often before the situation arose. Did Force and Wolfe have that instinct? If they did, they were behind him somewhere, tracking his movements.

The earring camera and the belt audio device were still

in place, so he could be traced. But if things went south, which seemed likely at the moment, he'd need backup right away.

But he couldn't turn and look.

Instead, he glanced at his watch to see it was around five in the morning. Dawn should break in about thirty minutes, so if they wanted to bury his body under the cover of darkness, they had miscalculated.

Josh parked the car in front of a motel set away from town that obviously catered to truck drivers, based on the humungous parking area housing at least five of the big rigs. A restaurant, trinket shop, bar, and gas station formed a partial horseshoe around a smaller parking area holding cars. "We're here."

"Picadelli's Motel," Raider read aloud, fixing his jacket more securely around Jonny's gun. He didn't like shooting a weapon he'd never used before, but having the cold metal against his hip gave him some sense of security. He opened the door, stepped out into the chilly morning, and stretched his back. "We can't be here for breakfast." Though, he was starving.

The other men exited the vehicle.

Jonny glared over the top of the car. "Give me my gun back."

It must've killed the enforcer not to make that demand in the car at least once. That's what he got for going with the freaky silent treatment the entire ride.

Raider smiled. "No."

Jonny's nostrils flared. Red crossed the hard planes of his thin face. "You and I are going to have a problem at some point. Thought I should let you know."

"That became inevitable the second you pressed a gun to my head," Raider returned, shutting his door quietly.

Eddie chuckled and stretched his thick body before

walking over puddles toward the bar and away from the car and motel. "I think you two are gonna be great friends. Well, unless I ask Josh to kill you, Raider. Then, not so much."

Josh kept walking toward the bar, not reacting to the words. Did he have a reaction? Raider studied the enforcer. "Hey, Josh? You don't talk much."

"Nope." Josh kept walking, his gait loose, his expression calm.

All right. Raider kept all three men in his sights. Were Wolfe and Force anywhere near? The coming dawn had lightened the sky enough that he could see, but no cars were driving their way. He might be on his own. "This is quite the distance to come for breakfast, but I'm hungry. Should we hit the restaurant instead of the bar?" The lights in the bar were turned off.

"Nope." Eddie reached the glass door and unlocked it with one key. He stepped inside and walked past a long bar toward the back.

Raider followed, his adrenaline flowing, his body instantly hyperaware and ready to fight. The glow from the cash register glinted off bottles of booze and showed red vinyl bar stools and a gleaming hardwood floor. Scents of tequila and wood chips filled his senses.

Eddie nudged open a door, and light spilled out. He motioned Raider inside a square-shaped room lined with shelves holding more liquor bottles and other supplies. One man in his forties, solid as a brick wall, stood to attention at the far end, and in the middle, another guy sat in a chair with his hands tied behind his back. Blood and bruises covered his face and had turned his white shirt a dark red. His head was down.

It took Raider a second to recognize him. "Oh shit." He stopped trying to appear disinterested and sighed as Sean looked up at him. The metallic smell of blood caught him, and he subtly coughed, shoving down bile. "What the hell are you doing here?" The damn farmer was supposed to be in a safe house right now.

Eddie grinned. "Good ole Sean came on the scene because he was protesting a new development in his farming community, and guess when the next hearing was?"

"Last night?" Raider grunted.

"Yep."

Sean blinked blood away from his eyes. "Do you have any idea what a condo development will do to the available water? We need that for crops."

Oh, Raider was going to kill him. Did Force even know the farmer was gone? If not, hopefully he hadn't told Brigid. She'd freak out. "So. This is awkward."

"Yes," Eddie agreed. "We know he gave you the journal, so we figured it'd be a long shot to actually catch him at the hearing. I'm surprised you didn't lock him down."

"I did," Raider said grimly.

Eddie lifted his head in a gesture to the guy standing at the wall. "Did you get him to admit anything else?"

"Just that he misses your dad," the guy said. "Seemed genuine."

Sean snorted. "You're not half the man your daddy was."

Eddie leaned forward, and Raider tensed. How the hell was he going to get Sean out of this without both of them taking a bullet to the head?

Eddie smiled. "Where's your daughter? If you're not locked down, neither is she."

"The hell she isn't," Raider returned, keeping his gaze on the wounded farmer. "She'll stay where I put her."

Sean lifted his head, sweat rolling down his damaged neck. His eyes were bloodshot and his nose definitely broken. "My girl does what she wants." He broke off to cough up blood, the sound wheezing.

Yeah. Definitely broken ribs and punctured lung in there somewhere.

Eddie smiled at the guy who'd done the damage. "Good job tonight, Tom. Looks like you just got a promotion."

Tom cracked his neck. "Thanks, boss. Want me to finish this?"

"Nope. You go on, now. Have a good night," Eddie said, his gaze returning to Sean, who was silently glaring.

"Okay." Tom strode out the back door, limping slightly. Maybe Sean had given him more of a fight than was first apparent. Two seconds later, an engine ignited, and then Tom was gone.

Jonny moved to Sean and punched him in the gut. Blood sprayed in every direction, covering Jonny's entire front, including his chin. Sean growled and tried to lift off the chair. "Make this a fair fight, P. Though you'll be crying."

Raider's legs bunched to intercede, but he forced himself to stay in place.

Jonny snarled. "Want me to handle him?"

"No." Eddie turned and looked at Raider. "This is how you earn trust, Raider Times. Take out that gun Jonny so kindly gave you and put one through this asshole's head. Nobody betrays me. Just think what a clear path you'll have with the daughter, then."

Shit. Raider drew out the gun just as Josh did the same, except Josh pointed his at Raider.

"Oh," Eddie added. "If you don't shoot Sean, Josh is going to shoot you. Make a choice."

Chapter Twenty-Nine

Brigid took a long pull on her straw and led the way into case room one, where Roscoe was already back to sleep on his plush bed in the corner. Angus was paranoid, to say the least, so nothing interesting had been left up on the board. "Okay. Why do you want to find Wolfe so badly?" She flipped on the lights.

Dana followed and took a seat, retrieving her laptop from the bag. "I figured your offices would be nicer than this."

"We're the rebels," Brigid said easily, also taking a seat. "Not exactly the gold star of HDD agents." For some reason, she was happy with that fact. Well, she would be if she hadn't signed a plea bargain basically giving away her life. But one thing at a time.

"Though that is a nice-looking dog," Dana said.

Yeah, he hadn't gotten enough sleep, apparently. "What do you have?" Brigid asked.

Dana opened her laptop, looking lovely in the glow of the screen. But at least she wore normal clothing and wasn't all fancy, though Brigid wished she could do that casual hair-pulled-up look. Her curly hair was tough to tame. "I need the Wi-Fi password," Dana said.

Brigid reached for the laptop and connected it to the system. "There. You can use the screen now, too."

"Thanks."

The elevator dinged, heavy footsteps sounded, and Malcolm West strode into the room. His hair was mussed and his eyes tired. "Hey."

"Hi." Brigid performed introductions. "What do you know?" Her lungs seized. Just how bad was the situation?

Malcolm shook his head. "Nothing. Raider went for a ride, and we don't know why. Wolfe left his phone, and Force is doing something to find Raider, but that's all I know. They didn't have time to talk."

Brigid's throat clogged. Raider was trained and he was smart. Same with Wolfe and Force. Everything would be all right. "Where's Kat?"

"Home with Pippa," Malcolm said, turning toward Dana. "Let's get some work done while we wait. What do you have?"

The elevator dinged again, and heels sounded. Nari poked her head in, her eyes clear, her hair perfectly in place. "Have you heard anything yet?"

"No," Malcolm said. "But I called you in just in case. For now, this is Dana, Wolfe's reporter friend."

"Hello." Nari moved inside and took a seat. Today she wore a pale yellow silk blouse with dark jeans. "I take it you have information for us?"

Dana nodded. "I do if this goes both ways. You need to have information for me, too."

Malcolm kicked back, and the scar above his eyebrow seemed more prominent in the early light. "That depends entirely on what you have. If you have information that helps, I promise we'll reciprocate."

"Okay." Dana typed in some keywords, and a face took shape on screen. "Meet Senator Scot Tyson from

Boston. I tugged on a string Wolfe gave me, and several stories unraveled, but I'm still working on them."

Brigid kept quiet about the fact that the senator and Eddie Coonan had a connection. The senator was in his early forties with a distinguished jaw, dark hair, and piercing blue eyes. "What did you find?"

"It's an interesting string and just a theory right now." Dana typed again, and documents came up on screen. "Wolfe gave me facts about a girl in Seattle, but it turns out that three women with connections to Tyson have disappeared. The first was a girl when they were both in high school." A picture of a cute blonde with wild hair and a couple of piercings came up on the screen. "Jacki Mint."

"She just disappeared?" Nari asked, leaning forward.

"Yes," Dana said. "There are accounts from other students about Scot and Jacki dating, but he denied it and there was no evidence. Plus, Jacki had run away before, so the local sheriff figured she'd run away again."

"It's possible," Nari said. "Though she hasn't shown up in twenty years?"

"Nope," Dana said, typing again. A woman in her early twenties, this one another blonde, emerged on the screen. She had sparkling eyes, a sweet smile, and was dressed in scrubs. "Dr. Annie Jones, who'd just started her residency in Seattle, where Scot was attending law school at the time. They dated, she disappeared, and this time he was questioned by the police. No evidence of any foul play was found."

Brigid took notes. She'd need to see if there were any records of Eddie traveling to Seattle during that time. Maybe the lost women had nothing to do with Tyson, or maybe he'd hurt them, or perhaps he'd had Eddie do his dirty work. Who knew at this point? "This is good research," Brigid said.

"I'm just getting started." Dana looked over at Brigid's notes. "I'm thinking your computer skills would come in handy right about now. Would you do a deep dive on these cases, as well as look for others?"

"Absolutely," Brigid said, her instincts humming. "What was the conclusion of the police concerning the doctor?"

Dana shook her head. "The case went cold. No evidence anywhere, and Scot left Seattle after graduating from law school. Took a job with a big firm in New York, where at least one more woman disappeared." Another blonde, this one in her early twenties, came up on the screen. "Lucy Wilcox, who interned at the law firm where Scot worked. Absolutely no connection found between them. Not a one."

"Isn't that a coincidence?" Malcolm asked, sarcasm heavy in his dark tone. "Three blondes, all disappear around the good ole senator. This guy is dirty. We have to prove it." His phone buzzed, and he lifted it to his ear. "West." His eyebrows rose, and he straightened up. "Well, shit."

Brigid stopped breathing.

The gun felt heavy and final in Raider's hand. Tom was gone, so that left him with three men to subdue. Eddie was probably armed, but he hadn't pulled a gun out, so Raider could knock him out quickly. Jonny P was unarmed, so again, fighting would be fine. But Josh seemed pretty damn comfortable with the gun in his hand. If Raider rushed him, he'd shoot. Even if Raider got to Josh fast enough, Eddie would have time to pull his weapon out and shoot him in the back.

None of Raider's options were good.

For now, he bluffed. He kept his gun pointed down and walked over blood spatter to the stubborn man. "Your daughter loves you, and I put you somewhere safe. Why in the hell would you risk that?" he asked, trying to buy time.

Sean's green eyes nearly glowed. "I figured I could handle it, and I still can. Why don't you go get a drink or something? You're not needed here."

Raider circled him as if enjoying the moment, but bile kept rising in his throat. He couldn't let Brigid's dad die. Angling his head, he checked out the bindings. Simple zip ties. Now all he needed was a knife. He looked toward the ceiling and each corner.

"What's the holdup?" Eddie asked, leaning back against the wall, his hands free.

"Lookin' for cameras," Raider returned. "This feels like a setup, Eddie. Me shooting this guy in the head could get me the chair." He pretended to look around, hopefully giving Force and Wolfe information—if they were in range. "This back room isn't a good place to do this, either. Too much splatter and forensic evidence."

"Oh yeah?" Eddie snorted while Jonny P barely smiled. "There's so much evidence in here already that I might have to burn the place down and rebuild."

Raider shook his head. "That's not how to do it."

"Then how?" Jonny P challenged.

"In the middle of nowhere, outside, where the elements wash away the blood," Raider said as Sean's glare got stronger.

Eddie pushed off the wall. "There are no cameras back here, and the ones out front were disabled before Tom had some fun with Sean. I can't afford a record of my being here, either." He drew out his gun, a silver Smith & Wesson 500, and aimed the barrel at Raider's head. "Josh? Go fetch the car and bring it around back. We'll either have one or two bodies for the trunk."

Raider's body chilled. Now probably wasn't the time to

note that Eddie had some serious issues and probably a complex or two. That particular gun was overkill for an indoor situation. Seriously so.

Josh immediately handed Jonny P his weapon and went out the back door, again without an ounce of emotion. The door shut, and thick silence spiraled through the room.

This was bad. He could shoot both men on a swivel, but one of them would get a shot off. Sean had remained still, his body tense. He'd be ready to move if necessary. Though his wheezing was a concern. If Raider didn't get the guy to a hospital pretty quickly, he was going to die anyway. Okay. His only chance was to put himself equal distance between the two men with guns, shoot one, duck, and shoot the other.

Yeah, he was gonna die.

A siren sounded in the distance.

Raider's head snapped up, and the entire room froze. "Not good." He stepped toward Sean. "Is this room soundproof?"

Eddie rushed for the door and slightly opened it. "No. We don't really use it much." He turned over his shoulder to glare at Raider, while Jonny P kept the gun leveled. "You're wired."

Raider jerked up his shirt to reveal his bare chest. "Don't be a moron. Your guys searched me, anyway." He looked around as if thinking rapidly. The sirens were getting closer. He leaned down toward Sean's face. "Just how loud were you?"

Sean sucked in air, and blood dribbled from his mouth. "I wasn't quiet." He snorted, his eyelids fluttering.

"Shit," Raider snapped, adrenaline bursting and swelling his veins. He tucked his gun in the back of his waistband. "Knife," he barked.

"What?" Jonny P burst out.

"They're here," Eddie muttered, still watching outside.

Raider clapped his hands hard. "Hurry up. We don't have time. One of you has a knife."

Eddie jerked his head, and Jonny P drew a knife from a holster at his calf. "Let's kill them both," Jonny P said, smiling.

"We don't have time for this," Raider urged.

Red and blue flashed through the opening in the door. Eddie shut it.

Raider angled around to make sure Sean was still breathing. Kind of. "Knife, damn it."

Eddie nodded.

Jonny threw the knife and Raider caught it, quickly sliding it through the bindings. Sean shook and opened his eyes.

Raider looked around. "Sean? You were robbed, and Eddie and I heard screams, came in and chased the guy off. Just be quiet until we can get to you in the hospital, and your loyalty will keep you safe in the organization this time. Eddie, we were just about to call 911. Got it? Sean, you don't know our names." He looked up as if panicking. "Damn it, Jonny. You're covered in blood." Raider turned to Eddie. "Is there somewhere one of us can hide in here? If they see that blood, we're dead."

"Cubbyhole behind the old Pac-Man machine. We keep cash there," Eddie said.

"Go," Raider said urgently, rushing to Jonny and handing him the gun and knife. "Take all the weapons." There was no way he'd get away with this, but with the cops outside, at least he had a chance to live through it. Had Force called the cops?

Jonny glared at Raider, took Eddie's gun, and jogged out of the room.

"Come out with your hands up," a man bellowed through a bullhorn. Raider jerked his head. Shit. Was that Force?

Raider looked himself over as if making sure no blood was on him. "You wanted on any warrants?"

"No," Eddie said, eyeing Sean. "Should we kill him?"

"No." Raider pretended to survey the scene again, his mind calming. "He'll back us. Act like you're in control with the cops."

Eddie hesitated and then nodded.

Raider leaned toward Sean's ear. "I'm so going to kill you for this," he whispered tersely.

"Bring it on," Sean wheezed, just as quickly turning his head and smacking a kiss on Raider's chin.

Raider reared up. He did not just do that.

Sean chortled, the sound painful. Then he slumped unconscious.

Crap. Raider shoved past Eddie for the door. He had to get Sean medical help. "Follow my lead." He moved past Eddie and opened the door, his hands up. "We heard screaming and caught a guy robbing this place. The bartender needs an ambulance. Now," he called out, facing two legitimate Collinsville police cars with doors opened and cops pointing guns at him. He blinked.

Force moved from one car and Wolfe the other, both wearing police jackets. Wolfe grabbed his arm and spun him around to face the wall, while Force ran inside. Eddie's hands went up in surrender, his expression oddly innocent.

Force moved for Sean and felt his neck. "He's alive. Call for an ambulance," he ordered Wolfe.

Wolfe finished pretending to search Raider. "You take these two in, and I'll wait for the ambulance with this bartender guy."

Good. Raider tried to measure Sean's uneasy breathing. Wolfe surely had some combat medical experience, and that would come in handy while the ambulance made its way to them. Hopefully it wasn't too late for the stubborn farmer.

"Roger that," Force said, motioning Eddie toward the door. "We'll see what really happened."

Raider glanced at Eddie, who glared. All right. This was going to be interesting.

Chapter Thirty

Raider sat in back of the squad car and watched the trees fly by outside as they headed into town. He didn't have much time.

Angus Force looked at them through the rearview mirror, playing the role of a small-town cop perfectly. "How about you boys tell me what happened tonight?"

Raider shrugged. "Heard a ruckus, went to investigate, and saw some punk beating up that old guy. We had to intervene."

Force frowned. "The door was unlocked?"

"Yep," Eddie said.

Force craned his neck to better see Eddie, taking a turn quickly as he drove closer to town and out of the boonies. "What were you doing at a bar at five in the morning?"

Eddie cut Raider a hard look. Yeah, this was looking like a disaster.

Raider hunched over. A tire company flew by on the right, while a gradual drop-off began on the left, punctuated by white pine trees and balsam poplar. "I don't feel well, man."

Force snorted. "Too bad. You'll be at the station in about fifteen minutes."

Man, Raider hoped Force was on the same wavelength as him. "I need out. Now."

"No. And if you puke back there, you're eating it up later." Force glared through the mirror, perfectly in character. "We're not some big city force—meaning we play by our own rules."

"Great," Eddie muttered, looking around the back seat.

Damn it. How was Raider going to get them out of this? Force was playing it straight, but the partition between the front and back seats was new and aluminum. Raider could kick it until he broke his ankles, and he wouldn't get to Force. What the hell should he do? "Come on, man. Roll down the window just a little." If he could get his hand out, he could unlock the door.

Force sighed and then stiffened, looking at his side window.

Raider looked at Eddie and then turned to see the black town car speeding their way. Shit. What was Josh going to do? The guy leaned out his front window, gun aimed.

Raider gave Force a warning look, just as the rear tire exploded.

Force bellowed and tried to correct, turning the car down the hill. "Hold on," he shouted.

Shit. Double shit. Raider planted his hands against the seat in front of him, trying to brace himself as they went over the bank. The car bumped and jumped, sliding sideways and hitting every rock on the way. Force jerked the wheel away from the bigger trees, but gravity took over, and they slid sideways before flipping back around. The car hit a massive tamarack tree head-on with a loud boom.

Force's head smashed back against the aluminum divider with enough power that it vibrated, while Raider and Eddie were slammed against the back of the front seat. Pain burst through Raider's shoulder. He turned to see

Eddie pushing himself to sit, blood flowing from his right cheekbone.

Raider's door opened a sliver. He turned and kicked it as hard as he could, using both feet. The tree cracked loudly, and branches rained down. Steam hissed from the crumpled-up engine area. He kicked again.

Eddie hit his shoulder. "Hurry up."

"I am." Dizziness slammed into Raider's brain, and he swayed but kept kicking. Finally, the door opened all the way. "Let's go." He scrambled out, stood on the uneven ground, and a branch jarred his injured shoulder. Pain hit first, and he fell on his ass.

Eddie fell out of the car and rose to his knees. "You okay?"

"No." Raider looked up the embankment to see Josh and Jonny P peering down. "We have to get out of here."

Eddie tried to stand and ended up bent over, heaving out air. "Jesus." He gestured to the cop in front. "He can identify us."

So could Wolfe, who'd been left behind, but apparently Eddie wasn't thinking clearly. Raider staggered to his feet and opened the front door. Force was hunched over the steering wheel, bleeding from the back of his head. Oh God. Was he alive? Nausea rippled through Raider's gut. His hand trembled when he reached for the pulse point on Force's limp wrist. Slow but steady. How badly was the agent hurt?

Raider drew the gun from Force's holster, and shoved him as gently as possible across the seat. Then he pressed the barrel against the seat near Force's ass and squeezed the trigger. The sound was deafening. He turned and slammed the door. "Took care of him." He looked up the long slope to the road. "We have to run. Now."

Eddie turned and stumbled over a rock, landing on his face.

Raider limped to him, grabbed his arm, and hauled him to his feet. "They'll be looking for this guy. We just killed a cop, Eddie. Run."

Eddie started to climb. They helped each other, balancing on rocks and downed trees, falling several times. Eddie heaved and moved to puke, and Raider grabbed his biceps and shook him. "Don't throw up here. Can't leave any evidence."

Eddie sucked it down and trudged up again.

Finally, they reached the road.

"We don't have much time," Josh said calmly as Jonny P opened the back door and urgently gestured them inside.

Raider's vision hazed, turned red, and then hazed again. He helped Eddie into the car and then fell in himself, his entire body aching like one pulsing bruise.

Josh peeled out, heading away from the town. "How bad you hurt?"

Eddie coughed. "Not bad enough to stop."

Raider shut his eyes and put his head back, taking inventory. How badly was Force hurt? Where the hell was Wolfe? Were they working with the local cops? This was about to go seriously south, if Force couldn't get the story straight. The news would have it soon. Everything inside him wanted to return and help Force get to a hospital. The guy hadn't regained consciousness even a little. "I have serious concerns about your organization," he murmured, trying to stay in character.

Eddie shifted his weight, moving the seat. "What the hell does that mean?" he wheezed.

Raider opened one eye, and morning light nearly cut his brain in two. "We go on a simple mission, and I end up killing a cop. I'm not impressed."

Eddie clapped him on the shoulder, and pain exploded

down Raider's torso. That shoulder was definitely out of joint. "Yeah, but now we're in bed together." His smile revealed bloody teeth. "You get me a hundred million dollars, and I'll show you how easy it is to clean it. For fifty percent, of course."

"Twenty," Raider countered, his lungs struggling to work.

"Forty."

"Thirty, and that's my final offer," Raider said, his body seizing in pain.

Eddie held out a hand. "Deal."

"Good. Drive me closer to a real town and let me out. I need to set the plan in motion." If he lived through the next couple of hours. "I'll be in touch."

Eddie grinned. "You have until tomorrow suppertime. Then I send Jonny and Josh after you."

Angus Force came to with blood sliding down his face and pooling on the seat of the cop car. His vision was blurry and his body oddly numb. Silence surrounded him and then sound came rushing in with the force of a tidal wave.

"Angus." Wolfe leaned over him. "Dude. Any neck or spine damage?"

"I don't know." Angus reached for the steering wheel and pulled himself to sit. The world spun, and his bones clattered against each other. He huffed in pain and sat for a moment. "Concussion for sure."

"Yeah. I got that." Wolfe clamped both hands on Angus's shoulders and hauled him from the damaged vehicle. "Can you stand?"

Angus fell back against the car. His ass burned. Had Tanaka shot him in the butt? "Give me a minute."

"Don't have a minute." Wolfe pivoted, heaving Angus

away from the car, and setting him down as gently as possible on a rock. "Need to wipe down the car best I can."

Angus looked around at the trees, which seemed to be spinning. He tried to think. "Where's Raider?"

Wolfe tapped his earbud. "In the car with Eddie. I think he's hurt but can't tell how badly. Should have a pickup location soon."

Angus blinked blood away from his eyes and surveyed the destroyed cop car. "Where's Sean?" That stubborn jackass. Why hadn't he stayed safely in police protection?

"Dropped him at the hospital," Wolfe said, finishing and turning toward him. "Guy was on his last legs and didn't have a choice."

Oh, this was a complete disaster. "Phone," Angus said.

Wolfe handed over his burner. "Any chance you can talk while running up the hill?"

The thought of even limping up the hill made Angus want to throw up. The incredible pain in his left side promised a couple of broken ribs. So far, he was breathing okay, so one hadn't pierced a lung. Yet. He took the phone and dialed quickly.

"Angus?" Brigid's panicked voice came over the distance. "What's going on? Is everyone okay?"

"No." He coughed, and blood spit out. Shit. Internal bleeding was a bastard. "Listen. We need help."

"What do you need?" Nari's voice came through the speaker, straightening his spine. "Where are you?"

Her voice helped center him. He'd deal with that fact later. "Quick rundown. Wolfe and I stole two police vehicles from the Collinsville station." Two out of the four the department owned. "The shift change is going to happen shortly, and they're going to notice. I need you to contact Fields and Rutherford and have the HDD take care of this." He leaned over and tried to gasp as a spasm took him.

"Angus?" Nari's voice rose. "What's happening?"

"Nothing," he groaned as Wolfe helped him to sit up again. "The HDD has to cover us with the cops, and it'd be perfect if they'd put out a bulletin about a local officer being shot and killed, with no other information." The HDD was never going to go along with this. "And they need to pick up Sean Banaghan, who's at the local hospital. Put him in a safe house until further notice."

"My dad? What are you talking about?" Brigid breathed.

"He was hurt, but he'll be okay. Get him out of that hospital if possible." Angus groaned.

"You think HDD will help us?" Nari asked, her tone tentative.

"Either that, or all hell is going to descend upon us and the agency. Use those words if you have to." Angus tried to sound more confident than he felt. "We're in a shitstorm here, but tell them we're close to breaking open a huge trafficking case." Close might be a lie, but he was willing to lie at this point.

"We'll make it happen," Nari said. "I promise, Angus."

Good. The shrink had connections beyond Angus's, and that was the most he could hope for. He clicked off and took Wolfe's offered hand to stand. He wobbled on his feet. "We have to get the hell out of here."

Wolfe looked up the long distance to the road above. "I have the other cop car up there. We can drive on I-90 for a couple of miles just to get free, and then we need to ditch it. Fast."

The local cops would be looking for it before HDD could intervene, provided HDD decided to help. Angus nodded and then instantly regretted the motion as pain dropped him to his knees.

Wolfe looked down at him. "This is gonna hurt. I'm sorry." He leaned down and hauled Angus over his shoulder.

The blood rushed to Angus's damaged skull, lights exploded, and he heaved. His stomach was empty, so nothing came out. Wolfe ducked his head and began running up the hill, holding Angus as tight as possible to keep from jostling him. Angus closed his eyes to avoid watching the uneven ground rush by.

Man, Wolfe was tough. Angus weighed about two-twenty and was mainly muscle. Wolfe ran full bore up the rocky hill without a hitch in his stride. He'd been a good choice to join the Deep Ops unit. The guy was as solid as they came. Physically, anyway.

They reached the cop car and Wolfe dropped to his haunches so Angus could stand and fall into the passenger side. Pain ripped up Angus's body. Then Wolfe ran around, jumped in, and peeled away from the embankment.

Angus tried to hold on to consciousness as long as he could. "Raider?"

Wolfe tapped his earbud. "Negotiating with Eddie, but he sounds funny. Like he's in pain. He hasn't given me any indication of the seriousness of his injuries."

Damn it. "We're going to need a doctor." In addition, they required treatment without leaving medical records. "Any thoughts?"

"Let's pick up Raider after they drop him off, and we'll figure out where to go from there." Wolfe looked at him, still driving fast, and his face wavered into two Wolfes. "Force?"

"Nope." Force finally let the darkness take him. But everything still hurt.

Chapter Thirty-One

Brigid typed quickly, making sure there were no reports of stolen police cars from the small New York town, her worry over her father and Raider turning to acid in her stomach. The day had been long, and her back muscles might never relax again. The elevator dinged its normal announcement of arrivals, and she lurched from her chair and into the main room.

Malcolm sat hunched over a stack of papers, while Pippa was setting up a nice buffet on one of the desks. It looked like chicken casserole, rolls, and Caesar salad, and it smelled delicious. Roscoe sat on his furry haunches next to Pippa, his intense gaze on the biggest dish.

Brigid nodded at the quiet brunette and then moved for the elevator.

Raider, Wolfe, and Angus limped off, and she stopped cold. "Holy crap." Blood and dirt covered them all. Her heart stuttered and then calmed. They were hurt, but they were okay. Raider was still alive. She nearly swayed in relief.

Roscoe barked once and leaped past her, whining as he sniffed around Angus.

"It's okay, boy," Angus said, patting the dog's wide head. "I'm all right."

"You sure?" Pippa asked, hesitating by the food.

Angus nodded and then winced, shutting his eyes. "I have to stop doing that."

Brigid, her throat clogged, gingerly reached out to Raider. He had bruises along the side of his face, these a brighter purple than the one that had nearly faded from her dad's punch. His arm hung at a weird angle, and blood seeped from his hip and his other thigh. "Raider?"

"I'm okay," he said, lines of fatigue and pain fanning out from his midnight-dark eyes. "Eddie let me off in a nowhere town so I could get to work, and these guys were kind enough to pick me up before I passed out again."

"My dad?" she asked, her voice trembling.

"Safe," Angus muttered. "And locked down more securely this time, even with his own doctor. We had to have him removed from the hospital, but he's okay now."

The elevator door closed. The men limped toward the food, while Wolfe kept a close eye on the other two as if expecting them to drop at any moment.

Pippa hovered and turned to unwrap plastic plates. "I thought everyone would need a good dinner."

Malcolm stood and studied the other men. "Are you sure we shouldn't go to the hospital?"

"No," Angus said shortly. "We've driven almost eight hours, all day, and we're not seeing a doctor. There can be no medical records about this right now." He jerked his head toward Brigid and then wavered before regaining control. "What's the news?"

Brigid resisted the urge to put her arm around Raider's waist to make him sit down. "Nari somehow got the HDD to step up and reach out to the local Collinsville cops, but we don't know the extent of their cooperation as of yet. Rutherford and Fields aren't responding to my calls." Which hopefully meant they were working the problem.

The elevator ground loudly and then hitched, opening with a more drawn-out ding than usual this time. Nari stepped out along with a gnarled bald man wearing a white lab coat, Snoopy pajamas, and cream-colored women's Ugg boots. He held an old-fashioned black doctor's bag in one weathered hand. Nari's jaw dropped. "Oh, good lord. You two need a hospital."

"No," Angus barked, sending the dog in a tailspin around him. "The next person who suggests a hospital gets shot in the knee." He limped to the nearest chair and dropped onto it with a groan. Roscoe yipped and ran to his side, setting his furry head on Angus's knee for reassurance.

Nari's lips tightened. "Very well. This is Dr. George Georgetown, and he has agreed to see you both and make sure you're not about to drop dead here in this crappy office."

George Georgetown? Seriously? Brigid studied the elderly man.

He smiled, revealing ill-fitting dentures. "I'm still licensed but haven't worked much the last couple of decades."

Nari, the most petite woman in the office, leaned down to take his arm and draw him into the main room. "We appreciate any help you can provide." Lowering her chin, she looked at Angus and then Raider. "I can't tell who is injured worst."

"He is," they both said, pointing to the other.

Raider rolled his eyes. "Force has a concussion for sure, and based on his breathing during the last several hours, I'd bet on a broken rib or two."

Angus didn't even turn. "Not to mention the burn along my ass from you shooting me."

Brigid gasped.

Raider patted her hand. "I had to aim close to you, and your butt was better than deafening you for life. But I didn't know I'd burned your ass. Sorry about that."

Angus waved him off. "I need to sit here for a minute.

You go first." He stroked the dog's head. "Doc? I think Raider's shoulder is out of joint. Wolfe offered to fix it, but Raider refused for some reason." His laugh was more of a wheeze.

Brigid finally gave in and grasped Raider's good arm. "We can use case room two as an examination room." The other case room was full of the documents she'd been printing out all day to create a better background on Eddie Coonan, his organization, and his ties to the senator.

Raider, surprisingly, let her lead him around the desks to the room.

Once inside, Brigid shoved chairs out of the way and helped him onto the table. "How badly are you hurt?"

"Not bad." His gaze softened. "Stop worrying, Irish. I'm fine."

The doctor closed the door and came forward, looking into Raider's eyes. "You have some bad contusions on your face. Any dizziness or nausea?" The doc took a light out of his bag and shined it in Raider's eyes.

"No." Raider's eyebrows drew together as he studied the older man.

Yeah, the old man didn't look like he had it together. Brigid cleared her throat. "What's up with the pajamas?"

"I like Snoopy," George said easily, taking out a pair of scissors and making quick work of Raider's shirt. "There we go." He probed along a bruise on Raider's clavicle before taking out a bottle of pills. "I see no internal damage or concussion, so take a couple of these, one under your tongue to dissolve. I promise you won't feel me put your shoulder back in place."

It showed how badly Raider hurt that he took the pills without question.

Brigid wanted to snuggle into his side, but she had to tell him everything first.

The doc looked up at her. "Help me get his pants off,

would you? I'm guessing stitches are needed based on the amount of blood on those jeans."

Raider snorted. "She's always trying to get my pants off."

He wasn't quite sure how he'd gotten home, but for sure, the world was a bright and sparkly place. Raider sat next to Brigid on his sofa and tried to eat a truly delicious casserole, when all he wanted to do was sing. "I haven't played my guitar for you yet," he murmured.

Her face pinkened, and she looked around the room. "I'd like that." Once again, she nudged his plate closer to him. "The doctor said you might need to eat after the pills he gave you."

"Huh." Damn, those were good pills. Raider grinned, feeling the lightness of the air around them. "I can't remember. How's Force?"

"He's okay. Concussion and possible internal bleeding, so the doc and Nari went home with him for the night to keep watch." Her phone buzzed, and she read the face before reaching for his remote control. "That was Wolfe. Said to check out channel two."

The screen came alive, and a very handsome African American reporter stood in the rain outside of the Collinsville police station. He was saying something, but his words sounded garbled. "What did he say?" Raider slurred, his body feeling heavy. Really heavy.

Brigid's voice sounded as if it came from far away. "He's saying that a police officer was killed and there's a manhunt on."

"Huh." Raider leaned back on the sofa and let the universe have its way with his body. "I only shot near Angus's butt. I didn't kill him." Something about the statement wasn't right, but he couldn't grasp what. Words were silly, anyway. He'd learned early on that actions mattered. Not words. He turned toward Brigid. "You are so pretty."

She sighed and stood. "Come on, Ace. Let's get you into bed."

Now that was a plan. He struggled to his feet and followed her into the bedroom, and when she helped him to undress, he reached for her.

"Later." She grinned and pushed him down on the cool sheets. "Unbelievable."

"With me." He grabbed her hand and tugged, and when she landed, he curled around her, ignoring his new stitches. "I like you, Brigid. You're sweet and honest and if I don't die in the next week, I'm really gonna ask you out. Play you a song or two, and maybe you could meet Miss A."

Brigid stiffened but didn't say anything. "Just sleep for now, Raider. You'll feel better in the morning."

He felt pretty damn good right now. But he let the sparkles and unicorns take him away for a while, and he dreamed of bright colors, sandy beaches, and a sky so blue it had to be painted.

A sound awoke him and he lay there for a moment, not moving. Where was he? Light filtered in through the window blinds, and a warm body was pressed next to him. He blinked and reality came rushing back. His shoulder ached, his hip hurt, and his other leg burned a little, but he could breathe without pain, and his head was clear.

What in the hell had been in those pills?

He partially turned to see Brigid lying on her side, a mass of hair curling down her shoulder and over the comforter. She made another soft sound, her pale face pinched. "Brigid." He ran his knuckles over her cheekbone. "Wake up, baby. You're having a bad dream."

Her eyes slowly opened, shamrock green and unfocused. She blinked.

He cupped her angled jaw, gentling his hold on her soft skin. "You okay?"

"Yes." She rubbed her chin. "Even a short time in a cell was too much. Sometimes I dream of small places where the walls keep closing in."

"You're safe now." He traced her full lips with his thumb, and his body started to wake up despite the aches. "I won't let anything happen to you again." Even if the unit disbanded, he'd make sure she ended up somewhere safe and on the right side of the law.

She leaned into his touch. "I won't break the law again, even for a good cause." Her eyes clouded. "Raider, I—"

His phone buzzed from the bed table and he reached for it, reading the face. "Force wants everybody in the office in an hour to plan the next phase of the op." Shouldn't Force be in bed somewhere? The guy definitely had a concussion along with internal bleeding.

Brigid sighed. "What's the next phase?"

"I have to go back in." The last person on this earth he wanted to see was Eddie Coonan. He could be ready in ten minutes, and it took about twenty to get to headquarters. That left them thirty minutes. Ducking his head, he swept his mouth against hers.

"What are you doing?" she asked, her voice soft.

"Taking a minute, or thirty." Moving carefully, he rolled over, right on top of her. Good. No big pains.

She chuckled and caressed his flanks, wiggling her butt and widening her thighs to make more room for him. "Wait a minute. How's your shoulder? The doctor said to refrain from using it and maybe wear a sling for a week or so."

His dick pounded against her soft panties. "The injury is an old one and won't even slow me down now that the shoulder is back in place." He'd initially injured it being tossed off a bridge. "Ibuprofen at regular intervals for the week is more than sufficient." He could still aim, shoot, or fight, and that was all that mattered. "For now, why don't you baby me?"

Her grin was all sauce. "I suppose I could—" A pounding on the exterior door jerked her head toward the bedroom doorway. "What in the world?" she breathed.

"Guys? I brought lattes. Let me in, or I'll break the door down," Wolfe called out, his voice way too cheerful. "I'll drive you to work."

Raider groaned as his body tried to adjust, but he just wanted to keep playing with Brigid. "I'm gonna kill him."

Chapter Thirty-Two

Exhaustion pulled at Brigid as she walked into the HDD bullpen, supersweet latte in hand. Wolfe had already dodged into case room one to deliver coffee to Angus, Malcolm, and Nari. Raider moved at her side, surprisingly graceful. "You sure you're okay?" she asked.

He nodded. "Yeah. This was nothing. I'm not ready to fight or go jogging, but I'm solid." A phone buzzed, and he drew two from his jacket pocket. "It's the burner."

She caught her breath as he stopped and pressed the button for the speakerphone. "Times here."

"Hi, Raider. It's Eddie." His voice sounded muffled over the phone. "I can't meet tonight—raincheck for tomorrow morning? Say around nine?"

Angus and Wolfe emerged silently from the conference room and stopped to listen.

Raider frowned. "What's going on? I don't like changing plans."

"What's going on is that my good friend Sean has disappeared from the local hospital, and I'm worried about him." Anger and tension rode Eddie's tone. "There's no chance you have an inkling of where he went, is there?"

Raider grimaced and leaned against his desk. "Dude,

I have no clue. I've been sleeping since, ah, our meeting yesterday. Have a raging headache."

"Must've been too much beer," Eddie said.

Man, he was careful over the phone. Was that a lesson learned from the tape recordings her father had hidden for years? Brigid swallowed, not moving too much.

"Yeah," Raider agreed. "Okay. I'll be at your bar at nine in the morning. Any chance you serve breakfast?"

"No. Eat before you get here, and don't be late." Eddie ended the call.

Raider pressed a button. He focused on Angus. "Are we sure we have Sean locked down this time?"

A perfect steering-wheel imprint had turned purple across Angus's forehead, and a sling held his arm against his ribs. Even his eyes looked swollen. "The records and the cameras at the hospital, should Eddie somehow get his hands on them, will show that Sean checked himself out and hopped in a dented 1990 blue Kia driven by a young-looking brunette with big boobs."

How was Angus even standing? Scolding him wouldn't work, and they were under a time crunch. "The brunette is an agent?" Brigid asked.

"Affirmative," Angus said. "Two other agents, one dressed as a doctor and the other a nurse, told Sean exactly what to do. Right now he's in protective custody with medical assistance whether he likes it or not."

Raider sighed. "We're running out of time for those girls. It's Tuesday, damn it." He slammed his fist on the table.

Urgency propelled Brigid toward her computer room, and she tried not to feel guilty that she was happy Raider would have another night to heal before going undercover again.

"Your plan?" Angus called out.

She kept moving. "By the end of today, I'll know every

connection between Eddie Coonan and Senator Tyson as well as everything I can find in their respective backgrounds." An entire day to herself in front of the computer was exactly what this case needed. "I may break a few laws."

"I've got you covered," Angus returned, his voice pained. "Do what you have to do."

She paused at her doorway and partially turned. "Is my father really okay?"

Angus grinned, splitting his lip open again. Then he winced. "Your father is a pain in the butt to the two agents and one doctor staying with him, but yes, he's safe."

"Good." Brigid opened her door, set down her coffee, and started to work three computers at once. Her phone buzzed, and she glanced down to see that it was Agent Rutherford calling. She ignored the call and turned back to learning everything she could about human trafficking while her other searches ran. Soon Agent Fields called, and she declined that call as well. She had much more important issues to work on than talking to those two.

What was there to report? HDD had been brought in on yesterday's fiascoes.

The phone buzzed again, and her palms started sweating, but her typing didn't slow. If she had something to report, she would. They needed to leave her alone.

Malcolm brought in tacos from home around noon, and she caught a glimpse of Nari walking by outside. Today the woman wore pressed gray jeans, a floral shirt, and designer boots. Brigid sighed and forced a smile for the ex-cop. "Thank you."

He looked her over, set down the tacos, and took the other seat. "What is your problem with Nari?" There was mild curiosity but no judgment in his low tone.

"No problem." Brigid tugged the paper plate toward her keyboard. "I like her. A lot." Which was the truth.

Malcolm lifted one dark eyebrow. "Uh-huh."

"I really do." Brigid took a bite, and flavor exploded on her tongue. She chewed and swallowed. "What are we, girlfriends now?"

Malcolm snorted and extended his muscled arms to stretch. "What's the deal, Bridge?"

The sweet new nickname warmed her throughout, but she knew the guy wouldn't let it go until she confessed all. "It's just that Nari's always so put together, you know? Pressed clothes, perfectly fit, her hair smooth and glossy."

Malcolm blinked. "So?"

"So, I knew you wouldn't get it." For some reason, he'd always been easy to talk to. The fact that he was an ex-cop and she an ex-con just made the situation more interesting.

"If you want to be put together like that, then do it." He reached for one of her tacos and bit into it.

"Right." She rolled her eyes. Her mom had tried everything to get Brigid to like dresses and dolls, but she'd been happy out with the horses and hay. A farm girl through and through, until she'd discovered computers.

Malcolm grinned. "Hey. Take it from somebody who was undercover for two years. You can become anybody you want. Or, you can decide that you don't like to shop and iron and just be you." He stood and tapped the top of her head. "I like the you that you are." Then he disappeared.

She turned back to her computers, her chest warming. How odd was it that a wounded and scarred ex-cop who ranked around ten on the dangerous scale had become her best friend? Smiling, she reached for the last taco.

After a day reading through the copy of Sean Banaghan's evidence journal, Raider's temples ached and his eyes burned. He needed a decent night's sleep with no pain or drugs. He sat at the far end of the conference table from

Angus, who'd kicked his head back and gone to sleep about an hour earlier. His light snoring competed with Roscoe's snores in the far corner. Every once in a while, one of them would let out a whimper.

Wolfe loped inside, munching on a Rice Krispies treat left by Malcolm. "Nari had a date and Malcolm walked her out. Brigid said she'll be ready to give a report in just a second." He pulled out a seat.

Brigid followed, her laptop in one hand and a treat in the other. Her eyes were bloodshot and her face wan, and she'd tied her thick hair on top of her head. Dark red curls cascaded down on either side of her face, giving her a fragile, feminine look. "Okay. I'm ready to talk. I found so much." In contrast to her eyes, her voice was animated.

His body stopped aching and started humming. Her natural scent wafted toward him, and he straightened in his chair.

She sat between him and Wolfe, typing on her laptop with one hand while eating the Rice Krispies treat with the other. "I had to create a diagram, and I hope this helps." Finishing the treat, she leaned over and gently prodded Force in the shoulder. "Angus? Let's go over this, and then we'll get you home."

Force opened his eyes and focused on the screen without moving a muscle. "Thanks for the hard work today, Bridge."

Her smile was cute. "Any time," she said. A series of numbers came up first on the screen. "First of all, this is rough, but I've created false bank accounts in the Caymans that total a hundred million under several fake corporation names." She swallowed. "There's no real money there, but you can make a false transfer and not get caught for a day. Hopefully."

She was the best, so Raider nodded. "I'll make it work."

"I hope so." She typed more. Then a cloud chart came

up on the screen. "I know this is goofy, but go with me here. The yellow clouds are known businesses of the Coonan organization, and the blue clouds are businesses that are or have been associated with Senator Tyson."

Raider studied the intricate chart showing clouds connected to more clouds connected to even more. "I take it the green clouds are where the two connect?"

"Yes. For instance, the Coonans purchased several old apartment buildings in a run-down area of Johnstown, and at that time Tyson was a county commissioner who voted to rezone the area to commercial instead of residential. The Coonans then tore down the buildings and built businesses." She sighed. "There are tons of examples here. Tyson went from being a lawyer to a hearing examiner to a county commissioner to a senator, and now he's running for president."

There were connections upon connections. "Anything illegal?" Raider asked.

She pursed her lip, her expression thoughtful. "I think there's a comprehensive pattern here that nobody has added up before, and it doesn't look good. But as for evidence of an actual crime? I haven't found it yet." She typed more, and a list of business names came up. "These are parent and foreign corporations that at one time had something to do with either organization but now are defunct. This one paid for Tyson's college and law school tuition with a scholarship program and then just disappeared." Her brow furrowed. "I'd love to tie it to the Coonans but haven't been able to do so yet."

Man, she was impressive. To do all of this in one day was amazing. "Nice job," he murmured.

She blushed a dusky rose and typed more. "Okay. This one is of the Coonan organization, in and of itself. These are the companies I've traced to them so far that deal with motels, bars, restaurants, laundromats, and even a couple of art galleries. Easy laundering opportunities. I've sent you all a report on this."

Okay. Now she was just turning him on. Raider adjusted his jeans. Smart girls. The best. "I can't believe you did all of this in one day." Her analytical skills intrigued the hell out of him.

She kept her gaze on the screen. "You need to study all of that before tomorrow." Then she typed more. "Here are all of the possible crimes, arrests, and interviews of Eddie and his closest enforcers. You'll notice a lack of evidence and convictions, but read them through."

Angus scrubbed both hands down his face. "How many reports did you generate?"

"Five." She typed more. "Here's a detailed timeline of Senator Tyson's life, missing women, and any hint that he was involved in the disappearances. During his time in law school and New York, I discovered travel itineraries for Eddie Coonan to wherever Tyson was at the time."

Wolfe leaned forward. "That's excellent."

"But not evidence of wrongdoing," she countered, her shoulders hunching.

Raider freaking loved how her mind worked. They had one more night together, and he was going to make sure she knew how amazing he thought she was. "That's four reports."

She nodded and documents flew across the screen. "The fifth report, and it's in all of your inboxes. A rundown on human trafficking and possible transportation and destinations, taken from that sheet I memorized at Eddie's." She ground a fist into her eye. "I need lubricating drops for my eyes. Keep forgetting to buy them."

Raider stood. "It's time for some sleep. I'll be here at five in the morning to get wired up again before flying to Boston."

She closed her laptop, her face turning pale. "That's the

other thing. I've tried everything all day to figure out a way to get into Eddie's computer system, with absolutely no results. I couldn't even get in through his phone, and I couldn't ping him." She looked up, her gaze somber. "He uses some sort of jamming equipment in that computer room. Once you're in there, we won't be able to see or hear anything."

Angus dropped his feet to the ground. "Wonderful."

Raider sighed. Exactly.

Chapter Thirty-Three

Raider hauled Brigid against him as he drove them home, his body settling at having her near. "If something happens tomorrow, I want you to know that the last week has been one of my best in years," he murmured.

She snuggled against him, her eyes shut. "Me too."

The woman sounded exhausted. He parked and lifted her out of the truck, ignoring his protesting shoulder and ribs while striding into the building and up to her apartment. She blinked several times when he set her down, and he couldn't help but slide his mouth against hers. Would she ask him in? He couldn't blame her if it was too much of an emotional risk.

She kissed him back, making a soft sound in her throat that shot right to his cock.

A sound clanked from somewhere in her apartment.

He went from aroused to alarmed in a second, shoving her behind him. His body went on full alert, and his focus narrowed. "Get down the hall."

The door opened, and the silver barrel of a gun emerged from the darkness.

"Down!" He bellowed, charging forward.

He smacked the gun out of his way and tackled the gunman, taking them both down to the floor hard. He grabbed the guy's shoulders and rolled them over, using the asshole as a shield in case there was another attacker. The guy punched Raider in the throat, and Raider secured his legs around his attacker's, pressing his forearm against the guy's neck and yanking his head down with his other hand to cut off the guy's air.

Pain lanced through his head and down his hip, but he let adrenaline shove it away. No pain. Only fight.

The attacker flopped against him like a landed trout. He was dressed in a silk suit with a tie that bunched up beneath Raider's chin. Was it one of the mob guys? How had they found him?

The hard tile bit into Raider's back, and he held on tighter.

"Raider!" Brigid yelled, flipping on the entryway light.

"Get out of here," he snapped, looking frantically around for another attacker. His gaze caught on a second man, this one leaning against the kitchen counter. His suit was a worn brown and his shoes scuffed with age. "Agent Fields?" he coughed out. The older agent with the grizzled salt-and-pepper beard just nodded.

Brigid shut the door and looked from one to the other. "Um."

Raider released his hold and shoved over the unconscious body of Agent Rutherford. The younger agent had blond hair and wore expensive suits. Guy hadn't fought worth shit, though. "What the hell are you two doing here?" Raider shoved himself to his feet and kicked the silver gun toward the living room. The two HDD agents acted as the liaisons between the HDD and the Deep Ops unit, a fact that nobody seemed to like much. As a handler, Raider really didn't like having handlers. Now more than ever.

Pain flooded through Raider once again, and he fought it. This wasn't the time to feel.

Fields finished unwrapping a peppermint candy and popped it in his mouth, eyeing his motionless young partner. "He's supposed to be the best fighter in his generation in hand-to-hand. Apparently not." Even his voice was grizzled, and his eyes had that weary look most agents earned if they survived decades in Homeland Defense.

Raider eyed the prone agent. He was breathing all right but hadn't regained consciousness. "Why did he have a gun pointed at me?"

"Didn't know it was you," Fields said around the peppermint. "We heard Brigid arrive, but there's no peephole, and she didn't come in. So, as usual, Rutherford led with his gun." Fields crunched through the candy. "Apparently that was a mistake." He didn't much sound like he cared one way or the other.

Rutherford groaned but otherwise didn't move.

Facts slammed together with a loud bang in Raider's head. He focused on the redhead, who was eyeing the scene like she wanted to run back out the door. "Brigid?" His voice remained calm and level. "Want to tell me why these two agents are waiting patiently in your apartment?" Fury spiraled from his gut up his esophagus, and he swallowed it back down faster than Fields had eaten the candy.

She bit her lip. "I was going to tell you in the truck, but then you carried me inside, and then I wanted to tell you, but then you kissed me, and, well . . ."

"You kissed her?" Fields snorted, the thick lines at the sides of his eyes crinkling. "Tough duty, Tanaka?"

Raider breathed in and then out deeply, calming every instinct he had to punch the older guy. He looked at Brigid, somewhat surprised when she met his gaze evenly. "So much for trusting your partner, huh?" God, he was a moron. All it took was a pretty face with green eyes, and he'd assumed he knew her—assumed that she was the person he'd read about on paper and then met. Hell. He'd wanted to save her and show her that she could use her skills with computers in an honorable way. His ego had certainly led the way on this one. The woman didn't need him as a savior.

She exhaled loudly, twisted her head as she stared at Rutherford. "Is he going to need medical assistance?"

"No," Raider said shortly, itching to grab the booze he had stashed back at his place. A shot of Jack would go down perfectly right now, but showing that weakness to the HDD agents wasn't going to happen.

In a surprisingly smooth move, Rutherford catapulted to his feet, ducked his head, and rushed at Raider, hitting him hard enough to lift him off his feet.

Ah, hell. Agony zipped through him like knives. Raider slammed his elbows down onto Rutherford's shoulders and angled in, hitting the sides of the agent's neck. Rutherford dropped like a stone, and Raider landed on his feet, leaping between the man and Brigid just in case. He'd choked the guy out; maybe the agent wasn't in his right mind yet.

Rutherford rolled again and stood, but this time, Fields grabbed his arm. "Knock it off," Fields growled. "I ain't taking you to the hospital tonight. Have a big date."

Rutherford straightened to his full six-foot-something height and brushed back his light hair, his eyes throwing daggers. It was the first time Raider had seen the spit-and-polished agent anything but perfectly put together. "At some point, you and I are going to finish this," Rutherford snarled.

Raider lifted a shoulder. "I've been fighting since I was seven years old. Something tells me you haven't." While the guy had decent moves, he'd learned in training and not in reality. Definitely not on the streets. "My shoulder was out of joint yesterday, I have seven stitches in my left hip, ten in my right thigh, the remains of a concussion, and

I just choked you out. If you really want to fight, this is probably your best chance." Man, he hurt right now. Bad.

Rutherford yanked his arm free.

"Everyone calm down," Brigid said, tossing her purse on the back of the sofa. "We're all on the same team."

Rutherford angled his head to see Brigid past Raider. "Don't forget what's at stake here, lady."

Heat spiraled through Raider, and he took a step toward the agent. "You're not threatening her, are you?" He'd be more than happy to choke the asshole out again. Maybe for longer than thirty seconds this time.

"He's not threatening me," Brigid said, moving forward and taking Raider's arm. "Well, that's not true. They threaten me all the time. I've been working with HDD for five years." Her voice lowered to soft and oddly sad.

Raider partially turned toward her, forgetting about the agents. "What about when I picked you up from prison two months ago and brokered such a good deal for you?"

She winced. "Staged. Orange jumpsuit and all." Her eyes glowed a dark green. "I mean, I did get in trouble hacking five years ago, and those records are accurate. But instead of going to prison, I made a deal with the HDD that I'd work for them instead. I was undercover for another case in the prison when Force found out about me and made the request for me to join the Deep Ops team."

She was a spy? A damn spy?

Agent Fields sighed. "Nobody trusts Force, and even though we have Nari on the team, we figured having one more mole wouldn't hurt. Brigid's job is to report back on everyone, especially Force. You know he's nuts, right?"

Raider took a step back from her, and her hand dropped to her side. Red hazed his vision, and he cleared it without changing his expression. "Why not just tell us the truth?"

Rutherford snorted. "Seriously? You're the crappiest band of misfits ever seen, and as soon as Force figures out his ghost isn't real, you're being disbanded. The only reason you're in place, Agent Tanaka, is because Force wanted you there. The juice you think you have at HDD isn't there any longer."

Raider swallowed. His ego was taking such a beating from every direction, he might have to rethink his vow to the damn agency.

Fields nodded. "Sleeping with the wrong woman can have worse consequences than you think. You have some seriously high-up enemies, my friend."

"We're supposed to fail," Raider said slowly, losing any illusion of elite status. He was just another agent, a cog in the wheel. Oh, he might be good at his job, but apparently that didn't mean shit. "Force is being appeased until we fail bad enough that even he won't have enough friends to keep the Deep Ops unit open."

"Yep," Rutherford said cheerfully. "It was a shock when the unit actually prevented the bombings weeks ago. Who knew? But you're one mission away from failure."

Fields sighed. "I'm sorry about this, Agent Tanaka. But you have to see how desperate Force is to find a dead guy, how lost Malcolm West is after leaving the police force, how irritated Nari is at being in the unit, and how shit-assed crazy Clarence Wolfe is. How could you think this was anything other than temporary?" His voice held so much sympathy, Raider wanted to puke.

It hit him then. While the leaders in the HDD wanted them to fail, they didn't have the power to make them stop. "Ah, hell. Lassiter really is alive." Force was correct, or no way would the HDD be allowing such a group to exist. "You're afraid Force will go public with that news, and that maybe, just maybe, people will believe him." It was a risk, either way. But putting Force in place with a bungling group that was bound to fail made for a better government plan. Maybe Miss A had been wrong. Perhaps he should've gone the other route.

No. Miss A was never wrong.

Brigid faltered next to his side. "I'm sorry I couldn't tell you the truth."

"How long?" Raider asked quietly, his chest aching more than the other injuries.

She blinked. "How long, what?"

It wasn't any of his business, but he wanted the full story. "How long do you have to continue your work for the HDD as your plea deal?"

She blinked and looked at Fields. "There wasn't a time limit."

So this had been hanging over her head for five years? The woman was too smart for that. "Your lawyer really sucked," Raider muttered. "The deal I thought I brokered for you was much better."

Her expression cleared. "I didn't get a lawyer. Federal law, treason, etc. They gave me two choices—prison or the HDD." She glared at Rutherford. "Let's just say they were very convincing."

Rutherford smiled, showing perfectly even white teeth. "We do our best."

Raider's fingers curled into a fist. One punch, and those teeth would fly across the room. All of them.

Rutherford's eyes gleamed a deep blue. "This is confidential, Agent Tanaka. I hope you understand that, if you want to keep your job."

Apparently his job wasn't worth what he'd thought it was. "If I've finally read this all right, I'm on my way out, anyway." He slid his phone from his back pocket and hit speed dial.

"Force," Force answered, his voice distracted.

"No." Brigid moved toward Raider, reaching for his arm.

He smiled. "Hey, Force, it's Raider. Apparently Brigid

is under servitude to the HDD, we've been set up, and everyone wants us to fail. How about we meet for a drink tomorrow after I survive infiltrating Eddie's organization? I can happily explain everything to you, and by the way, I'm pretty sure your dead serial killer is actually alive." He clicked off before Force could answer. Then he turned and looked directly at Brigid. "Like I said. There has to be somebody you can be totally honest with in this business."

She swallowed, her skin so pale her lips looked white. "I didn't have a choice."

There was always a choice. He'd been her handler for two months, making a complete ass of himself as he tried to help her find the right path. She could've confided in him at any point. They were a team, a complete unit, and they were supposed to be working together. And, even more important, they'd slept together. That meant something to him, if not to her. "Well, this does make the mission easier," he murmured.

She faced him bravely. "Meaning what?"

"I thought you'd be worried about me tomorrow, so I was worried about you." He tried to gentle his voice but didn't have any luck. "Guess we're just playing games here. Good to know."

"You want to play games with me? Oh, bring it on." Her chin lifted, and damn if there wasn't challenge in those emerald eyes. "Give it your best shot, Tanaka."

Chapter Thirty-Four

God save her from men and their egos. She kept her gaze on Raider but spoke to Agent Fields. "You're up-to-date on all of the escapades, especially since you're the ones who secured my dad from the hospital. I have nothing new to report on Angus Force's search for Lassiter, Wolfe's craziness, Mal's PTSD, or Nari's snooping. Now go away so Raider and I can fight."

Raider's chin lowered, giving him the look of a sleek tiger about to pounce. "The last guy I fought was knocked out. You sure you want to play?"

Heat pooled in her abdomen and her breath quickened. Yeah, his sense of control and obvious intelligence, not to mention the sexy good looks, had intrigued her from the beginning. But this sense of danger, of a rebel just beneath those nice clothes, had drawn her quicker than a calf to its first salt lick. She could sense the fiery deadliness at home in him, and deviant that she was, she wanted to feel the flame. "Oh, I want to play," she murmured.

Fields cleared his throat and clapped his partner on the back. "I think that's our cue to leave. Like, right now."

Raider's gaze met hers, those black eyes blazing. It was as if the other two men had disappeared.

Until Rutherford opened his mouth again. "Banaghan? Don't forget I could have you back in a cell on an island in the middle of nowhere with the snap of my fingers."

Raider pivoted in a purely graceful arc and punched the agent in the middle of his face as if aiming for the refrigerator behind him. A loud crack echoed, the man fell back, and Fields caught him before he could impact the tile again. "You ever threaten her again, and I'll rip your throat right out," Raider said. The threat was all the more frightening for the calm and centered way it was delivered.

Brigid took a step back, her heart pounding from slow to painfully fast.

Rutherford struggled to stand on his own, both hands covering his nose. Blood dripped down his lips and through his fingers.

"Let's go. Now." Fields dragged his young partner to the door, opened it, and quickly disappeared.

Brigid wanted to follow. Oh, she'd thought of challenging Raider, but right now, he wasn't himself. At all. "You just assaulted a federal agent," she snapped, heat sliding up her spine.

"You should leave, or I'll assault another one," he snapped back, his lids half-lowered.

"You're in my apartment," she snapped. Then she blinked. "You'd hit me?"

Slowly, so slow and sexy, he shook his head. "No. I definitely wouldn't hit you." Then he cocked an eyebrow. "Or maybe I would."

Her breath caught. "What do you mean by that?"

"Girl"—his Southern drawl rolled out so fast it thickened the air in the room—"I've never met a woman in more need of a good spanking than you."

Her mouth dropped open so fast her skin stretched. He did *not* just say that. There was *no way* he'd just said that.

His smile was pure masculine sin. "So that's how to get you to stop talking."

Her lips snapped shut. Spirals of heat, sharp and tingling, circled down her torso to land hard in her abdomen. Her panties grew wet. This should not be turning her on, but right now, everything about him was just so wrong and sexy and somehow right.

Her body was a moron. "I signed a contract and couldn't tell you the truth." They had to find a common ground; surely he'd understand that she'd had to follow the rules.

"I don't give a fuck about contracts right now," he growled. "Some things, including friendship and becoming lovers, trump all contracts. You lied to me."

Yeah, his rules were all his own. Not society's. Why had it taken her so long to realize that fact? "I like you."

Instead of softening, his expression sharpened. "I don't like you very much right now, Brigid. Tell me to leave, and I will. Now."

Her gaze dropped to the obvious bulge in his jeans. Her breasts tightened. "You don't want to leave." A slight tone of triumph entered her voice.

"Didn't say I wanted to leave. I said a smart girl would toss me out. Right now." He crossed his arms, pulling his T-shirt tight over those strong chest muscles. "It's your choice, but if you let me stay, the talking will be kept to a minimum. I want you, there's no hiding that. But I don't trust you, and I ain't going gentle."

That drawl. Solid, authentic, Southern sin. A shiver took her, and she barely hid it. "I've never said I wanted gentle." She was caught in the moment, in the challenge of handling his anger. Even so, in the very back of her mind, a warning hummed. This was no ordinary man, and she was out of her depth.

Warnings had never worked before with her.

"If you're sure, take off your clothes." Lust and anger burned in his eyes.

"No." The word came as naturally as breathing.

He smiled, and desire beat harder inside her. "Your legs are twitching. You want to run? Want me to catch you?" He looked like he wanted to hunt her down.

Yeah, she'd like that. But she looked around the tiny apartment. "There's nowhere to run."

"Exactly," he murmured.

Her legs trembled this time, and she flashed back to when they'd been wrapped around his strong hips. "I want you, but I think we should handle some of the anger between us first." She wasn't a complete dumbass.

"Oh. I can fuck you with lies between us but not anger?" A muscle ticked in his jaw.

Yep. That aroused her even more. She was so screwed up. "Tell you what, Ace. A small wager, if you will." Her voice came out all breathy, darn it. She angled into the living room.

"What's that?" Excitement darkened his high cheekbones.

"You have five seconds to catch me. You win, do what you want with me." Even the words weakened her knees. "You lose, and we sit and talk out your feelings for an hour. A full hour."

"My feelings? I'm pissed. There they are. All out." He leaned back against the counter in a casual move. "But I like the first part of the wager. So, I'm in."

"Good." She moved farther away, putting the sofa and coffee table between them. "Go."

In a surge of graceful power, he came right over the sofa, as she'd known he would. Instead of dodging to the side, she lifted the cheap table, let him plow into it, and shoved him back onto the sofa. She paused in one second of triumph before pivoting to run, making a fatal mistake. In one smooth motion, he flipped the table over, came at her, and pinned her against the wall with the table legs on either side of her. "Five," he murmured, his face close to hers.

Her heart hammered so quickly her skin hurt. "I think that was six." It wasn't. It was five seconds.

For the briefest of moments, those dark eyes softened. "We both know it was five seconds, Brigid. No more lying."

"Fine," she burst out. "No more lying. But no stupid spanking, either." The words were sexy, the reality not so much.

"You said I could do anything with you," he reminded her, his breath minty on her face. "Remember?"

She winced, even as her body went full burn and ready for him. Think, damn it. "We have a dangerous mission tomorrow. Surely you don't want to spend tonight in such a way?"

He threw the table to the left, where it hit the wall by the door and splintered into several pieces. "No. I want to spend it like this." Moving in, he took her chin and leaned down to kiss her. Hard and fast, anger and power in the movement. In the firmness of his touch and the depth of his kiss.

He was everything and more, not holding back in the slightest. It was how she'd wanted him from the first time she'd seen him all uptight in that nice suit. But now, oh now. She wanted it all. Not just him physically, but the rest of him. He'd love as intensely and completely as he did everything else.

But it was too late. She'd lied to him, and he was all about control and loyalty.

His tongue thrust into her mouth, tasting of mint and Raider. He dominated in that simple touch, curling her toes and escalating her need to unbelievable heights. She lifted her hands and immersed them in his thick hair, curling her fingers and digging deep.

He growled into her mouth, and she quivered, pressing her body against his harder one. The power there, the danger, she'd seen it firsthand. Every time somebody had challenged him, had threatened her, he'd taken them down with moves as graceful as they were deadly.

His hands clamped on her hips, and he twisted her, spinning her to face the wall.

She gasped, her hands pressed against the faded wallpaper. Turning her head, she rested her heated cheek against the coolness.

He tilted her head even more to the side, elongating her neck. His breath blew over her ear, and she shivered as his talented mouth slid down. A lick of his tongue to the sensitive skin where neck met shoulder spiked more arousal in her.

With one smooth and oddly gentle movement, he pulled her shirt over her head. Then his hands, those calloused, strong, big hands, cupped her breasts over her cotton bra. Her nipples hardened, and her knees weakened, forcing her to lean back against him. He pinched her through the material, the bite just enough to shoot shockwaves to her clit. She gasped, her eyes closing. "Shouldn't we go to the bedroom?"

His mouth was suddenly at her ear again, while he ground his erection against her backside. "Bad girls who lie don't get the bedroom."

Oh man, she might orgasm right now from the dark tenor of that Southern timbre. "What do they get?" she asked breathlessly.

"Bent over." He snagged her around the waist, pivoted, and bent her over the sofa.

She jerked her head to the side to avoid suffocating in the cushion. "This is a furnished rental."

"So?" He planted one hand over the small of her back to hold her in place and loudly unbuckled his belt.

What was her point? That hand was so damn warm. "Um, mice often live in rentals. They love couches." She couldn't grasp a complete thought.

He paused. "You don't have mice."

"You don't know that," she groaned, only pure will keeping her from burying her face in the cushions. "The hantavirus is a killer."

His bark of laughter was as unexpected as how quickly he lifted her and strode for the bedroom. "You are such a pain in my ass."

Was that affection? She could swear there had been affection in that pained statement. Then the world spun, and she found herself flat on her back. His big hands yanked off her jeans and panties before he lifted her and planted her squarely on her hands and knees.

Facing the wall.

"Oh," she murmured. Well, all right. He had mentioned helm of the bobsled that first night. Amusement took her, battling with the overwhelming desire. "Should this be so much fun?" It took her a second to realize she'd spoken out loud.

"No." A hard smack to her butt punctuated his response, but that was definitely humor in his tone. Heat spread from his palm across her back and down her abdomen to land between her legs.

Her head dropped and her body burned for him. If they could laugh together, even while fighting and having wild sex, they had a chance. For what, she wasn't sure. But it was there, and she'd figure it out later. His clothing rustled, and then his hand slipped between her legs.

"Ah, Irish." He bit the back of her shoulder, not so gently. "You're wet and ready. Like getting spanked?"

"I liked your laughter," she said, giving him the truth and moving against his hand. He felt so good.

He was silent for a moment, stroking her even higher. "Then I'll laugh more often."

So sweet. Even pissed at her, he had a sweetness hidden in all that toughness that shot right to her heart. And even now, he was taking time, making sure she was ready for him. Whether he liked it or not, Raider Tanaka was a good guy.

"You're ready," he rumbled, sliding his hand around her body to press her neck to the bed. "Down and vulnerable, baby." A condom wrapper crinkled.

She didn't feel vulnerable. Oh, she was open to him and unable to move, but that hungry and dark tone promised she had power. He pressed against her, and she held her breath, her eyes rolling back in her head when he pressed the tip of his penis inside her.

So big and full.

Then he drove into her, his hands clamping on her hips to hold her in place. She lost her breath, her eyes opening wide. God, it was so much. No hesitation, no fear.

"More," she whispered.

"Gladly." He gave her no more time to become accustomed to him and started thrusting, hard and fast, a nearly impossible tempo.

Pleasure surged through her, rolling an orgasm quick and burning through her body, making her climb higher for the next one. He leaned over her, his tight stomach warm on her back, his fingers threading through hers on the bedspread. And somehow, he powered harder into her. Deeper.

She arched her back to take more of him.

Her breath caught, the world paused, and then she exploded. She cried out and stiffened, riding out the sharp waves into unreal pleasure. He kept hammering, his powerful thrusts lifting her hips, prolonging her climax until she couldn't take any more. Then his fingers tightened on hers and he tensed, whispering her name as he came.

She blinked, completely overcome. What now? Where did this leave them?

Chapter Thirty-Five

Raider drove the rental care toward Eddie's bar, conducting a quick final check on the camera and audio belt. His burner phone was on speaker on the seat next to him. "You hear and see?"

"Affirmative," Wolfe said from the motel room down the street. Force's head had been too damaged to fly, and the gnarly doctor had been quite insistent he stay in DC. When Nari chimed in, Force had growled but agreed. "You sure you want to take a gun in? They'll probably confiscate it," Wolfe said.

"Maybe." It was a gun he could afford to lose. "Eddie and I bonded the other day, so maybe I can keep it."

Wolfe sighed. "Fair enough. I can be there in minutes. Happy hunting." He clicked off.

Raider pushed a button and erased the last call. He tried to settle into character, but his mind kept going to Brigid and the night before. He'd pushed her hard, and she'd met him every time. They'd gotten only an hour or so of sleep, but his body had never felt so relaxed. Even his injuries weren't bothering him, he was so satisfied.

Physically. Emotionally, he'd shut down. Oh, he liked her, and he'd have sex with her if she wanted, but his time of trusting her was over. She was loyal to HDD, her bosses, and not to their unit or him. It was that simple. He'd lost.

Never in his life had he had so much fun while having excellent sex, and he'd been angry with her. Still was. What was it about the sexy redhead that just tunneled beyond his good intentions? She'd lied to him, which meant he couldn't trust her, so why the hell was he wanting to get back into bed with her right now? Maybe take her to a movie? Sure, he got it. The HDD had scared the heck out of her, and she had signed a contract.

Why didn't she know she could trust him? She should have. If nothing else than to get her a better contract.

Damn it. He had to get his head back into the game. He parked out front of the bar, squared his shoulders, and sank himself into the persona he'd created. Every other concern in the world faded away. Nothing existed but right now.

Adopting his swagger, he stepped from the car and crossed the wet ground, glancing down the sidewalk. Nothing out of place. He pushed open the door and strutted inside the darkened interior where several down-and-out-looking men hunched over drinks at the bar.

The bald bartender gave him a chin jerk in acknowledgment.

So Raider continued past the patrons to the back door, which opened immediately.

Eddie motioned him inside, finishing a phone call and sliding his phone into his back pocket. A bruised lump was raised over his right eye, and an already yellowing bruise covered the entire left side of his face. He looked Raider over. "You look like shit."

Raider grimaced. "It's been a rough week." To say the least. "You're the one who tried to blow me out of a boat."

"Yeah. Sorry about that." Eddie clapped an arm around Raider's shoulders and led him toward the poker table. Josh stood post at the back door, his expression inscrutable as usual. Eddie steered Raider beyond the table and to the one door they hadn't gone through together yet. He punched numbers into the keypad, shielding it with his body. The door clicked open. "After you."

Man, he hoped he didn't get shot. Raider strode inside and stopped short at seeing the neat bottles of alcohol lined on metal shelves. "All right. We drinking?"

Eddie shut the door and snorted, taking out his silver gun. "You armed?"

"Yeah." Raider turned to face the threat. "So?"

Eddie shrugged. "Just checking. Do you have the account numbers?"

"I do." Raider handed over a folded piece of paper with the false accounts Brigid had built. Hopefully she was as good as advertised.

"All right." Eddie studied him and then tucked his gun away again. "You're gonna like this."

Doubtful.

Eddie looked up at a bottle of vodka on the top shelf. "Open."

What the heck? A wisp sounded, and one side of the far shelves of booze slid outward, revealing an opening. "Nice," Raider said, meaning it.

"Just wait." Eddie led the way into a small room surrounded by concrete. A safe had been built into the wall in the far side, which explained the hidden room.

Raider looked around. "We're getting into a safe?" The door snicked closed behind him, obviously controlled somewhere else.

"No." Eddie waited for a moment, and the smooth concrete wall rolled to the side. "This way."

Raider followed him down a flight of stairs to another doorway at the bottom. His heart rate increased as he studied the devices around it. "Those are bombs."

"Yep." Eddie punched in numbers on another keypad,

the door opened, and he walked inside. Raider shook his head, gathered his courage, said a silent prayer, and followed the mobster. Once past the doorway, he stopped short, letting out an involuntary whistle. “Holy cow.” He looked sideways at Eddie. “This is like NASA.” And it was.

Eddie shut the door. “Thanks.”

They stood on a small dais above several rows of computers in front of wide screens set along the walls. Several techs typed away, a couple wearing headsets. The room was silent, save for the sound of keyboards and a slight hum. “Brigid would love this,” Raider said, reaching for his burner phone.

Eddie stopped him with a head shake. “The second you left the poker room, all electronics jammed. You can’t call her from here.”

That’s what he’d figured. Raider feigned disappointment. “She’d love this setup.”

“Well, if this works out and I don’t shoot you in the head, then you can invite her next time. She makes websites and shit like that, right?” Without waiting for an answer, Eddie strode down the steps to the main floor. “Any chance you share her?”

“No chance,” Raider said, throwing a little more Brooklyn into his tone.

“No problem.” Eddie held up a hand in surrender and then strode over to a twenty-something kid dressed in khaki pants, a button-down, and metal-rimmed glasses, to hand over the folded paper. “This is Rex. It’s his domain.”

The kid nodded bleached blond hair and took the paper from Eddie. “Hey.” He leaned down and typed in the series of numbers.

Raider moved toward him. “Wait a minute. I need to understand what you’re doing.”

Rex scoffed. “Right.”

Raider shook his head. “I mean it.”

Eddie sighed. "That's fair. All right." He looked down at the paper. "It appears you have seven accounts here, and we'll transfer funds into, what? Say fifty of our businesses? Some shell and some real?"

"Probably about a hundred businesses, since this is a new venture," Rex said evenly, typing away. "No offense, but no trust yet."

Eddie grinned. "Oh, we can trust Raider, here. He killed a cop for me yesterday, and I'm sure he'd hate for me to let that news out."

"You have no proof," Raider countered, playing along.

Rex snorted, a sinus-filled sound. "I could create some in about five minutes while role playing any online game with my other hand."

"Cute," Raider said, his chin up. "Now explain what you're doing to earn your thirty percent here, or I'm gone."

"Fifty percent," Eddie said, watching the numbers flash across the screen.

Raider didn't even try to fake surprise. It was expected. "We had a deal," he reminded Eddie.

Eddie shrugged. "You didn't really think I'd take this kind of chance for anything less than half, did you?" He shook his head. "And now that we're in bed after the cop killing, well. I'm taking fifty, or I'm taking all of it and calling it a day." He jerked his head toward Jonny P and another armed foot soldier on the other side of the dais. They'd been out of sight before Raider had descended the steps.

Raider sighed. "Fine. Just explain what's happening. Then I'll decide if I want to invest the rest of my funds with you." He leaned in, keeping his voice hushed. "And don't forget that I have the other half of the journal and evidence, Eddie."

Eddie flashed his teeth. "I haven't forgotten. But I went

through what you gave me, and none of it is catastrophic. Especially after all this time."

Raider let his own teeth shine. "You didn't think I'd give you the good stuff up front, did you?" Yeah, he liked throwing Eddie's words back at him.

"No." Eddie straightened. "Okay. Rex?"

Rex typed more, read, typed more, and then nodded. "The money is there, and I've traced at least two of the deposits to the Lagaretoes in Thailand and the Norts in India." He looked over his shoulder. "You're dealing in more than drugs and antiquities, my friend."

Raider let his face go stony. He couldn't overplay his hand. Those trails had been added by Brigid early this morning after Angus had come up with the idea. Perhaps they could get Eddie to give them the information they needed. "Wrong."

Eddie eyed him. "I know those organizations. You're part of the game."

Fuck, Raider hated that term when used with human trafficking. None of this was a game. He was going to take these assholes down if it was the last thing he ever did. "I don't know you well enough to discuss my other businesses, Eddie." He didn't have to force hardness into his voice this time.

Eddie's gaze turned calculating. "Maybe we can do more than launder money together."

That was the plan. "We'll see." Raider pointed toward the screen. "Now explain what's happening." Eddie had just received confirmation that the money was dirty, so if he was ever going to trust, it was now. Before he found out the actual money wasn't going to arrive in the other accounts. For now, it was all numbers on a screen.

Eddie nodded. "All right. Here's the deal. We'll take your funds and funnel them through our businesses in small amounts, watching for any alarm bells on the way.

For this kind of transaction, we'll use hair salons, a couple of nonprofit organizations, several churches, art galleries, and so on. It should take about a week or two, and then we'll form several corporations together and plant seed money. You can use the corporations to create new businesses or cash out. But I figure you have enough cash."

"I do." Raider scratched his head as if the concept was overwhelming, which it would be to anybody unfamiliar with laundering money.

"We do cash differently, for obvious reasons," Rex said while still typing away.

"Right." Eddie rolled his shoulder back and winced. "That tumble down the mountain yesterday was a bruiser." He rubbed his upper arm. "How's your head?"

Perfect opening. "It's fine. A little dizziness, but nothin' I can't handle." As if to emphasize his point, Raider leaned back against the stair railing.

"Tough man." Eddie's nod came with a grin of what appeared to be approval. "Okay. Back to business. With cash, we obviously need to take more time and use even more businesses. It's easier to keep from getting caught, but it's a lot harder to accomplish for that reason. How much cash do you want to move?"

"Let's just work on one project at a time," Raider said, counting the computers in the room. He needed to get his watch into one at some point. There were several empty consoles, but he couldn't just sit down and start typing, could he?

"Fair enough," Eddie said. "By the way, where's the evidence I want?" His eyebrows wriggled. "Does the pretty redhead have it?"

Raider scoffed. "Of course not. It's still with my friend, who's unreachable."

Eddie shrugged. "Yeah, it's not the insurance policy you think. I'm not too worried about the evidence."

In other words, Eddie might still shoot him in the head. But the senator was worried, and that might or might not matter to Eddie.

Raider glanced at Jonny P, who hadn't stopped watching him since he'd arrived. The guy definitely wanted to take a piece or two out of Raider's hide. "I think he likes me."

Eddie smiled.

"What's up with the explosives outside the door?" Raider had clocked enough to blow up the entire building.

"The whole room on every side is wired," Eddie said easily. "Can't have this kind of evidence in the cops' hands, now can we?" He shot Jonny P a hard look. "We had a cop infiltrate our organization a year or so ago, and I've never forgotten the betrayal."

Every cell in Raider's body went cold as ice. "Is that so? What happened to the guy?"

"Jonny P took care of him," Eddie said, gesturing carelessly.

Raider barely kept a snarl from ripping his lip. "Interesting. How did you find out? I'm always watching over my shoulder with my enterprises."

"People make mistakes. Anybody leading two lives always has a trail back to their real one." Eddie watched a big screen in the corner. "For instance, your woman's father. He's on the run, but I'm gonna find him."

No, he wasn't. But that didn't mean he'd fail to find Brigid's real life. "I'm sure you will," Raider said. "Unless, of course, those explosives accidentally detonate. That happens, you know."

Eddie just grinned.

Rex's typing didn't pause. Apparently the computer guru had accepted the risk of being blown up with the job. How much did a guy like him make, anyway? It couldn't be enough to remain in bed with Eddie, but once in, always in. "How long is this going to take?" Raider asked, drawing in a large breath as if in pain. Which he actually was.

Eddie read the screen. "We're staying here until Rex confirms the transfers. Should only be a couple of hours?"

Rex nodded.

Raider cleared his throat. "In that case, I'm taking a seat." He chose a chair a couple down from Rex in front of a PC with a smaller screen. "Any chance this thing has solitaire on it?"

Chapter Thirty-Six

Brigid paced the small computer room, her eyes gritty after a long day of working on the computer, reading and listening to all of the evidence her dad had collected, and trying to forget the fact that Raider was in a secured room with Eddie Coonan. Hopefully. Or maybe he'd been shot and left for dead.

She eyed the plain black coffee Wolfe had left for her that morning before leaving with Raider. No whipped cream. No sprinkles. She'd shoved down tears the second she'd seen it. Oh, why hadn't Wolfe just yelled at her? It'd be so much easier to handle than the plain, unflavored coffee.

Apparently the soldier was angry after hearing of her betrayal. She gulped down more tears.

Angus Force had been absent all day on doctor's orders. Apparently his internal bleeding had gotten worse, and he'd had to visit the hospital late the night before. Now he was cranky and at home, according to Nari. Brigid felt a little guilty that she was happy not to face him yet.

Her phone dinged, and she lunged for it on the desk, lifting it. "Raider? Hello?"

"Helloooo, Irish Rose," Raider drawled, his voice low and slurred.

She sat down, her entire body stiffening. "Raider? You okay?"

"You know what I like? You." He snorted out a laugh. "Usually. I mean, not right now, because you lied. But you make the cutest noises when you sleep. I hope we can sleep together again."

She looked around the vacant room. "What's happening right now?"

"Hey—" There was a scuffle and Raider's swearing dimmed in volume.

"Brigid? It's Wolfe."

Relief filled her so quickly she almost slid off the chair to the hard floor. "Thank goodness. What's going on?" Her mind kicked back into gear. "Is he *drunk*?"

"Um, yeah. Completely snockered," Wolfe affirmed, amusement lightening his usually gritty tone. "He and Eddie tied one on, bonding all afternoon. From what he spilled on his shirt, it's a combination of tequila, Irish whiskey, and I'm guessing peppermint schnapps."

Brigid winced. "Ugh. That's a fatal combination."

In the background, Raider could be heard singing "Danny Boy." She pressed her ear harder to the phone. "You know, I think this is the first time I've heard that song performed with a Southern accent." Actually, the man had a pretty decent voice. Maybe she could get him to play the guitar and sing for her when he got home. If he ever forgave her, that was.

"Dude, shut up," Wolfe said, his voice directed away from the phone. "We don't want to get kicked out."

Raider's voice lowered in volume, and he moved on to a Beyoncé song.

"Damn it," Wolfe muttered. "I may have to just knock him out. You never should've lied to us."

"I know," Brigid said, her gaze straying to the plain coffee that was now ice cold. "You can yell at me later.

For now, don't hit him. He's had too many hits to the head lately. A skull can only take so much."

"I don't yell," Wolfe muttered.

Yeah. He just gave mean coffee. She glanced at the computer. "Are you guys coming home?"

"No. We're sending the USB to you via courier, and we already dropped it off. Should be there in just over an hour," Wolfe said.

Her chin dropped. "He managed to get the information?"

"He did," Wolfe affirmed as Raider crooned a Kenny Chesney song about better boats in the background. "He played a computer game for a while, faked dropping a bunch of stuff, and shoved the flash drive in the right port. He managed to type and get what you wanted—we think. As soon as you confirm, we'll plan from there."

Okay. Good. Excellent, really. "Then he and Eddie drank all afternoon." Their lives were weird.

"Yes." Wolfe sounded bored. "As soon as you know anything, call me. I'd love to get out of here." Something clanged, and Wolfe swore. Loudly.

"Hey, baby. Put a ring on it," Raider sang into the phone. "We're engaged, and I haven't given you a ring yet. That was an oversight. I bet you'd like diamonds and emeralds. You know, something Irish and pretty but not in the way when you type." A ruckus sounded. "Knock it off, Wolfe," Raider slurred. "All the single ladies, you know, all the single ladies—"

"Damn it." Wolfe growled, apparently once again having taken possession of the phone. "Call me with an update." He disengaged the call.

Brigid drew the phone from her head and just looked at it.

Nari poked her head in the doorway. "Heard the phone. News?"

Brigid jerked her attention back to the moment. "Yes.

Raider is all right, and the flash drive should be here in just over an hour." She looked up at the shrink, wondering if she could come clean before Raider or Force told on her. "He did it."

Nari smiled. "Excellent. He's good at the job." She opened the door wider and handed across some notes. "Angus and I have been studying Senator Tyson and trying to profile him a little bit. Here's what we have so far, but it'd be nice to meet the guy once. Just to get a feeling for him."

Brigid would rather use a Commodore VIC-20 for a month than meet that man in person. "Think we should bring Dana in? She's been tracking down everything she can about him."

Nari slowly nodded. "Sure. Let's wait and see what you find on the flash drive and then go from there. I do think we'll bring her in, but let's get our ducks in a row first." Her dark gaze narrowed. "You're pale. Everything okay?"

It had been so long since Brigid had spent time with friends. Since she really had a friend. "No."

The elevator dinged and heavy footsteps echoed. "Brigid Banaghan! Get your ass out here," Angus Force bellowed.

Nari jerked around.

Brigid immediately stood, blanching. So much for a reprieve.

Nari stepped out of the doorway, her heels clicking angrily. "What in the hell are you doing out of bed? The hospital only released you about three hours ago."

Brigid fought the temptation to hide and walked out of the room, taking in a furious Angus. He stood tall near his office, his arm in a sling and his hospital wristbands still in place. A bandage covered his left temple, and his face was pale and pinched. "Can we talk about this later?"

Roscoe sat on his haunches, looking from Brigid to

Angus and back. He whined softly. Kat was with Pippa and Malcolm, so at least he was safe from the tirade.

Angus strode into his office, limping only slightly. "Get in here. Now."

She gave a curious-looking Nari an apologetic look and then followed Angus, shutting the door and taking a seat. He remained standing on the other side of his messy desk. "Are you the one who faked your personnel file?"

"Yes," she murmured. "It's easier to remember it if you're the one doing it."

His green eyes darkened. "Do not get cute with me."

She wasn't aiming for cute.

Even battered and bruised, Angus Force was a scary guy. "Tell me all of it. Right now." His voice was low and so soft it sent chills up her back. Would he fire her? Make her leave the team? Panic swirled around in her stomach.

"I was working for a nonprofit fighting child pornography, and I hacked into the wrong computer. All of that is true." She couldn't leave. The team needed her, and she needed them. The thought nearly shocked her into silence. Only the intensity of her boss's expression kept her talking. "But it happened five years ago and not recently."

He swallowed. "You made a deal with the HDD."

"Yes. I've been working for the agency for five years, and we've done some good." There was still so much more to do.

"How'd you end up here?" He didn't move, although all the color had leached out of his rugged face.

She had to physically bite her tongue to keep from suggesting he sit. He'd probably snap her head off if she even tried. "Agent Rutherford came to me and gave me a cover ID. He didn't tell me why, just told me to watch you and the other members of the team and report back." She cleared her throat. "There hasn't been much to report. We've worked hard."

Angus's head lifted. "Have you told them about Roscoe's drinking problem?"

She frowned. "No. Of course not." That was irrelevant.

"What about Wolfe keeping a kitten in his pocket most of the time?"

She shook her head. "No. That has nothing to do with the team." Why was he asking such odd questions?

"What about Nari going on different dates and spending way too much money on shoes?" Angus growled.

Okay. "No. Those are things that friends know about each other. They have nothing to do with a unit or work." She wasn't here to betray anybody.

Angus's nostrils flared. "How about Malcolm? Have you said he balances his time between here and home and works from home a lot to be with Pippa?"

"No." Who the heck cared? "A lot of people telecommute these days." The stubborn male was going to fall down if he didn't sit, but she didn't say a word. A whine sounded, and then a scratch, and the door opened. Roscoe padded in, looked around, and moved to sit by her side, watching Angus.

Angus didn't twitch. "What about me, Brigid? What have you told those bastards about me?"

The words held meaning to him. She could tell. "Just that you work hard and keep a good balance between the Lassiter case and whatever other case we're working on." She leaned in. "I haven't said anything about how grumpy you get about Nari or how you two circle each other." Though what was the deal there, anyway?

His jaw ticked. "What about my drinking?"

"You all drink. It's social and personal and has nothing to do with the job." He was listing the oddities or perceived weaknesses that could hurt the team. "I don't want to do anything to harm anybody here, Angus." She absently patted Roscoe's head, looking for comfort. "Everything I reported back is also in the official reports. I don't want to leave. I like it here." Her voice broke on the last.

"Why?" His voice did not break.

She thought about it, tugging the dog closer. "We're a good team, and we're making a difference. I like everyone." She pressed her lips together and then forced out the words. "It's the first time in forever that I feel like I'm home."

"Did you sleep with Raider?"

Heat circled into her face. "I don't think that's any of your business." She'd pretty much opened herself up to him, and he was still giving her a hard time. Enough was enough. "You have to believe me. I wouldn't hurt the team."

"I don't believe a word you say." He rocked back on his heels and quickly regained his balance, his face still hard.

She didn't say a word. Nope. Not one word about what a stubborn jackass he was being. And his words cut deeper than she would've expected. But she held his gaze.

"Raider said something about coercion," Force snapped.

"Yes," she sighed. "They scared me with treason and Guantanamo and all of that, and I signed an agreement basically saying I'd work for the HDD without an end time, and that they could send me back at any time if I didn't follow directions." Which, frankly, she might have violated by not reporting everything Angus had just asked about. "Rutherford likes to threaten, but Fields is okay."

Angus studied her for several moments, making her feel like a fruit fly on a slide. "I'm a good profiler, and I didn't see that you were a mole. I mean, I thought I got you released and not that you were a plant."

"I'm sorry." She tried to hold his gaze, but it was difficult. The elevator dinged in the other room. "That should be the USB. Do I still have a job or not?"

Nari knocked and poked her head in. "We have a problem."

"Great." Angus limped around the desk and followed

her into the bullpen. "Brigid, your job is temporary. You're almost out of here."

Brigid patted Roscoe and did the same, halting at seeing Rutherford and Fields. Her chest ached. Agent Rutherford had bruises along his neck from having been choked out, in addition to a swollen nose and two black eyes.

"What's going on?" Angus snarled.

Rutherford smiled. "You've been running too many unsanctioned ops, and we're here to pull you back. You are now officially off the Eddie Coonan case. Recall your team members."

Brigid's lungs seized. Called off the case? Why?

Angus stared down both men. Fields looked off to the side, his mouth turned down. Rutherford, the prep-school asshole, met his gaze with triumph. "Who got to HDD?" Angus snapped.

"Watch yourself, Force," Rutherford warned.

Angus set his stance like one of those cowboys in an old Western. "Off the case, huh? Just who exactly has the juice to pull us off like this?"

The senator. The guy who already had an impressive mantle of power. Brigid kept silent. Oh, she had more digging to do. For now, while she still had a job.

Chapter Thirty-Seven

The USB was delivered about thirty minutes after the two agents had left. Brigid took it immediately to the computer room, her mind spinning. Angus had been locked in his office making phone calls, often yelling rather loudly. At least she hadn't been shown the door. Yet.

She inserted the USB, typed in commands, and watched information travel across the screen.

Her door opened, and Angus stalked inside, somehow even grumpier looking and paler than before. "Did Raider get the information?"

"I think so." She pointed to the lines of code. "It's encrypted, and it's going to take some time to decrypt it." She would gladly spend all night on the project. "How did your calls go?"

"Not well. Apparently the senator has some powerful friends. We're supposed to stop working the case immediately, or we're going to get shut down altogether." He wiped a hand across the long bruise on his forehead and then blanched. "Rutherford would love to shut us down."

She looked at the code, needing to decipher it. "You want to back down?"

"Don't know how." His gaze focused again. "Those girls are being brought in two days from now, and I'm not shutting anything down. And you should've made a better deal with HDD—like the one we thought we got for you."

"I know," she sighed. "But I was scared and didn't have a lawyer." Truth be told, she would've done anything to avoid being sent to Guantanamo for treason. "It hasn't been too bad. This is my first major undercover op, and I hate it. I mean, I like the team and my role, but it has totally sucked having to report on you." She swallowed, wanting to ease the pain she saw in his eyes. So she opened her drawer and took out a small bottle. "I sent you the reports a few minutes ago, and this is aspirin, if you'd like some."

He took the bottle but his gaze didn't soften. "You can finish this case, and then you're out. I can't have people I don't trust here." He snapped open the top and downed three pills before handing it back. "We're probably all getting fired, anyway."

"Not if we bust Eddie," she said, using her best old-cop imitation voice.

He didn't even crack a smile. "Nice." He looked at the screen. "How long is it going to take you?"

She turned back to the challenge, her adrenaline starting to flow, tears pricking the back of her eyes. "All night. I'm hoping I can read it by morning, but I can't guarantee it." Though she wouldn't sleep until she had answers for them.

"Okay. What do you need?" he asked.

She blinked. "These computers are all I need."

He planted a heated hand on her shoulder. "Did you eat dinner?"

"Wasn't hungry." Had she eaten all day? She couldn't remember. "I'm fine."

He sighed. "I'll go get food and coffee for you. It's going to be a long night."

She couldn't help it. Tears welled in the back of her eyes, so she kept her gaze averted. "Thank you."

"I need your mind clear so you can work." He leaned away. "In fact, tell me what you're going to do."

His distance hurt. She'd gotten accustomed to being part of the team, and that had been a huge mistake. She tried to clear her head and answer his question. "How much do you know about classical ciphers, Python, and working the reverse?"

"Nothing."

"Then I don't have time to get you there. Someday we'll chat about public key cryptography and then my programs." Concern washed through her as he wavered. "Go rest, Angus. You need it."

He stared at her for a moment and then turned to limp from the room, his movements painful to listen to.

She took a deep breath and got to work. If the last thing she did at Deep Ops was to save those girls, she'd be okay. The night flew by as she worked all three computers. Coffee and food appeared at her elbow a few times, and at some point, the dog ended up on her feet, keeping her warm.

After midnight, the outside office grew quiet, and she kept pushing, unraveling somebody else's work. A challenge that thrilled her in a way most people would never understand. But after several hours, her hands ached, her butt had gone numb, and her vision began to blur. She drank more coffee, trying to keep herself awake.

Angus poked his head in around one in the morning. "You need more coffee, food, sugar?"

She blinked and turned away from the computer. Her legs ached. She'd been tensing them while working, again. "What are you doing here?" The guy could barely stand.

"Nari and I have been here all night," he whispered. "She just fell asleep in the bigger chair in my office. What do you need?"

"Nothing." She had a sports drink somewhere, she was sure of it. "Go home."

He shook his head, and that odd purple-striped bruise shimmered. "I wouldn't leave you here alone."

Exhaustion and frustration took her, and tears filled her eyes. "Oh, Angus. I'm so sorry." She sniffled.

He took a step back, his eyes widening. "I know, and I figured we'd talk about it later. While you were working, I got my hands on all the reports you filed about the team. They were positive and didn't reveal any of our, well, idiosyncrasies."

She chuckled on a sob. "I want you to trust me again. This is the best team ever, and I'd never do anything to hurt you. I'm just so sorry."

He frowned and gingerly limped toward her, patting her awkwardly on the shoulder. "It's okay, and I'll let the rest of the team know the truth. We've all been undercover, and we get the job. If I didn't trust you, you wouldn't be sitting here right now with my only family spread across your feet."

Her heart burst, and she quickly wiped away the tears. He was just so funny—the tough guy couldn't handle tears. "I'm forgiven?"

He patted her harder, and her teeth rattled. "You're totally forgiven. I promise."

"Raider is still mad at me." She sniffed, her attention already caught by the second monitor. "So is Wolfe."

"I'll make sure they know all the facts," Angus said, backing toward the door. "But it's up to them, you know?" He closed the door quietly, obviously running from the emotion in the room.

"Well, at least he isn't mad any longer. Right, Roscoe?" She pivoted, already lost in the scrolling code. The dog started to snore louder, and she fell back into the challenge of the hack.

* * *

Raider shoveled in the cheeseburgers and fries that Wolfe had found for lunch, sitting at the small round table in their crappy motel room. The place was probably owned by Eddie. "I can't believe you let me sleep that long," he said, reaching for another burger.

"You were seriously drunk." Wolfe munched contentedly on a chicken sandwich. "It's good that you and Eddie bonded. Did he tell you anything of use?"

Raider shook his head. "Not really. Just a lot of talk about loyalty with threats thrown in."

"Normal guy stuff." Wolfe jerked his fries away before Raider could attack them. "Do you remember singing about putting a ring on Brigid's finger?"

Raider paused in the middle of chewing and looked up at the ceiling. "Vaguely?" He winced. "I didn't make too much of an ass of myself, did I?"

"Nah. You're a happy drunk." Wolfe took a drink of his soda. "What's up with you guys?"

Raider finished his third burger. "I'm not sure. We pretended to be engaged, then we hooked up, and then I found out she was lying to us all." He munched on some fries. "Turns out she signed a deal with HDD, and they scared the crap out of her. I need to have another talk with Rutherford and this time use my fists."

"Hmm." Wolfe lounged in the chair, his body too large for the rickety wood. There was no doubt he'd crash down in short order. "Seems like you care for her. Why not just protect her?"

"I am going to protect her," Raider countered, sucking down his sugary drink and trying to dispel his headache. Even so, it felt good to talk things out with somebody he trusted. "But she's not my type, anyway."

Wolfe chewed thoughtfully. "What's your type?"

"Organized, mellow, kind." Raider kept eating.

"Sounds boring." Wolfe rolled his neck. "Though she

shouldn't have lied to us, right? I guess it's up to you whether she's worth the risk or not."

He didn't need more risk in his life. Raider looked at the clock. "I wish she'd call and tell us the information is good. We need to get out of here and find those girls."

"Then take out the senator," Wolfe muttered. "Did you read all of the copied journal?"

"Yep, and according to Force, there's nothing about the guy on the tapes. We'll need to dig deeper or trap him, somehow," Raider said, his mind finally awakening. "For now, he and Eddie think I have some evidence on him, so that does give us an advantage."

Wolfe crumpled his wrappers together just as Raider's main phone rang.

"Hello." Raider put the phone on speaker and set it beyond his burger.

"Hey. It's Force with Brigid here." The guy sounded exhausted.

Raider exchanged a look with Wolfe. "All right. Did I get the correct information?"

"Yes and no." Her voice ran through him like a potent wine. Soft and sweet with a hint of Ireland. "You downloaded information about twenty-three shipments, and we have the origination points, train and cargo shipments. For twenty of them, we have destinations and even cargo hold numbers. It's a great find. But I can't identify what is in which shipments and there are three shipments with no destinations."

Raider sighed. "Chances are, those are even more protected, which means they're the humans and not the drugs." Crap. "Suggestions?"

"Was there a main computer in the room? One that seemed to direct the entire business?" Brigid asked.

Raider scrubbed both hands down his face over his

three-day shadow. "Yes. It was manned by a guy named Rex who seemed to be in charge of the entire outfit."

"We need a download from his computer," she murmured. "He must have files not on the main server, and those are the ones we need."

Wolfe shook his head. "There's no way they'll let you get to that computer."

Raider ran through possible scenarios. "Not willingly."

Force cleared his throat, the sound tinny through the phone line. "Can you get into that room yourself? Say wait until after dark and break in?"

"Not a chance," Raider said. "You wouldn't believe the security in this place, and even if I could get past it, the entire building is wired. I'd rather not take that chance." He stared at the phone. "Brigid? How long will those fake bank accounts keep Eddie's guy occupied?"

"Did he seem pretty good?" she asked, worry coming through.

"Definitely," Raider said. "If he is as good as you, how long do I have?"

Quiet ticked for several moments. "If he's as good as me, it depends. If he's suspicious, he's already had somebody go to one of the new accounts and try to withdraw. If he isn't, then you might have until tomorrow, but I wouldn't count on it. Fake money is easy to decipher if you know what you're doing."

Wolfe tapped long fingers on the table. "I think Eddie is suspicious across the board. We have to assume he has discovered the truth or will soon. What's our play?"

Raider's gut churned. The picture of little Hathai wouldn't leave his mind. He had to find her and the other kids. "I have to go back in. If we're going to find that shipment of girls, I have to find the destination of that cargo hold. It could be any port in the country." It appeared that Eddie's businesses were all over the world, so there was no way to guess. Eddie was excellent at keeping his hands clean while others did the dirty work.

"This is a bad idea," Brigid protested, her voice rising.

"Yeah," he agreed. "We don't have any other options. Eddie might trust me, he might not—either way, he'll let me back in. The question is what to do at that point. You're going to have to send me explicit directions about what to do with the master computer, Brigid. We can pick up another flash drive on the way to Eddie's."

Wolfe sipped his drink. "There's no way you're going to have the opportunity to use another flash drive without them noticing. It's a miracle it worked the first time."

Raider's chest heaved and reality settled in. "I know." Thinking as rapidly as his pounding brain would allow, he started laying out the plan. "Here's our only chance. I'll call Eddie and arrange to meet for a late dinner or drink." No matter which way he looked at it, there was no way he wouldn't get shot.

Chapter Thirty-Eight

Brigid's restlessness was going to make her brain explode. After talking to Raider, she'd taken a short nap and then worked all day, even collaborating with Dana on the angle with Senator Tyson. They sat at the conference table, with Nari at the end, her heels up on the table, a file in her hand. "That senator is a jackass."

Brigid looked up. "Can you believe he's running for president?"

Dana pushed papers across the table. "Oh, he's never making it to president. We're taking him down first."

That was a nice thought. Brigid yawned. Her stomach rumbled.

Nari perked up and slid the glasses up her forehead. "Hey. How about we go grab dinner? Raider and Wolfe aren't in play for a couple of hours, and we could use a break. There's a sports bar and restaurant just five miles down the road."

"Sounds good." Dana shoved the copy of the journal away from her. She grinned. "No government unit has ever trusted me, or any reporter, this much."

Brigid snorted. "We're not your average governmental unit."

"That's the truth." Nari laughed. "Hey. Why don't we pretend, just for two hours, that we're not in a unit? We can't get anything accomplished until Raider goes in, so let's just take a couple of hours off."

The idea sounded lovely, but Brigid couldn't get rid of the empty feeling in her stomach about Raider. Yet she did need dinner. "You sure you're not mad at me?"

"Nope. I totally get it," Nari murmured.

Well, that was fair. Brigid relaxed a fraction. "Why don't we call Pippa and see if she wants to join us? Girls' night out. Well, girls' two hours out."

"Good idea," Nari said. "That way Malcolm can go check on Angus. The stubborn ass finally went home an hour ago when the doctor gave him the choice of home or another ambulance. Can you believe him?" She slipped into a light-colored leather jacket and clip-clopped from the room.

Dana grinned. "Maybe there can be girl talk. What is going on between those two, anyway?"

Brigid rubbed her chin. "I'm not sure. Either they truly don't like each other, which is possible, or sexual attraction is making them crazy. I can't decide." She stood and headed for the door. "I'll drive because I won't drink anything. I'm tired, and I need to be as clearheaded as possible the second Raider gets the additional information." Because he would. He had to succeed and live through this.

"Excellent. I could use a glass of wine," Dana said, her blond hair up in a ponytail as she worked.

Wine might help, since Brigid planned to grill the reporter, just a mite, about Wolfe.

"Pippa is in," Nari said, shutting off the light in her office. "Malcolm will drop her off and then take dinner to Angus and make sure he's still alive. Win-win."

Brigid smiled, but a part of her wanted to curl up in a chair and sleep for an hour. Or just sit there and worry about Raider. They had so much to talk about, and she hated the plan for the night. But what other choice did they have?

Being one of the good guys kind of sucked sometimes, especially when most of the other good guys thought she was a bad guy.

The drive was made in silence, and they'd just been seated at a nice booth in the back of the comfortable sports bar, which had mounted televisions everywhere showing different sporting games, when Pippa appeared.

"Hi." She sat next to Brigid. "We were already on the way to see Angus when you called. I'm starving." The brunette's hair fell in natural waves to her shoulders, and her eyes sparkled. She'd dressed in jeans, flowy shirt, and denim jacket.

"How are you?" Nari asked.

"Great," Pippa said. "Not having a cult chasing me has really eased my anxiety." Her soft chuckle was contagious. "I still don't love crowds or loud places, but who does?"

It was nice to see the woman out and about. They ordered drinks, wine for everyone but Brigid. She ordered a hot chocolate. Might as well splurge.

"So," Nari said, sipping a rich-looking merlot. "No shoptalk. Only girl talk."

"All right." Brigid jumped right in. "What's going on with you and Angus?"

Nari coughed delicately. "I meant you and Raider."

"Too late. You first," Brigid said, sipping her chocolate and letting it warm her from the inside out.

Nari rolled her eyes. "Nothing is going on. He doesn't like me being foisted on him by HDD, and he doesn't like psychiatrists at all. Plus, he's just a grumpy bastard in general."

"But a cute one. Sexy and growly," Dana said, taking a sip of her chardonnay.

Nari blushed a little. "Well, yeah. But not sexy enough to get beyond the grumpiness."

They'd see about that. Brigid faced Dana. "And you and Wolfe?"

"Just friends." The reporter took a healthy drink of her old-fashioned. "Don't get me wrong. That man is fine to look at, but he has some serious issues, and I'm busy with my own right now. Plus, he laid it out there that we're just friends, and I've never found it a good use of time to change somebody else's mind."

Wow, she sounded balanced. "That's just smart," Brigid murmured. But they'd make such a nice couple, and both deserved to be happy. She'd never acted as a matchmaker before, but why the heck not? Once things slowed down.

"Pippa?" Nari asked. "How's life shacking up with the super-sexy Malcolm West?"

Pippa all but beamed with happiness. "It's awesome. I mean, he leaves his socks everywhere and it does drive me a little nutty, but he makes up for it in other ways."

Brigid smiled, even though her chest felt hollow. What would it be like to have that kind of relationship with a man? A good man who only wanted the best for you. Could she have that with Raider? Would he ever completely forgive her? Even if he did, he would always work for the government and probably not the unit, especially if they were being shut down. Where did that leave her? The HDD sent her wherever they wanted, and she had no choice in that.

"Brigid?" Dana asked, her cheeks rosy. "Your turn. That Raider is one sexalicious dude."

Brigid snorted and then coughed. "You are such a dork."

"Yep," Dana said happily. "It's nice to be making friends."

Yeah, it really was. Hopefully Brigid would be able to keep these friends. "All right. We slept together, he was amazing, he found out I was working undercover for the HDD and had lied to him, he got pissed, and now I think he's not interested except for sex."

The table was quiet for a moment.

"That's a lot," Nari finally said.

"No kidding. Geez. Too bad you can't drink right now," Dana agreed.

Pippa patted her arm. "He looks at you like you're a chocolate chip cookie and he hasn't eaten a sweet in a year. Don't worry, it'll work out."

Brigid turned to Pippa. "Now *that's* what you say in this situation." Grinning, she turned back to the other two women, who were both looking at her over the tops of their glasses. "Take notes. You guys need to work on your comforting skills."

They laughed and ordered another round, and this time, Brigid ordered extra whipped cream. Wolfe was totally ruining her when it came to sweet drinks.

This was such a bad idea even Raider couldn't find a silver lining. He opened the bar door and walked inside, Wolfe on his heels and looking like a bulldog about to find a steak dinner.

Eddie sat at a table near the back next to Jonny P, eating what appeared to be a large bowl of spaghetti. He looked up with a smile on his face that quickly disappeared as he caught sight of Wolfe.

Raider approached. "Eddie, this is Wolfe, my associate." He purposely didn't look at Jonny, who'd already pushed his jacket back to reveal a gun in his holster. The guy all but vibrated in place, ready to enforce Eddie's word. Was it good or bad that Josh the Bear wasn't around? "Where's Josh?"

"Off on private business again. Doesn't tell me where." Eddie's square face hardened, making his nose look more broken than usual. "I didn't say you could invite a friend."

"Who says I'm a friend?" Wolfe asked, his voice low and even grittier than usual.

Eddie looked him over and turned back to Raider. "You have about five seconds to explain, or Jonny here starts shooting."

"It's been too long," Jonny agreed congenially. "My trigger finger is starting to itch." He seemed more dressed up than usual in gray slacks and a button-down shirt, and his blondish-gray hair was smoothed back. Maybe he had a date later. Raider's research showed that Jonny liked petite blondes and seemed to fall in love fast.

Wolfe drew out a chair, flipped it around, and straddled it. "I work for Mr. Times's partner."

Eddie stilled. "You have a partner."

Raider tried to blush and took the other seat. "Yeah. A normally silent one, but he wasn't happy with the amount of funds I let you transfer yesterday, and he sent Wolfe to gather more information. To meet you."

Eddie leaned back, looking from Raider to Wolfe. "I don't do business with silent partners. We meet, or no dice."

Wolfe smiled, and the sight was chilling. "I'm the face and voice of my boss. The only chance you'll ever have to meet him is in hell, and hopefully none of us are going there for a while." He turned and faced Jonny P directly. "Up to you."

Man, Wolfe was a frightening bastard when he wanted to be. Raider aimed for an earnest expression. "I've done business for five years with Wolfe and my partner, and that's how I've built the organization so quickly. Too quickly, since we need your help laundering the money."

"For now," Wolfe interjected.

Raider leaned in. "The Thailand and India projects are mine. My partner wants nothing to do with those kinds of enterprises." If he could get Eddie to open up about the trafficking, maybe they wouldn't need to hit the computer. "You and I have that in common and maybe could expand our business relationship beyond laundering." He kicked back as if this were a casual meeting about office supplies. Being too eager with Eddie would tip him off.

Eddie looked at Wolfe. "What's the name of your boss? Maybe I've heard of him."

"He has no name, face, or voice," Wolfe said. "I'm it. All you've got. If you want fifty percent of the funds"—he cut Raider an irritated look—"then it's me or nothing. I can be a good friend to have, Eddie Coonan."

If that wasn't a threat, Raider didn't know what was. "I like you, Eddie. I think we could do some very profitable business together."

"You should've told me you had a partner," Eddie said, his expression harsh. His frown cleared. "With him throwing in Wolfe here, he doesn't trust you?"

"Oh, he trusts me," Raider said easily. "Otherwise, one of us would've killed the other by now."

Wolfe nodded. "True statement. We're great partners to have."

Eddie's cheek twitched. "You want me to convince you to work with me?"

Wolfe shrugged. "It appears we're already working with you. I'm here just to make sure it's a good idea."

"And if it isn't?" Jonny P asked, his hand inching for his weapon.

Wolfe didn't blink. "Must we really throw threats back and forth? Obviously we all know our jobs, are successful, and have no problem taking care of the competition." He looked at Raider. "Do they have any idea how much you enjoy making bodies disappear?"

Raider straightened his shoulders. "I've kept my hobbies to myself. Thanks."

Eddie tossed his napkin on his half-eaten spaghetti. "My answer is no. I don't work with people I haven't met." He pushed back from the table. "I'll get you your half of the money we worked yesterday, within two weeks. Other than that, we're done."

Wolfe sighed heavily and drew out a square black box with a blinking red light above a round blue button. "Plan B it is, then."

Eddie paused. "What's that?"

Wolfe eyed the blinking light. "My boss has some impressive connections in the government, and this is a prototype that has great potential. That button? If I push it, those explosives Raider told me about will go kaboom."

Jonny P snorted. "You're serious."

"Yep." Wolfe looked deadly serious. "In fact, any explosive device within a half block, other than old-fashioned dynamite, which you don't have, will detonate."

"Bullshit," Eddie said, his chin lowering. "My explosives are beyond the shield, as we call it. It's a fantastic jammer."

"Yeah. Government. Can get beyond your jammer." Wolfe cocked his head. "Wanna bet on it?"

Eddie's mouth compressed into a thin line. "If this building comes down, you die."

Wolfe twisted his torso and confiscated Jonny P's gun while still holding the detonator in his free hand. "I'm ready to die, Mr. Coonan. Are you?"

Chapter Thirty-Nine

Malcolm came to pick up Pippa just as Brigid finished her lettuce wraps. They were exactly what she needed. "How's Angus?" she asked.

"Stubborn and cranky, but he enjoyed the chicken-and-rice dish." His dark green eyes sparkled, and in his black jacket, he looked like a badass. Several women had tracked his progress across the restaurant, but he hadn't seemed to notice. Droplets of rain clung to his dark hair. He held Pippa's coat out for her. "It's raining. Did you have fun?"

"I did," she murmured, her face rosy from two glasses of wine.

"Good." He looked around. "You guys leaving?"

Nari waved him off. "I'll get the check—you two go ahead. We need to return to the office in case Raider or Wolfe has news."

Mal nodded. "Okay. I'll be in bright and early, but if anything breaks, let me know right away. I'll be there." He put his arm around the pretty brunette and they headed for the door.

"I like her," Dana said, finishing her wine. "They make a nice couple."

"They really do." Nari signed the check. "Okay. Our two hours are over. Time to head back to reality."

It had been a nice two hours. Brigid scooted from the booth and led the way past the other patrons, opening the door to a light rain. Darkness had just started to push away the light, and it was an easy trek across the parking lot to Raider's gleaming truck.

She clicked the fob to unlock it, and two men emerged from behind it.

Nari immediately stepped up to her side, her heels clicking. "What do you want?"

Brigid looked rapidly around, but nobody else was near. The bar was off the main drag, and the parking lot well lit. Should she scream? Wait a minute. She looked closer. "Josh the Bear?"

Josh's eyebrows rose. "Yep." He pulled out a snub-nosed pistol. "Our truck is behind yours. Let's take that one, Luke."

What was happening? Had Raider been found out? Wait a minute. No way could Josh have traced Raider back to the HDD. This wasn't making any sense.

Luke, a dead ringer for Idris Elba, looked at Dana. "She the reporter?"

"Yep," Josh said, gesturing at them with the gun.

Ah, crap. Josh had followed Dana. Brigid looked for a way to run back to the restaurant without getting shot, but no avenue presented itself.

Dana stepped up on Brigid's other side. "If it's me you want, leave them." Her voice shook, but she tried to push herself in front of Brigid.

"No," Josh said. "I could shoot one or even two of you, but I'd rather not. Just come with us, we'll have a discussion, and I'll let you go."

"Bullshit," Nari said, kicking up so fast her leg was just a blur. She hammered Josh in the wrist, and the gun flew out of his hand, dinging a Buick. Her shoes were in the dirt, and her bare feet brutal. She kicked Josh beneath the jaw and pivoted, nailing Luke right in the balls.

Brigid froze for a second and then bunched and ducked, head-butting Josh as hard as she could in the gut. He doubled over with a pained *oof* and grabbed her shoulders, throwing her against the truck. She impacted with a loud crunch, and pain ripped down her arm. "Run, Dana," she yelled, falling to her butt on the wet dirt.

Dana turned to run for help, but Luke was on her, grabbing her by the ponytail and sling-shotting her against the truck. She hit next to Brigid and dropped with a cry of pain. Brigid scrambled to her feet as Nari and Josh traded blows, Nari clearly winning. She dropped him to his knees and did a quick spinning kick to his head that knocked him against the post of the streetlight.

Brigid went for Luke, who was reaching for his gun. He pivoted and punched her in the cheek. Stars exploded behind her eyes, and she fell fast, landing on Dana. Dana grabbed her and hauled them both to their feet, where they tried to balance each other.

Luke whipped out a square object and pressed it to the back of Nari's neck. The thing crackled, her head jerked, and she flopped to the ground.

"Nari," Brigid cried out, rushing to her friend.

Josh caught her around the waist as the other guy grabbed Dana. He carried her easily around the truck to a larger red one and tossed her in the back seat, then followed her in, quickly grabbing zip ties from the back-seat pocket and securing her hands.

Dana landed next to him, and he did the same to her while the other guy ran up front and jumped in the driver's seat, quickly speeding away.

Brigid reached for the door handle with her bound hands, pulling wildly.

"Childproof," Josh said calmly as the driver slowed down to meander sedately onto the main road.

It had all happened so fast. Brigid tried to catch her breath and leaned forward to look beyond Josh to Dana. The reporter had mud in her hair and a bruise forming on her chin, and her eyes were dazed. "You okay?"

Dana swallowed. "Yes. You?"

No. Her head felt like she'd hit a truck, which she had. And her right arm felt like one long bruise. "I'm good." She leaned back and struggled to shove fear away so she could concentrate. "Josh? This is a bad idea. Let us go."

"Nope."

Was he armed? If so, could she get the gun with her wrists tied together? She shifted her weight and inched toward him.

"Don't make me tase you," he said conversationally, staring straight ahead. "It didn't look like a pleasant experience."

They'd left Nari unconscious in the parking lot in the rain. She was so small; would a driver see her before hitting her? Panic snatched Brigid's breath away, and she tried to breathe normally. In and out. Nari would be okay. The unconsciousness couldn't last long. The woman could seriously fight and was probably recovering even now. Maybe she was already up and calling for help. "What do you want from us?" she gasped.

"Me? Nothin'." The guy was as solid as a rock and just as steady.

Okay. This was crazy. The driver turned onto the Interstate, driving toward DC.

"Where are we going?" Dana asked, her words slurred.

"You'll see," Josh said.

Brigid looked behind him to see normal traffic. What if Raider needed her back at her computers? This was a disaster. "We've made a copy of the journal and tapes, Josh.

Even if we hand them over to Eddie, he'll never know whether we still have the information."

Josh nodded. "We've known that since the beginning. Good thing it's close to the end."

Chills flashed down Brigid's spine.

Raider stood. "Let's go into the back room, Eddie. I promised Wolfe here that he could see where the money went and how it's being laundered. Once he's satisfied, we can get back to making ourselves very rich men." Without waiting for an answer, he turned as if all was normal and moved toward the back door.

Eddie soon stood next to him to punch in the numbers. "I'm going to kill you for this, Times. Just thought you should know."

Raider sighed. "Get in line, buddy. If this doesn't go well, my silent partner will make sure we're all buried in a ditch together somewhere. This guy is brilliant but nuts. Trust me that you don't want to cross him."

Eddie opened the door, walked inside and looked at the camera. "He should fear me. And he will by the time I'm done with him."

Fair enough. The shelves opened again, and Eddie led the way inside with Raider, Jonny P, and Wolfe taking up the rear. Raider's body settled into the operation, even as adrenaline sharpened his focus. They walked onto the dais, and the door shut quietly behind them. Today, only five techs were working inside the facility.

"Show me what's happening," Wolfe ordered.

"Fine." Eddie walked down the stairs and moved toward Rex, who was typing away wearing a set of earbuds and dancing in his seat. Would the HDD try to hire him after all of this was over? Raider tried to read the code flashing across the screen as Wolfe came abreast of him.

The cocking of a gun behind them had Raider stiffening and turning. The bald bartender stood beneath the stairs holding a semiautomatic weapon, barrel pointed at Raider's chest.

Rex tugged out the earbuds and turned, his eyes earnest beneath the wire-rimmed glasses. "Man, I hope I read your signal right on the camera."

"You did." Eddie turned and yanked Jonny P's gun from Wolfe's hand.

Signal? There hadn't been a signal. Damn it. Raider edged away from Wolfe in case there was an opening one of them could take.

Wolfe lifted the black box in the air. "I'm ready to see the fire of hell. Anybody else?"

Raider sighed. "I'd rather not die, but I guess it's not a bad way to go."

Wolfe signaled subtly, and Raider exhaled to settle his body. This was going to hurt. He barely signaled back. Then he counted. Before he could hit three, Jonny P pivoted and smashed the box out of Wolfe's hand. It flew toward Raider and slapped the floor, skidding several feet. Raider dove for it just as Wolfe lunged for the guy with the weapon.

The weapon discharged, and Jonny P landed on Raider, scrambling for the box. Another gun fired, this one even louder, and a bullet chipped the concrete near Raider's head. He and Jonny froze, the box just out of reach. Turning, he looked over his shoulder to find Eddie had a gun pointed at him.

Wolfe and the bartender grunted and coughed, fighting fiercely for the gun, while Rex slid down beneath his computer table as if his body was boneless. His eyes were wide but focused, and he kept hold of his mouse as if just waiting to get back to work.

The bartender grunted and Wolfe growled, punching each other fiercely. They fought for the gun, and it triggered, spraying bullets toward the computers.

"No!" Raider bellowed just as a bullet hit Rex in the neck, spraying blood out the other side to cover the floor. The computer tech died instantly, pitching forward, his face planting on the hard concrete.

Wolfe hit the bartender in the gut, and the guy kicked Wolfe in the leg, sending him back.

Eddie partially turned and aimed, just as Wolfe secured the gun and fired, hitting Eddie. The mobster flew back and landed on a computer monitor, knocking it over the table to the floor, where it shattered.

Wolfe turned and hit the bartender over the head, knocking him out cold on the floor. "Get the box," Wolfe ordered.

Jonny P pushed off Raider and partially lifted himself, his hands up.

Raider breathed out. Okay. He reached for the box just as Eddie came over the table and fired the gun. Red burst across Wolfe's chest, his eyes widened, and he dropped.

"Wolfe!" Raider turned and jumped to his feet to reach his friend. The world halted, and panic overtook him. The room hazed.

"Stop," Eddie ordered. "Jonny?"

Jonny shoved Raider to the side and leaned down to take the box. He flipped it over to read the bottom. "Made in China?"

"You're fuckin' kidding me," Eddie muttered, blood flowing from a wound in his left shoulder.

Jonny slid open the compartment to reveal two AA batteries. "This is a remote control for some kind of toy." He tried to hide it, but incredulity showed on the sharp angles of his face.

Raider coughed. Was Wolfe dead? He couldn't be. His eyes were just closed for a minute as he sat against the far wall, his hands limp. Raider dragged his attention back to the mobsters. If he was going to help Wolfe, he had to get those guns. "It's for a miniature Bumblebee Camaro. Thing drives like a dream."

"I'm going to kill you." Eddie pointed the gun at Raider's head, right between the eyes.

Shit. This really hadn't worked out. Raider's shoulders settled, and his body relaxed. "Before you do, tell me about Treeson. You knew him as Albert Jones."

Eddie blinked. "The narc? Ah, damn. He was yours? I had Jonny cut him apart piece by piece."

Anger blew through Raider so quickly he almost stopped breathing. "Where's his body?"

Eddie shrugged. "Doesn't matter, since I'm going to kill you. But he's in a vacant lot in the Deacon neighborhood. I'm building a bar there next year. Now. You ready to die?"

An image of Brigid, laughing at something he said, filtered across Raider's vision. The perfect image to take with him into the afterworld. He tried to look for a way out, scanning the room, wanting somehow to see her again.

Eddie smiled, blood dripping from a cut in his lip. "Any last words?"

Raider focused. "Yeah. Never underestimate a wolf."

Eddie began to turn, but it was too late. Wolfe lifted his powerful weapon and shot him dead center in the chest. Jonny P scrambled for the gun, but Wolfe fired again, hitting Jonny P in the temple. He went down without another sound.

"Shit." Raider ran to Wolfe and skidded on his knees. "How bad you hurt?"

"Dunno." Wolfe gingerly dropped the gun and let Raider lift his shirt.

Raider sucked in air. "Okay. Right shoulder, through

and through. You're going to be okay." Yeah, but he was bleeding a lot. Raider yanked off his shirt. "Keep that against the wound." Then he took the flash drive from his pocket and ran to the main computer, ignoring the dead tech beneath it. He drew out the paper Brigid had given him and quickly typed in the necessary commands, thankful the kid had still been logged on. The download only took a minute, but felt like hours. Finally, he released the USB. "Got it. Let's go."

"Okay." Wolfe struggled to his feet, his hand over the bloody rag.

Raider's phone buzzed, and he lifted it with one hand while propping his good shoulder beneath Wolfe's to help him walk. "Got the info, boss. We're on our way."

"Good." West sounded both pained and furious. "We have a problem."

Of course they did. "What is it?"

"Brigid and Dana were taken an hour ago. Get here fast." Raider jerked as Wolfe did the same, having heard Angus. Then, for the first time that crazy night, Raider finally felt fear.

Chapter Forty

There was little traffic on the road, which was a damn good thing. Angus Force wasn't happy. Not one inch of him felt good. Or even decent. His brain still pounded against his skull, his liver seemed to be having difficulty working with his kidneys, and his left leg had gone numb days ago. But none of that, not *one* bit of it, compared to the rage in his chest that Nari had been left helpless in the mud and two of his own taken. Dana was working with the team, so that made her his, too.

They'd been gone for more than two hours. Two whole fucking hours.

Worse yet. He'd read through every one of the reports Brigid had filed about the Deep Ops team, and every single one was positive. She'd betrayed nothing, and he hadn't had the chance to tell the rest of the team that she was clean. One of them to the end.

And either somebody had hit Nari in the head, or she'd struck a rock on the ground, because all she could remember was that Dana was the target. That the mysterious guy she couldn't remember had wanted the reporter.

He followed the directions to Dana's apartment that Wolfe had left for him after arriving in DC via the private plane, bleeding like a stuck pig and then disappearing and refusing to answer his damn phone. Finally finding the sprawling apartment building that housed a myriad of urban professionals who worked in DC and the outlying areas, Angus parked and eased himself from the vehicle, careful of his numb leg.

Ducking his head against the rain, he hustled up the stairs to apartment 3A, where he knocked loudly.

"It's open," Wolfe called out.

Okay. So the guy was alive. Angus shoved open the door to a modern-style living room with cut glass, hardwood floors, and comfortable furnishings. "You couldn't answer your damn phone?" he snapped.

Wolfe looked up from a white plush sofa, a remote control in his hand. Dana Mullberry's face was frozen on the screen. "She was on camera for years, and her last interview was just a month ago. She does both print and live podcasts."

Angus studied him as he would an injured animal. "You're bleeding on her white sofa."

"I have it bandaged." Wolfe returned his attention to the screen, his clothes a wild mess and bristle along his hard jaw. "I've been going through all of her recent interviews, research, podcasts, and stories. Nothing stands out as suspicious."

Angus looked at the smiling blonde on the screen. Intelligence shone in her moss-green eyes, and her facial structure looked fragile. "She's smart, and so is Brigid. They'll be all right, Wolfe." But would they? As far as he knew, neither of the two knew how to fight.

Wolfe shook his head, his entire body a long, tense line. "I should've been here. I promised to back her up, and I wasn't there. And somebody took her." He threw the remote, and it slammed against the wall, sending a picture of a calm, peaceful lake crashing down.

"They were out to dinner," Angus said, his vision graying. "There was no way to know they'd be taken."

Wolfe shook his head. "I don't know which case this is about. Who wanted her and why?" Standing, he dripped more blood onto the sofa, his hands curling into fists and cracking his already damaged knuckles. "Has Nari remembered anything else?"

"No." Angus swiped both hands down his face. "She's at the hospital now, and they're keeping a close eye on the head trauma. She knows her name and so on, but the last week is still a blank." He'd never forget the sight of her dark hair on that hospital pillow, her long lashes resting on her pale face. "I stopped by there on the way here. The doctor will call me if there's any change." He desperately wanted to be there with her, but he had a job to do.

Wolfe looked around the pristine apartment again. "I haven't found a thing. Not one."

"That's okay. I've called in an HDD tech, and she's going through all traffic pictures right now. Let's work the case from the office."

"Fine." Wolfe stormed by him, smelling like blood and gunpowder.

Wonderful. Angus followed him, and the drive back to the office was made in angry silence. Finally, they arrived and made their way down to their floor. Hopefully the tech had found something.

The elevator door opened to the sound of a commotion. A bruised and battered Raider Tanaka was yelling at the purple-haired and furious Agent Frost, while Malcolm and Roscoe watched from a safe distance.

"What the hell is going on here?" Angus bellowed, limping out of the elevator.

Frost pivoted toward him. "This jackass thinks I'm a hacker, which I am not. I'm a techie, and that involves a totally different skill set."

Raider's chin lowered, his eyes blazing. "Then be a techie and get me my information. Who took them and where did they go?"

Angus's temper competed with his sympathy. "Malcolm? You have anything to say?"

The ex-cop, his body tense in case he needed to step in, shook his head. "No update from the hospital. Agent Frost has called friends and connections to use traffic cams, but there aren't any cameras around the restaurant from which they were taken, so we have no idea what kind of vehicle was used. We don't even know where to start."

Agent Frost turned toward Wolfe. "Any type of lead with the reporter's records? A trail to follow on a story?"

"No," Wolfe said shortly, fury cascading off him. "What about the flash drive we took from Eddie's? Anything?"

"I. Am. Not. A. Hacker," Frost said, her pointy chin turning red. "So, no. There are, however, several hackers at HDD, though none as good as Brigid."

"We've been taken off the case," Malcolm reminded him quietly. "There's no guarantee HDD will take us seriously or decrypt the information. The senator has some juice."

Angus nodded, his mind reeling. "We have until tomorrow. If we don't get Brigid back in the next several hours, we'll have to turn over the flash drive." Unless he could find a hacker and bring them here. That was an idea. "Raider? You have to have some decent contacts at HDD. Reach out and get me the names of a couple of hackers."

Agent Frost's light eyebrows rose in her youthful face. "What then?"

"Then we kidnap them," Wolfe said grimly, heading for the computer room.

Raider's jaw set. "Works for me." He limped after his friend.

* * *

Brigid's headache traveled to her stomach and made her nauseous as they drove past the homes in McLean, Virginia, and finally parked on the brick-and-stone circle driveway of an imposing stone mansion with wide windows and a curved shingled roof. She tried to fight when Josh pulled her out of the truck, but the guy was too strong. He prodded them both toward the front door.

Brigid looked wildly around, but trees and shrubbery enshrouded the home, giving it privacy. If she yelled, would anybody hear?

"You yell, and I'll knock you out," Josh said mildly.

Was he a mind reader, or what? They reached the door, Luke opened it, and they walked into an opulent living room. Josh nudged them down stairs that led to a basement gym. Oh, this wasn't going to be good.

Barbells, two treadmills, a jump rope, a long mirror, and other exercise equipment were scattered about the space. "Sit," Josh said.

Brigid eyed Dana and then went to sit on a padded bench, keeping her back to the wall. Dana sat next to her.

Footsteps sounded down the stairs, and Senator Tyson entered the room wearing a tuxedo and perfectly shined shoes. "I was in the middle of a fund-raiser," he muttered.

"Figured this was your place," Dana said, sitting straighter, a bruise marring the right side of her face. "The 'for sale' sign outside is quite a show of confidence. Sure you're moving to Pennsylvania Avenue?"

"Yes," the senator said. "I'm fairly confident."

Brigid looked from Josh to Tyson. Her body temperature plummeted. "Raider isn't going to trade the journal and evidence for us."

"Yes, he would," Tyson said, straightening his tie. "But I'm sure you made copies. I don't believe there's enough evidence in that journal, or what's left of it, to hurt me. Your daddy was gathering materials against the Coonans to gain his freedom. I was an afterthought, and not even a big one at that time. Wasn't even in public service yet."

Good point. "Then why take us for Eddie?" Brigid studied Josh, whose intelligent eyes scanned the room and then focused on the doorway.

"Oh." Tyson coughed. "I see. No. You were an afterthought. It's the reporter I want."

An afterthought? "Is that a fact?" Her voice shook. That meant she was expendable.

"Affirmative. In case I need leverage with what's left of your HDD unit. And I would like to know what's in the second half of that journal. But it's Dana's sources, who she's talked to and what she's said, that I require first."

"About the missing women," Dana breathed.

"Yep. We've been following you for a while and were surprised when you first visited the hole-in-the-wall HDD unit and the Irish rose here." Tyson double-checked his cuff links and looked her over. "I do like blondes, but unfortunately I have a nasty temper. It's usually an accident, to be honest. They shouldn't make me mad."

Oh, there was no way he'd let them free after this. Brigid's lungs stopped working, and she struggled to breathe. She was going to die, and she'd never gotten a chance to tell Raider how she really felt about him. He'd never know. She calculated the distance between her and the door. Even if she got past Josh, where would she go? There had to be a phone somewhere.

"You won't make it," Josh said, not looking at her. How did he do that?

Tyson chuckled. "Even if you did, I own the police in this town already. A combination of money and blackmail. Get to a phone, call 911, and I promise you'll disappear quickly."

Her palms grew clammy. They needed to get free and run. Brigid looked around the basement room. No windows, probably concrete block as the foundation. This wasn't looking good.

Dana cleared her throat. "Did you kill them?" she asked, softly.

Was she after a story or what? Of course, the longer the guy talked, the longer they'd stay alive. Brigid looked at the man.

He shrugged. "Depends on who you're talking about."

"The girl in high school," Brigid threw out.

"Yeah. We had a fight, I pushed her, and she hit her head. That really was an accident." He smiled as if in fond remembrance.

Brigid's stomach lurched.

Dana straightened up. "The doctor in Seattle?"

The senator looked into the distance as if remembering. "She was the love of my life, I'm pretty sure. The night she died, I learned I shouldn't drink tequila."

"And the intern at your law office?" Brigid croaked.

"Oh, her." The senator shared a look with Josh. "She had stumbled upon a case and some evidence we didn't want anyone to see. I'm not even sure how she died."

"You?" Brigid looked at Josh.

He didn't say a word.

"Any other girls?" Dana murmured.

"Nope. I've removed other obstacles from my business and political life, but you'll never find those connections." He grinned, his teeth sparkling as if he was in a campaign poster.

Josh didn't return the smile. There was a connection here that Brigid couldn't quite put her finger on. "Eddie Coonan's business is in trouble, which you obviously know because I'm here, and you would like the journal. But Josh, why are you here?" Shouldn't the enforcer be protecting his boss right now along with Jonny P?

Josh glanced at her, no expression in those sharp eyes.

Tyson fixed his cummerbund and then looked up, his thick eyebrows rising. "Oh. I see. No. Josh doesn't work for Eddie. Not really."

Brigid's mouth dropped open. "Josh works for you." Her mind clicked facts into place like a good code. "Every time Eddie flew to wherever you were when a woman disappeared, Josh was with him." Holy crap. Josh was the one who helped the senator—and worked for him. "Does Eddie know?" she asked.

"Of course not," the senator said easily. "I put Josh in place years ago to keep an eye on my investments." He shrugged. "And take Eddie out if necessary." He straightened and looked around. "This room is soundproof, with only one locked exit, and armed men are on the other side. This is my wife's favorite room, so I suggest you don't break anything. Stay here and behave yourself. Josh, bring the blonde. It's time she and I had a talk." He turned and strode out of the room.

"No!" Brigid jumped up between Dana and Josh, but he swatted her away like she was nothing. She hit the side of the treadmill and fell. Even though Dana fought the enforcer, he dragged her out and slammed the door, sliding locks into place.

Brigid ran to the door and tried to open it, twisting frantically. The senator killed blondes. She had to get out of there. She started tapping on the walls. Hadn't she seen a movie where the good guys broke out through the Sheetrock? But this was all cinder block or cement. Damn it. She swung out and hit the stationary bike. The one with the screen. Wait a minute. Her heart galloping, she jumped on and pressed the start button.

The screen flared to life. Oh, it was one of those subscription streaming bikes, which meant an Internet connection. All right. She could do this.

She explored the app. Damn it. No communication method. Only bike rides, live streaming classes, and other apps. But where there's one app, she could find another. She followed the trail to a social network created for athletes and downloaded the app, her mind screaming. As soon as it downloaded, she created an account, and on any network, she could send a message.

Holding her breath, she sent a message via email to all the members of her team. There was no guarantee they'd see it or even open an odd message. It might even look like an advertisement or promotion.

Dana screamed from somewhere in the house, and Brigid stopped breathing.

Chapter Forty-One

Raider paced the hub of the office, his mind misfiring in every direction. Malcolm and Wolfe were in with the tech trying to find any sort of lead on the traffic cams, and Angus watched him pace, finally sitting in a chair. "You need to calm down."

"I can't." Raider shot a hand through his hair. "She's in danger. I never let her off the hook. I mean, sure, I was going to forgive her, but I'm such an ass. I couldn't just say it was okay." His body felt as if horses had dragged him for miles. "I never told her how I felt. She doesn't know."

"She's smarter than you. Sure, she knows," Angus said wearily, putting his head back. "I just called and checked on Nari. She can't help—no memory. We have to find them."

"We know Eddie doesn't have them," Raider said, increasing his pace. "Dana could've been working on any story. If the senator has them, why not call with a ransom demand? He has to want that journal, but I'm sure he knows we've kept a copy." He growled, frustration eating at him. "After seeing the first half, he must realize it was about the Coonans and not him."

"So he didn't take them," Angus said.

"He's all we've got," Raider countered. "We don't know

anything about Dana's other stories. Only this one. We need to track that bastard down."

"You're tilting at windmills," Angus said. His phone dinged, and he glanced down. "Telemarketers. On email."

Twin dings sounded from the computer room. Raider paused and looked over his shoulder. That was odd. Then his phone buzzed. "Wait a minute." His heart leaped into his throat, and he yanked out his phone, scrolling through email and reading. His legs nearly gave out. "It's Brigid with a location. We have to go. Now."

It took them too long to suit up, and they broke speed limits galore on the way there. Malcolm drove, being the only one without bullet holes, concussions, or broken bones. They wore outdated bulletproof vests and had armed themselves with guns, knives, and even a couple of grenades Angus had somehow secured last month. Roscoe wore his FBI vest and looked bigger than normal. But would they get there in time?

It had been over thirty minutes since Brigid had reached out, and he couldn't be sure how long her message had taken to get to him via some social networking site. She had to be alive. Fear caught him around the throat, and he calmed himself, going into battle mode. No emotion, just rational thought.

They parked two blocks away. "Wolfe and Raider, you take front," Angus said. "Malcolm and I will take back. This is shock and awe, but try not to kill the senator. We're in enough trouble right now."

Raider cut Wolfe a look. If the bastard had hurt either woman, he was going to bleed.

Forgetting all of his aches and pains, Raider crept low around the stone wall and surveyed the front of the house. High-end, brick and stone, no security visible. It was a nice neighborhood of rich people, and no doubt the senator didn't want guards everywhere. However, there would be plenty inside, he was sure.

He looked at Wolfe. The guy had fresh bandages in place, his breathing was shallow, and dark circles shadowed his eyes. But there was nobody else on earth Raider would want backing him right now. "You good?"

"Yep." Wolfe withdrew his weapon and studied the house. Twin windows showcased darkened rooms on either side of the main door. "I say we go in through glass."

That would definitely be shock and awe. Raider studied the angles. "Keep your head down and try to lead with your shoulder. Your good one." He'd do the same. "On three. See you inside." He bumped forearms with Wolfe and stayed low, putting himself in position. Then he counted, took a running start, and fired his gun at the top of the window. The glass cascaded down, and he timed his entry perfectly after the glass had scattered over the shrubs, landing just inside and rolling by a dining room table already set with fancy china.

A man with an automatic machine gun ran around the corner, firing wildly in Raider's direction and hitting the china cabinet. Chrystal blasted apart, its shards flung every which way. A piece cut into Raider's hand, and he winced, raising his weapon and firing.

The guy went down, still spraying.

Raider ducked low and crept around the corner, stopping as more gunfire erupted at the back of the house. Another armed guard turned the corner, and Raider took him out with a shot to the knee. The man yelled in pain, fell, and Raider ran forward to hit him with the butt of his pistol, knocking him out.

He incapacitated two more men before reaching an office where Wolfe was grappling hand to hand with the senator, who was putting up a surprisingly good fight. Dana was tied to a chair, her shirt undone, blood flowing from several cuts along her arms. Raider drew his knife and rushed to release her, pressing her shirt to her wounds. "How badly are you hurt?" he asked, leaning down to check her eyes.

"I'm okay," she gasped, tears on her cheeks. "Brigid is downstairs past the kitchen. Get to her. Fast."

Raider looked up just as Wolfe threw the senator onto the desk and slammed his head into the heavy oak. "You got this?"

"Got it. Get Bridge," Wolfe snapped, punching the senator square in the mouth.

Raider ran down the hallway as more gunfire came from the back of the house. When he found the stairs, he crept down, gun out, and turned the corner at the bottom. A kick came out of nowhere, knocking the gun from his hand. "I don't have time for this shit." He moved with his knife, taking down a guy the size of a muscled rhinoceros, and plunging the knife into his arm. Then he pressed his forearm against the guy's neck, effectively choking him out. "You're gonna have a headache," he muttered, looking wildly around.

He saw just one locked door. He stood and rapidly disengaged the locks, praying he'd find her alive on the other side.

Brigid held the ten-pound weight to her side, ready to swing it. The door to the gym opened, and she ran forward, trying to halt in the last second. "Raider?"

He was like a bruised avenging angel in a black bulletproof vest, looking like the baddest of all badasses. And he'd come for her. He pivoted, took the weight away, and grabbed her up in a hug. "You're okay."

She hugged him back, leaning away. Blood flowed from his temple over the bruises on his face, his injured arm hung wrong, and he had a split lip. "You look terrible." She chuckled through her tears.

"You look amazing." He put her down.

"Dana—"

"Is okay. Wolfe is with her," Raider said, running his hands down her arms. "Are you hurt? Any injuries?"

"No," she coughed. He was there. He'd gotten her message.

He leaned forward and touched a bruise on her cheekbone. "Who did this?" His voice went so low and dark, she shivered.

"I think some guy named Luke?" There had been a couple of skirmishes. "Oh, and guess what? Josh is really working for the senator and not Eddie. Can you believe it?"

"Eddie's dead," Raider said flatly, taking her hand and leading the way up the stairs, his gun out. "Stay behind me."

"Clear," Angus called out loudly. Roscoe barked several short yips before Wolfe gave another clear call.

Raider kept his arm over her shoulder and herded her toward an office at the back of the house. Several prone men, some bleeding, lined the way, and she averted her eyes. She and Raider moved into the office, where the senator was sprawled on his desk, groaning. Wolfe slipped his shirt over Dana's head, his vest flung over a chair.

Brigid ran to her, hugging her. "Are you okay?"

"I am." The reporter hugged her back, but her arms were bleeding. "Nice job getting the word out."

Brigid coughed and looked around. "What now?"

Angus surveyed the scene. "Anybody have a phone that still works?"

"Yeah." Malcolm entered the room, a cut across his temple, his phone in his hand. "Who do you want me to call?"

Angus smiled at Dana. "Nobody. I want you to stream

live. What do you say, Ms. Reporter? How would you like to break the biggest story of the year right now and right here?"

Dana blinked. "I'd love to." A slow smile spread across her face. "Am I talking to you?"

Angus nodded.

"Wait," Wolfe said. "I thought we wanted to stay under the radar."

"Most of us do," Angus agreed. "You guys remain out of the shot—I'm going public because it's time. Lassiter needs to find me." He reached over and hauled Senator Tyson off the desk. "And this guy is going public right now so whatever high-up buddies he has can't bury this."

The senator wavered on his feet, his eyes glassy and his nose bleeding.

Dana tugged Wolfe's big shirt down to her thighs.

Wolfe took the phone from Malcolm, punched a few buttons, and pointed it at the trio.

Dana smiled for the camera. "This is Dana Mullberry, and I'm reporting to you live from Senator Scot Tyson's house, where he kidnapped me and tried to torture me for information." She gestured to Angus. "This is Homeland Defense Department Agent Angus Force, and you might recognize him as the FBI profiler who took down the famous serial killer Henry Wayne Lassiter." She paused. "Boy, do we have a story for you."

Raider drew Brigid out of the room. "This is going to take a while. We're running out of time to find those girls. I have the flash drive from the main computer at Eddie Coonan's. Do you think you can decrypt it here, or do you need your computers?"

"I need mine."

Malcolm jogged out, avoiding the camera. "The HDD is on its way, as are a million other agencies and news outlets. If we're gonna get out of here, we'd better do it right now."

Raider took Brigid's hand, whistled for the dog, and ran for the front door, which was surprisingly intact. "Our truck is just down the block. We'll have to send somebody to pick Angus up later."

"Angus is going to be busy," Malcolm returned, running out into the night with the dog on his heels.

"Good point," Raider said, keeping a strong hold on Brigid's hand. They jogged down the street, and Malcolm jumped into the driver's seat.

Raider paused and turned her to face him. "I love you. Wanted to say it in case we get blown up or something. Sorry it took this for me to realize it and say the words." Without waiting for an answer, he picked her up and placed her in back of the truck with him. Roscoe leaped into the front and barked three times.

Loved her? As in really loved her? Everything inside her turned to Jell-O.

Mal drove the truck faster than he should, but Brigid didn't complain. The sense of urgency hadn't left her, and she wouldn't be able to take a deep breath until she'd decrypted that flash drive. There was such a small window to save those girls, and she wasn't sure she could make it. When was the last time she'd slept?

Malcolm looked at them in the mirror. "Did either of you see Josh go down?"

"No," they said in unison. Had Josh the Bear survived?

She rested her head against Raider's shoulder and let her eyes close. Within a second, he was carrying her out of the elevator at headquarters. "I slept," she mumbled.

"Yep." He carried her right into her computer room and handed over the flash drive. "Agent Frost was here, but she probably cleared out once the broadcast went live. I would have."

"No kidding." Brigid took the flash drive and went to work, smiling gratefully when Raider left and returned with freshly brewed coffee. Taking just a second, she downed the entire cup, and then repeated the steps she'd taken with the earlier flash drive, hoping the tech hadn't added any bombs. There were a couple of different cyphers, but she went at them, while Raider checked on her once in a while with more coffee or just a hug.

Suddenly, the code flashed on the screen and then unraveled.

She sat back and blinked. "Raider?" she whispered, her voice gone for some reason.

"Yeah?" He opened the door, his face bruised and his eyes exhausted. "You got it?"

Elation caught her and spun her around. "Yes." She really did. Right there. "Three shipments, two Port of Los Angeles, and one Port of Seattle. Times, cargo numbers, and plans to retrieve." Smiling, she printed the information off and handed it over. "Call the FBI."

"Gladly." He smiled, took the paper, and then disappeared.

She'd done it. They all had. The FBI had plenty of time to save those girls and get them home. She looked around. For so long, she'd done what the HDD had told her, fearing repercussions. Not anymore. Finally, she was home.

It was time to face her handlers, no matter the cost.

Chapter Forty-Two

When Raider fetched the document he'd spent an hour printing off, there was so much pain in his body that he'd turned numb. Numb wasn't a bad place to be, truth be told. Malcolm and Wolfe were wrapping things up with the FBI and SWAT teams in case room one, Brigid was still in the computer room, and he had a short time to get everything in place. The elevator dinged, and Angus Force escorted a battered and bruised but still walking Sean Banaghan into the bullpen.

Raider tapped the papers into order on his desk. "Hey. I thought you had a collapsed lung?"

"Nope," Sean said. "Just a couple of bruises and broken ribs. No big deal."

Man, the guy was tough. Raider looked at Force. "Your dog is snoring in your office."

"Hey." Force limped by him, pain etched into the lines bracketing his mouth. "I have a couple more phone calls to make, and I need a shot of Jack Daniel's. Give me a sec." He shut the door to his office.

Sean wore a Red Sox hat, green sweatshirt, and jeans, his boots looking right at home on him. His green eyes sizzled above the bruises on his face. "You look like you lost a game of chicken with a semi."

"Feel like it, too." Raider gestured to Wolfe's desk, which faced and abutted Raider's. "Have a seat."

Sean looked around and dropped into the chair. "Where's my girl?"

"In her computer room. I think she's asleep," Raider said, dropping onto his chair and letting all of his bruised bones clatter together. "She's amazing, man. Just deciphered a computer code very few people in the world would even attempt, and in about five hours, a bunch of terrified women and girls are going to be saved from a horrible fate. She *saved* them."

Sean smiled. "She's a smart one, she is."

She was beyond smart. Sweet, kind, intelligent, spunky, and beautiful. It was way too early, but Raider wanted to plan a visit for her to meet Miss A, maybe at the end of summer.

Sean cleared his throat. "I guess you could date her. You don't seem so bad."

High praise, indeed. "I think that's up to her." Raider grinned. He'd definitely jumped the gun, declaring love so soon, but it was true, so why not say it? To think he'd thought he wanted somebody pliant and predictable. Ha. Brigid was neither of those things. Though he'd probably have to date her for a while and convince her that nice guys who followed the law were better than rebels without a clue.

Sometimes he had a clue.

Force limped out of his office and sat in Mal's chair, wheezing when he moved. "Just heard from the hospital. Nari is better and her memory is returning, which is good. Dana's online podcast has a zillion hits already, and she's busy typing up an exposé for the AP, so we might be okay."

Sean studied Force. "Did you get hit by a train?"

"Close enough. I let the whole team know that Brigid didn't betray us at any point, and I apologized profusely to her for not being nice. Then she fell asleep." Force put his head back and groaned. "Is it just me, or are these cases getting harder?"

"You'd better be nice to my girl," Sean muttered, rubbing a bruise on his chin.

Raider prodded the bruise on his temple. One of the many bruises on his temple. "Every member of our team, except Roscoe, has some sort of damage, so yeah. It's getting worse."

Force opened one eye. "Not Malcolm. He remained intact during this one."

Raider shook his head. "Nope. He took a knife to the ribs and left thigh. Wolfe stitched him up a couple hours ago, and there was swearing. A lot of swearing. West can string expletives together in a truly impressive fashion."

"Huh." Force gingerly prodded the long steering-wheel-shaped bruise on his forehead. "The dog always manages, somehow. We should take lessons."

Raider snorted. "That dog is freakin' nuts. Though, he was all business on the raid."

Force smiled. "Yeah. He was the best before we got blown up the final time. He can still get serious when needed." He gestured toward Sean's baseball cap. "You're off the hook, in general. Going to stop being an ass and take your daughter to a game?"

Sean nodded. "Yeah. She's coming home for Christmas, and I think she's bringing this big bruise of an agent over here."

Raider perked up. "She said that?"

Sean grinned. "I believe she said she'd consider it. Play a little hard to get, man."

Force snorted.

The elevator dinged, and Raider straightened, looking around. "Everyone who should be here is already here." He reached for the gun in his waistband. "We need better security."

"We don't have any security," Force retorted.

The dog padded out of the office and sneezed several times, his gaze on the elevator.

It opened to reveal two men.

"Ah, shit," Force muttered. "What are you two assholes doing here?"

Agents Rutherford and Fields strode inside, all grace and no injuries. Well, Rutherford still had a light bruise across his throat and two black eyes, but they looked like they belonged on him.

Rutherford's eyes blazed. "Do you have any idea of what a clusterfuck you've created? Going live with that reporter?"

"Yes," Force replied, not moving an inch. The guy probably hurt too much to breathe.

Rutherford shook like a puppy about to spring. "You've broken so many protocol rules that I can't name them all. We're going to get you shut down if it's the last thing we do."

"Meh," Raider said, not giving a shit right now. "We're too public, and we just gave the HDD and the FBI one of the biggest busts in recent history. You don't want to shake us loose, or the public just isn't going to understand."

Rutherford's teeth ground together so hard he had to have a headache. Seriously.

Brigid emerged from her computer room, her hair in wild curls around her shoulders, and her eyes cloudy. She rubbed them. "Why the yelling? It's early in the morning, and we haven't slept for days. No yelling."

God, she was adorable when grumpy. "Come here, sweetheart," Raider invited. "You can sit with me and face the mean agents."

Her smile was beyond cute.

Rutherford coughed. "You were undercover. This isn't real. There's no way *miss loves a rebel* here would go for you, Tanaka. You moron."

Brigid paused, turned, and pretty much snapped. "Listen, you slicked-back prep boy, my-dad-is-a-powerful-lawyer, every-rich-kid-in-every-bad-teen-movie jackass, I do love him. And he is a rebel."

God, she was amazing. Raider kicked back to watch. Wait. Love. She'd said love. His chest heated and warmed his entire body.

She moved to him, plopping herself on his lap. "For goodness' sake, just look at him. He went undercover, took down a mob family that has been in play for a century, destroyed your plan in one second, and came for me through mobsters and glass and machine guns, without hesitation. He's a rebel, and he's exactly everything I've ever wanted."

Sean jerked his head. "And it looks like he got the girl." The farmer grinned.

"Yeah," Brigid said softly, turning toward Raider. "He totally got the girl."

Brigid slung her arm around Raider's neck, wanting to punch both agents. Finally. She was no longer terrified of them or what they could do. She had power, too. They were just so clueless. Raider was a hero, and a badass one at that. She glanced behind her; Wolfe and Malcolm had emerged to watch the fireworks.

Wolfe hurried up with a huge latte covered in more

sprinkles than she could count. "You were sleeping, or I would've brought you this. Sorry about the plain coffee yesterday." He shuffled his feet, bruises on his face, his head hung.

"Thank you," she said, grabbing for the treat. "I'm sorry."

"Me too." His smile was oddly sweet. "We're friends again." Relief covered his huge face.

The team was battered, wounded, and obviously solid. Good. This was her team, and that mattered. Even her dad was there.

"This is the best day ever," she whispered to Raider.

He coughed. "Okay." Then he nudged a stack of papers toward Sean. "Hey. You're the only one who can walk without crying right now. Will you please hand these to Agent Fields?" Raider looked at the older agent, who was watching the scene unfold while chewing what looked like a cough drop. "Sign these. Now."

Rutherford didn't wait. Instead, he strode forward to grab the papers and started reading. He looked up. "Not a chance."

Brigid looked at Raider. "What is it?"

"An amendment to your plea agreement," he said, not looking away from the agents. "It basically ends it, says you've done your job, and that all charges against you are dismissed. You're no longer obligated to the HDD."

Angus nodded. "You're free, Brigid. You can do anything you want."

Her heart leapt. "I want to stay here. To work with the team." To be a part of something good that included a wild dog and silly cat.

"You got it. You sure?" Angus reached for her hand, his grip tight.

She laughed. "Of course. This is my team."

"Thank God." He released her and slumped in his chair again.

"No," Rutherford said, again. He looked around at the wounded group. "You're all freaking crazy."

"Well, yeah," Wolfe agreed, leaning back against the wall.

"Maybe so." Raider lowered his voice. "Sign these papers, or we go public with everything we have on this unit, how you've operated it, and how you blackmailed and scared Brigid into signing a bad plea deal. The HDD has enough public relations problems that by the time I'm done with you, you'll wish you'd never met us."

"I already wish that," Rutherford shot back. "That's extortion, Agent Tanaka."

Brigid straightened. "See? Total bad boy." She kissed him on his bruised temple. "I'll go public with the fact that you collect miniature tea sets, Rutherford. Your BuyOnline account isn't secure."

"Those were for my nieces," he gritted out.

Her smile even felt mean. "Not by the time I'm done with you. It'll be a fetish." She looked at Fields. "And you. A serious involvement with Buffy, Angel, and the Avengers." She shrugged. "But it's the Whedonverse, and Joss Whedon is awesome. So I can't argue with your choices."

Fields just kept chewing. "Think they'll ever make a sequel movie to *Serenity*?"

"No," she said sadly. "I don't think so."

"Me either, but I can't help but hope," he said, grabbing the papers from his partner and striding forward to take a pen off the desk and quickly sign. "There you go."

"Hey—" Rutherford started.

Fields calmly turned around and headed for the elevator. "We lost this one. Sometimes it happens. Now I want waffles." He entered the elevator and turned around. "Hurry up, or I'll leave you here with them."

"This isn't over," Rutherford snapped, turning on his polished loafer and following his partner.

"I hope they get stuck," Wolfe muttered.

Brigid shuddered. "The bad guys are all gone." Then a thought occurred to her. "Where do you think Josh the Bear is?"

"Dunno," Raider said, stretching his legs and wincing. "The guy didn't exist until he worked for the senator, so maybe he's moved on to another life. Could turn into a model citizen, or he might start his own crime organization. Dollars to donuts, we'll never see him again."

Weird. Definitely weird.

Roscoe barked once at the elevator and then flipped a perfect U-turn in the air, running full bore for Angus's office.

"Stop him!" Angus bellowed, turning in his chair. "I left the Jack Daniel's out."

Wolfe and Mal both grabbed for the dog, but he leaped between Mal's legs and was on the bottle in a second. Then, in a graceful dodge, he tipped it up, backflipping toward his bed and out of sight. Moments later, Wolfe emerged with the empty bottle. "He got it all."

"Damn it." Angus shook his head. "Somebody put on some Metallica. He likes to dance when he's drunk." The dog emerged, already shaking his head and tail in direct opposition to each other.

Sean stilled, watching the pooch. "Um, alcohol kills dogs. Shouldn't we take him to the vet?"

"No," Brigid answered, trying not to smile. "He's been to the vet several times, and the vet says he has the liver of an old sailor. He'll dance for a while, flirt a little with me, and then pass out."

"Unbelievable," Sean muttered.

"I know. We're working on it." Angus sighed. "Nice job with the plea agreement, Tanaka."

Brigid's heart filled. "I agree. Thank you." He'd thought of her, even after this crazy week.

"Of course." Raider snuggled her closer. "Force? Is there some sort of HR form we have to sign to be dating in the same unit? I mean, we are dating. Nice and slow."

Okay. Her badass was a dork sometimes. She could live with that—he was sexy and cute. "Screw HR, and we are not going slow."

His gaze sharpened. "Oh?"

Her heart rate picked up. This was probably a private conversation, but the team was in on everything, anyway. "Yeah. The way we're going, we won't survive the next op. So no going slow. We're in love, and we're moving full speed ahead."

Sean gave him a sympathetic nod. "She's a little like a steamroller. Her mama was like that, too."

Brigid ignored her father. "I'm tired of our crappy apartments. We're going to move to a nice place." She looked over her shoulder at Wolfe and Malcolm, her heart almost bursting with excitement. "You both own twenty acres in Cottage Grove, right?" Their cottages were right next to each other, and the acres spread out from there.

"Yep," they answered in unison.

"Would either of you sell us an acre? I'd like to build out there." Then she'd be close to Wolfe, Mal, and Pippa. It sounded perfect.

"Sure," they said in unison.

Vulnerability caught her way too late. She looked down at Raider. "I mean, if you want to."

He kissed her, with so much promise in the touch that she was instantly reassured. "Of course, I want to. We can buy whichever acre or acres you want, and we'll start building immediately. We can even invest in a farm up north to visit on weekends, if you want. I love you, Irish."

For the first time in her life, she could say those words to a man with no hesitation. Doing so in front of her father and the trusted people of her team meant even more. "I love you, too."

Read on for an excerpt from
Rebecca Zanetti's next Deep Ops novel!

BROKEN

Clarence Wolfe strode up to the entrance of the super-secret sex club as if he had done so a million times before.

Down the street and partially hidden by branches from a sweeping cherry tree, Dana Mullberry ducked lower in her car and pressed her binoculars to her face so hard her skin pinched. What in the world was Wolfe doing at Captive?

She swallowed. Her heart rate, already thundering, galloped into the unhealthy range. It had taken her nearly a month to find out about the club, an additional two weeks to track down the location, and yet another month to finagle an invitation to the casual play night as a guest. And the ex-soldier, the beyond hunky badass who'd relegated her immediately to the friend zone, was walking inside like he owned one of the coveted million-dollar memberships?

She shook her head. Once and then again. When she could focus once more, there Wolfe prowled through the binoculars, his powerful body illuminated in the full moon-light. She swallowed.

He'd followed the rules for the night, too. Male doms were to wear leather pants and dark shirts, females any leather outfit, and subs were to wear corsets and small skirts if they were female and knit shirts and light pants if they were male. Apparently, Wolfe was a dom. Figured.

She'd assumed she'd chuckle at seeing guys in leather pants, but there was nothing funny about Wolfe's long legs, powerful thighs, and tight butt in those pants.

In fact, he looked even more dangerous than usual, and she would've bet that wasn't possible.

Where in the heck had Wolfe found leather pants? Was he really some sort of dom who went to clubs? He did not *like* people enough to spend time with anybody in a dungeon. She giggled, the sound slightly hysterical, so she cleared her throat.

What now? She looked down at her tight green corset and black skirt that was as long as she dared. At the very least, it covered the still healing knife marks on her upper thighs that she hadn't told anybody about. Not even her doctor. The criminal who'd cut her during an interrogation was behind bars, so why did it matter?

Forget the nightmares. They'd go away soon.

Her more immediate problem was that Wolfe had just walked through the front door of the mansion that housed Captive. Her source was inside that place, and she'd spent a lot of time gearing up for this.

But would he blow her cover?

She'd been sitting in her car for an hour watching people arrive. Okay. She might've been gathering her courage. This was so outside her experience. She hadn't even known sex clubs existed until that movie came out about BDSM.

But her boss at the *Washington Post*, where she used to work, had once said she'd do anything for a story, and he'd been right. Well, mostly. Okay. She could do this. In fact, why not look at the fact that Wolfe was inside as a positive? His presence gave her unexpected backup.

Yeah. That was the idea. Forget the fact that the sexiest man she'd ever met was in a sex club right now. Yep. Good plan. She slid from her car and pulled her skirt down as far as she could, which still barely covered her butt.

Her heels tottered on the uneven sidewalk as she clip-clopped by a high stone wall that no doubt protected another zillion-dollar mansion. Then she crossed the street, her head high, shivering in the chilly breeze as she reached the front door and knocked.

"Hello." A man in full tuxedo opened the door. He was about six feet tall with curly blond hair, and he was built like a linebacker. "Can I help you?"

There was no way anybody could get by this guy if he didn't grant access. She handed over her gold-foil invitation.

He accepted the paper and drew a small tablet from his right pocket, scrolling through. "Ah. Miss Millerton. I see that you answered the questionnaire and have signed all of the necessary documents." He smoothly slid both back into his pocket. "A couple of quick questions."

She forced a smile, feeling way too exposed in her scant clothing. Hopefully the questions weren't about her fake name or cover ID. "All right."

"What's your safe word?"

"Red," she said instantly.

"Good. If you need help, who do you yell for?" His voice remained kind but firm.

She blinked, thinking through the documents she'd read online. "For anybody, but especially the dungeon monitors." The words felt foreign in her mouth. Should she ask him about Albert? Or was that taboo? She didn't want to get kicked out before she found her source.

"Good." The guy opened the door to reveal a rather ordinary-looking front vestibule with another wide door behind him. "Go ahead and have fun, sweetheart."

Fun? She nodded and tottered on her heels to the door, which, somehow, he reached first and opened for her.

"Thank you," she murmured, instantly hit by a wave of noise and heat. Music blasted from the ceiling, and in front of her, a palatial living room had been set up as a dance floor on one side and a full-length bar on the other. Bar. Definitely bar. She could have a drink and maybe talk up the bartender. A quick glance around the darkened room, highlighted by deep purple lights from high above, didn't reveal Albert's location. She didn't see Wolfe, either. Good.

She made her way through a crowd of people in leather and other gear, finally reaching the bar.

A six-foot-tall woman dressed in a full leather outfit leaned over, her full breasts spilling out the tight V-neck. "What can I get you, hon?"

"Tequila. Shot," Dana said. Should she ask for a double? No.

"Sure thing." The woman poured a generous shot and pushed it across the inlaid wood. "You a guest tonight?"

Dana nodded and tipped back the drink, sputtering just a little. "Yes."

The woman grinned, revealing a tongue piercing. "You new?"

"Yes." Dana coughed.

"I'm Jennie." She tilted her head and poured another shot. "Mistress Jennie."

Oh yeah. Dana had tried to memorize the appropriate lingo from the online sites. She accepted the second shot, her hand shaking. "Thank you." Was she supposed to add the "mistress"? The website hadn't said.

"You bet. Just have some fun, and remember you don't have to do anything you don't want to do. The play rooms are all over the house, and if there's a red sign on the door, it can't be closed. You can just watch if you want," Jennie said, moving down the bar as somebody caught her attention.

Good advice. Definitely. Dana took the second shot and let the alcohol heat her body.

"Hello." A man appeared at her elbow. "We haven't met."

She partially turned. The guy was about fifty with shrewd eyes and an iron-hard body. He wore leather pants and a red leather vest that showed muscled arms. "I'm Dana."

"Charles." He held out a hand to shake and kept hers a moment longer than necessary. "You here to explore a little bit?"

Oh crap. "I'm just here to ease my way in." She tried for a flirtatious smile, but her lips refused to curve. "In fact, I was looking for my friend Albert Nelson. Any chance you know him?"

Charles slid closer to her, his pupils dilated. What was he on? "No. But I could make you forget him." He took her hand again, and she tried to pull back, but he just smiled. "How about we go check out some of the rooms? I could show you around."

"No, thanks." She forced her smile in place as panic began to rise.

"Come on—" Charles began.

"She said no." Charles's hand was instantly removed from hers, and he was tossed toward the dance floor, barely catching his balance before he collided with two people slow dancing.

Dana gulped, tasting tequila on her lips as she looked up, knowing the voice very well. "Wolfe." Only training kept her from blanching at the raw fury in his sapphire blue eyes.

He leaned in, his full lips near her ear. "What the hell are you doing here?"

She shivered and dug deep for her own anger. Then she

pressed her hands to her hips. "What are you doing here?" she snapped back.

His gaze swept from her revealing top, down to her toes, and back up to her blazing face. "Subs don't use that tone, baby. One who does ends up over a knee. Quickly."

Oh, he did not. She glared. "I am not a sub," she whispered.

"You're dressed like one." His dark T-shirt tightened across his muscled chest as he leaned closer again. His buzz cut had grown out to curl a bit beneath his ears, giving him a wild look.

"There weren't many options," she hissed.

"Wolfe." A man also dressed in leather, his brown hair slicked back, moved up beside Wolfe. He was about forty with tattoos down one arm. "I see you found a friend. Finally going to play?"

Wolfe didn't look away from Dana, his gaze morphing from furious to calm in a second. How in the world did he control himself like that? "I'm normally not a public player, as you know."

What the hell did that mean? Dana began to ask, but Wolfe subtly shook his head.

The man held out a hand. "In that case, I'm Master Trentington. How about I show you around tonight?"

"That's kind of you." Dana shook his hand, her lip trembling annoyingly. "But I was actually looking for a friend named Albert Nelson. Do you know him?"

Trentington reluctantly released her. "I do, but he's not here tonight. I'd love to play your guide in his stead."

"No," Wolfe answered before she could, angling his body closer to her and almost between them. He glanced over his shoulder at Jennie. "Spare cuffs?"

Jennie grinned, reached under the bar, and tossed over a pair of bright pink wrist cuffs.

Wolfe snagged them out of the air and snapped them on Dana's wrists before she could blink. They were fur lined and well sized, but felt restrictive nonetheless. "We've already reached an agreement," he murmured.

"Well. In that case, have fun." Trentington moved to leave.

"Charles was being pushy again," Wolfe said quietly. "It's time you kicked him out."

Trentington sighed and turned toward the dance floor. "Thanks."

Dana looked down at the pink cuffs. She kind of felt like Wonder Woman. "Why did you—"

"They show ownership," Wolfe said, clipping the cuffs easily together.

Her abdomen rolled, and her head snapped back. "Excuse me?" She tugged hard, but they wouldn't separate, effectively binding her wrists together. She eyed his shin. With her heels, she could do some damage.

He chuckled, the sound low and dangerous. It slid over her skin, burning her from within. "Right now, you're playing a sub, no doubt for a story. But I'm playing a dom, and if you kick me, I'll toss your ass over that bar and beat it."

His words slid right through her to pulse between her legs. For Pete's sake. That scenario was not sexy. But the idea of Wolfe's hand anywhere near her butt sent her already sensitive body into hyperdrive. Oh, she'd handle him later. For now, she had work to do. She leaned closer. He'd said "playing." "Are you on a job?" she whispered.

"Yes." He glanced around. "Who's Albert Nelson?"

"My story," she said, looking again. "I scared him off last week, but I know he's a member of Captive, so I came here to ask him questions." Maybe to scare him into answering. At this point, she didn't care. Finding out who'd killed her friend was all that mattered. "Your job?"

"Confidential. You know a guy named Clarke Wellson?"

"No, but I could do a background check later," she murmured. They'd helped each other on cases before.

Wolfe glanced down at her, his gaze warming. "You look incredible."

"Thank you." It was nice he'd noticed, although the outfit wasn't really her style. She was more a jeans-and-flannel type of girl. She shuffled uneasily in her heels. That way he had of switching topics had thrown her ever since they'd met. "Okay. I'm going to mingle and ask questions. You?"

He smiled, the sight daunting. "I just cuffed you. No dom would allow a sub to mingle."

Allow? Oh, heck no. She blinked. "Then uncuff me."

"No. Last time you didn't have backup, you nearly died." He crossed his arms, somehow scouting the entire room while also watching her.

Her back teeth gritted together. "You're not in charge here, Wolfe."

"The cuffs say otherwise," he said, angling his head to take in the dance floor.

She couldn't help it. She really couldn't. For months she'd chased this story, and she was here pretty much tied up because of a guy who only wanted to be her friend. She kicked him, as hard as she could, right in the shin.

He stiffened, rapidly pivoted, and both broad hands went to her hips before she could blink. She was in the air, halfway to the bar, before she even thought to struggle. Uselessly. Wolfe's hold was unbreakable. Oh, he wouldn't *dare*.

A heavy thud sounded from behind Wolfe. A woman screamed.

Wolfe dropped Dana to her feet and shoved her behind him, angling toward the dance floor. He looked up to a balcony high above.

Dana inched behind him, staring down at the dead man

Visit us online at
KensingtonBooks.com
to read more from your favorite authors, see books
by series, view reading group guides, and more.

Join us on social media
for sneak peeks, chances to win books and prize packs,
and to share your thoughts with other readers.

facebook.com/kensingtonpublishing
twitter.com/kensingtonbooks

Tell us what you think!

To share your thoughts, submit a review,
or sign up for our eNewsletters, please visit:
KensingtonBooks.com/TellUs.

on the ground with a bullet hole in his head. His eyes were wide open and frighteningly blank. Her stomach lurched, and she coughed. "That's Albert," she whispered.

Wolfe looked over his shoulder at her. "Well, shit. That's Clarke, too."

Sirens sounded in the distance. Wolfe grabbed her bound wrists. "We have to get out of here. Now."